I0760565

EXCAVATING THE BURIED HEART

EXCAVATING THE BURIED HEART

Estelle Tudor

Inlustris

First published in the UK in 2024 by Inlustris Publishing, Wales

Cover designed by Inlustris Publishing ©
Interior formatting and design by Inlustris Publishing ©
Edited by Jordan at L. Newton Books ©

A CIP catalogue record for this book is available from the British Library.

Paperback ISBN 978 1 915950 14 7

E-book ISBN 978 1 915950 15 4

Hardback ISBN 978 1 915950 16 1

Written in British English, so spellings/grammar choices will reflect that.
Triggers: Some mild swear words are used in the text and there are themes of abandonment and cheating.

For all who—despite their broken hearts—still believe in the magic of love.

"Your heart was broken…but your spirit never was."

Kent, UK – 10.30pm.

Mia Davenport drummed her fingernails on the desk in time to the ringing of the FaceTime call. Calli was late, but then Calli was always late. Her cousin on her American mother's side was perennially late for everything. Mia's Aunt Junie joked it was because her only daughter had gotten too comfy in the womb, and didn't make an appearance until 17 days after her due date. That kind of entrance set a precedent.

Seventeen rings later—*very apt*—a face appeared on the laptop screen.

"Oh!" Mia sat up straighter. "You're not Calli," she said, noting the handsome face of the man smiling at her from across the Atlantic. His black curly hair flopped charmingly over his brow while piercing blue eyes sparkled with amusement.

"I'm Josh," he said in a deep, slightly Southern, voice, "Ash's colleague." He referred to Calli's fiancé. "Calli's running late" – *of course she was*. Mia smiled to herself – "Ash has gone to pick her up, so they asked me to let you know."

"Oh, right," Mia said. "I'm Mia, by the way," she added.

"Hi, Mia, nice to finally put a face to the name," Josh said with another smile, and Mia found herself strangely flustered. *You have a boyfriend*, she reminded herself sternly. Loyalty meant everything to her, but she still had eyes in her head didn't she?

"Nice to 'meet' you too," Mia replied. "Tell Calli to give me a call later."

"Will do. I'm just setting up card night while I wait for her and Ash." Josh held up a deck of cards, and a small pang of FOMO worked its way through Mia. She'd loved joining in Thursday night card night with Calli, Ash, and their friends on her last visit to New York in Calli's old, cramped-but-cosy, apartment, but she'd never met Josh before, so he must be a new addition to their friend group.

"Well, I'll leave you to it. Have a great night," Mia said with a smile and for a brief moment their eyes met across the distance of thousands of miles and held.

"You too, Mia," Josh replied.

With an awkward wave, Mia disconnected from the call and let out a long breath. *Focus, Mia*, she chastised herself and closed her laptop lid, before pushing back from her desk in the sunny bedroom her boyfriend, Henry, had said she could use as her study area when she'd recently moved in.

Her phone beeped with a text message.

Hey, Cous, sorry I missed you! Stav had me working late. I've just got out now. So… what did you think of Ash's new colleague?????

Mia rolled her eyes at the amount of question marks. Calli and her continual matchmaking.

That sucks! Josh seemed very nice but I have a boyfriend remember?

Not that Calli needed the reminder. She'd even met Henry, although, admittedly, the pair had never seemed to hit it off, which pained Mia.

More like a roommate. When was the last time you and Henry spent any proper time together?

Mia stared at the message with a frown. When *was* the last time she and Henry had gone out? She'd suggest a date night to him when he came home from work.

Her eyes flicked to the clock on her laptop. He was late again; just like every other night that week. Her fingers typed a hasty reply:

He's the newest partner and still finding his feet. I'm sure when he finds his rhythm, he won't have to work so late.

Even to Mia's eyes, the message seemed defensive, but she didn't want to admit to herself that Calli had a point. But, even so, she certainly wasn't going to throw away a two-year relationship on a couple of doubts...*or a piercing pair of blue eyes*.

Calli came back with a few moments later. Then:

I'll FaceTime you in ten, you can join in remotely with card night. You can be my wingwoman. Grab yourself a glass of wine, and chill.

Mia's shoulders relaxed as she texted back:

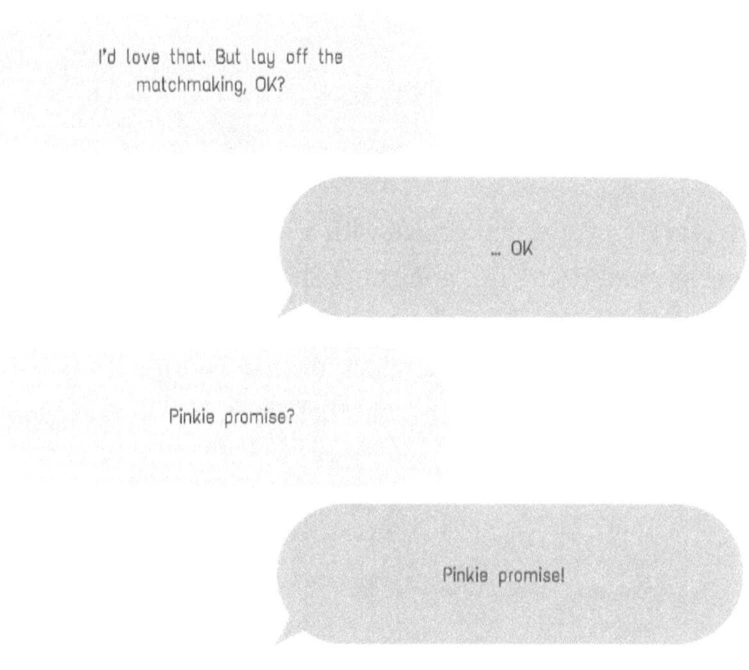

Calli's text came back with a crossed-fingers emoji.

Mia took her laptop and went down to the kitchen to select a crisp white wine from Henry's ample collection and poured a large glass. She settled on the sofa, flipped open the lid of the laptop, and took a sip of the wine while waiting. Despite the time difference, she could manage an hour to join in the fun, and, with Henry being late, it would offer a welcome distraction.

So thus became the weekly Thursday transatlantic card night. One that Mia spent the week looking forward to.

Mia hurriedly hid her dig kit inside the laundry basket, followed by her grimy t-shirt, shorts and socks. Her boots—thankfully still hidden in the boot of her car—would have been a dead giveaway to what she had been up to the past eight hours.

She stepped into the shower and turned on the rainfall showerhead as Henry's voice filtered in from the landing.

"Darling, where are you? We have reservations in an hour."

"In the shower," Mia called back, furiously scrubbing the dirt from beneath her nails. She winced; her manicure was ruined, but she couldn't have passed up the opportunity to be part of an impromptu dig. It was a great experience and could only add an extra layer of interest to her C.V.

So why are you trying to hide from Henry where you've been today...and will be tomorrow? Mia heard Calli's voice questioning her in her head, and she nibbled on her lip. Why was she exactly?

She didn't have time to answer her thoughts as Henry came into the sleek white-and-chrome bathroom. Through the misty glass panels of the double shower, she watched him loosen his tie. Perhaps distraction was in order.

Mia slid open the door and tossed him a teasing smile. "Care to join me?" she asked, one eyebrow raised.

"Really, Mia, you are going to flood the floor," Henry snapped, barely looking at her.

The teasing smile evaporated from Mia's lips and she pulled the door closed with a muttered, "Sorry."

"Don't pout, darling," Henry said through the glass, "we don't have time for fun and games, and besides I took a shower at the office."

Again? Mia thought. But instead, she simply said, "Of course. I'll be out in five minutes."

She finished washing and conditioning her hair, before swiping a hand over the long length of it, drawing away the excess water. By the time she stepped out, Henry had vanished.

Sighing, Mia cast a look at the laundry basket and her things stashed there. Deeming them safe for now, she wrapped a fluffy snow-white towel around her damp frame and padded out into the bedroom.

Henry stood, shirtless, at the open doors to the floor-to-ceiling mirrored wardrobe, one that encompassed an entire wall. He had—grudgingly, Mia sometimes thought—given her a third of the space, bemoaning the fact that his designer suits would now be squashed into the other two-thirds. He'd given her a wink as he'd said it, but still she felt like a guest in his house at times.

Mia gave herself a mental shake. She was being mean; living together was still new for both of them and would take adjustments. If the cold, clinical house wasn't exactly her style, she hoped that she could soon add a touch of her own flair and make it into a home...for both of them.

Henry turned; a dove-grey shirt in hand. “I thought you could wear the black dress tonight, the one I chose for you at that chic little boutique—we want to impress the Fellowes’ don’t we.”

His snappiness seemingly gone, Mia determined to keep his good mood, so gave an agreeable smile. “That’s a good choice.” She joined him at the wardrobe and slid out the long, black satin square-necked dress. A bit plain for her usual taste, she would wear it if it kept Henry happy and his business prospects high.

He leant in, and she turned to meet his lips. But his grazed, instead, over her brow. “Good girl,” he said. “Now Mr Fellowes is the one with the money but Mrs Fellowes is the one with the trousers, if you take my meaning.”

Mia knew what was expected of her. “Leave it to me. I shall make small talk with Mr Fellowes and leave his wife to you.”

Henry slid on the shirt and gave her an approving smile. “Perfect.” He deftly buttoned up his shirt, and added gold cufflinks. “Oh, and perhaps don’t bore him with talk of your little hobby. We want to keep his interest, not send him to sleep over the entrée.”

Mia fought hard to keep the smile on her face, and in that moment knew exactly why she had hidden her tools and not told Henry where she had been that day.

He didn’t even wait for her answer, instead walking away to select a tie from his vast selection. Mia stared at his back and forcefully pushed away Calli’s remonstrative voice in her head, and set about drying her hair and getting herself dressed.

Henry wasn’t totally against her career, he’d even encouraged her to apply for an internship at two prestigious American colleges. He approved of the academic side of it...though not the practical side of it. The part she loved most, if she were being completely honest.

Mia slid the dress over her black underwear and was struggling with the zip when Henry was there, easing the zip into place. She wanted to arch into his touch, but his earlier rebuff still stung.

"Thank you," she murmured and turned to face him. He studied her critically, rather than with desire.

"I think you should cut your hair, but for now you'll just have to wear it up," he told her, "but not in that braided thing you do; a nice simple twist will be appropriate."

"But I thought you liked my hair long," Mia said, spirit drooping. Even if he didn't, she certainly did, despite the pale-blonde locks reminding her of her absent mother.

"You're a prickly thing tonight," he told her, pulling her closer to him. He tilted her chin up and gave her a quick kiss on the lips. "I did like it...but I want to be taken seriously at the firm and need to be seen as sophisticated—in all parts of my life."

Mia, caught off-guard by the kiss which did the job of softening his words, said, "That makes sense, but let's talk of it another time; we don't want to be late."

His eyes flicked to the glass clock on the dresser. His brows pulled together, his grey eyes darkening. "Damn. Quickly finish getting ready. I'll meet you in the car."

He pulled his Armani suit jacket from its hanger and thrust his arms through it as he strode from the room.

Mia turned to survey herself in the mirror. Her long, almost waist-length, hair hung in thick ropes. The dress did nothing to flatter her, but Henry was adamant about her never upstaging the client's wife, so she dismissed the little pang of vanity. Not wanting to irritate Henry further, she grabbed her hair and twisted it deftly up to the back of her head in a knot and secured it with hairpins.

Mia slicked on a muted rose-pink lipstick and a touch of mascara before grabbing her bag and slipping on low-heeled black shoes.

Henry was already messaging Mia's phone, hurrying her up, as she descended the stairs. Not bothering to waste time in replying to him, she let herself out of the house and locked up. The engine running, she opened the door to his Tesla and got in. Mia had barely put her seatbelt on before he pulled out of their driveway.

During the short drive to the restaurant, Henry coached her on suitable conversation topics and compliments. Mia resisted the amused urge to tell him that she hadn't forgotten from the last time they had entertained prospective clients of his investment firm.

They parked up and headed inside, Henry striding ahead and entering Buchanon's restaurant to give their name. Mia followed, somewhat out of her depth, but pushed a smile onto her face as the maître d' showed them to their table. Mia frowned in confusion at the five seats around the circular table, but had no time to question Henry as Mr and Mrs Fellowes were led their way.

"Smile, Mia. You look like a deer caught in the headlights," Henry said out of the corner of his mouth, before plastering on the charming smile he reserved for the wealthiest of his potential clients.

Automatically, Mia smiled and shook hands with the older couple as the introductions were made. They had just sat down with Mr Fellowes approving the wine, when a cloud of familiar perfume wafted around Mia and she turned to see her friend,

Nadia, heading their way. That explained the fifth seat.

Nadia, another partner at Henry's firm—albeit, a junior one—apparently had no one to dictate her dress code. She breezed in wearing a thigh-length emerald-green velvet dress that hugged every curve and set off the glossy highlights in her long, loose sable hair.

"Sorry I'm late, everyone," she said, smiling around at them each in turn. She took her seat between Henry and Mr Fellowes and waggled a hello to Mia across the table.

Mia smiled back, confused as to why neither Henry nor Nadia had told her she would be joining them too.

"That's quite all right," Henry said, a benevolent smile on his face, and Mia's eyebrow rose. He usually abhorred lateness.

Over the meal, Henry schmoozed Mrs Fellowes, while Mia did her best to converse with Mr Fellowes, but Nadia, having far more experience, kept taking over. In the end, Mia excused herself and sought refuge in the restroom.

Coming out of a stall, Nadia was leaning over the sink, reapplying her bright red lipstick. She focused on Mia in the mirror, and rolled her brown eyes.

"God. That Fellowes is a dry old stick, isn't he?" she said. "Good job he's rich."

"I thought he was quite funny," Mia said as she washed her hands, "with his anecdotes about his dog."

Nadia smacked her lips against a tissue she pulled from her beaded handbag, then pouted. "You and animals, Mimi, truly. You think anyone who likes them must be a good person."

Mia watched her friend in amusement. "Well, it's usually a good indicator," she said drily.

Nadia tossed her lipstick back in her bag and snapped the clasp closed. "I don't know why Henry dragged you out to this...

it's not really your thing is it? I'm sure you'd much rather be at home watching old episodes of *Time Team* or something."

In truth, Nadia was right about that, but it still rankled. "I often come along to help Henry with his clients," Mia said.

Nadia raised one perfectly plucked eyebrow. "Hmm, he never told me."

Mia laughed. "Why would he? You both have your own clients." As she said it, she wondered why Nadia was here for this particular dinner.

"Oh, but we are working together closely on this portfolio. Didn't he say?" Nadia said, a slight smirk to her lips.

Mia slowly shook her head.

Nadia leant in and patted Mia's bare arm. "Why don't you tell Henry you've got a headache or something and leave the buttering-up to us. It must be torture for you," she said, her eyes wide and sympathetic.

The thought tempted Mia. "I can manage," she said, knowing Henry would not be too happy with her if she pulled a stunt like that and lost him his clients in the process.

Nadia flipped her hair back. "On your own head." She sighed. "Come on, let's go and charm them and make some money." Smiling in her cat-like way, she strode out of the restrooms. Mia followed, already regretting her decision to stay. She wasn't cut out for this shark-eat-puppy world.

She caught up to Nadia as she was speaking to Henry at the bar. "...has a headache. Send her home, Henry."

Henry dragged his gaze from Nadia's earnest face and inspected Mia.

"You are looking a bit peaky," he said.

Peaky? Outraged more like it, Mia thought as she shot a glare at her friend. Apparently, Nadia thought throwing her friend under the bus equated to doing her a favour, but Nadia didn't even notice the glare as she was already rifling through her bag.

"You can take my car, Mimi." She held up the keys to her Audi. "I'm picking up my new car tomorrow, so just leave it on your street—I'll get the garage to collect it from there."

Mia stared from one to the other. "I'm fine," she protested, but neither of them seemed to hear.

Henry took the keys from Nadia. "That's quite a good idea. I know you have an early start at the university tomorrow," Henry said with a smile. "I will make your apologies to the Fellowes'."

Guilt settled in Mia at her mild deception. Yes, she would be working *with* the university, though not at it. Deciding retreat was the best option, she accepted the keys.

"How will you get home?" she asked Nadia.

"Oh, I'll make sure she gets home safely," Henry said, and Nadia let out a little laugh.

Mia looked from one to the other, then smiled. "That's kind of you," she told Henry and leant in to kiss him. He deflected her at the last moment, turning instead to accept the tray of mocktails from the barman.

Flushing, Mia stepped back with a murmured, "Good night then. Good luck with the Fellowes'."

"Night, Mimi," Nadia said, with an airy wave, and headed back to the table.

"Don't wait up, it'll probably be a late one," Henry told her, gesturing to the drinks. "I think the old chap might be a tough nut to crack, but I'll work on Mrs Fellowes until she gives him the green light." He smiled as though Mia would approve of his aggressive stance.

With a slightly sour taste in her mouth, Mia smiled back and repeated, "Good luck."

Carrying the tray, he walked away from her. Mia watched him for a moment, at the picture the four of them made—the epitome of a successful business dinner—before heading out of the restaurant and into the car park.

Inside Nadia's car, Mia pulled out her phone and texted Calli in New York.

Hey, Cous, are you free for a FaceTime later?

She gave a wry smile; she might as well make the best of her banishment by soaking up some Calli-therapy.

Calli's reply came swiftly.

Of course, but what happened with the 'big, important dinner'?

Mia's fingers hesitated over the keyboard before answering:

Still happening... but without me.

Wanna talk about it?

Mia smiled fondly at her phone. That was what she loved about her cousin. Yes, she had a fondness for prying, *and* matchmaking, but ultimately would respect Mia's privacy if she didn't feel like talking.

Nah, it's all good. I'll log on in half hour, OK?

Okie dokes - look forward to it

Mia put her phone away and belted up. She drove herself home, the scent of Nadia's lingering perfume filling the interior of the red Audi, and indulged herself by playing her friend's *The Best of the 00's* CD at full blast; memories of teenage summer holidays in Greece making her smile.

The next day, Mia stood, ankle-deep, in mud, staring down at the two letters in her hand. Normally, the only part of excavations she didn't enjoy—muck seeping into her socks—would have given her the ick, but the letters she kept intermittently pulling from her shorts pocket drew her mind away from the discomfort.

Her heart leapt into her mouth at the thought of what life-changing opportunities they contained. The official-looking letters had come that morning as Mia had been leaving but for some reason, she hadn't wanted to open them on her own. She'd taken them with her, deciding to open them with Henry after she had finished at the dig and hoped he wouldn't be too late, and she wouldn't have an agonising wait to find out what was inside the missives. Considering he hadn't returned until well after midnight after the business dinner, she gauged that he would probably be home normal time tonight. She hoped, at least.

"Mia, those artefacts won't reveal themselves," Conrad, the

site manager, reminded her, and she slid the letters back into her pocket with a sheepish look.

"Sorry, Conrad, I'm a bit distracted," Mia admitted, and the older gentleman smiled.

"I can see that," he said. He perused the site nestled on the outskirts of the university grounds, and then gestured to the car park with his auburn-haired head. "Go on, I'll finish up. I can see you're itching to go and share your news."

Conrad, for the past four years, had been a sounding board for her dreams and had given her a sterling review to add to her academic ones when Mia had applied to the New York City University archaeology department—and the Los Angeles one (on Henry's urging)—applying to be a summer assistant to professors there. And *both* letters had arrived at the same time. Her stomach was in serious knots.

"Thanks, Conrad, appreciate it." Buoyed up on securing the Fellowes' promises to invest, Henry had left early to be the first in the office and laud his win. Perhaps, she could phone him when she got home and entice him to join her for lunch. The wait would kill her otherwise.

As Conrad waved her thanks off with another smile, Mia collected the tools from her dig kit, wiped them off and stowed them in the leather roll-up bag. She climbed out of the excavation hole, waved to the students she'd been mentoring, and grabbed her denim jacket and bag.

On the short drive home, Mia thought of Henry and, aside from the stress he'd been under in securing the Fellowes deal, how attentive he'd been lately, dispelling all her doubts, and even Calli had conceded he was stepping up. They'd gone out at least once a week—even managing a weekend away—and he'd been so supportive of her desire to make use of her dual citizenship and apply for jobs in America. She'd preferred New York to be closer to Calli, but Henry had encouraged her to try L.A too—the company he was a partner in had a branch there and he hoped to further his own career. Perhaps, with the Fellowes deal under his belt, management would approve a transatlantic transfer.

Mia nibbled her lip. If she were being honest with herself, she'd delayed opening the letters because she was scared she'd have to make an impossible choice. She wanted to carry on supporting Henry, truly, but didn't want to put her own preferences aside in the process. She'd already sacrificed so much in the pursuit of harmony at home. But, with a happy sigh, she admitted there were worse problems to have.

They would work it out. Together.

She parked up on the road, noting another car—a perky red Mazda—already in the drive behind Henry's black Tesla. She didn't recognise it but thought it was probably one of Henry's colleagues. Perhaps, Mia thought happily, he had decided to have a working lunch at home and, though disappointed she'd have to delay her news for a bit longer, it would give her time to settle her nerves.

Mia stopped briefly on the pavement to stroke her neighbour, Mrs Higgins' tabby cat, Mortimer. He hopped over on his three legs, tail out for balance, and gave a little meow of greeting.

"Good afternoon to you, sir," she said, and he purred beneath her hand.

She left the cat on the pavement and carried on along the drive and let herself into the house, setting her keys down on the marble side table; the only piece of furniture in the stark white entry foyer.

She tilted her head as strains of classical music filtered down from upstairs. *Strange*, Mia thought, knowing Henry never put music on when he worked. With a shrug, she made her way up the stairs, intending to pop her head around his office door and let him know she was home.

The music muffled her footsteps as she walked along the tiled upper hallway. She paused as she could tell from the open doorway of his office that he wasn't inside, and neither was the unknown colleague.

Her heart hammered uncomfortably in her chest when Mia realised the music was coming from the ajar door of their bedroom. On feet turned suddenly leaden, she forced herself to make the rest of the journey along the hallway and pushed open the door fully.

Mia blinked and then blinked again at what she was seeing. Henry's naked torso rose up from beneath the white silk sheets, covering the figure beneath him. She must have made some sort of noise as the song ended, because Henry stiffened then straightened; revealing the woman beneath him. Now, Mia thought, she truly was going to be sick.

"*Nadia*," she said, her voice an anguished whisper as she took in the flushed but sated face of her friend. Her *lifelong* friend. Her mind raced a million miles an hour. Of course, that must have been Nadia's new car in the driveway—the one she told Mia about the night before, as she had casually, yet, coldly perfectly orchestrated her removal from the cosy business dinner. *Oh my god, this could not be happening*.

"Mia? What are you doing home early?" Henry snapped, as if this was all *her* fault. His grey eyes flashed in his handsome face, while his usually perfectly styled dark brown hair was mussed as if a pair of hands—red-nail-tipped hands—had raked through it.

"What the hell, Henry?" Anger pushed through the shock. Pushed through the normally gentle and agreeable demeanour that Henry favoured. Mia glared at them both. *Nadia* had introduced them, for god's sake! *I've found the perfect guy for you, Mimi. He's just started at my office.* What a fool she had been. "No, please don't get up," she added as Henry made to push up off the bed and get out. "I'm going to do what you obviously prefer me to do—leave. Oh, and Nadia? You two are *perfect* for each other." Mia aimed the last words at Nadia, and Nadia had the good grace to flush with acknowledgement as she pulled up the sheet across her chest. Her long dark brown hair swung around her face covering her red-smeared mouth. But it couldn't sear her face from Mia's mind; that was branded there forever.

God! Mia turned on her heel as Henry called after her. She made it to the front door and claimed her keys before Henry appeared at the top of the stairs, now wearing a pair of silky grey boxers. *Ugh.* The ones Mia had bought him.

"Mia, wait! We can work this out," he said, but Mia speared him one final look, mustering every last ounce of disdain.

"What for, Henry, I was never what you wanted was I? It's over. It was over the minute you and Nadia betrayed me," she said wearily now. Knowing she had not only lost the man she had believed herself in love with, but her best friend too. He had tried to mould her into a demure, composed partner, but obviously what he truly desired was the polar opposite.

Pride prevented her from letting him sweet talk her into staying and listening to his bullshit excuses. Mia left him calling after her, yanking open the door, and running out to her car. She didn't care that she was leaving her belongings and clothes behind. She had her laptop, dig kit, and university notes in the boot of her car. That was all she needed right now. She started the ignition, and peeled off from the kerb, sending a silent apology to Mortimer as he jumped in alarm on the pavement. Mia glanced in her rearview mirror; the cat was now arching his back and hissing at Henry, who stood in his boxer shorts watching her go.

Mortimer had never liked Henry. Perhaps, she should have taken note.

"Thanks, Dad," Mia said, later that night, as she accepted the cup of tea from her father. He had made it to her liking; tan coloured, with a splash of milk and drizzle of honey to sweeten it.

"I don't like leaving you, are sure you'll be all right?" Stephen Davenport asked for the second time, taking a seat next to her on the squashy sofa in the living room. They'd already had the same conversation that afternoon.

"Dad, it's your honeymoon. I'll be fine, I promise." She smiled at him, it was a trifle watery, but it was still a smile. Mia had driven straight to her family home twenty minutes away, and sought refuge in her father's hugs. Her dad had recently remarried, and she loved Alice; the sweet widow her father had met at an art class and fallen quietly in love with.

Mia's mother, Mae, was a self-confessed free spirit and, after she and Mia's dad divorced when Mia was eight, had continued her travels around the world, before recently re-settling in her native Miami.

"I know, Mouse, but I'm sure Alice won't mind delaying it for a bit," Stephen said.

"Absolutely not, Dad. This cruise has been booked for months. I promise I'll be fine. I've got some holiday time due to me, so I'll hibernate here for a bit. Conrad will understand." Mia patted her dad's hand, but he regarded her worriedly with his blue-green gaze; the same colour as Mia's own eyes. Her long thick, pale-blonde hair was courtesy of Mae.

Stephen sighed. "Fine, but if you want me to pay a little visit to that goddamn idiot before I go, just say the word."

Mia said sadly, "He's not worth it. Neither of them are."

"You are worth a thousand of them, especially that Nadia. To think, I treated that girl like she was my own daughter. Didn't she have us fooled?" Stephen pulled Mia into a one-armed hug, and Mia rested her head on his shoulder.

"Didn't she just," she murmured.

They sat in silence for a few moments before Mia's laptop, sat on the coffee table, started ringing with an incoming video call. It was Thursday, Mia remembered dully.

"There's Calli. I'll give you some privacy." Stephen stood, and collected the mugs, before making his way into the kitchen.

No sooner had Mia accepted the call, and Calli took one look at her face than she was shouting, "Ash, get in here!" She took a closer look. "Something's wrong with Mia."

Calli's fiancé, Ash, joined Calli on the screen immediately. He must have had his brown-black hair cut recently and it was now cropped close to his head on the sides and longer on the top. As his brown eyes crinkled in concern in his olive-skinned face, Mia couldn't even get out the words to tell him it suited him. Her throat was suddenly clogged with the tears that she had held back. She wished she was with them all, needing her real friends right now.

"What's wrong with Mia?" Mia heard Josh's deep voice in

the background.

"I don't know," Calli murmured. "Mia? Did you get the letters? Did they turn you down?"

The letters. Mia had completely forgotten all about them. Mutely, she shook her head, and suddenly the tears were rolling down her face. "It's—it's Henry," she managed.

Calli's light-brown eyes hardened. "What has he done?" she almost snarled.

It all came out, every shameful little detail. How she'd had the letters, been so excited to share the contents with Henry. Of what she'd discovered when she'd gotten home, and now she couldn't even bear to open the letters.

"That sonofabitch. And that two-faced Nadia, too!" Calli said heatedly before Ash shot her a warning look.

"I—I know. What am I going to do, Cal?" Mia sniffled.

"I'm getting on a plane," Calli said, and Ash raised his eyebrows at her.

"Calli, you can't go now—you've got work remember? And an audition next week." He gave Mia an apologetic look.

"It's OK. I appreciate the sentiment, but Ash is right. You can't just get on a plane, Cal, because I made a horrible choice in boyfriends."

"That bloody weasel—I'll tear him apart." Calli did snarl this time, and Mia smiled through her tears.

"Dad already offered to have a little chat with him," Mia said, and Stephen called in the background, "We can tag-team him, Cal!"

"Damn straight, Uncle Steph!" Calli said, and pushed her mass of brown-gold curls off her face. Two spots of colour stained her brown cheeks. "Seriously though, Mia. Open those letters. I *know* they've accepted you. Pick one and leave, and don't look back. Don't let what's happened ruin your future, OK?"

Mia delved into the pocket of her shorts and pulled out the two letters. "I'll do it, but I need a minute."

Calli's face softened, her eyes sympathetic. "Call me later, all right?"

"OK. I don't think I'll be up for card night though," Mia said, knowing that she could do with the distraction, but seeing all the faces she cared for, and separated by thousands of miles when she needed them the most, would be too hard.

"Come to New York and we'll do a special card night in your honour," Calli said softly.

"Maybe," Mia replied, feeling as though all her dreams had turned to dust. "Speak to you later."

"See you, Mia," Ash said, while Calli blew her a kiss.

Mia disconnected the call and sat back against the cushions of the sofa. Alice came in through the back door from her bingo night, and Mia listened absentmindedly to her stepmother's muted conversation with her father in the kitchen. Making a decision, she picked up her laptop and carried the letters upstairs to her childhood bedroom. She sat on her bed and stared down at the letters, tracing her fingers over the typed address. The address she'd never live in again. Had barely even *begun* to live in, only having moved in with Henry a little over six months ago. Nadia had even helped her move in, for goodness sake—had their affair even been going on then? Mia pushed the horrifying thought away. She would go mad with the wondering otherwise.

Had she been wrong in wanting to share the contents with someone special, have someone be excited for her for a change, help her choose between the cities if need be, or console her if it went wrong? Mia's lungs constricted, and her hands trembled so violently that the letters fluttered to the floor. If she'd arrived home at her usual time, she wouldn't have discovered the truth. *How long would it have carried on?*

I can't breathe, Mia thought, and fumbled with her laptop to bring up an app she'd used before when flying. It helped her to focus on deep breaths until the sensation passed. A video call came in as she was sucking in a breath and getting no benefit. Her fingers pressed accept in her clumsy attempts at finding the app.

"Mia, are you all right?" Josh's concerned face filled the screen. She gasped and he must have realised what was happening as he said, "Look at me."

Mia did so, desperately locking eyes with the man who she'd never met in person, but through the weekly card night's banter had become her friend.

"Copy my breathing," he instructed. "Nice and slow." She tried to emulate his calm, slow breathing and finally, she found her natural rhythm. "That's it, eyes on me," he said in his soothing Southern drawl.

"Th-thank you," Mia got out, after her heart rate had returned to normal. "That one came out of the blue."

Josh's bright blue eyes crinkled in sympathy. "Panic attacks have a habit of doing that," he said. "But yours was totally understandable. I guess you aren't doing too good?"

Mia grimaced. "If I'm being completely honest? Not good at all. I don't want to worry my dad or Calli, so..."

"So, you're putting on a brave face?" Josh said.

"Something like that." She bent down and retrieved the letters. "I probably should open these."

"Want some company while you do?"

Mia considered Josh through the screen, and it was as though they were in the same room. “Thanks. I’d appreciate that.” She took a deep—albeit slightly shaky—breath and opened the one with a Los Angeles postmark. “Dear Miss Davenport, thank you for your application...we are pleased to offer you the summer internship...” she trailed off, not at all excited by the offer. That was what Henry had wanted for her. Wanted for himself.

“Open the other one,” Josh encouraged and Mia did so, pausing before she read the contents. “It’ll be OK,” Josh added. “The worst thing that could ever happen to you has happened, right?”

Mia pondered on that. “You’re right. Getting betrayed by the two people who I thought would always be there for me—yes, that’s pretty up there with the worst.”

Josh, thankfully, kept any pity he might have felt out of his gaze. “Then read it. I’m right here.”

Mia closed her eyes, then decided by delaying it, she wouldn’t change the outcome. She opened her eyes and met Josh’s in a flash of blue before she lowered her gaze and scanned the letter. “I got it,” she said, then louder, “*I got it.*”

“Congrats, Mia. Now, you’ve got a decision to make. I’m sure whichever one you choose will be an awesome place for a fresh start.”

“I never wanted L.A. Henry...Henry encouraged me to go for it.”

“Don’t think about what he wanted. What do *you* want?”

“New York.” Mia didn’t hesitate. “I want New York. I want to run in Central Park with Calli, join your card nights, go to shows on Broadway, take in the sights and sounds...I want New York.”

"Then come. We'll all be here for you. You need to think about *your* future now," Josh said, and suddenly Calli and Ash popped up in the background.

"Come on Josh, we've started! Oh, Mia, hi." Calli muscled into the frame. "You OK?"

Mia managed a genuine smile for her cousin. "I will be. I'm coming to New York," she said and Calli's scream echoed through the screen.

"*Yes*! We're having tequila tonight!" She gave a little shimmy and Ash let out a groan.

"Some of us have work early tomorrow," he muttered.

Calli gave a wicked grin. "Not all of us." She and Ash moved out of view as Calli negotiated how many shots she could get away with.

Josh and Mia exchanged an amused smile. "Tell Calli I'll call her with the details...and thanks for being there today."

"Anytime," Josh said. "See you in New York."

"I'll look forward to it," Mia said. "Bye."

"Bye, Mia."

Mia disconnected the call and laid back on her bed, the letter from New York still in her hand. She was moving to New York. She let out a small smile. *She was moving to New York.*

A tentative thought formed in her mind. Perhaps she could take a trip and reconnect with Mae too while she was over there. Henry had never encouraged her to do so, and Mia had never pushed too hard because there was—admittedly—a lot of unresolved issues between her and the woman who had birthed her, and subsequently eased out of her life like a butterfly on the wind. Henry had thought Mae Vega's bohemian nature didn't align with the persona he was trying to cultivate. God, what an idiot she'd been, Mia thought, disgusted at herself and how easily she had been manoeuvred.

Well, none of that mattered now, Mia thought with a gasping sob. She pulled her legs up to her chest and curled up into a tight ball. She fell asleep with tears tracing down her cheeks, the New York letter clutched tightly in her hand.

CHAPTER THREE

Mia scanned the bustling terminal at JFK and sighed. She should have expected it. Of course, Calli was late.

Still shaky from the turbulent landing, she started walking, pulling her two large cases behind her. Her laptop bag bumped along her hip as she weaved her way through the crowd and towards the exit. She'd text Calli and get an Uber instead.

"Mia?"

Mia turned at the familiar deep drawl. She took in the tall, athletic-looking man who stood before her wearing blue jeans and a tight dark-grey tee, and immediately recognised the tousled black curls and bright blue eyes set in the handsome angular face. "Josh, hi!" She abandoned her cases, and, needing a moment of human contact after her brush with near-death, stepped forwards and hugged him, inhaling a fresh sea salt and coconut scent that clung to his skin and clothes.

Taken by surprise perhaps, Josh stiffened briefly, before he returned the hug, encircling his arms around her and giving a gentle squeeze.

Mia pulled back and flushed. "Oh my god, sorry! I *hate* flying and that landing was a doozy. I was so relieved to be on safe ground and see a familiar face."

He grinned down at her. She only came up to his chin despite her long-legged frame. "No worries at all," he said easily. "This your luggage?" He gestured at her two grey suitcases.

"This is it," Mia said. "My dad collected my things when Henry was at work, so I had clothes to bring with me." She'd had no wish to ever set foot in the sleek, soulless house again, and nothing, besides her clothes, toiletries, and a few books, belonged to her anyway. Josh gave her an understanding look and Mia fell into step beside him as he commandeered the cases and headed for the exit.

"Calli was running late, so I offered to come and get you," Josh explained and Mia laughed.

"When isn't Calli running late? I hope Ash is prepared to wait for her at their wedding."

Josh made a noise of agreement. "Don't worry, I'll be on hand to calm him down. He asked me to be his best man."

Mia looked at him questioningly. "They've set the date then?"

Josh nodded. "They were discussing it last night. I'll let Calli fill you in on all the details."

Not too long ago, Mia had harboured ideas of getting married herself, thinking Henry was near to proposing, but of course, his secretive—and alternately attentive—nature was because of an entirely different reason. One she didn't care to dwell on right now. Ash and Calli had been engaged for a year, and Mia had been waiting for them to finalise the details of their wedding, and now she was in New York, she'd be able to help Calli out with the preparations.

"I'm so happy for them," Mia said quietly, and Josh gave her a sideways look.

"How are you holding up?" he asked as they headed out into the bright summer afternoon and towards the huge car park.

Mia pushed her long sheet of pale-blonde hair over her shoulder, and was grateful she'd settled on a loose linen white shirt and blue jeans as the early summer sun heated her face. She gave a small shrug. "I don't really know," she admitted. "I've kind of become numb—as if it didn't, in fact, happen, and I'm simply going on holiday. I know it's not healthy to bottle stuff up, and not deal with it, but I genuinely don't know how to reconcile with what happened."

Josh stopped amongst the rows of cars and popped the boot of a white Prius. He placed her cases inside and closed the lid. "That's understandable. Trauma can affect people in different ways. But you're right, it's not healthy in the long term, but right now, you need to do what's best for you." He leant on his car and looked at her. "I'm always here to talk if you ever need it."

"I appreciate that," Mia said, and though this was the first time they had ever met in person, no awkwardness presented itself. It was as if they'd always been friends. "I might hold you to that—probably after one or two cocktails." She attempted a laugh but it fell kind of flat.

Josh pushed off the car and squeezed her shoulder in a comforting gesture. "Come on, let's get you to your new home."

Mia slid into the front passenger seat when Josh held the door open for her. Calli and Ash had insisted she stay with them for the duration of her internship—which would initially be a few months over the summer—with a view to staying on longer if both parties were mutually happy. Mia couldn't wait to get started on assisting with Professor Marlowe Deacon's latest archaeology project. She hoped there would be fieldwork involved too, but mostly it would be administrative.

The drive to the apartment block opposite Central Park where Calli and Ash lived took forty-five minutes from the airport, and Mia found the time passed quickly as she and Josh chatted easily. She discovered the reason for his smooth drawl was because he'd been born and raised in Texas. He'd attended college in New York and had stayed after he got a job at the law firm where Ash worked too.

"So, your mom and Calli's mom are sisters?" Josh asked as they headed into the city.

"Yes, Mae loves travelling and after she met my dad at Stonehenge, decided to put down roots—it didn't last though. When I was eight, she told me she felt like a bird in a cage." At Josh's sharp look, Mia hastened on, though she didn't know why she was defending Mae's behaviour. "She wasn't *intentionally* trying to hurt me, that's just who Mae is. She set off travelling again and I stayed with my dad."

"That's tough on a little girl," Josh remarked.

Mia pondered his words. "It was for a time, but I carried on."

"Another thing you bottled away?" Josh said quietly.

Mia frowned. Never having thought of it like that before. "I guess I did," she admitted. "But I'm thinking about trying to rekindle our relationship while I'm here."

"Is she in New York?"

"No, she's back in Miami where she grew up. She's living with Aunt Junie—Calli's mum. I might take a trip down and see her after I've settled in." *And when I can face another flight*, she added mentally, suppressing a shudder.

"That'll be good—for you both, I suspect," Josh observed.

"Yes, maybe," Mia said quietly. They pulled into the

underground car park beneath a smart apartment block. “Do you live close?” she asked as he parked up and turned off the engine. Never having asked before, she was enjoying finding out more about him.

He turned to her with a smile. “Very close.”

Mia raised one eyebrow in question.

“Here,” he said. “On the same floor as Calli and Ash. Ash got me the place when their neighbour moved out.”

“That’s handy for card night,” Mia said.

“Among other things,” Josh said. “Ash and I carpool most of the time. We have movie nights, and there’s a karaoke bar down the block that Calli’s always dragging us to. Not that I take part.” He grimaced.

“Us? Do you have a partner or a roommate?” In the six months Mia had known Josh—admittedly only through video call—she’d never seen him bring anyone to card night.

“By ‘us’ I mean me, Ash, and our other friends. But to answer your question, I don’t at the moment. I split up with my girlfriend last year, and I don’t want—or need—a roommate,” Josh said lightly.

Mia winced. “Sorry, that was nosy, and sorry about your girlfriend. Breakups are rough.” She knew that only too well.

Josh flashed her a smile. “It was mutual, so no hard feelings.” He opened his door and got out, and Mia took the opportunity to take a deep breath then slide out after him. He got her luggage out of the boot, and said, “Come on, we’ll take the elevator up to the lobby first. I want you to meet Lou.”

“Who’s Lou?” she asked intrigued.

“You’ll see,” he said with a wink, and Mia decided to go with it, and followed him over to the lift.

They rode the lift up to the lobby and the doors opened onto a clean, spacious foyer with a curved wooden desk set back from the glass-fronted entrance doors. A bank of mailboxes filled the opposite wall. Mia hadn't visited Calli in over a year, and her cousin had been in her own apartment at that time—only moving in with Ash when they got engaged—so Mia inspected the area with interest. Her gaze landed briefly on the older man behind the desk, before her attention was grabbed by a tiny chihuahua emerging from behind the base of the desk with a tiny yap.

"Oh," Mia said and stepped out of the lift, pulling her luggage. She abandoned her cases and bent down. "Well, hello."

"Meet Lou," Josh said. "I know you love animals. He's a bit grumpy—" he broke off when the tiny dog approached Mia and she scooped him up.

"Aren't you the sweetheart." Mia let out a giggle when he licked her face eagerly. "You're simply misunderstood, aren't you?" she crooned, and the dog gazed back up at her with adoring dark-brown eyes as if to say, 'Now, here's someone who gets me'. Mia then spoke to Josh. "The secret is to look them in the eyes—not in a dominating way, of course—and let your gaze soften until it sneaks past their guard and into the pure soul all animals have. Show them you want to be friends. And just like that" – she nuzzled the dog, who licked at her again – "love at first sight."

Josh made a strange noise, and then cleared his throat. "I see."

Mia smiled at him, then once again noticed the older man waiting patiently behind the lobby desk, a welcoming smile on his face. "Oh, I'm sorry," she said. "How rude of me." She walked over and extended her free hand. "I'm Mia Davenport."

The man clasped her hand. "Hello, cara mia," he said in a

slightly accented voice.

Mia laughed. "I can see where Lou gets his charm from."

Josh's eyebrow rose at that statement. "Mia, this is Carlos, concierge extraordinaire. Carlos, Mia is Calli Vega-Lamone's cousin from England. She'll be staying with her and Ash Sharma for a little while."

"A pleasure to meet you," Carlos said, his brown eyes sparkling beneath his head of neat grey hair. "Miss Calli did mention it to me."

"Lovely to make your acquaintance too," Mia said.

"Shall we get you upstairs and settled in?" Josh asked, and Mia nodded, looking forward to unearthing the box of tea bags in her suitcase and making a big mug of honey-sweetened tea.

With a wave to Carlos, Mia made to walk over to the lift, then gave a little laugh as she realised she still held Lou. She turned back and handed the dog to the grinning concierge.

"You are most welcome to take Lou out for a walk any time you like, Miss Mia." He leant over the desk with a wink. "My friend runs a little delicatessen down the block and he always slips in a bit of extra bacon for Lou with my morning bagel."

"Oh, I would love to take Lou out." Mia scrunched her nose at the tiny dog. "It's a date—not that I'm dating at the moment, but for you, sweet Lou," she said, pausing to tickle him under the chin, "I shall make an exception."

Carlos crinkled his face. "A lovely young lady such as yourself not dating? It's a tragedy," he said.

Mia was acutely aware of Josh waiting behind her, but she gave a delicate shrug. "It's more a tale of betrayal," she said softly, then in a more bolstering tone, "but I am in the best city in the world, and I intend to concentrate on my career and on making new friends."

Carlos' face smoothed out, and he gave an approving incline of the head. "Well, with friends such as Josh, and Lou, here, I think you're off to a great start."

Mia smiled. "I couldn't have put it better. Bye Carlos, Lou," she said, and then with Carlos', "Bye, Miss Mia," and Lou's little yip, Mia joined Josh and entered the lift when the doors opened.

Mia leant back against the wall, one hand on the handle of her larger suitcase. "Thanks for introducing me to Lou, there's something soothing about animals, isn't there? I feel back to my pre-bumpy-flight self now."

"While I love animals as much as any sane person, we'll have to agree to disagree about how soothing Lou is—especially when he's nipping at the laces of my running shoes." Josh gave a comical grimace. "But I'm glad you're feeling a bit better. You hate flying that much, huh?"

Mia shuddered. "Give me a disintegrating jeep rattling apart over the desert, or even a rusty boat in the med, over flying miles above the ground in a metal tube, any day."

The lift doors pinged open on the fifth floor, and Josh said as they exited, "You've had a few adventures of that type then?"

Mia grinned. "A fair few." The smile fell from her face. "But I think this'll be my toughest adventure yet."

A comforting hand fell on her shoulder, and she looked up at Josh gratefully.

"Come on, let's go and see if your cousin has finally made it home." He gestured to the right-hand door of the two apartments on that floor.

"I can't wait to see her."

Before they had even knocked, the door was wrenched open and Calli was barrelling out of the apartment with a high-pitched squeal.

"*Mia*!"

And Mia found herself enveloped in the familiar, comforting arms of one of her very favourite people in the whole world.

Then the tears came.

"Oh my god, you brought proper tea bags! And *please* tell me you brought my favourite caramel chocolate."

Mia smiled at Calli's excitement. The tears had ceased—from both of them, but Mia thought Calli might start up again when she rifled in her bag and brought out a couple of jumbo-sized bars of the chocolate.

Calli seized them eagerly. "Gimme!" she said, then her face fell comically and she handed them back to Mia. "You'll have to ration them. I cannot be trusted." She exchanged an adoring look with Ash, a soft smile on her lips. "We've set the date, Mi—the venue we wanted had a cancellation. We've only got a few weeks to prepare, so I can't eat my weight in chocolate now!"

Ash smiled back at her; his dark brown eyes dancing. "Eat the chocolate, Cal, you're beautiful no matter what."

"You are such an enabler, Ash," Calli wailed, her eyes creeping back to the chocolate bars. "Oh, all right, maybe one." She gracefully accepted the bar off Mia, who viewed the exchange with fond amusement.

"I'm so glad I'm here to help you with the wedding preparations," Mia told her cousin.

Calli beamed. "I'm going wedding dress shopping Saturday morning, and *you* are coming with me. I need all the help I can get." She peeled back the wrapper and broke off a row of the chocolate and handed it to Mia. "Give Josh a taste, Mi, I bet he's never had anything so sweet."

Mia's mouth parted in shock—all thoughts of wedding dress shopping fleeing from her mind—thankful Josh was behind her and couldn't see her face. She gave a weak laugh, as Calli regarded her innocently, and snapped a square of the chocolate off. Turning in the bar stool she was sitting in at the kitchen counter, she offered it to Josh.

Instead of taking it from her, he leant forward and Mia had no choice but to pop it into his open mouth like he was a baby bird. He closed his eyes as he chewed, making an appreciative noise in the process. Mia's cheeks heated and she swivelled back around in time to catch Calli grinning at Ash.

When Calli noticed Mia's frowning look, she shrugged as if to say 'what?'. Calli loved to match-make, and that thought was enough to fill Mia with a hollow foreboding. *Not this time,* she thought dully. She was done with romance for the foreseeable future.

"You're right, Cal, it's delicious," Josh finally said, having finished eating the treat.

"Told you," Calli said.

Mia rolled her eyes, the affection for her cousin overtaking the frustration at her obvious attempt at playing cupid. "I'm surprised customs don't charge me import fees—the amount of bars I've brought over here for you, over the years."

Calli giggled. "Why do you think I invited you to stay so

many times?"

"Charming," Mia said, but her lips twitched.

"Let's have a proper cup of tea, then you can unpack and rest, Mi. For tomorrow, it's Thursday—and you know what that means?"

Mia smiled in genuine anticipation. "I can't wait. I have been looking forward to attending an in-person card night for so long!"

Calli let out a squeal and hopped off her bar stool to give Mia another squeezing hug. "It's gonna be fab. You guys make yourselves comfy," she said to Ash and Josh and they wandered over to the sofa. "Come on, I've got something to show you." She pulled Mia off her stool and across to the cupboard beneath the kitchen sink. She opened it and reached in, pulling out an ornate black-and-gold teapot. "This was Nanna Prim's. Mom brought it over last time she visited, and I knew it would be perfect to have a 'proper brew' in it."

Mia's lips twitched at Calli's attempt at an English accent. "It's perfect—I think I remember it from when I visited her once. Didn't she have it on a shelf in her kitchen?"

Calli pursed her lips. "Probably, you know she liked her collections."

Mia recalled her nan on Mae's side. Having very little to do with Mae during the last sixteen years since Mae had left Mia when she'd been eight—and with living in England—family visits to her American nan had been scarce. She hadn't known Nanna Prim as well as Calli had.

Side-by-side, Mia and Calli brewed up a pot of tea, and let it steep. "Cal," Mia said, lowering her voice so they wouldn't be overheard. "I know you were only teasing, but don't try and instigate anything between me and...anyone, OK? You're as bad as Simi: '*Stop watching P & P on repeat, and living off lemon sorbet, lady, and get out there and find your own Darcy—oh, and find one for me while you're at it*'," she mimicked, but not unkindly, Mia knew her old university friend only had good intentions.

Calli stopped pulling teacups off the hooks from where they hung beneath a narrow white shelf. "I always thought Simi was so wise." She pursed her lips in agreement, then, seeing Mia's face, continued hurriedly, "You're serious? I know you said no more dating, but I didn't think you were dead set against it." Mia winced as her cousin's voice rose in tone at the end.

"*Shh*," she implored. "But yes, I'm completely serious—I don't have the mental capacity for it right now." Or the inclination. The whole thing made her slightly nauseated if she was being honest with herself. "I want to enjoy my time here, with no complications." *Or further heartbreak.*

Calli stared at her for a moment, then gave a jerky toss of her head. "OK, I'm sorry. I only want you to be happy." Mia understood the weird phenomenon that happened when people coupled up and wanted everyone around them to be just as happy, but Mia would rather live vicariously through *their* happiness, than risk again the heartbreak of what happened when things went wrong.

"I am happy—being here with you, and about to start a new step in my career." She nudged Calli with her hip, and Calli nudged her back.

"OK," Calli said, but the assurances belied the look in her eyes; the worried, disbelieving look.

"Shall I pour?" Mia asked.

Calli's eyes cleared. "Sure, I think it's only right."

Mia poured out four cups of the strong tea, added a jug of

milk, sugar sachets and a pot of honey to the tray and carried it over to the coffee table. She sat in one of the armchairs, opposite the sofa occupied by Josh and Ash, while Calli curled up in the other one. "Just a splash of milk for me, Mi," Calli said.

Mia made Calli's tea, then looked at the men. "How do you take yours?" Josh asked. "I'm more of a coffee guy, usually, but I'm game to try in honour of your arrival."

"Splash of milk and a drizzle of honey," Mia said.

"Sounds good," Josh agreed.

"Me too," added Ash.

Once they were all sipping on the tea, Calli spoke to Mia. "Now, I told you about getting you a trial shift waitressing at the restaurant?" Mia nodded. She had a small stipend from the internship, so she'd happily agreed to Calli's suggestion to try and get a job working with her part-time to top up her income. "OK, I'll take you with me to my shift on Friday. When do you meet your professor?"

Mia set down her empty tea cup, feeling a bit better—everything always seemed a bit better after a cup of tea. "Monday morning, at the university."

"Ooh great, you'll have time to settle in a bit. Do you still like running?"

"Yes, even more so lately," Mia said but didn't elaborate.

Calli met her eyes in understanding—running had always been Mia's emotional release. "Perfect. There's a group of girls I run with in Central Park called the Park Valkyries." Calli grinned. "Safer in numbers, right?"

"That's a great idea," Mia said.

Ash set his own cup down. "I could get used to drinking that," he said, then added, "the running group is a great idea. I'm much happier Cal has company to run with when I'm at work."

"Do you run, Josh?" Mia asked.

"When I have the time. Ash and I work until six usually Monday to Friday—except for Thursdays for card night, when it's four—so I either go pretty early or on the weekend. Otherwise, I make use of the running machine in the gym down the block from our office."

Mia nodded. "How was the tea?"

Josh tilted his head in thought, swirling the remnants of the tea around as if he could somehow see into his future. "It's an acquired taste," he said eventually in a neutral tone.

Mia laughed, while Calli said, "We'll make a tea drinker of you yet, won't we, Mi?"

Mia met Josh's bright blue eyes. "Oh, definitely," she agreed.

Josh set his cup down next to Ash's not looking convinced in the slightest, then stood. "I'd better get going," he said. "But, Mia, it's been lovely to finally get to meet you in person. I'll see you tomorrow at card night." He gave her a smile, which she returned.

"Likewise, Josh—and thanks for collecting me from the airport."

"Anytime," he said, then said his byes to Calli, while Ash got up and walked with him to the door asking him something work-related.

Mia debated having another cup of tea when she sensed Calli's eyes on her. "What?" she asked.

Calli's light-brown eyes were thoughtful in her pretty heart-shaped face. "Nothing, just thinking what a shame it is."

"What's a shame?" Mia asked.

"Oh nothing," Calli said hastily. "Anyway, why don't you go unpack and rest for a bit. Ash made lasagne and we'll have it for a late dinner."

"That sounds great," Mia said, then decided to do as Calli suggested and unpack at least. She had no idea what time her body thought it was but her phone told her it was 7.30pm, New York time. "Too late to call Dad in the UK, but I'll shoot him a text so he knows I arrived safely. I'll give him a ring tomorrow."

Calli stood when Mia did. She helped Mia with her luggage and showed her into the second bedroom.

It was a brightly lit room from the setting sun coming in through the large windows. A double bed sat in the middle of the room against the far wall, dressed with a geometric black-and-grey print duvet set. Bedside tables were placed on either side set with two squat lamps; one on each. On the wall opposite the windows was an open door revealing a small walk-in closet, while next to it was a dressing table and chair with a mirror above it.

"Hope it's OK?" Calli asked. "The dressing table isn't quite big enough to use as a desk, but you're welcome to use the dining table when you need to—oh, and you'll have to share the bathroom because there's only one, but Ash is a bit of a neat freak, so no random bits of stubble or seats-up here."

"It's perfect, Cal, thanks. I appreciate you letting me stay. The uni offered me a room on campus as part of the internship package, but I had enough of dorms in my own student days."

Calli pulled a face. "Same. But now look at us—total grown-ups."

Mia winced. "Well, *almost*. I'll be back at Dad's when I return to England," she said.

"Then stay here! I'm sure you'll find a job—or sweet-talk the professor into giving you a full-time position."

"I might," Mia said, "but it's early days yet." Secretly, that was high up on her list of wants, but she wouldn't be making any firm decisions yet. There was still time.

"Well, if you decide that's what you want—you'll always have a place here, for as long as you need it," Calli said, then gave her a quick hug. "So glad you're here, Mi."

"Me too."

They exchanged a smile, before Calli said, "I'll leave you to it."

"Thanks, Cal."

After Calli had gone, Mia sat down on the bed and shot off a quick text to her dad, and one to Simi—who had stepped up seamlessly as best friend and confidante after he'd learnt about Nadia's betrayal—before plugging in her phone charger in one of the outlets.

Mia unpacked her clothes and shoes and set her toiletries, makeup, and hair things on the dressing table. Finally, she pulled out her laptop and flipped open the lid, bringing up the web page for NYCU. She re-read through the information for the archaeology department, soothing herself by going over the now-familiar words.

Excitement replaced the nerves. She had made that first step—she was here, in New York—and on Monday she'd make the second step, by meeting the professor face-to-face. Mia had interacted with him and a few other faculty members during the online interview process, but was eager to connect with Professor Deacon in person. His career on the Roman Era and the British Celts had interested her for a long time, and Mia looked forward to helping him in the department, and learning from one of the best.

She carefully closed her laptop down and took another deep breath. It was going to be OK, she reassured herself.

New York would be a completely fresh start for her—one she could enjoy by looking to her future while dealing with the past. Both her own, and academically.

Mia kicked off her canvas shoes and laid back against the cushions. She'd close her eyes for a little while, and do as Calli suggested, and rest. But her body overruled her mind and believing it to be nearly 1am, it pulled her down into a deep sleep in moments.

And not even the sounds from the busy New York street outside was enough to disturb her.

"Morning." Calli emerged from her room, the greeting mingling with a yawn. "Did you sleep well? I tried to wake you to eat last night, but you were like the dead."

Mia grinned at her cousin's appearance. Her thick gold-brown curls exploded around her face, while she bleary-eyed shuffled towards the kitchen area. "Good morning. Surprisingly, I did. I woke at 4am and watched the sunrise. Then called my dad and had a nice long chat with him."

"How's Uncle Steph—and Alice?" Calli asked, fiddling with the coffee machine.

"Fine," Mia said. "They've just returned from their honeymoon cruise in the Caribbean and enjoyed themselves immensely."

Calli turned with a smile. "I'm so glad he found someone, he's such a lovely guy."

Mia thought fondly of her dad, who had been the best dad she could ever have wished for. When Mae left, he had given Mia all the attention, and distraction with various activities, as he could. "It's almost like he waited until I was settled before he focused on his own happiness," she mused. "He shouldn't have waited though—look how that turned out. Now, I'll be the one cramping his style if I go home."

Calli poured a cup of steaming coffee, and then joined Mia on the sofa. "Don't be so hard on yourself. None of us can see into the future. You, and your dad, thought you *were* settled. It's not your fault Henry couldn't keep it in his pants." Mia winced, and Calli's face dropped in horror. "Sorry, Mi, that was insensitive. You know what I'm like before I've inhaled two cups of coffee."

Mia gave her a reassuring smile. "It's OK, you're not wrong. And I thought it was *one* cup you needed?"

Calli shuddered. "It's two now. What with working at the hotel restaurant, keeping up with auditions—and now a wedding to plan, having two cups of coffee is going to be my baseline before I function in the morning."

Mia grinned. "Well, I'm here to help with the wedding prep, and if I get the job, then I'll be on hand at work to boost your spirits. I can't help with the auditions though. Any luck there?"

Calli lowered her mug from the huge gulp she had just taken. "Some. I had a small role in an independent musical—only in the ensemble, but no big breaks yet."

"Well don't give up hope, you're an amazing dancer, and you'll get there," Mia said, rubbing Calli's arm encouragingly.

Calli's eyes lit up. "Ooh, maybe you *could* help me practice—you're a good dancer too, remember that dance we put together that summer—what were we, 16?" She laughed, and Mia joined in, recalling the memory.

"Oh, yes, what did we call it again?" Mia thought a moment, then clicked her fingers. "That's it; a Paso Salsa smash up."

Calli's eyes twinkled. "That was a good summer," she said. "I know things didn't work out with Mae, but we did make some great memories."

Mia thought of those heady few weeks in Miami when she had just turned 16. Calli invited her over for her birthday celebrations and they'd spent a week choreographing a routine with some of the local boys. Calli's mum owned a dance-bar on the beachfront and they'd put on a little dance show as part of Calli's Sweet Sixteen party. The visit had been going so well until Mae had phoned to say she wasn't going to make it after all; deciding to prolong a trip to Nepal instead. All the joy had left Mia as she experienced the same feelings of childhood abandonment again. She'd been hoping to see Mae as it had been years since their last reunion. But Mae did what Mae did best.

"That's Mae for you," Mia said simply, and gave a careless shrug. But it still stung even after all these years.

Calli nibbled on her lip, then said in a bolstering tone, "Anyway, what I was thinking, if we push the dining table out of the way, you could help me choreograph a small piece. I need to put something together for an audition coming up soon."

Mia buried the past deep. "I would like that," she said.

"Great." Calli stood and returned to the coffee machine to refill her cup. "Want one?" she asked.

Mia shook her head. "I've had three cups of tea already," she said with a laugh. "I'll be bouncing around the place."

"Ooh wanna go and run off the caffeine?" Calli asked looking up at the kitchen clock on the wall. "The Valkyries'll be running in half an hour."

"That sounds amazing," Mia said. "I could do with moving about and getting some fresh air."

Calli toasted her with her mug. "Perfect. I'll get dressed and meet you out here in twenty."

Mia stood. "Great, I'll change too." She'd put on a pair of silky pyjama bottoms and a tank top when she'd awakened early; in time to witness the beautiful sunrise paint the metallic-and-glass New York skyline molten copper. Ash had appeared around 6.30am, and then hurried out to work, and Mia had done a bit of computer work before Calli showed her face at 7am.

The two cousins separated off into their rooms. Mia changed into a pair of black-and-silver patterned fitness leggings, and matching racer-back top. She laced up her black running trainers on her feet, before dividing her long hair into two, and braiding them on either side of her head.

Back out in the kitchen, Calli was dressed similarly, but her curls had been tamed back into a low ponytail. She was filling two water bottles at the sink when Mia joined her. "All set?" she asked.

"Yep, looking forward to meeting your friends," Mia said.

Calli passed her one of the water bottles and together they headed for the door. Calli locked it after them and pocketed her key in a zip-up armband around the bicep of her right arm.

They both chatted with Carlos and Lou for a few minutes with Mia promising to take Lou out soon, before they headed out onto the bustling Manhattan street. Mia stopped and absorbed all the familiar sights and sounds.

Her happiness was short-lived as a woman wearing huge sunglasses and a designer pant suit elbowed her out of the way. "This is a side*walk*," she said snippily, and Mia flushed.

"Sorry!" she called after the woman, who glared at her over her shoulder.

Calli looked at her in bemusement. "It's like you've never

been here before," she said, pulling Mia along, out of the way of more people who hurried along the pavement, and over to the crossing.

"Sorry," Mia said with a sheepish smile. "But every time *is* like the first time. I love it here."

Calli shot her a fond look as they crossed when the walk sign lit up. "I know you do. But it's New York, remember; everything moves at a much faster pace, and not everyone likes to stop and stare around on the sidewalk."

Mia shrugged self-consciously. "I can't help it. It just awes me every time."

Calli tilted her head and leant in with a mock whisper. "It has the same effect on me, but I'm too cool to show it" — she gave Mia a teasing hip-bump — "Why do you think I stayed here after college?"

"Oh, I don't know, because of a handsome man with dark hair and dark eyes?" Mia joked.

Calli's eyes softened as they made their way into Central Park. "He is the main factor, admittedly. But I wouldn't want to live anywhere else." Her eyes tracked over to a group standing near a tall tree. "And here's another reason why. Come and meet the Valkyries."

Mia smiled pleasantly and followed her over to the group of women. Calli made the introductions, and Mia's head swam trying to remember all the names.

"Don't worry," a petite redhead with sparkling hazel eyes said. *Dotty*—Mia thought, hastily. "You'll get used to us. Get Calli to add you to our WhatsApp group. That way you can know who's running and when. We make it a rule to have at least five of us running at any one time, and never after dark."

"That's sensible," Mia said.

"Dotty, and Claudia" — Mia focused on the tall, dark-haired woman Calli gestured to — "work at the restaurant, so you'll get to know them well."

"Great," Mia said and smiled around at the other six women stretching and chatting. One, a cool-eyed platinum blonde, gave Mia the once over as if sizing her up. Mia increased the intensity of her smile, then thought she was probably trying too hard—but two-and-a-half years of people-pleasing Henry and his ilk was hard to let go of. The woman gave her a curt nod, and carried on stretching.

Mia nibbled her lip but philosophically reasoned that she couldn't be friends with everyone, and she'd find her way soon enough.

"Shall we go?" Claudia asked, and after murmurs of assent, they all set off at an easy pace, before incrementally increasing it, but all stayed within the group as they ran. Mia thought they were all like a well-oiled machine, and soon the familiar—almost meditative—state filled her as her feet pounded in the rhythmic pattern her body was used to. She shared a grin with Calli as they followed the curving paths, and was almost fully content.

They finished their run and waved goodbye to the other Valkyries at the park gates before Mia and Calli headed back to the apartment building.

"You can take the first shower," Calli said as they headed into the lobby, then added, "Hey, Josh, what are you doing here? Bunking off work?"

Josh leant against the desk, a large manila envelope in his hand. He was dressed in a light grey suit, white shirt, and a cobalt-coloured tie that brought out the blue of his eyes. Now why had Mia noticed *that*?

Bemused at herself, she met Josh's eyes and smiled in greeting.

"Because, someone in their infinite wisdom sent this to my home address instead of the office." He held up the envelope. "Thanks for letting me know it was here, Carlos."

"No problem," Carlos said.

Mia bent down to pick up Lou, and Calli gave her a wide-eyed look.

"*Of course* he adores you," she said, with a shake of her head. "You and your weird affinity with animals."

Mia giggled when Lou licked at her cheek. "I adore him too," she said.

"Hmm," was all Calli said, giving the dog a side-eyed look, then spoke to Josh. "Mia and I have been for a run with the Vals."

"How was it?" Josh asked, looking at Mia.

"Wonderful. The girls are a great bunch, and it felt *good* to run."

"That's terrific," Josh said with a flashing, white-toothed smile. "I'd better get back to the office. See you both later?"

Calli gave a merciless grin. "Be prepared to lose, Cavanaugh," she told him. "Oh, and Give Ash a big kiss from me," she added with a wink.

He laughed. "I'll leave the PDA's to you, Cal. I'm sure Ash would appreciate my restraint."

"Spoilsport," she said with a jokey pout.

Mia set Lou down and he wandered around the back of the desk to Carlos.

"See you later, Josh," she said.

Josh gave them both a wave, then pushed out through the lobby doors and out into the street.

Mia found herself staring after him, but was thankful Calli hadn't noticed, being too busy checking their apartment's mailbox. God knows she would have had some teasing remark for her. In another time, and situation, Josh would have been someone Mia would have enjoyed getting to know better, but as things were, she hoped they would become good friends instead.

Mia said goodbye to Carlos and joined Calli at the lift doors. Inside, Calli rifled through the stack of letters.

"Bills," she said morosely, then, "oh, this one's for you." She handed Mia a photo-image postcard, and Mia's heart started to beat uncomfortably harder in her chest.

She stared down at the picture of a temple, and couldn't help the bitter twist of her lips as she said, "It's from Mae."

"But I thought she was in Miami with Mom," Calli said.

"She is. She has a stack of postcards from her numerous travels she uses instead of writing me a letter using ordinary stationery. I mentioned it to her once when I was a little girl that I collected all the postcards she sent me and put them in a scrapbook." Until Mia got older, and wiser...and sad about it all. When it became less of an adventure, and more of a catalogue of another month, another year, when she didn't see Mae. *Look, look at all these wonderful things I'd rather be doing...these places I'd rather be...than be with you.*

"Oh, Mi. Perhaps Aunt Mae thinks it's a way of maintaining a link between you both." Calli leant into her, and looked over her shoulder. "What does she say?"

Mia blew out a long breath and flipped the postcard over. It was short and succinct as ever. "Junie tells me you're in the states. I hope you'll visit. M," she read in a dull voice.

"Well, shit. She does know postcards are not like telegrams and not charged per character, right?" Calli said.

The knot of tension in Mia's chest unravelled as she let out a bark of a laugh. "Oh, Cal," she said, shaking her head, "trust you to keep it real."

The lift doors pinged open and together they walked out. "Someone's gotta," Calli said and pulled Mia in for a hug, then released her hastily. "Ugh, we're both sweaty. Shower!"

"*Calli.*"

"Keeping it real, remember," she said and unlocked the door to the apartment.

“I fold.”

Mia placed her cards down and sat back, not at all mad that she was doing horribly. It was being there in person with all the faces she’d come to know through the video calls, and enjoying the camaraderie between them all, that was the real win.

“Me too.” Calli gave Mia a narrow look. “You were supposed to be my good luck charm,” she moaned at her.

Mia shrugged innocently but couldn’t help her smile. “Sorry, Cal.”

Calli grumbled and got up to pull out more beers from the fridge. Mia scanned around the table at Ash, Josh—who seemed to be doing remarkably well considering the amount of green, red, and black chips still sat in front of him—and their friend, Benito, who, Mia had just learnt, was Dotty’s husband, and Claudia’s brother. The remaining players were Ash and Josh’s work friend, Lance and his fiancé, Nicolette, and Sylvie—a widowed older lady who lived in the apartment block whom Calli had befriended.

Dotty and Claudia didn't enjoy cards, so gave the nights a miss, hence why Mia had never 'met' them before.

"Josh, you are killing it tonight," Lance said good-naturedly, folding. He shook his head, setting his longish blonde hair swinging, his grey eyes on Josh's pile of chips.

"Perhaps Mia is *my* good luck charm," Josh returned with a wink at Mia.

"Hey, no fair. I have dibs on any luck from Mia," Calli returned and passed out the beers, before rubbing the top of Mia's head jokingly like one would rub the stomach of an ancient statue.

Mia laughed, enjoying herself immensely. "Well, Josh *did* pick me up from the airport," she reminded her cousin.

"That's low, Mi," Calli said, shaking her head as if in disappointment, "holding my affliction against me."

"Being perennially late is not an affliction, my love," Ash said. "I think it's kind of endearing."

"Aww, you do?" Calli skipped around the table to plop herself in Ash's lap, almost scattering his smaller pile of chips. She leant in and gave him a smacking kiss on the lips, eyes wide open.

Ash eyeballed her suspiciously. "Hey, stop peeking at my cards," he said and Calli huffed out a laugh.

"Busted."

"You won't think it's endearing when she's late for your wedding, Ash." Sylvie cackled, her brown eyes twinkling, and fanned out her cards in front of her, revealing a full house.

The others sat back, faces painted in arrays of surprise. Mia hid her delighted giggle behind her beer.

"Well played, Sylvie," Nicolette said, toasting the older lady with her beer bottle. Her black bob swung around her face, as her green eyes lit with humour.

The group broke up and as Ash and Calli chatted with the others, Josh and Mia collected up the empty bottles.

"A bit of that good luck sneaked over to Sylvie, huh?" Josh said, a twinkle in his eye.

"I couldn't be shown to be playing favourites now, could I?" Mia returned, leaning back against the counter. "Sorry to burst your winning streak."

Josh shrugged easily. "I'm still ahead of the others."

"What's the prize again?"

"At the end of the year we all go out for a meal—and whoever had the most wins all year has their meal paid for them, and tickets to a game or show of their choice. The others all chip in," Josh reminded her.

"Sounds great. Shame I only just officially started," Mia said.

"Perhaps I'll share," Josh said, and for a moment their eyes met in a quick flash of blue, and blue-green.

Mia dipped her head. "That's very generous," she said lightly, and with a quick smile at him, moved away to clear away the remnants of the snacks.

The night broke up soon after with most having work the next day, and Mia happily waved them goodnight when they left, leaving her with Calli, Ash and Josh.

Mia yawned. "I think I'm going to call it a night too, I've been up since four," she said.

"Of course, I totally forgot." Calli gave Mia a hug.

"Goodnight, guys," she said to Ash and Josh.

"Night, and good luck at your trial shift tomorrow," Josh said.

"Thanks," Mia said, "and thanks for tonight everyone—it was great fun." Then stifling another yawn and, with a wave to them all, she made her way into her room and got ready for bed.

She replied to a funny meme text sent from Simi, then set her alarm and put her phone on charge.

Her first full day in the city that never sleeps had been a good one, and she hoped it would set a precedent for the rest of her time there. But her *body* needed sleep, craved it in fact and, with the moon shining behind the curtains, Mia closed her eyes.

"I'm impressed," Stav—Calli's boss at the restaurant of the Central Hotel—said approvingly at the end of Mia's trial shift.

Calli bounced on her toes behind him, giving Mia a double thumbs-up. Mia hid her grin and focused on the slender brown-haired man.

"Thank you. I have four years' previous experience and my old boss would be only too happy to provide a reference," Mia said. Working through her university years at the local restaurant was coming in handy now.

Stav focused his hazel eyes on her. "Pass on his details, but it's only a formality at this point. You've shown me you're efficient, polite, and adaptable. You're the kind of wait-staff we are looking for."

Mia smiled. "I'll be working part-time at the university but as soon as I know my schedule I can let you know. But I'm free until Monday."

"Fine, I'm sure we can work around it." Stav held out a hand. "Welcome to the team. Why don't you come for a shift tomorrow afternoon? The dress code is a white shirt and black skirt or trousers."

Mia shook his hand. "That sounds great. Thank you."

"Send me your old boss's details, and your schedule as soon

as you can." Stav passed her a business card, which she pocketed.

When Stav had left, Calli flung herself at Mia. "*Yes*, another step complete," she said, hugging her tight. "Are you OK to get back home? I have another two hours of my shift yet."

"Sure," Mia said as they pulled apart. "I'll get the subway. It'll be good practice anyway. Going back and forth to the uni and to here. Thanks for getting me the trial, Cal."

"A pleasure—anyway it was entirely selfish as you know," Calli said with a wink, then added, "Oops, better go," when Stav returned.

"See you later," Mia said, then with a smile on her face, exited the restaurant, crossed the lobby of the hotel, and stepped out onto the sunny street. She found the subway and joined the lines of people descending the steps down from the pavement.

Mia didn't have to wait long and once settled onto the train, she pulled out Stav's business card and input the details into the contacts on her phone. Things were going well; she'd secured another job, so would be earning enough to support herself and contribute to Calli and Ash's rent, she'd made friends with the Valkyries so she could keep fit, and had the weekly card night to look forward to. All she needed was to meet the professor and settle into the department.

If she still had a hollow pit in her stomach every time she thought of home and her life there, Mia determined to bury it deep as though it was a relic that had served its purpose. It felt like a different life, one someone else had lived.

Resolutely, she put her phone away, and watched out for her stop, concentrating on the here and now.

As Mia was ascending back up to street level, her phone

pinged with a notification and she pulled it back out.

She smiled at Josh's message.

How did it go?

Good. I got the job.

She added a thumbs-up emoji.

That's great, congrats! Calli will probably have the tequila out tonight in celebration.

Ha, probably. Pop around later and help me keep her in check.

Mia texted back, a grin on her face.

That I can do.

Great, see you later.

Mia pocketed her phone, pushed open the door to the apartment block and greeted Carlos. He was chatting to another similarly-aged gentleman wearing a well-worn grey felt pork pie hat, which he doffed at Mia.

"Ah, Miss Mia, I was just telling my friend all about Lou's new best friend," Carlos said.

Mia stopped and bent down to pat Lou when he appeared from around the back of the desk. She straightened and held out her hand. "Hello, I'm Mia."

The other man clasped her hand and brought it up to his lips. "Giovanni," he said.

"Giovanni owns the delicatessen down the block, and previously held the title of Lou's other best friend." Carlos leant in conspiratorially, eyes twinkling. "All down to the bacon."

Giovanni chuckled. "He is not wrong, but I am happy to give up my position to such a lovely young lady. I hope I will see you at the deli soon? My bagels are award-winning."

Mia dimpled out a smile. "How about tomorrow?" she asked. "I can bring Lou for a little walk, and you and I can have breakfast, Carlos."

Carlos beamed. "It would be an honour," he said.

"Great. Lovely to meet you, Giovanni."

"Gio, please," the man said, and Mia smiled again.

"Gio. See you tomorrow," she said and leant down again to pat Lou before she made her way over to the lift to call it.

The gentlemen waved at her as Mia entered the lift. Yes, things really were working out. What need for romantic relationships did she have? She could find fulfilment in all the other kinds of relationships. That was far safer.

Back in the quiet apartment—both Ash and Calli still at work—Mia brewed a cup of tea and brought up Simi's blog. Her friend worked at the archaeology department in Oxford cataloguing finds, but he assuaged his boredom of the sometimes-dry material by creating fun and informative blog posts. Ones that usually had Mia snort-laughing at the in-jokes she'd spot beneath the official jargon.

She pulled out her phone and texted him a photo message of

her in front of the blog post with a big thumbs up.

He replied almost immediately with a photo message of his own. Mia stared at his familiar grinning face beneath his cloud of black hair—as he toasted her with his giant coffee cup emblazoned with 'Nectar of the Gods'—and experienced a reminiscent pang. Things were so much easier when she'd been a student. Before she'd met Henry. She and Simi and their group of uni friends had gone on many field trips and adventures; camping out beneath the stars, shivering beneath threadbare blankets, and finding such rare and amazing artefacts that made the often harsh conditions so worth it. She had loved fieldwork. *Loved it.* But Henry had disapproved and, besotted, she'd allowed him to persuade her to take a desk job.

Slowly, Mia closed the lid of her laptop. Now was her chance, her chance to do what she wanted to do, pursue the career she chose. If only she had been able to see Henry for what he was, before the betrayal had forced open her eyes and *made* her see.

Mia finished her tea pensively, before pulling out the makings for that evening's dinner. She'd wanted to surprise Calli and Ash and cook for them as a 'thank you'.

As an afterthought, she texted Josh.

I'm making steak for dinner, you're welcome to join. Might be a good base for that tequila.

She didn't have long to wait for his reply.

Sounds good, on both counts. What time do you want me?

7pm?

Mia knew he and Ash finished at 6pm, so thought that would give them enough time.

Look forward to it.

Mia set her phone down with a smile then prepped the large potatoes and put them in the oven to bake. She tenderised the steaks and marinated them in a chilli-and-peppercorn sauce while the potatoes continued to bake. She made a salad and pulled out the crusty loaf she had bought from the bakery two blocks over that Calli raved about. Calli was right; the fresh bread smelled divine, and she couldn't resist cutting off the end and smothering it in the butter she had pulled out ready to make a garlic butter spread with.

She was nibbling on the last bit when Calli entered the apartment and let out a groan, kicking off her low-heeled black shoes. She sniffed the air in an exaggerated fashion.

"Does my nose deceive me?" She zeroed in on the kitchen area. "Mia, you are a goddess!" She danced over to join Mia. "But you didn't have to do all this, silly. You're our guest."

"Uh-huh," Mia said, waggling the butter knife at her. "If I am to live here, I'll be pulling my own weight." She narrowed her eyes. "And that includes chipping in with the rent *and* cooking some nights."

Calli pouted, but her face softened. "Oh, all right, if it'll make you happy and I'm not complaining, not when it looks and smells so delicious in here."

"Good." Mia booped her on her nose. "Now go and get cleaned up while we wait for Ash—oh, and I invited Josh too. Hope that's OK?"

Calli searched Mia's face slowly, then said, "Of course, Josh is like family too." With a small smile playing around her lips, she headed for the bathroom.

Mia stared at the closed bathroom door for a moment before turning to the task of making the garlic bread.

"That, was excellent," Ash said, dropping his napkin onto his empty plate. "Are you sure you want to continue in archaeology? You'd make a great chef."

Mia dipped her head self-consciously as Calli and Josh added their compliments. "I'm sure. I do like cooking though, it's a great de-stressor, but archaeology is my passion."

"Well, as much as I don't want you to be stressed, Mi, I'm all for the end results," Calli said with a fond smile. She stood and started clearing the plates and instinctively Mia went to help.

"Sit, we've got this," Ash said and helped Calli with the plates.

Josh collected the glasses from the wine they'd had with the meal, and leant in. "I agree. It was delicious. I was brought up on a ranch, and I have to say those steaks were perfect."

Mia flushed. "That is a compliment then."

He smiled at her and set the glasses next to the sink where Calli was loading the dishwasher.

Once the kitchen had been set to rights, and Mia, Josh and Ash had settled themselves in the living area, Calli came over brandishing a bottle and four shot glasses.

Mia and Josh exchanged a look, twin smiles on their faces as

Calli shouted, “Tequila time!”

“Just one, Cal. Remember we’re wedding dress shopping tomorrow,” Mia reminded her, and Ash added, “And we’ve got a meeting at the office.”

“How could I forget?” Calli’s eyes sparkled. “But OK, just one,” she conceded with a faux-pout. She poured out the drinks and passed them around.

They toasted to Mia’s securing the job, and tossed back the drinks, chasing them with a bite of lime.

Mia sat back against her chair and took in the others’ happy faces, joining in with the exasperated laughter when Calli said, “*One more*?” A hopeful eyebrow raised.

Mia awoke early the next morning, surprisingly refreshed; her body now adjusted to the time difference. She dressed in one of her favourite dresses; a yellow-and-pink floral cotton summer dress with a full scalloped edged skirt that hit at the knee, and triangular-shaped cut-outs at the waist. The vee-neck top had wide straps, leaving her arms bare. She twinned it with a pair of pink suede wedge sandals, and a straw handbag. She'd lightly curled her hair and pulled half of the wavy tresses up to secure it at her crown with a pink hair ribbon, and left the rest loose to flow around her shoulders almost to her waist.

She added a touch of natural make-up and pink lipstick, and a pair of dangling circular woven-straw earrings adorned with tiny pink and yellow tassels, and made her way out into the living area.

Calli peered at her blearily. "Do you have to look so sunny this early," she groused. "Ash was the same—up, showered, dressed, and out the door before I could even un-stick my eyelids."

"First cup?" Mia asked, indicating the mug in Calli's hand.

Calli lifted it in a salute.

"I'm going to grab a quick breakfast with Carlos and Lou while you get ready," Mia told her, and Calli watched her from over the rim of her coffee cup.

"Only you could make friends so fast," she said with an affectionate smile.

Mia smiled back, though it was tinged with a hint of sadness. Friends had been thin on the ground lately, with Henry slowly extricating them from her life. He'd even started on about Simi and how he wasn't a good influence, but thankfully, she'd held her ground there. Knowing what a true friend her university pal was. It was a shame she hadn't seen Nadia for what she really was. "Lou is a great recommendation," she finally said. "I'll see you in an hour."

"Enjoy."

Mia left her cousin to her morning ritual, and headed down to the lobby to collect Lou. The little dog danced daintily as she secured his lead.

"Now, Giovanni's is down the block on the left. You can't miss it. Ask for the usual times two, and he'll take care of you," Carlos said with a smile.

"Got it," Mia said with a smile of her own, and leading Lou, she exited the apartment block.

She walked along the pavement, keeping her steps slow and small to allow Lou, trotting beside her, to keep up. He gazed up at her with adoring limpid chocolate brown eyes as she murmured to him what a good boy he was.

Outside the delicatessen, Mia stooped to pick him up before going in. Carlos had been right; she couldn't miss it. The sign outside declared it to be *Giovanni's* in bright red and green curling letters.

"Ah, bella Mia, lovely to see you again, and buongiorno, Lou." Giovanni came around from the counter and tickled Lou under the chin. Lou bore it with great dignity, obviously knowing that bacon would be his reward.

"Buongiorno, Gio," Mia said. "May we have the usual please times two?"

Giovanni dimpled out a smile. "It would be my pleasure." He packaged up two bagels. "And some extra bacon for Signor Lou, of course." He handed over the bag, which Mia slid over the wrist of her free hand, and then set the cardboard coffee holder containing two cappuccinos on the counter before her. Mia pulled out her debit card to pay, but Giovanni shook his head.

"This one's on me—a welcome to New York."

"Thank you, Gio," Mia said with a smile, picking up the coffee holder. "Have a great day."

"You too, enjoy your breakfast with Carlos," Giovanni said, then held the door open for her as she manoeuvred her way out past a customer coming in.

On the street, Mia set Lou back on his feet and, carefully carrying the container of coffees and the bag of bagels, set off back towards the apartment block, the little dog scampering loyally by her side. The sun shone down on Mia's face and a smile blossomed beneath it.

"Good morning."

Mia stopped on the pavement as Josh descended the steps of the apartment block. He was dressed in light grey trousers and a white short-sleeved shirt with narrow pale blue stripes, and carried his briefcase. Mia presumed he was on his way to work.

"Good morning," she replied with a smile.

"You look very pretty," he said. His eyes flickered over her dress, then up to her face.

"Thank you," Mia said. "I'm about to have breakfast with two fine gentlemen, then I'm off wedding dress shopping with Calli, so thought I'd dress up a little for the occasion."

Josh informed Lou, "Aren't you the lucky one." A smile twitched at his lips when Lou let out a little grumbling noise.

Mia laughed. "He's waiting for his bacon, but you've been very patient, haven't you, sweetheart?" She dropped her gaze to the dog, then back up and caught a flash of something indecipherable in Josh's gaze.

He cleared his throat, then said, "Have fun. I'll see you later."

"Bye Josh, have a good day."

He nodded at her, then carried on towards the underground car park, and Mia headed into the apartment block and set the coffee and bagels down on the desk.

"Here we are," she said.

Over bagels and cappuccino, Mia and Carlos chatted about archaeology and how his great-niece was interested in the subject. Mia promised to get the girl some information from the university and to give her a call to chat further with her.

The lift doors pinged and Calli emerged, looking fresh and put together in a skirt and cropped jacket ensemble in a sky-blue colour.

"Ready?" Mia asked, wiping her hands with a napkin.

Calli managed a smile, a touch of nerves in her eyes.

"It'll be fine," Mia reassured her, then said to Carlos, "Thanks for breakfast, Carlos, Lou," she said.

"Thank *you*," Carlos returned. "Next time tell Gio it's on me."

Mia smiled. "I'll look forward to it." She linked her arm

through Calli's, and waggled a wave to Lou, before they headed out to grab a taxi to the dress shop.

Inside the cab, Mia nudged Calli, "So what style are you looking for?"

Calli pursed her lips. "Something quite traditional, but more of a drapey, flowy skirt instead of a full one, I think. I like the high-neck lace top with sleeves but I don't know if that will be too hot."

"That sounds beautiful, but probably worth trying on a few options. Are we meeting anyone there?"

Calli shook her head. "Not this time. I want it to be you and me today," she said, then laid her head on Mia's shoulder.

"Oh, Cal," Mia said, overcome.

"Don't get all sentimental on me—yet. Let's save the tears for the dresses," Calli said with a laugh, but when she straightened and looked at Mia, emotion swam in her eyes.

"Sure. I can do that," Mia agreed, thankful she remembered to put a small packet of tissues in her bag. "How come Josh and Ash had to work today?"

"They're working on some big contract so are doing a bit of overtime to keep on top of it. I think they're only working this morning though," Calli said.

"I see," Mia said. The taxi pulled up in front of a shop, covered in faux ivy and blossoms. "Oh, this is beautiful," she exclaimed, and Calli beamed.

"Isn't it?"

They paid the driver and paused on the pavement to stare up at the building. Mia squeezed Calli's hand. "This is so exciting," she said.

Calli squeezed back. "Thank you for being here, and doing this with me."

"You might be my cousin, but in truth, you're the sister of my heart, Cal. There's nowhere else I'd rather be."

"Oh, Mi, I couldn't have put it better myself." Calli sniffled then took a deep breath. "Shall we do this?"

Mia squealed. "Absolutely!"

They entered the shop and were immediately met by a tall smiling woman, dressed in a navy blue dress, with brown hair twisted into a neat chignon. "Welcome. My name is Lisette."

Calli smiled back. "I'm Calli Vega-Lamone, I have an appointment today."

"And this is?"

"My cousin and maid of honour, Mia Davenport."

"Your—your maid of honour, Cal?" Mia stared at her cousin in shock.

Calli laughed. "Well of course. I might not have officially asked you, but there's no one else who could fill the role."

"Oh," Mia said, eyes filling again.

"Champagne!" Lisette said and clapped her hands together. A younger woman emerged from the back carrying a round silver tray with flutes of sparkling pale gold liquid. "This is Frances, and will be assisting us today."

Mia and Calli accepted the glasses and said hello to Frances. The petite woman, dressed similarly to Lisette, with a crop of short curly light-brown hair smiled back at them.

Soon, Mia and Calli were perusing dresses in Calli's favoured style and narrowing the selection down to three to try on.

Mia settled herself on the white velvet tufted sofa in front of the changing area to wait for the grand reveal, and sipped on the rest of her champagne. The curtain twitched and then was pulled back, and Calli emerged with Frances and Lisette trailing after her.

Mia set her glass down beside her on the floor and slowly stood. “Oh, Calli,” she said taking in the high-necked lace top of the long-sleeved gown, and the sweeping skirt in a waterfall of ivory silk. “You look like a princess,” she whispered. The ivory made Calli’s brown skin glow, and brought out the blonde highlights in her mass of golden-brown coloured curls.

“This is it,” Calli whispered. “This is the one I dreamed about, and it doesn’t feel hot at all.”

Lisette brought her hands up to her chest. “That is the magic moment, when it feels *right*.”

“It’s more than right—it’s perfect,” Mia said. “Ash is a lucky man.”

“Isn’t he?” Calli said, lifting her head like a queen before dissolving into delighted laughter.

More champagne was brought out and the dress was toasted. “To finding the one—*and* the right dress,” Mia said with a wink, and Calli grinned in response.

“Now, have you thought of bridesmaid dresses?” Lisette asked, once Calli had changed out of the gown. “Might I make a suggestion?”

“Of course,” Calli said.

“We have recently taken a new shipment of gowns and I believe they will suit your needs perfectly. They will echo your dress in that they are silk, but in a lovely shade of gold that will complement all skin tones and hair colours.” As she spoke Lisette directed Calli and Mia over to a rack of dresses. She pulled out one and showed it to Calli.

It was a long fitted gown whose skirt flared out slightly as it reached the bottom and was made from a drapey silk. The bodice was heart-shaped with thin lace straps all in the gold colour Lisette had mentioned.

"Try it on, Mi, so I can see it properly," Calli urged.

Mia looked at Lisette who said, "This way, Miss Davenport."

"All right," Mia said with a smile at Calli and set her champagne down. She followed Lisette over to the changing room, and slipped out of her cotton dress and into the slinky gown. She scrutinised herself in the mirror and noted it did enhance her pale skin and blonde hair giving it all a warm glow, while skimming over her body in a flattering manner.

Mia pulled back the curtain and Calli gaped. "I want all eyes on me," she said, a twinkle in her eye.

Mia flushed. "All eyes *will* be on you, Cal," she protested.

Calli laughed. "I'm teasing," she said then turned to Lisette. "It's perfect. I'll need four."

"Of course. See Frances before you leave and she will make an appointment for your other bridesmaids to come in for a fitting, but I think this one fits your maid of honour like a glove."

Mia got changed back into her summer dress and while she was waiting for Calli to finish up with Frances, she wandered over to the display of formal gowns for hire. She stopped before one gown. It was forest green and gold and gave her warrior queen vibes with its full skirt. Though sleeveless, with only two twisted fabric straps holding it up, it had an organza cape that flowed from the back. A gold metal belt cinched in the waist and finished the look to perfection.

Her phone rang while she was gazing at the gown. "Hi," she said, answering Josh's call.

"Hi, Ash asked me to call. He didn't want to interrupt Calli if she was still trying on gowns. He wondered if she'd like to meet him for lunch?"

"She's finishing up now," Mia told him. "Hang on." She spoke to Calli and relayed the message.

“Absolutely. I’ll meet him at his office,” Calli replied.

“Did you get that?” Mia asked.

“Sure did,” Josh replied. “So how did it go? Was it successful?”

“Very,” Mia said. “Ash is going to be a mess—but in a good way.” She ended with a laugh.

“That sounds promising,” Josh replied, a smile in his voice. “So how about you?”

“Oh, yes, Calli picked a gorgeous dress design for the bridesmaids too.”

“That’s good, but I meant, did you want to meet for lunch?”

Mia stopped her trailing fingers over the green gown. “Sorry,” she said regretfully, “I have a shift at the restaurant today—my first official one.”

“No problem,” Josh said. “Rain check then?”

“Of course,” Mia said, so grateful that she had already found a wonderful bunch of friends, and settled so seamlessly into New York life.

“Ready?” Calli asked.

“Sure,” she replied, then spoke into her phone, “I’ve got to go, Josh.”

“OK, see you later,” he said.

“Bye.” Mia hung up, and she and Calli took their leave of Lisette and Frances and went outside to wait for the Uber Calli had booked.

“I’ll drop you off at the apartment then carry on to Ash’s office if that’s OK?” Calli said once they’d settled into the car.

“Of course,” Mia replied, and Calli relayed her request to the driver.

Calli sat back with a contented sigh. “I am so glad that part is settled. Now I can concentrate on everything else.”

"Is there anything you need me to do?" Mia asked.

"Everything at the venue is taken care of. They have a wedding organiser in-house and you tell her what your colour scheme is and they do the rest. All we have to do is choose the menu, and what extras we want in the night, and they magically make it happen." Calli patted Mia's arm. "So you, my maid of honour, shall be responsible for the bachelorette party."

Mia smiled. "Any preferences? Loud and rowdy or respectable and restrained?"

Calli gave a wicked grin. "A bit of both?"

"We can do that," Mia said, echoing Calli's grin.

The grin slid off Calli's face. "Joking aside, what I would really like is to have it in Miami. Mom is coming here for the wedding, but she's offered to host the bachelorette at her bar. You'd need to liaise with her to finalise the details."

Mia blinked. "O-*K*," she said slowly, putting her own sentiments about Mae aside. She *had* planned to visit her anyway, perhaps this would be the perfect avenue to do so.

"You sure?" Calli said.

Mia eyed her beloved cousin seriously. "Of course. This is what you want, and I will make it happen."

Calli leant in and pressed a kiss to Mia's cheek. "You're the best. Oh, we're home," she added looking out of the window.

"Go and enjoy lunch with your fiancé and I'll call Aunt Junie later and set things in motion," Mia told her.

Calli blew her a kiss as Mia got out and headed into the apartment block intending to get changed for her shift.

She greeted Carlos and Lou before riding the lift up to the fifth floor, all while her stomach twisted itself into a knot. Seeing Mae wasn't going to be easy, but just like moving to New York, it was the first step in fixing the mistakes of the past in order to secure the bright future she wanted.

She just needed to take another first step.

CHAPTER EIGHT

Mia's first official shift at the restaurant Saturday afternoon went well, and her second on Sunday too, even if Stav seemed to take a shine to her. She put it down to him trying to help her acclimate to her new role and brushed it off.

She had arranged with her Aunt Junie the details of Calli's bachelorette trip, liaising with the other bridesmaids; Dotty, Claudia, and Nicolette, and some of the Valkyries who were able to make the trip, and had finalised the flights. They were to head off in a few weeks for the long weekend which perfectly coincided with some planned renovations to the restaurant so they wouldn't have to worry about booking time off work. Mia was both excited and apprehensive about the trip. She looked forward to seeing Aunt Junie and getting to know all the girls better, but there were two blips on the horizon—one, she hated flying, and two, she would be seeing Mae for the first time in years.

Mia pushed away those two worrying aspects and instead focused on the professor, who sat before her, going over her portfolio of work.

"Hmm...so you've mostly concentrated on Egypt and Greece—but you did a stint at the Roman fort at Caerleon too, if I remember correctly from our online interview?" Professor Deacon zeroed in on her; his brown eyes keen in his ruddy, bearded face.

"Yes, in my third year. I helped with restoration at the site."

"Very good." The professor closed her file, and leant back, steepling his fingers beneath his chin. "You came highly recommended from your department—not only because of your professionalism and passion in the field, but I'm told you have a pretty way with words?"

"Oh, well, I have been asked to write up infographics, and I used to jointly run the student blog with my friend, Simi—he writes a blog for Oxford now. You may have seen it?"

"Journals are more my style," Professor Deacon declared. "But I have something different in mind. I don't go in for flowery prose usually, but in this case, we need to *sell* it, and I believe you are just the person for the job."

Mia was intrigued, and even more so when he showed her an image of an incredible recent discovery and revealed what he required of her.

"I'll get started right away," she told him, and he stood.

"Excellent, that's the sort of enthusiasm I expect. Now, I'll show you to your office—more of a glorified broom cupboard, I'm afraid, but at least it has a door and a desk." He led her out of his office and down the corridor. He stopped at a wooden door and opened it. He held out his hand. "Miss Davenport, I am looking forward to working with you."

Mia smiled and shook his hand. "And I with you, sir," she said.

"Very good," he said. "Your schedule is on your desk—but I'm a flexible man and if you need to shufty things around a bit, just let me know."

"Thank you," Mia said. He returned to his own office, and Mia hid her squeal of excitement as she inspected her 'office'. The professor wasn't kidding when he said it was more of a cupboard. The desk almost filled the width of the room and she had to squeeze to get around it to the chair. On the walls were pinboards and narrow shelves. She would make it work.

She pulled her laptop out of her bag and set it on the desk before taking a seat and opening the lid. She started a new document making notes on fundraising ideas, and also planned out the presentation the professor wanted her to put together.

When Mia had the bare bones, she took a look at her schedule and then emailed Stav with her availability. She'd probably be working long weeks, but it would be worth it, and with the extended weekend coming up in Miami to hopefully decompress it would all be fine. As long as she and Mae could be civil. For Calli, she would certainly try.

A tap on the door had her looking up to see a broad, tall man with shaggy bright-blonde hair standing in the doorway.

"Hello, I am Axel," he said in a heavily accented voice. "I work for Professor Carnley in Scandinavian Studies, down the hall."

Mia stood and offered her hand. "Hi, Axel, nice to meet you. I'm Mia—Mia Davenport."

He shook her hand in a firm grip. "Nice to meet you too, Mia. Professor Deacon mentioned you would be starting today, so I thought I would come and introduce myself. Besides me, there is another who helps Professor Carnley—Pieter works Thursdays and Fridays."

“Ah, I see. There’ll only be me part-time—apparently, Professor Deacon has never had an assistant before?”

“Not as long as I have been here. I am from Sweden, and Pieter, Germany. We both started last year, but I might stay on—if I can get my girlfriend to join me here.”

“I’m only here for the summer but potentially longer if it works out,” Mia said. “Does your girlfriend not want to move?”

“She is considering it. When she comes to visit in a month’s time, I am going to try and convince her.”

“Well, good luck!” Mia said, knowing how easy it had been for herself to make the decision to move her whole life, but she could understand it might not be as straightforward for everyone else. Especially if they had a good life where they were.

“Thank you.” Axel nodded. “Well, if you need anything, I am just down the hall.”

“Great, thanks,” Mia said and turned back to her work when Axel left, mentally adding another potential friend to her growing list.

“Knock knock.”

Mia blinked behind her reading glasses as the door opened and Josh popped his head around the apartment door. “Not disturbing you, am I?” he asked, gesturing at the laptop and papers spread out before her. In between shifts at the restaurant, hanging out with the others, and early-morning runs, she’d put together an idea for a fundraiser. After the professor’s go-ahead, she was now finalising the presentation, and the finer details of the event.

Mia blew out a breath and sat back in the dining chair. “No, come on in, I’ve been at it for hours,” she said.

Josh entered and closed the door behind himself and joined her at the table, taking a seat beside her. "Cal asked me to come over and help you set up for card night. What are you working on?"

Mia turned the laptop so Josh could see the screen. "I'm putting together a presentation for a fundraiser the department is organising. This was found in a small village in England last month and Professor Deacon got excited enough to believe there might be more to be found." Mia tapped the screen on a small image next to the text she had been compiling. Josh studied the ring in the image; a twisted silver-coloured metal with two curling pieces holding precious green and amber-coloured stones. Mia turned her head with a smile. "It might've been Queen Boudicca's," she said, then blinked as her glasses brought Josh's bright blue eyes into sharp focus. She pulled the glasses off, slightly disconcerted.

"Queen Boudicca? She was that Celtic queen, right?" Josh asked, interest colouring his tone.

"She was Iceni; one of the Celtic tribes. Her story always fascinated me, and now I get to be a part of it," Mia said, her voice awestruck.

"You love it, don't you?" Josh asked.

Mia smiled. "I'm a total geek for history, but for me, it's more than that. Take this ring for example. Say it *was* Boudicca's, think of all the battles it witnessed, the history being made by the hand that wore it, then it was lost, covered in soil, trodden over by thousands of feet until one day, a farmer bought a new plot and was doing some irrigation work and what does he find?"

"The ring," Josh said, appearing totally invested.

Mia wiggled in her seat, delighted. "Its story isn't over—it's like Boudicca's hand is reaching out across the centuries, and we archaeologists take that hand and hold it for a while. Her tragic story is never forgotten. She is never forgotten."

Josh fell silent, and Mia glanced at him sheepishly. "Sorry, I tend to get a bit sentimental...but don't tell the professor. He'd be aghast. 'There's no room for sentiment in archaeology, Miss Davenport'," she mimicked in a deep, booming voice, recalling his notes on her presentation draft.

Josh laughed. "He sounds quite formidable."

Mia gave a fervent nod. "Oh, he's a character all right, but his enthusiasm for the subject is unrivalled. It's a great honour to work with him. Although..." she hesitated.

"What is it?"

"He's entrusted me with this whole presentation. He's hoping to raise funds to put an expedition together and if it goes well, he's promised me a spot on the dig. I'd love to do a bit of fieldwork, it's been ages since I have been on a location dig. Henry never liked me to—" Mia broke off with a flush. "Never mind." She waved a hand airily.

Josh gave her an understanding look. "Sounds like you're well overdue then. I'm sure you'll do an awesome job in raising funds. But if you need any help—I can put in a word at my firm. They're always looking for things to sponsor. It's good for business."

Mia brightened. "Thanks, and that would be great. I can get you tickets when I've finalised the details. Let me know how many you'll need."

"Sounds good." Josh indicated her notes. "Do you need any more time now, or shall we set up? The others will be here soon."

Mia saved her document and closed down her laptop. "No, my brain is mush," she said with a smile. "I'll finish it up tomorrow." She gathered up her papers and slotted them into a box folder. She stood and collected both the folder and laptop. "I'll pop these in my room, then I'm all yours," she said.

Josh cleared his throat, then said, "Great." He noticed her T-shirt. "What does that say on your top?" he asked.

"I Dig You," she said with a grin, then flushed. "I mean, that's what it says. It was a gift from my old uni friend, Simi."

"He sounds fun," Josh said with his own grin.

"Life's never dull with Simi around," Mia said, then went into her room, and set the laptop and folder on her dressing table before inspecting her appearance in the mirror.

She'd bundled up her long hair on top of her head in a messy bun, and had chucked on a pair of grey sweats and the cropped pale pink slogan tee, after finishing work at the university. With a fond smile, thinking of Simi, she pulled her hair out of its bun and finger-combed it into loose waves.

Mia left her room and joined Josh in the dining area, where he was setting out the green baize tablecloth on the round dining table.

"I'll sort the nibbles, shall I?" Mia asked.

Josh stared at her then blinked. "You took your hair down," he said.

"Oh—yes. I had a bit of a headache brewing so thought I'd relieve some of the tension," she explained, feeling suddenly exposed beneath the gaze he ran intently over her hair.

"I like it down," he said, and then turned back to taking the decks of cards out of their container.

OK. "Thanks," Mia murmured, then giving herself something to do, she pulled out bowls and started decanting pretzels, potato chips, and popcorn into them.

Josh joined her in the small kitchen area—made smaller by

his tall presence—and opened the fridge, removing two bottles of beer. He lifted one up, one eyebrow raised in question.

"Sure," Mia murmured, and accepted the bottle when he popped the cap and passed it to her. She nearly dropped it when their fingers inadvertently brushed. God, Mia, she thought, your brain really is mush. She took a long sip of the cool beer to cover her discomposure.

"God, I needed that," Josh said, taking a long swallow himself.

"Rough day?" Mia asked.

"You could say that. Ash and I have been working on this complicated case—both parties insist the artwork is theirs, but with no legal contract drawn up…the battle continues."

"Oh that's right, you work in acquisition contracts. Fine Art, especially, is your forte?"

Josh nodded. "I loved art in high school, and toyed with making it my major, but my dad encouraged me to go for something more secure. So I took law, with some art classes, and now I combine the two." He smiled, but a touch of wistfulness filled his gaze, and Mia wanted to ask, to probe deeper but held back, not wanting to overstep. He carried on, "Not exactly the creative outlet I craved, but still, it keeps me busy and puts a roof over my head."

Mia took a sip of her drink, pondering his words and what they revealed. Had he put his own dreams aside and settled? "It's great when you get to do what you love for a living," she said, wondering if he was truly content with his own career path. "I always knew I'd be an archaeologist. Although, I fancied myself as the adventuring type—and I was for a while—but life forced me down a different path and I ended up doing part-time desk duty in the archaeology department at Canterbury

University."

"So what made you go for the internships over here?" Josh asked, leaning back against the counter.

Mia pursed her lips in thought. Because she'd wanted more? More excitement, maybe. To push herself. "I was at my desk when the two opportunities came in and I thought 'Why not?'. I told Henry, and, to my surprise, he was keen—especially the L.A one. With my dual nationality, it would be easy for me to settle here if I wanted to. Now I think, he only encouraged me, because his work has an office in L.A., and probably wanted a bit of the L.A.-lifestyle himself." She shook her head bitterly. Would he have invited Nadia over on the sly? Mia's ex-friend had always fancied herself as a model, and would probably have taken full advantage of the opportunity.

"That's shady," Josh said. "But you always wanted New York?"

Mia gave a genuine smile. "I did. I love it here, and I missed Calli. In truth, I'd been feeling out of sorts—you know, stagnant. Things were a little weird with Henry and I...I know why now, but then I just thought he was under a lot of stress at work." But it turns out it was something or some*one* else he was under, she added darkly to herself. She gave a mental shake and carried on. "I thought if I—or we, depending on him—took a few weeks away then maybe things would somehow re-centre themselves." Her laugh was bitter when it came. "Funny really, it's because of the letters that I discovered the pair of them. I left the university dig site early so I could go home and open them with Henry."

Josh's eyes crinkled with sympathy. "Shit, Mia."

"Exactly," she said, and took another long pull of her drink. "But hey, if fate hadn't intervened, I'd probably be miserable and unaware in L.A right now." She laughed and noted it was a trifle forced, but she determined to push away her pain when the apartment door opened and Calli and Ash came in playfully bickering over who was carrying more groceries.

Josh gave Mia's shoulder a reassuring squeeze then moved across the apartment to jokingly referee.

Mia sipped on her beer, the knot of anxiety beginning to unravel enough that, soon, she was able to join in with the banter.

CHAPTER NINE

Plans for the fundraiser quickly took shape, and Professor Deacon pulled some strings with contacts of his. Within a week they had a selection of items—both real, and replicas—to auction off. Josh had spoken to his boss, who had bought tickets for them to attend with a view to perhaps making some bids himself.

Mia found her rhythm and committed to regular shifts at the restaurant on Tuesdays, Wednesday afternoons, and Saturdays, with alternate Sundays off. Although, her suspicions about Stav had come to fruition when he had asked her out and Mia had frozen, stammering out she wasn't dating at the moment. She hoped he would let it drop; not wanting to have to find another place to work so soon if things became awkward.

Mondays, Wednesday mornings, Thursdays, and Fridays Mia spent at the university. She ran early mornings with the Valkyries and even managed a few nights out with Calli, but it was the Thursday night card nights she still looked forward to the most.

Tonight, she had to concentrate on the Fundraiser. It was the Wednesday evening of her third week in New York and the university lecture hall had been booked and the tickets sold out. Mia had gone back with Calli to the bridal shop and hired the ethereal forest-green dress, knowing it would be perfect for her to do her presentation in.

"Calli, can you zip me up?" Mia backed out of her room but was met with silence. She turned her head, searching for her cousin and let out an, "*Oh,*" of breath when, instead of Calli coming to her aid, Josh stood next to the kitchen counter, alone. He'd already dressed for the event in a dark green—almost black—velvet jacket, black shirt and trousers.

They stared at each other for a long moment, until Mia remembered she was standing with her bare back exposed, and turned abruptly, her long hair whirling about her.

"Need assistance?" Josh asked. His gaze lingered on the dress, his eyes widening in appreciation.

"Yes, please," Mia said, feeling stupidly nervous for some reason. "Calli was supposed to help, but..." she trailed off.

"She had to go and collect her dress from the dry cleaners. She'll be back soon," Josh supplied.

Mia swallowed as Josh approached her. "Right."

"Turn," Josh said softly as he towered over her, and Mia noticed his sea salt and coconut scent had been exchanged for something dark and spicy this time.

She slowly turned and, after the merest of hesitations, Josh brushed her hair out of the way. Mia held back the shiver that threatened to erupt when his fingers accidently touched her bare skin. He carefully tugged up the zipper and smoothed it into place.

Mia faced Josh with a grateful smile, highly aware of the

flush staining her cheeks. "Thank you. I know fashions were a bit different back then, but not that different that I would have gotten away with half falling out of my dress," she said, then could have smacked her hand to her forehead in horror. "I—I mean, I was having trouble with the zipper."

Josh stepped back with a smile, and took in the floor-length forest-green dress, with draped front, and gold-coloured metal rings embellishing the twisted straps. "It's a beautiful dress," he said, and Mia felt beautiful in it.

"Isn't it?" she said, then grinned. "It has pockets."

Josh gave an appreciative laugh. "Ah, yes, the holy grail of dresses—must have pockets."

Mia laughed in delight. "I'd better finish getting ready," she told him.

"Sure. Take your time. I'll hang until Ash and Calli get back."

Mia returned to her room and leant against the door when she closed it. Her skin was still tingling from where Josh had touched it and she needed to take a few deep breaths to settle herself. She was acting ridiculous and knew it. *Of course, his fingers had to touch her, how else was he to zip her up otherwise?*

Exasperated at herself, Mia went over to the dressing table to pick up the gold metal belt that went with the dress. She cinched it at her waist, before taking a seat and selecting a few pieces of loose hair to braid—momentarily wincing when she thought of Henry wanting her to cut it. Almost defiantly, she twisted two chunky braids up to encircle her head and pinned them, leaving the rest of the braids to mix in with the loose locks. Finally, she clipped tiny filigree clasps to the flowing braids, and then added coppery-green eyeshadow to her lids, lengthening mascara to her lashes, a touch of blusher to her cheeks—not that she needed it—and a slick of shimmery pink gloss to her lips.

Mia stood proudly, as though she were a warrior queen herself, and slid on gold leather flat cage sandals, tying the straps around her ankles. She picked up the small gold clutch bag and put her phone and other necessary items in it, before she once again made her way out into the living area.

This time, Josh openly gaped at her appearance, before recovering and clearing his throat. "Now, that, is an outfit. Your hair looks amazing."

Mia smiled shyly. "Thank you. I thought I'd better get into character. The professor told me to 'sell it'."

"I'm sure you'll raise more than you need for the excavation," Josh said, and set down the bottle of beer he'd been holding.

"I hope so," Mia said, and then turned as Calli and Ash hurried in, Calli with a dry-cleaning bag slung over her shoulder. "I know, I know," she said, catching Mia's eye. "I'll be five minutes tops."

Mia laughed. "Don't rush, honestly. I need to go on ahead anyway to help set things up."

"Do you need a lift?" Josh asked.

Mia shook her head. "Thanks, but no. Axel is coming to pick me up."

"Axel—is he the big, Viking-looking one?" Calli turned in the entrance to her doorway. "Or is that the other one?"

Mia's lips twitched at the description. "Axel does have long blonde hair and is quite tall, so I guess you could call him that."

Calli raised an eyebrow, mouth opening, and Mia shot her a warning look. Calli deflated, the probably-suggestive comment about her new friend dying on her lips. "Right, well. See you there!" she said, gave Mia a little wave, and headed into her room, Ash following with an indulgent grin. Calli popped her head back out briefly to say, "You look killer by the way!"

"Thanks, Cal," Mia said with a smile.

Silence fell in the room until Josh said, "A Viking, huh?"

"Axel and Pieter are from Europe—they work with another professor in the department but they pitched in with the fundraiser," Mia explained.

"Ah," Josh said.

The intercom buzzed, and Mia hurried over to answer it.

"Miss Mia, a gentleman is here for you," Carlos said, then with a hushed voice—one that still carried well into the apartment, added, "I am so glad you are dating. You need to enjoy yourself."

Oh dear god, Mia thought with a wince. "Oh—ah—thanks, Carlos, but he's a colleague," she corrected him. A colleague who had a girlfriend.

"Right, of course. He said he would wait outside," Carlos said a touch of disappointment tinging his tone.

"I'll be right down," Mia said, then closed her eyes briefly before turning around. She smiled at Josh, who studied her with intense eyes. "I'll see you at the fundraiser," she told him.

He picked up his bottle again. "I look forward to it, Killer Queen."

Mia let out a breathy laugh, and Josh grinned. She opened the door, let herself out, and took the lift down to the lobby.

"Well, Lou, would you look at our Miss Mia," Carlos said when the lift doors opened and she stepped out.

Lou gave an agreeable yip, and pranced over to her on his tiny paws.

"Sorry, Lou-Lou, no picky-ups today, I have to get going." Mia crouched to run a hand over his tiny back. "We shall have a mini date tomorrow...if that's OK?" she directed at Carlos.

"Oh, indeed. Go and enjoy yourself now," Carlos told her.

"It's work, but it should be fun," Mia told him with a smile. He rounded the desk and walked down the steps with her to hold open the door for her.

"Have a good night," he said.

"Thanks, Carlos," Mia replied and looked across to the kerb when a car horn beeped. Axel leant out of the window of a bright yellow Volkswagen Beetle.

Mia made her way over and Axel hopped out with a smile. He wore a smart blue shirt over his broad shoulders, tucked into trim black trousers. "Nice car," she told her colleague.

"Nice dress," he countered in his Swedish accent, then, "I just picked it up. Now I am planning on staying here, I thought I might as well get a car."

He opened the passenger door for Mia and she slid in, carefully lifting the skirts of the long gown, before buckling her seatbelt.

Axel settled himself in and he said. "We have to pick up Pieter and his girlfriend on the way if that is OK?"

"Sure," Mia said. "We've got time. As long as we are in position before the guests arrive. I don't want Professor Deacon losing it tonight."

Axel chuckled. "I thought Professor Carnley was tough, but he is a pussycat in comparison."

"Professor Deacon is definitely more of a bear."

They laughed companionably together, stopping to pick up Axel's German-born colleague, Pieter, and his glamorous girlfriend, Annika.

"That is a very beautiful gown," Annika said, casting an experienced eye over Mia once they had reached the university and had gotten out of the car. Tall and sylph-like with cropped blonde hair and pale blue eyes, Mia could see how Annika was such a successful model.

"Thank you, and you look fabulous," Mia said, taking in the black mini-dress, seemingly made up of hundreds of criss-crossing satin straps.

"Oh, this? It is *Dominica*," Annika said as if Mia should know who she was talking about.

"Lovely," Mia said, not overly up on designer brands.

Pieter took Annika's arm and helped her up the many steps to the function hall entrance. Her sky-high Louboutin's—even Mia recognised those—clicked as she walked, with a flash of their red soles.

"I will park the car and then be in to help you finish setting up," Axel said.

"See you in there," Mia replied and followed the others up the steps.

Inside, she wasted no time in checking the list she'd left pinned on the noticeboard and mentally ran through everything in her mind. The chairs had been set up as she'd requested; in rows in front of the stage. A microphone and stand were placed front and centre, a display table for some of the items was positioned where she had asked, and a screen hung along the back of the stage wall.

"Ah, Miss Davenport, nice and early, I see...and looking *quite* the part." Professor Deacon emerged from the storage room, and gave Mia an approving nod. He wore his usual tweed trousers, but for the event he had paired it with a tweed waistcoat over his white shirt, finished off with a jaunty checked bowtie.

"Anything you'd like me to do?" Mia asked.

"No, no, the wait staff have the champagne and nibbles ready to go after the event. Pieter is in the storage room and he, and Axel, will bring out the items lot by lot. So all I need you to do is place that lovely torque around your neck, and prepare yourself for your presentation."

"I need to go to my office and collect my notes and the torque, but Axel is here, he's just parking his car," Mia informed him.

Professor Deacon nodded, then mumbled something to himself and wandered back into the storage room.

Mia headed through the function room, and out into the corridor before going into the faculty department. Inside her office, she unlocked her desk drawer and removed the pewter replica torque the professor had referred to. She placed her handbag in the drawer and locked it.

She studied the necklace, running her fingers over the hammered metal, tracing over the twisted curls at the end with her fingertips. She hooked it around her neckline, and each of the two curls sat either side of her neck, just touching her collarbones. The dress framed the torque perfectly as if it had been made to complement it.

Mia picked up her notes, scanned over them, and concentrated on her breathing for a few minutes, trying to banish any nerves. You've done this countless times before...*in and out*...these are your peers...*in and out*...this is just another step in the next stage of your career...*in and out*...this is a subject you love...*in and out*.

More in control, Mia left her office, taking her notes with her.

"There you are, the prof is getting ready to start." Axel met her on the stairs, and Mia followed him back down.

"Tell him I'm ready," she instructed Axel.

Instead of going into the main seating area where the guests had all now taken their seats, she waited backstage to be introduced by the professor.

"Ladies and Gentlemen," boomed Professor Deacon moments later from the stage. "Thank you for attending our department's fundraiser. As you may—or may not know—a remarkable discovery was recently made in a farmer's field on the outskirts of what is believed to be the final battle of Queen Boudicca and her fateful army. But I shall leave the details to my far more eloquent assistant, Miss Mia Davenport."

Mia took a deep breath and swept out onto the stage, channelling Boudicca, and hopefully exuding the same type of confidence as the queen would have had. "Thank you, Professor Deacon," she said with a smile, as the professor stood aside. Gentle applause filled the room, and Mia scanned her eyes over the guests. She noted Calli sat next to Annika, along with Ash and Josh in the second row. She smiled at Calli and Ash, and her eyes briefly met Josh's and he gave her a smile.

Encouraged, Mia glanced down at her notes and began, clear and crisp. "It all began with a hand. A hand that fisted into the air followed by a battle cry." She paused for effect, and noticed the room had fallen silent, rapt. "And on that hand?" She clicked the button on the podium and the screen behind her flashed up with a blown-up image of the ring. "We believe it was this. This ring has been dated to 61 AD and was—as the professor stated—discovered in the exact location of that final battle. It is the most exciting discovery made in recent years, and could lead to unearthing many more important artefacts and relics." Mia again paused.

"Professor Deacon plans to put together a team as soon as

possible, so the site will be excavated properly and thoroughly. But in order to do that, we need funds...and that is where you come in. Tonight, we have for you a collection of replicas, and some real pieces that have been kindly donated for you to bid on and own. Imagine, you could own a piece of history" — she smiled around at the guests — "and *be* a part of history in the making."

Mia paused one final time. "And so, how did it end? It ended with a heart. A heart that, though filled with the grief of defeat, had thundered with the strength and desire to do what was right for its people. And that, my friends, is what we" — she gestured at the professor — "desire to do. Do what is right and preserve the stories of the past for the generations of the future. Boudicca's story is legendary...be a part of her next chapter."

Mia pressed the button again, and an artist's rendering of what Queen Boudicca might have looked like filled the screen behind her; her pose strong and proud. Inexplicably, tears filled Mia's eyes and she hastily blinked them back, knowing the professor wouldn't approve of the sentiment. He had been generous in allowing her a bit of creative flair with how she worded the presentation, so she didn't want to push her luck.

After a moment of complete silence, the room erupted into appreciative applause.

CHAPTER TEN

A beaming Professor Deacon joined Mia on stage.

"Beautifully put, Miss Davenport," he said after the room had quietened down again. "And with you dressed like a queen yourself, what a perfect segue into starting the bidding" – he gestured at the torque on Mia's neck – "with lot number one, a replica of a Celtic torque necklace that would have been worn by a noblewoman from the Iceni tribe, created by Abigail Trowse, a student of metalworks here at the university."

Mia stepped to one side, her heart suddenly racing, buoyed up by the emotion of her presentation and the powerful image still up on the screen. She looked into the audience and noticed Calli dabbing at her eyes with a tissue. *Oh god,* she thought, knowing that if she continued to look at the pride on her cousin's face, she'd be bawling too. So instead, she trailed her gaze along the row and stopped on Josh. His face appeared frozen, his eyes intense on her. Heat worked its way slowly up her cheeks, and her heart moved in a strange cadence. After a long moment, Mia smiled at him, and he slowly returned it.

She focused her attention on the professor, seeing the bidding had begun in earnest.

"Is the lovely lady included too?" a French-accented voice called teasingly from the audience, and Mia's smile stiffened on her face.

The professor frowned, but said in a jovial tone, "No, no, my good sir, simply the necklace," and laughed. But Mia knew him well enough now to know that it sounded forced. The professor was angry—on her behalf, she thought with some affection.

Mia acknowledged his ire with a small dip of her chin before looking out into the crowd. The bidder that had spoken inappropriately—a classically handsome man with chiselled features and thick brown hair styled neatly off his face—raked his eyes over Mia as if he sought to genuinely own her, and not simply the torque. Disgust curdled through her stomach, but she kept a polite expression on her face.

"Pity," he said, and gave a mock sigh. "Oh, well, I shall increase my bid regardless."

The bidding continued until the Frenchman—Monsieur Raoul Soreni—was the victor, buying the torque Mia wore for a considerable sum.

Mia relinquished the torque to Axel for him to box up. The blonde Swede frowned and muttered, as he leant in to accept it, "Do you want me to remind Monsieur Generous of his manners?"

Mia shook his head, touched by his offer. "No, it's fine," she said. "Unfortunately we must be pleasant to our benefactors...even if they are not in return."

Axel muttered something in Swedish but moved away to help with the next lot.

Mia, standing aside as the next lot was brought out and set

on the table, noticed Josh regarding Monsieur Soreni with revulsion. That was all she needed; her friends coming to blows at the auction with the bidders. But thankfully, the gentleman sat the other side of Josh spoke causing Josh to focus on him and respond.

The auction continued without a hitch; the professor, Axel and Pieter, had it down to a fine art, and soon all the lots were sold for very handsome amounts.

"Thank you! How kind you have all been. My colleagues and I welcome you all to enjoy some champagne and nibbles, and mingle about in the smaller function room. A slideshow will show in the background for those who are interested in what your generous funds will pay for." Professor Deacon finished to the polite applause of those assembled.

The guests stood and filtered into the next room, and Mia let out a long breath. Professor Deacon followed the departing guests, talking in his big booming voice.

"That went well," Axel said, and Pieter nodded.

"It really did," Mia said, pleased. "I don't know about you guys but I could do with a glass of champagne."

"You deserve it, that presentation was incredible," Pieter said.

"Thank you. I wasn't sure if the prof would let me get away with it. You know how he is; *fact over flourish*, Miss Davenport." Mia giggled, but she had grown to genuinely like and respect the professor.

Pieter and Axel chuckled, and the three of them descended from the stage and crossed the room, heading for the champagne reception. The men were hailed by people they knew and went on ahead.

Mia stepped into the room and accepted a glass of

champagne from one of the hospitality students who had volunteered to help out. No sooner had she done so than the winning bidder of the torque, Raoul Soreni, stepped into her path. He held out a hand, and instinctively Mia clasped it to shake it, but he pulled up her hand to press a soft-lipped kiss to the back of it. "Ah, ma belle, Mademoiselle Davenport," he said.

Mia extricated herself as politely as she could manage. "Good evening, Monsieur Soreni."

"Call me Raoul, please. And may I call you Mia? Such a beautiful name." He smiled charmingly at her and she gauged him to be around thirty.

"Of course." Her own smile was tight. "Thank you for your generous bid tonight, it will help our excavation greatly."

He leant in closer; too close for comfort, but Mia refused to back up and show her unease. "Ah, you will find I am most generous...in all my pursuits." He offered a business card, and once again, she automatically accepted it. "My card. If you ever want to take a break from—what is the word? Ah, yes—*mucking* around in muddy fields. I could offer you a far more lucrative career path."

Mia knew he wasn't talking about a position that would interest her in the slightest. Nausea roiled in her stomach. She recognised the interest in his eyes, but she also recognised the type of man he was. The same as Henry. Hindsight was a great revealer and had honed her mind enough that Mia could clearly see Raoul's character, even if she had been previously blind to Henry's.

She pocketed the card, and said in her brightest voice, "That is so kind of you monsieur, but I enjoy *mucking* about in muddy fields. Do enjoy the rest of the evening, and merci beaucoup for your generous bid." Mia fixed him with her most glowing smile, and moved on.

The smile turned brittle on her face as she glided away, but she relaxed when Calli ran up to her with a little squeal. "*Mia*! That was beautiful," she said. "I got so emotional. Thankfully, Ash had a tissue but you should have warned me!"

Mia laughed a genuine laugh. "Sorry, I didn't realise you would be so affected."

Calli swatted her on the arm. "Hey, I'm not an unfeeling monster. It was poignant and so powerful...especially with the visuals."

Annika sauntered over to join them, a glass of champagne in hand. "Calli, here is the name of that designer I was telling you about before the auction began." She offered Calli a napkin with a name written on it.

Calli's face turned strained, but she took the napkin anyway. "Thank you, Annika, but, I'm happy with my style," she said neutrally, and Mia was proud of her cousin's restraint in not putting the woman—whom she'd only just met that night—in her place with a snappy retort.

"Of course," Annika said with a quick eye-flick down to Calli's purple sheath dress.

Calli ignored her and spoke to Mia. "Josh said he'd find you as soon as he could get away, but he and Ash are networking with their boss."

"OK," Mia said, grateful that Josh convinced his boss to come in the first place and support the auction.

"Your boyfriend is very handsome; he could be a model," Annika remarked to Mia, then took a sip of her champagne and pulled a sour face.

Calli's gaze laser-focused on the side of Mia's face as Mia answered, "Oh, Josh? He's just a friend."

Annika raised one perfectly arched blonde eyebrow, fixing Mia with a disbelieving look. "My mistake." She shrugged elegantly. "He watched you most intently. Speaking of which, I must find Pieter." She set the champagne down on the tray of a passing server and wafted away with an airy wave and a cloud of Dior perfume.

Mia waited a beat then said, "Don't, Cal."

"What? It's not my fault if people make assumptions." Calli shrugged innocently, and a flush burned up from Mia's collarbone.

"There's nothing *to* assume. He's only being friendly. He's like it with everyone," Mia said defensively.

Calli choked on her champagne. "Sure, Mi."

"He *is*. He knows I've been through a shitty time, and is being a good friend. He's considerate and gentlemanly. Just like a *friend*."

"OK, OK, put down the sword," Calli said, and set her champagne glass down. "That," she said, pointing an accusing finger at the flute, "really is bad. Your prof was a bit stingy with the drinks' budget."

Mia gave a reluctant laugh. "The department is trying to *make* money, not spend it."

Calli shook her head sadly. "Well it's a good job it wasn't a wine-tasting evening then." She side-eyed Mia. "That French bidder was a high-roller wasn't he, *and* a bit forward?"

Mia squirmed uncomfortably, thinking of the business card stuffed in her pocket. "A bit," she agreed, deciding not to bring up the conversation she'd had with him. Hopefully, she would never encounter him again.

"Hey, what's up, you're not still mad about Annika's comment?"

"What? Oh, no, my mind wandered then, sorry," Mia said, then added when the professor beckoned her, "duty calls."

"Go ahead. We're probably going to make a move soon anyway. Ash has an early meeting tomorrow." Calli leant in to press a kiss on Mia's cheeks. "Congratulations, this was great fun."

"Thanks, Cal. I'll see you at home."

Mia moved through the mingling guests and joined Professor Deacon. "Ah, Miss Davenport. Absolutely sterling presentation, if a bit whimsical," he said, bowing his bearded head. "But it worked. We have raised more than enough funds—we need approval from the university board, of course, but then we can set things in motion."

Mia smiled. "Thank you, Professor. That's very exciting."

"I'll want you with me, of course. You will be invaluable to the team," he told her, then moved away when someone hailed him.

Excitement fizzed through Mia at the thought of finally getting to do some fieldwork. With the smile still on her face, she turned away and nearly bumped into someone coming the other way.

"Oh! I do apologise," Mia said and found her forearms gripped by a pair of warm, strong hands, steadying her.

"My fault," Josh said, smiling down at her, and Mia relaxed.

He released her and they moved to one side to talk. "I've been looking for you to congratulate you. That was such a great presentation, Mia—*really* great, and by the looks of it, the fundraiser was a huge success?"

"Thank you, yes. And thank you for getting your office involved, your boss made a few bids, I noticed. Professor Deacon is very pleased. All we need is the green light from the board and we'll be off."

"My pleasure." Josh smiled. "And that's terrific news. When do you think you'll be going?"

"Not for a few weeks, definitely after Calli and Ash's wedding. We'd have to get all the proper permits sorted, arrange machinery, accommodation, and assemble a team first. But if I know the professor, he'll hurry things through. He'll want to get first dibs on the site for certain."

Josh tilted his head in thought. "And for good reason. I have never been more moved by a group of people. By watching your presentation, no one could be under any illusions of the passion and joy you have for the subject. The site couldn't be in better hands."

Mia blushed. "Then my job here is done. If I can inspire just one person to pursue what they love, then I'm happy."

"You inspired me," Josh said softly. "You were the epitome of a warrior queen up there, I could almost visualise the painting. All you'd need is a sword in hand, and the image would be complete."

"Why don't you paint it then?" Mia challenged, equally as softly.

Josh rocked back on his heels, his eyes intense. "Mia, would you-" he broke off when she took a sudden step sideways, as Raoul Soreni cut through the crowd of remaining guests, positioning herself so she was hidden from view by Josh's tall frame. Josh turned, a frown—aimed at the French collector—marring his handsome face. "Everything OK? I spotted Soreni cornering you after the auction. He was out of line with his comments." He angled himself so Mia was shielded further.

Absentmindedly, Mia toyed with the business card in her dress pocket. "It's fine. He passed on his business card, and urged me to contact him if I wanted a change of scene." She let out an empty laugh. "I've only just arrived in New York and barely begun to follow my passions, and he wants me to skip off to France and do a one-eighty on my career."

Josh considered her for a moment. "Mia—I know it's not my place, and tell me if I'm overstepping...but Raoul's known for being a bit of a playboy. I've had plenty of contractual dealings with him."

Mia's cheeks flushed, and her words came out a little harsher than she intended. "Thanks for the warning, Josh, but I'm not some green girl whose head gets turned by a French accent, a hefty bank balance, and a wink." *Oh, but you did for a posh English accent, ambition, and silky words.* The pain of that knowledge still hurt, and was the main cause for her misplaced resentment in answering Josh.

"Shit, Mia." Josh's hand hovered between them as if he wanted to clasp her arm. "Sorry, that came out wrong. I wasn't implying you *would* take him up on his offer, I just intended to let you know what sort of man he is. The number of pieces of artwork I've had to transfer over to disgruntled exes of his is quite staggering. Although, they're disgruntled no longer when they see what the art is worth."

Mia's embarrassed anger evaporated. "Sorry, Josh. I know you were only trying to be a good friend. Potentially dating someone is a bit of a sore point at the moment," she admitted, "in that, I have no desire to do so, and I'm tired of being bombarded by everyone else thinking I should just get over it and date already." She gave Josh a brittle smile. "But I assure you, Raoul Soreni is the last man who I would break my dating drought for. I'm familiar with men like him." She crumpled the business card up in her pocket until it was a tiny glossy, embossed, cardboard ball.

Sympathy flashed through Josh's gaze before it vanished and was replaced by something less discernible. "I understand. The conversation is off limits." He smiled gently at her. "Can I give you a lift home? Ash and Calli took an Uber already."

Mia, keen to get their easy-going camaraderie back, jumped at his offer. "Thanks. I'll just tell Axel he doesn't need to wait for me."

"I met him earlier, he's a great guy," Josh said.

Mia gave a genuine smile. "He's a lot of fun to work with, but we don't get to do it often enough. He reminds me a little of my friend, Simi. Great banter and sense of humour, but unexpected taste in vehicles."

"Perhaps I'll get to meet this famed Simi one day," Josh said.

"Oh, you never know," Mia said, with a smile, thinking of her old friend who she knew would love Josh, and would more than likely think up a nickname for him. "There's Axel now."

Mia moved away and spoke to her colleague, and noticed the crowd of guests had thinned out. She found Professor Deacon and he was only too happy for her to leave.

"You worked very hard tonight, Miss Davenport," he said. "I shall see you tomorrow."

"Goodnight, Professor," Mia said, and he waved her away with a smile.

She re-joined Josh. "I have to collect my handbag from my office," she told him.

"Lead the way," he invited.

Mia took him through the faculty area and up to her small office. "I won't be a moment," she said, opening the door. He leant on the doorframe as she went over to her desk and unlocked her drawer.

"You've settled in nicely," he said, eyes on the noticeboard filled with papers and photographs, and the plant on her desk.

Mia retrieved her bag. "It's been easy to. I feel at home here, and everyone is so friendly and welcoming."

"Do you think you'll stay here full-time if they offer you a position?" Josh asked Mia, his eyes lit with genuine interest.

Mia perched on the edge of her desk. "I told myself I wouldn't make hasty decisions ever again, so I'll wait and see whether they offer me a permanent position first, then I'll have a good long think about what it means for my future."

"And what do you see in your future?" Josh asked.

The small room suddenly shrank even smaller. "I don't know," Mia admitted, her voice a husky whisper. "But what I do know is, it's far brighter than what it would have been if I'd continued down that other route." She stood, and gave Josh a weak smile. "How about you?"

"My future?" Josh tilted his head in thought. "Perhaps my own firm one day...or I might take your advice and become a tortured artist, painting away the sunlight hours in my garret." He grinned, as though already brushing away that idea.

Mia laughed, the uncertain clouds dissipating. "Well, we have time yet," she told him, joining him at the door, hoping—yet not wanting to push him on the subject—that he would start painting again. She had died inside, inch by inch, by denying herself doing what she loved in order to please Henry. Sometimes, you had to do what pleased *your* soul, regardless of other people's opinion of it.

"That we do," Josh said, his tone easy, but his eyes serious. He stepped out into the hallway and Mia followed him, pulling her office door closed behind her.

Together they headed for the car park, Mia only too happy

to avoid encountering Raoul again. Men like that tended to see 'no' as a challenge.

Josh opened the passenger door to his car and waited until Mia got in before he closed the door, and rounded the car to get in himself. He caught Mia mid-yawn.

"Tired?" he asked with a smile.

"Incredibly," Mia agreed.

"Being a warrior queen is quite exhausting, I imagine," he observed, pulling out of the car park, and heading into the perennial New York traffic.

"Ha," Mia said. "I'd settle for being a fairytale princess right about now—preferably Sleeping Beauty."

"Well, you've got the beauty bit down," Josh said, then gave her a quick sideways look. "I—ah—meant with your blonde hair and your large eyes..."

"Oh right, of course," Mia said, startled.

They fell silent, and Mia stared sleepily out of the window.

"And not to mention your affinity with animals...that's totally a prerequisite of being a princess, right?" Josh broke the silence, a teasing tone in his voice.

Mia turned, readily taking the bait. "Oh absolutely." She gave a little giggle. "I can definitely see Lou doing my housework."

Josh laughed. "Only for you," he acknowledged. "Anyone else and he'd wreck the place."

They exchanged an easy smile, and soon they were chatting away as normal until they arrived back at the apartment block. They made conversation for a few minutes with the night concierge who had taken over from Carlos. Mia missed Lou's adorable face but looked forward to taking her little animal sidekick out for a walk the next morning after a long, and hopefully, restful night's sleep. *Although*, she hoped, with a wry smile to herself, *it wouldn't be as long as a hundred years.*

And she would do her own waking up, thank you very much.

The next evening, Mia fanned out a pack of playing cards and peeped at Calli, Ash, and Josh from over the top of them. "OK, I eased you all in, but be prepared," she said, with a wide smile. "I'm reserving all my luck for myself tonight." She was still pleased from the successful fundraiser, and was looking forward to a fun night with her friends.

Calli grinned back. "Ooh a challenge, I like it. Welcome back, Mia."

Josh and Ash lifted their beer bottles and toasted her.

They were finishing setting up for card night when Mia's phone rang. "Oh...that's weird. It's my dad," Mia said, with a frown. It was late for him to be phoning.

"Say hi to Uncle Steph for me," Calli said, pulling out bags of tortilla chips.

"Hi, Dad," Mia said, and for some reason, her heart had begun to pump faster in her chest. Her dad making a late-night call did not bode well. She listened to her father talking as though his words were being shouted at her from the end of a very long tunnel. She sank onto the sofa, nausea battling with the adrenaline. "No—no, thanks for telling me, Dad…no, I'll be OK," her words came out in a whisper. "Calli's here."

A hand landed softly on Mia's shoulder and she blinked up at Josh as she disconnected the call and dropped the phone to her lap. "What is it? What's the matter?" he asked.

"I—I can't," Mia said, and stood, her phone thumping to the floor. "I feel sick." She rushed past him, heading for the bathroom, with Calli hurrying after her.

Mia headed for the toilet and knelt, clutching the bowl, but nothing came out.

"Mia! You're scaring me. What's wrong?" Calli came in behind her and closed the door.

"They…they, *oh god*, I can't even say it." Mia stared at Calli and her cousin crouched down next to her, searching her face.

"Say it, Mi, get it out."

"*They're getting married*," the words burst out of Mia in a wail. She collapsed into Calli's arms and sobbed.

"Shit," Calli muttered, then crooned, "That's it, let it out, let it all out."

Mia cried until numb. Her father's words replayed in her mind. A mutual friend had told him and he wanted to tell Mia before she learnt about it on social media. He knew she'd blocked Henry and Nadia—but she still spoke to other friends who knew Nadia. It was only a matter of time until someone stirred the pot. He'd stayed up late so he could catch her when she came home from the university.

"Better?" Calli asked, releasing her, and sitting back and Mia noted the banked anger in her cousin's face. She pulled Mia up. "We are *not* going to give him the satisfaction of you sitting on the bathroom floor and crying all night. You, me, and the girls are going to 80's night and you are going to sing and dance, and drink if you want. What you are *not* going to do is wallow, OK?" Calli's tone brooked no argument.

Mia, numb and in shock, could only jerk her head in a parody of acquiescence. She needed something to distract herself with or she might have a panic attack.

"That's my girl," Calli said. She linked her arm through Mia's and led her out of the bathroom. Josh and Ash stood, questions on their faces. "She's had a bit of a shock; the weasel and the snake are getting married. So we are going to have a girl's night instead," Calli told them. "Sorry to ditch card night but this is an emergency."

Ash came over to join them, and handed Mia her phone before rubbing a comforting hand along her arm and said, "Don't worry about card night. Are you all right?"

Mia blinked and forced a smile. "Sure. I need to get out of my own head for a bit, that's all."

"OK," Ash said, concern in his gaze.

"I'll look after her," Calli said. "Come on, let's get ready." She led Mia over to her and Ash's room, and Mia caught Josh's eye.

"OK?" he mouthed.

She gave a slight shake of her head and a shrug.

"We'll come and meet you at the bar later," Josh said. "Walk you home."

Mia gave a small smile, and Calli said, "That's a great idea."

In Calli and Ash's room, Calli wasted no time in pulling out dresses and setting them against Mia. "This one is perfect. You're a bit taller than me, but it'll be fine."

Mia knew better than to argue and put on the stretchy strappy hot-pink bodycon dress, feeling as though she were taking some semblance of control back into her tumultuous life.

Calli then added bright 80's-style makeup to Mia's face, and fluffed up her already curled hair and sprayed up the front into a swooping curve, leaving the rest to bounce around Mia's face and body. "Now these." She shoved a pair of sky-high black shoes with hot-pink heels at Mia. "Thank goodness we're the same size in shoes. So much fun to share stuff." Calli's grin was over-bright and her voice higher than normal and Mia knew she was doing her best to buoy Mia up, while controlling her own anger.

Mia slipped on the shoes and winced. "Why would you want to torture me, Cal?" she moaned.

"If you're thinking about your feet, you're not thinking about anything else." Calli turned from the mirror where she was sweeping electric blue eyeshadow over her lids. The colour perfectly matched the tight skirt and crop top she wore in a shiny fabric. She smiled at Mia with lips slicked with an iridescent gloss.

"True that," Mia said with a small smile, using one of Simi's phrases.

Calli pulled Mia over so they stood side-by-side in the floor-length mirror. "Perfect," Calli said, taking in their appearances; an updated 80's style. "Let's go." She opened the door and ushered Mia out.

Mia self-consciously tugged the hem down on her dress as she walked out and when she looked up, her eyes clashed with Josh's. He slowly set his beer bottle down, and his eyes widened fractionally. "You—ah, you look nice," he said.

"Correction, Josh. She looks *hot*. Henry's a fucking idiot," Calli said.

"*Calli*," Ash said, but she shrugged.

"I said what I said."

"She's not wrong," Josh added quietly, and Mia flushed. Josh picked up his drink and took a long swallow while Mia turned away to hide her embarrassment by putting her phone and wallet in her small black clutch bag.

"I've texted the girls, they're going to meet us there," Calli said, missing the heat enflaming Mia's cheeks, "so it's just you guys tonight. Sylvie's having dinner with her sister anyway."

Ash came over and kissed her. "Right. Have fun. We'll see you there later."

"I'll save you a cocktail." Calli winked, then picked up her handbag. "Ready, Mi?"

Mia turned around, clutching her bag. "See you later," she told Ash and Josh. Josh watched her over the rim of his bottle for a moment then lowered it and replied, "See you later."

The girls left them to prep for their impromptu boys' night, and made their way out of the apartment, down the lift and out onto the street. The karaoke bar was on the same block, so thankfully Mia didn't have to totter too far.

"I'm going to need a cocktail if only to numb the pain of these shoes," Mia told Calli ruefully as they pushed the door open to Kocktails.

"Beauty is pain," Calli said wisely, as though she were an oracle, and Mia laughed a genuine laugh.

"So says you," Mia said, shaking her head as they headed to the bar. But Calli was already letting out a squeal and aiming towards Dotty, Claudia, and Nicolette who were sitting on barstools, sipping bright blue cocktails.

"Ooh, Mia, that dress is fabulous on you. No wonder you run so fast, your legs go on forever," Dotty said.

"Thanks, Dotty," Mia said and took a good look around the bar, grateful that Calli had neglected to tell the girls the reason for their spontaneous night out. She wanted to forget the awful reason herself. Flashing neon lights lit up the karaoke stage and pointed the way to the restrooms, while padded booths, chairs and tables filled up the remaining space around the stage and bar. The elevated dancefloor hung above a bank of booths, and the stairs leading up were highlighted in strips of neon green, pink, and blue.

"Drink?" Claudia asked, leaning in towards Mia.

"What are you having?" Mia asked.

"This is a *Blue Lagoon*," Claudia said lifting her tall glass.

"Sounds good," Mia said. Now she was out, dressed to the nines, with 80's music pumping, she felt a little better. A few cocktails and a dance would be exactly what she needed to stop thinking about anything else for a while.

"Yassss, Mia!" Calli said, and Mia grinned.

Soon, the girls were giggling and sipping on cocktails, and putting their names down for a go on the karaoke, but first, they headed up to the dancefloor and joined in with the other revellers in dancing to 'What a Feeling'.

"Iconic!" Calli shouted over the music. Her dance training kicked in, as she created a little circle around them from the others on the dancefloor, and showed off her moves.

Mia clapped along with everyone else, a rush of affection for her cousin flowing through her as Calli lit up the dancefloor. She was so glad she had come to New York...even more so now after the phone call. But truly, there wasn't a city like it. And there weren't people like it either.

She chatted to other girls, and drank more than was sensible, but the haze slicking over her mind was like a veil separating her two lives. The one before New York, and this far more pleasing one.

"Mia! You're up!" Dotty grabbed Mia and pulled her away from the bar where she had been chatting to a veterinary student about dogs. Mia waved apologetically to the girl before allowing Dotty to push her up on the stage behind the microphone. *What had she agreed to sing?* Oh, yes, that was right. She giggled at herself, and the ironic song she had chosen under the fog of that first couple of cocktails.

The music started and Mia began singing in a heartfelt tone. Calli, Claudia, Dotty and Nicolette swayed and whooped from in front of the stage. As Mia got to the chorus of the Foreigner song, she noticed Ash, Josh, Benito, and Lance had joined the girls. Josh caught her gaze and for one charged moment she couldn't look away. Then she was laughing self-consciously and finishing the song with gusto.

"Sing it, girl!" Calli shouted.

Mia took a shaky curtsey, then hopped down off the stage, laughing as Claudia caught ahold of her when she wobbled into her. "I'm quickly going to the powder room," she told her and, feeling like a million dollars, threaded her way through the club-goers to the restroom.

Inside, Mia used the facilities, then washed her hands, running cold water over her wrists in an attempt to cool herself down. The exertion combined with the alcohol was the cause of her heated cheeks, she told herself wisely, and certainly—*most certainly*—not for any other reason.

Mia left the restroom. Calli and the others were no longer near the stage. Thinking they were probably at the bar, she made her way over. A young man in a lime green shirt placed himself in her path.

"You sing well," he told her, leaning on the bar and fixing an 'obviously interested' look on his face. No neon sign needed here, Mia thought, trying to hide her grimacing smile. Finding humour in it was far better than succumbing to the frozen fear that lurked beneath the cocktail cloud.

"I had lessons as a child," she told the man, "but I wouldn't say I sang well."

He leant in. "I could *show* you," he said meaningfully, and this time the humour fled. Mia winced at the cheesy line as he hi-jacked the lyrics of the song, she had sung, into his pick-up line.

"No, thank you," Mia said as politely as she could, looking past him and trying to locate Calli in the crowd. She made to manoeuvre herself around the guy, but he stood firm.

"Aww, just one drink then."

Mia shook her fuzzy head, frustration rising. "I'm trying to get to my friends."

"The lady said no."

Relief speared through Mia as Josh appeared next to her at the bar.

The guy gave a disappointed look, then stepped back. "Sorry, bud," he said and turned away.

"Are you OK?" Josh asked, concerned eyes searching her face.

Mia nodded, but said, "Why is it, when I say no, I get ignored? But when you, Joshie, come in like my knight in shining armour, does it work?" Mia narrowed her eyes and waved a hand around. "Is it some sort of bro code that has its origins firmly in the caveman era?" She began fumbling in her handbag, knowing in some still-functioning part of her mind she wasn't being historically factual with her terminology.

"What are you doing?" Josh asked.

She retrieved her phone and then tapped the side of her head with one finger. "Always working," she said. "Siri, research craveman bro crode." She stumbled over the words.

Mia waited while the results came up. "I did not say...*dear god...craving* men..." She let out a long-suffering sigh. "Even Siri is against me."

Josh's lips twitched when Mia scowled at him, but he merely said, "Ready to go home? Calli and Ash are waiting by the exit for us. The others had to go."

"I think I better," she agreed.

"Woah," Josh said, as Mia stumbled forward on her sky-high heels, and caught her around the waist. He helped her through the crowd and over to the exit.

"Mia! There you are," Calli said. "Are you OK?"

"Perfectly," Mia said enunciating the word precisely. "Except for these torture devices on my feet, and conspiring phone ass...issitants." She aimed a look at Josh, trying her best to affect a composed and cool-headed demeanour. "Thank you for your help."

He gave a worried frown. "Of course."

Ash held the door open and the four of them exited onto the New York street.

Mia took a deep breath of the nighttime air and, buzzed by too many cocktails covering the layer of heartbreak she had hidden for the night, tottered over to the edge of the kerb. "I *love* New York!" she announced loudly, and a few indistinct yet irate shouts echoed back from buildings across the street. She pointed at Calli and Ash, "And I love you..." She spun in a circle. "And you, Joshie, I..." she trailed off, blinking up at him then carried on, "you are my newest and very bestest friend." She giggled and booped him on the end of his nose and continued on her uneven journey.

The others caught up with Mia as she stumbled and Josh said, "Shit, Cal, how much did she drink?" and scooped her up into his arms.

"Only a couple. As much as me...I think," Calli said.

"I might have had maybe one or two...or three more," Mia told them, flopping her head against Josh's chest. "I made many newest friends tonight, but you," she lowered her voice to what she thought was a whisper, "but you are still my bestest."

Josh looked down at her. "And you're my bestest," he said, bright blue eyes unreadable. "Let's get you home."

Calli and Ash went on ahead to open the apartment block's outer door.

"You always smell so good," Mia murmured. "You remind me of Greece...sea salt on the breeze...and blue, blue, blue." Her eyes fluttered closed as Josh continued to carry her.

Mia woke in the night to a small hand smoothing her hair back from her brow. She looked up; Calli sat beside her on the bed. "Are you all right?" she asked.

Mia groaned and closed her eyes. "I'm broken, Cal," she whispered.

Calli muttered something indecipherable beneath her breath, before shuffling down so she and Mia were almost nose to nose. "Look at me."

Mia fluttered open her eyes, and took in the steely glint in Calli's brown-eyed gaze.

"You are *not* broken," Calli said. "Everything around you fell to pieces, but you are still standing—still making strides to a future you want."

"Then why do I feel so terrified?"

Calli stroked her cheek. "Because you believe it'll all go wrong again. But you have to trust yourself this time."

One tear pushed out of the corner of Mia's left eye. "But how can I trust myself when I make such crappy decisions?"

A flash of anger crossed Calli's face, illuminated by the chink of moonlight coming through the curtains. "You weren't to blame for *their* choices, *their* actions, Mia. You made decisions based on what personas they presented to you—Henry can be suave and charming when he wants to be, and her, well, she was a manipulative little snake, but she was great at acting as your best friend. How were you to believe they were anything else than what they showed you? You were fooled, we all were."

Mia sniffled. "But I'm scared I'll be fooled again. I know you think I should start dating, and try and move on that way...but every time I think about it, I freeze, and go into self-preservation mode. Stav asked me out and when I turned him down I thought that was the end of it, but then he asked again the other day and I panicked. I couldn't even come up with a reasonable excuse this time."

"I'm sorry for being pushy." Calli sighed. "I thought if you found someone genuine who would treat you as you deserve then you would find your happiness again...and as for Stav, I'll take care of him."

Mia gave a watery smile. "Don't do anything that will cost you your job," she said.

Calli grinned. "Don't worry, I won't, but as for your reaction, perhaps it's time you speak to someone," she ended gently.

"A therapist you mean?" Mia sat up slightly.

"Sure. I know you Brits don't go in for exploring your feelings as such, but here it's the norm. Ash knows a good one—he had a few things to work through, and was so much better for it."

"Ash?" Calli's fiancé was always so calm and content, perhaps that was why.

"I'll get him to give you the number. Dr Carroll is kind, and great at what she does."

"All right," Mia said finally, knowing she couldn't go on as she was forever. Yes, focusing on her career and friends was fine, but long term, she would have to address the deep-rooted reasons of why she was still so traumatised.

"Great." Calli leant over and pressed a kiss to Mia's brow. "Try and go back to sleep." She climbed out of the bed.

"Cal?"

"Yeah?"

"Thanks for watching over me," Mia said softly.

Calli smiled. "Always."

Calli quietly left the room, and Mia stared at the door for a few moments. The events of the night before were a bit hazy, but she vaguely remembered Josh carrying her safely home. It seemed he was good at watching over her too.

The next morning, Mia nursed a cup of tea while staring out of the large living area window. She'd emailed the professor and told him she would make up her hours next week, and he had been fine with her doing that, and taking the day off.

The sights and muted sounds of everything still carrying on as normal far below her filled her with a detached sense of comfort. Ash had left for work early, and Calli had gone on an audition—fresh-faced despite the couple of cocktails she'd had at Kocktails—and feeling confident of getting a call-back, thanks to the nights Mia had helped her choreograph a dance piece for the audition. Even with the vague sense of ease, Mia had a pocket of contained energy in the pit of her stomach that yearned for release.

A tap came at the apartment door before it opened and Josh

entered. “Morning,” he said, seeing her curled up on the sofa. “I wanted to check you were all right.”

A brief burst of embarrassment filled Mia as she took him in. He was dressed in casual clothes, and he appeared clear-eyed despite the obvious concern displayed on his face.

“I’m OK,” Mia said. “A bit of a self-inflicted headache and a touch of humiliation but that’s about it.”

“You’ve got nothing to be humiliated about, Mia,” he told her with a kind smile.

“Oh? I distinctly remember you having to *carry* me? And something about me shouting in the street.”

Josh laughed. “Carrying you was no hardship, and you’re just happy to be in New York.” He shrugged it off, but Mia had to say her piece.

She stood and moved over to the kitchen area to pour a cup of coffee for Josh, just how he liked it. “Seriously though, thank you, Josh. You never make me feel like an idiot for my actions.”

Josh moved over to her and gently pulled her into a hug, and she sank into him. “That doesn’t ever need any thanks,” he said. “I’m here for you. I’ve got your back.”

Mia took a deep inhale, and his scent loosened something within her. “I appreciate that,” she said and stepped back. He crinkled a smile at her.

“So, what’s your plans today?” Josh asked.

She bit her lip. “I *need* to run, but none of the Valkyries are available today.”

“I’ve got the morning off work. I’ll run with you,” he offered and picked up his coffee from the counter to take a sip.

“You will?”

“Sure. I could do with a good run too. Get changed and I’ll meet you in ten.” Josh set his coffee cup down on the counter.

“Thanks,” Mia said, stupidly feeling tears prickle the back of her eyes.

“Anytime.” He left the apartment and Mia headed into her bedroom, and took a deep breath.

She changed into black leggings with a purple stripe, and tight-fitting purple vest top. She pulled her hair up into a high ponytail, and laced up her running trainers. Back in the kitchen, she filled up her water bottle before making her way out of the apartment, and locking the door behind her.

Josh was already coming out of his apartment, dressed in grey sweats and a white tee. “Oh, I forgot my water bottle,” he said and ducked back inside, leaving the door open.

Mia hovered in the doorway, realising she had never been inside his apartment before. It had the same layout as Calli and Ash’s but Josh had made it his own with dark wood furniture, and a deep-green sofa and chairs. A widescreen TV partially filled the wall the sofa faced, flanked by two pieces of artwork of misty forests, but it was the easel set before the wide windows that caught her interest.

Without thinking, Mia found herself stepping inside, drawn by the outline of a woman taking centre stage on the white canvas. Despite it only being the bare bones, it held movement; a breath waiting to be exhaled.

“Josh,” Mia said, moved, and he turned from the sink, water bottle in hand.

He tracked her gesture. An expression crossed his face and she recognised it from card night; the look he wore when he didn’t want to give anything away. “Oh that, it’s nothing,” he said.

“*Nothing*?” Mia said incredulously, unable to comprehend how someone with such obvious skill could dismiss it so easily.

He twisted the cap on his water bottle and wiped the neck with a cloth. He blew out a breath. "Sorry, it's just every time I try to carry on with it, I hear my dad's voice in my head. Telling me I shouldn't be wasting my time and should be focusing on my career instead."

"I'm sorry, Josh," Mia said, beginning to understand his reaction. When someone constantly told you your passions were a waste of time, you started to believe it yourself.

He met her eyes. "My dad's not a bad person; he's just a traditional guy, and wants the best for me. He had nothing growing up and worked damn hard to provide for me and my mom and now he owns a successful ranch. I think the terror of me ever struggling like he did drives him to be a bit hard-headed sometimes."

Mia wanted to go over to him, to comfort him as he had done for her so many times, but something stopped her. He held his posture rigidly, almost defensively. But she was the last person to judge someone's family. "I get it," she told him, instead. "But you are successful in what you do, a little time spent painting won't take you away from that, surely?"

His gaze wandered over to the easel, and he stared at the image for a long moment before shrugging. "Perhaps, I am too scared to try. I haven't completed a painting in years." He rolled his shoulders back, as if shrugging off the conversation, and looked at her. "All set?" he asked, changing the subject.

Mia recognised her cue. All right, she'd let it drop, as he had done when she'd requested to drop the topic of her not dating at the auction. She nodded, but the contained feeling from earlier still buzzed through her, and if she didn't run it off soon, she'd combust.

"Let's go then," Josh said, and his usual smile was back on

his face.

She led the way out of the apartment and Josh followed her, locking up after himself. Together they made their way over to the lift.

Inside, Mia leant against the mirrored wall, and closed her eyes, her own problems rushing back in. Why did she feel so stuck? Everything around her was moving at lightning speed; everyone else could deal, and move on, while she was frozen in time. Even though she was making steps towards the future she wanted, were they still too small to be noticeable? She needed to run, and break out of the box she'd confined herself in.

The lift stopped moving and she opened her eyes to see Josh watching her. "Sorry," she said, "I'm a bit in my own head today."

"It's fine, Mia. You've gone through a massive trauma, you don't need to apologise." Josh gave her an understanding smile before stepping out of the lift and Mia followed him.

Mia rallied herself enough for Lou's obligatory pat and crooning hello. And then with a smile for Carlos, and a promise to join him for a bagel breakfast soon, Mia headed outside with Josh and blinked in the sunshine.

Together, they crossed the street and headed into the busy park.

Mia stretched out her legs, and Josh did the same before they started jogging. But it wasn't enough for Mia and soon she was increasing her stride until she was sprinting along the pathways, her muscle memory kicking in. Josh kept pace and, in that moment, she appreciated him more than ever.

Her breath laboured after a while and she stopped to lean against a tree and rehydrate. Josh joined her. "You're fast," he observed.

Mia swallowed a gulp of water and stared out across the park; at the mums and dads pushing strollers, the couples walking hand-in-hand, and older people chatting on benches. "I did cross-country in high school—it was a great release for all that teenage angst," she said, endorphins fizzing through her veins and improving her mood slightly.

She sat down on the grass and Josh followed suit. "Feeling a little better?" he asked.

"For now, but I'm under no illusion that I need to work things through properly. Calli suggested I speak to a therapist and I think she might be right. I mean, how can I say to someone, 'Here, take these pieces of my broken heart and put it back together for me, thanks'." Mia leant her head back against the tree. "*I* have to fix it first. It's not fair on anyone else otherwise."

Josh was silent for a moment then said, "They say time heals all wounds, but sometimes you need more than time. Speaking to a therapist is a good idea. Even if it's just to un-bottle everything."

"You're right." Mia sighed. "I *do* bottle everything up because it's simply too painful to deal with. I not only lost the man I thought I was in love with but my best friend...my *oldest* friend too." Her voice thickened as she spoke the last sentence.

Josh murmured, "That's the part that truly hurts isn't it?"

Mia blinked back her tears at his astute comment. "I'd only been with Henry for two and a half years, but Nadia...Nadia, I'd known since we were *five*. God, she was like a sister to me, not by blood but by bond—but obviously, the bond meant more to me. She even called my father 'Dad'." Mia played with her water bottle as the pain sliced through her. "She would say: 'You don't mind, Mimi, do you?' She grew up without a dad, so of course I was happy to share my amazing dad, but now all those memories are tainted, every sleepover, every giggling night out, every shopping or cinema trip."

Josh listened attentively as she let it all out. "I should have seen it coming though. When a boy we both liked in sixth form asked me out I said no, because I knew she liked him too. She had no such qualms though when he asked her out next. 'You don't mind, Mimi, do you?' she'd said. Would she have said that about Henry too? '*You don't mind sharing, Mimi, do you*?' God. All I was to them was someone to use until someone better came along. I see now that Henry was keeping me around for my U.S. status; a stepping stone in his career." Nausea welled up inside Mia and she took a small sip of her water, trying desperately to erase the bitter taste. "I'm such a doormat. Such a goddamn *mess*."

Josh placed a gentle hand on her arm. "It's not your fault they made it messy," he said.

Mia sniffled. "And now they're getting married...they chose each other instead of me." She paused, the realisation filling her in a suffocating wave. One she had to battle back with slow, even breaths. The sensation eventually passed. "Him, I can understand now, but her? She played the long game."

"You deserved so much better from both of them."

Mia looked up at him through watery eyes and their gazes met and held. He pulled her in then for a one-armed hug, and she clutched him, breathing in his familiar scent of sea salt and coconut, now twinned with the male sweat of their run. "I'm going to run again now," she said.

He released her. "Then run. I'll be right behind you," he promised.

"Thanks, Josh."

He smiled, his eyes bright, and Mia stood and headed for the pathways. She ran, knowing her friend would indeed be right behind her, keeping her in sight. She ran until her lungs burned.

If only she could outrun her heartache as easily.

“Ah, Miss Davenport—just the person. I have some great news.” Professor Deacon met Mia on the stairs leading up to the offices the following Wednesday morning.

She gave him a polite smile. “Morning, Professor.”

“We have been given the go-ahead by the department. They were impressed with the fundraiser and the interest it generated for the university and for archaeology itself.” He beamed at her through his beard.

“That’s fantastic,” Mia enthused.

“Indeed, indeed, but there is one slight snag; we will need to find some local archaeologists, and volunteer students. We have ample funds for the machinery, and surveys and permits, and of course recompense to the farmer, and for accommodation and amenities etc but flying a whole team from the states will take us over budget.”

Mia brightened. “Leave that to me, sir. I know exactly the person to help us.”

“I knew I could count on you—and if you could secure us

somewhere to stay local to the site?" Mia nodded at the request. "Oh, and make sure there is a pub nearby that does some homecooked food, eh?"

Mia laughed. "Of course. It'll be top of the list."

"Very good," Professor Deacon said. "I want us over there no later than two weeks, please?"

Mia did the quick calculations in her mind. On Friday she was flying to Miami with Calli and the girls for the long weekend, while the boys were going to Texas to stay on Josh's family's ranch, and then the following Saturday was the wedding. It would be a rush but she could make it all happen.

"Certainly. I'll book the flights, sort out the accommodation, and get in touch with my contact," Mia said.

"Splendid," the professor said, and then carried on down the stairs while Mia made her way up to her office. She wasted no time in powering up her laptop and composing an email to Simi. He'd been hankering after fieldwork as much as she had been, and now she was about to make him an offer he couldn't refuse.

Smiling to herself, she hit send, and leant back in her chair, imagining her friend responding to her email with an image text of him beaming his acceptance.

Cruising on her good mood, she brought up the information for the farmer who owned the land where the ring had been found, and read through it. Her eyes widened as she scoured the list of what the property entailed. She'd hit the jackpot she realised, and sent off another email, this time to the farmer.

Mia finished off her morning's work by searching up flights, and sent the information over to the professor for his preference. Knowing she couldn't do much else until Simi and the farmer replied, she closed her laptop down and stowed it away in her bag before readying to leave for the day, only working the morning on a Wednesday.

She had another session with Dr Carroll that afternoon, and a shift at the restaurant that evening. Her first session with Dr Carroll had been successful in that she had unburdened herself freely to someone who had no prior knowledge of any of the other parties involved, and could just say everything that she had held inside for so long.

They'd briefly touched on Mae, and Mia was surprised to find that Dr Carroll believed Mia's reactions tied into her mother's abandonment too. Mia had balked at going too deep into that area, knowing she'd be seeing Mae in a few days' time and didn't want to have raw wounds exposed when they came face-to-face again.

Mia spoke to a few colleagues on the way out of the university before heading for the subway to catch the train back to the apartment. She'd grab some lunch before going to Dr Carroll's Manhattan office and hopefully make some more progress on the shitstorm Henry and Nadia had left her in the wreckage of.

She had come to enjoy her time riding the subway. With her earphones in and playing an eclectic mix of songs on the Spotify playlist she shared with Simi, Mia could people-watch to her heart's content. If she secretly yearned for what the couples riding the train obviously had, she merely put it down to her interest in the stories humankind had created for millennia. The lingering glances, shared secret smiles, and brief touches all spoke more poignant words than an ink and quill ever could.

With Sia's 'Unstoppable' playing, Mia exited at her stop and carried on up to street level. So lost in the music, she didn't see Josh coming up on her side from the direction of the underground car park until he touched her on the arm.

Mia jolted and turned to him with a startled laugh, removing her earbuds. "Sorry, hi," she said.

"Hi. Good song?"

"A bit of Sia," she said with a smile.

"Nice," Josh said.

They walked into the apartment block, spent a few minutes with Carlos and Lou before getting into the lift.

"So, I've got some news," Josh said as the lift doors closed.

"Oh? Do tell," Mia said.

"I'm going to London."

Mia's lips parted in surprise. "What? To stay?"

Josh leant back against the mirrored wall, and Mia could see her reflection as she looked at him. Why did she look so sad?

He gave a brief smile. "Just for the summer. Ash was offered the position but he's got the wedding and his honeymoon so declined. They offered it to me instead. I'm to observe how they run things in the London office, and see if we can implement things here. I've got a Zoom meeting with them this afternoon."

"So, we'll be in England at the same time then," Mia said.

Josh's eyes flickered, then he smiled. "You got the go-ahead for the dig?"

Mia nodded happily as the lift doors opened and they stepped out. "Yes, I received the news today and spent the morning sending emails, searching for accommodation, and looking up flights."

"When do you leave?"

"The prof wants to be over there in two weeks. How about you?"

"Same. I go the week after Calli and Ash's wedding." They stopped before the apartment doors and fell silent.

"I'd better go and grab a sandwich, I've got a session with Dr

Carroll this afternoon." Mia broke the pause, gesturing awkwardly at her door.

"How's it going?" Josh asked gently.

Mia blew out a breath and glanced away. "She thinks I have abandonment issues." Her laugh was shaky. "I think she might be right," she added in a whisper.

Josh set his briefcase down and quietly pulled her in for a hug, his chin resting on the top of her head. They stayed that way for one long moment, with Mia closing her eyes and listening to the steady, comforting drum of his heartbeat.

They eased back, Josh searching her face. "You need company while you make your sandwich?"

She smiled up at him. "Thanks for the offer, but I'll be OK. I think Cal is home. You go and get ready for your meeting."

"If you're sure?"

Mia pulled her key out of her bag. "I am. I'll catch you later."

He gave her another searching look, before answering. "Catch you later."

Mia let herself into the apartment, and Calli came out of her bedroom, her face a picture of unrestrained delight. "Guess who got the part?" she screamed.

Mia dropped her bags and rushed over to her cousin to grip her arms. Together they jumped up and down on the spot. "Not Iris again!" Mia said, referencing one of their favourite films, *Beaches*, and she and Calli burst into peals of laughter.

"Not this time, hand-walker! It's me, Calli Vega-Lamone!" Calli let Mia go and twirled away, ending with a flourish and began singing 'The Wind Beneath My Wings'.

Mia burst into applause. "Brava, brava!"

Calli collapsed onto the sofa and Mia joined her. She gave her a shoulder bump. "So, when do you start?

"After my honeymoon. Oh, Mi, it's all worked out so perfectly." Calli let out a contented sigh.

"I'm so pleased for you, Cal. I have news too—we got the green light for the dig, so I'll be off when you're enjoying your honeymoon."

Calli beamed at her. "Fab news. And Josh is off too, Ash texted me that he's accepted the secondment to the London office."

Mia said, "I saw him outside, he's got a Zoom meeting this afternoon with them."

Calli fell silent, and Mia could hear the cogs whirring in her cousin's brain. "Well, at least you'll both have some company over there."

Mia hid her smile. "England's not *that* tiny, Cal. I'll be a two-and-a-half hour drive away from London."

"Oh right, but it's still doable...you know, if you get lonely."

"I'll be *working*—and so will Josh." Mia stood and moved over to the kitchen area. "Celebratory sandwich?"

Calli hopped up from the sofa to join her, distracted as Mia had hoped. "With extra mayo?"

"Oh, 1000%." Mia smiled, and pulled out the makings for doorstop-sized chicken-mayo sandwiches.

"I'm in," Calli said, and took out Nanna Prim's teapot. "I'll brew."

As Mia compiled the sandwiches and listened to Calli singing quietly to herself, she thought that yes, everything was working out nicely. Her path was become clearer and the thorny parts were less visible. She only hoped she wouldn't encounter a tangle of them further along her journey. But she was used to surprise attacks now, so would still keep prepared. Perhaps she should speak to Dr Carroll about that analogy. The doctor would probably tell her that she still had her fight-or-flight response switched on, but maybe, Mia thought, just maybe the doctor could teach her how to put it on pause.

She gave a wry shake of her head as she plated up the sandwiches. She set them on the dining table and took a seat opposite Calli. It was a certain *aspect* of her life that was truly on pause. An aspect that she missed, but didn't, in equal measure. The risks far outweighed the rewards as far as Mia was concerned.

"Are you not eating that?" Calli's question had Mia looking at her hands and seeing she had stopped with her sandwich halfway to her mouth.

Mia laughed. "Give me a chance," she said, and pulled herself out of her head and concentrated on eating her sandwich. There would be time enough later to analyse the route her thoughts had taken and why.

"Spoilsport." Calli pouted, then poured out the tea.

Mia laughed. "You'll miss me when I'm gone."

Calli sobered. "You know I will, but it won't be for long. We'll all be back together at the end of the summer."

"Hopefully," Mia said. "The professor has never had an assistant before, he might not want me to continue afterwards."

"Then, my girl, you better make yourself indispensable." Calli lifted her teacup and gestured at her with it.

Mia lifted her own cup. "I can but try," she agreed and took a sip.

"That's the spirit." Calli grinned in approval. "Oh, I forgot to tell you—I've had the best idea for an activity at the bachelorette."

"Uh-huh?" Mia said slowly, wondering what nightmare was about to unfold.

Calli pointed at Mia. "You" — and then pointed at herself — "and me, are going to unleash the Paso Salsa routine."

Mia was thankful she had already swallowed her tea; a vivid vision of it spurting out of her nose floated into her mind. "Oh, no, no, no. You know I love you, Cal, but...just no."

"Too late. I spoke to Mom already and she's sneaked it into the last night's schedule. She even has one of the boys from that summer working for her—you remember Enrique don't you?"

Mia narrowed her eyes. "Not slick, Cal, truly."

"What?" Calli blinked her brown eyes at her innocently. "He's a great dancer. He gives lessons at the bar, and Mom dotes on him."

"Then you partner him," Mia said.

"Oh no, he's the perfect height for you. I'll dance with his husband, Diego." Calli stood and cleared the plates.

"His husband?"

"Yeah, they got married last year."

"Oh, right." Something loosened inside Mia now she knew Calli wasn't up to her usual matchmaking tricks. She huffed out a resigned breath. "OK then, for you, I shall dust off my dancing shoes."

Calli let out a squeal and tackled Mia in a side bear hug. "You're the best," she said.

Mia leant into her. "Please do me one favour—*don't* record it."

Calli giggled in Mia's ear. "I cannot promise that, but I shall strongly encourage people to enjoy the performance in the moment and not through the lens of their phone cameras."

"Thank you," Mia said as Calli released her.

"I'm going to finish packing—*eek*, we've only got two days until we leave!" Calli said, heading for her room.

"You carry on. I need to leave for my appointment," Mia told her.

Calli stopped and turned around. "Hope it goes well," she said sincerely and blew her a kiss.

"Thanks, Cal," Mia said and air-grabbed the kiss and placed it over her heart.

They smiled at each other before Calli pirouetted into her bedroom, and Mia collected her handbag, and let herself out of the apartment.

CHAPTER FOURTEEN

"Here." Calli thrust a squat glass half-full of amber liquid at Mia.

Mia accepted the glass with a trembling hand. "We could have driven. Miami's not that far. Make it a girls' road trip," she rambled. She stared around the busy terminal, and out of the window at the planes taking off and landing.

Calli rubbed small circles on her back. "It'll be fine, Mi. It's a shorter flight than the one you took from London. And I'm here, and the girls."

Dotty, Claudia, Nicolette, and the Valkyrie girls all gave her sympathetic looks, although Audrey—the cool-eyed blonde Valkyrie that Mia had never seemed to click with—rolled her eyes and said, "I think she's going to need something stronger."

Calli shot her a glare. "Not helpful, Aud."

Audrey shrugged, while Mia did her best not to wonder if Audrey was actually right. She took a deep, bolstering breath. "OK." She *could* do this. She sipped on the brandy and channelled the illusion of calmness...until their flight was called. "Oh god."

Calli took the glass off her and set it on the bar. "Come on. You're braver than you think, Cous."

As if in a dream, Mia let Calli escort her through the gate and the elevated tunnel and into the plane. *Don't think about it, don't think about it*, she chanted in her mind as they found their seats—Mia taking an aisle seat and buckling her seatbelt tightly. She tried to take deep, even breaths but they lodged somewhere between her lungs, as Calli patted her hand from beside her.

Mia's phone beeped, and desperately hoping it was something she could distract herself with, she opened up the message. It was a video from Josh. When Calli turned to speak to Dotty on the other side of her, Mia inserted her Earbuds, pressed play, and his soft Southern accent filled her ears.

"I know you are probably panicking right now, but focus on me and breathe, OK?" Josh then proceeded to take slow, deep breaths and Mia instinctively copied him, remembering the time he had brought her back from the brink of a panic attack before she had come to New York. "That's it, eyes on me," he said, and Mia couldn't help but smile, even though it was a recording and he couldn't see her.

She focused on his bright blue gaze, and the one black curl flopping over his forehead, and didn't even notice the plane take off.

Mia blinked when Calli tapped her arm with a smile. She pulled out one of her Earbuds as Calli said, "See. You did it! Now we are going to enjoy a movie, have a drink and relax OK?"

Mia flicked her gaze to her phone when a message notification popped up.

Rewatch as necessary.

"OK," she told Calli.

Calli beamed at her, then leant forward to pull out the info card from the seat pocket. While her cousin was busy, Mia texted Josh back:

Josh… thank you. M x

There was nothing else to say. He had known what she had needed and when, and had saved her from herself and her spiralling fear.

Anytime. Enjoy yourself x

Fondly, Mia noted the little 'x' he had added in response to her own—knowing it was more of a British-ism, and Americans didn't routinely add 'kisses' to the end of their messages—and put away her phone. Calli's excitement was infectious, and soon Mia was only half-aware of the fact she was suspended in a huge metal tube flying thousands of feet above the land. She watched the latest *Jurassic Park* movie, and sipped on a white wine spritzer, but couldn't hide her relief when they touched the tarmac, thankfully this time with no turbulence at all.

"Can I kiss the ground or would that be deemed weird?" Mia said, eyeing up the runway lovingly out of the tunnel window.

Calli gave her a side-eyed look, her lips twitching. "You're British, eccentricity is your thing isn't it?"

Mia hip-bumped her. "I think it's rubbing off on you," she said, but she laughed easily. Her feet were on the *ground*.

"Hey," Calli said, but then considered the statement with a purse of her lips. "Actually, you're not wrong."

They'd only brought carry-ons for their short trip, so they sailed through, and out of, the airport easily.

"OK. Are you *kidding* me?" Calli said, staring at the hot-pink stretched limo outside. After scanning the board, with her name written on it, held by the chauffeur, she directed at Mia, "Did you do this?"

Mia shrugged, pleased by her cousin's reaction. "We all chipped in, but yes, it was my idea."

Calli squealed and pulled her in for a quick squeeze. "O.M.G, this is going to be the best!" The driver opened the door and she scrambled inside, and Mia heard her muffled, gleeful shout of, "Champagne!" from inside.

"She'll behave," Mia told the driver as she passed him after the eight other girls had climbed in and settled themselves into the long seats.

"She'd be the first then, Miss," the driver said with a smile.

Mia smiled back, then climbed in and the driver closed the door after her. She found a champagne flute pressed into her hand, and as she sipped the pale gold bubbly liquid she had serious concerns about the state of her liver after the weekend would be over. However, the glowing look on Calli's face would make it all worth it.

"Oh, look," Dotty said, leaning in to Mia and showing her the screen of her phone. "Benito sent me this. The guys have been horseback riding."

Mia took in the group of men in the shot, all on horses in various colours of chestnut and palomino. Ash was on the horse next to Josh, his face wreathed in a big smile beneath his cowboy hat, and all of them appeared dusty but happy.

Mia took in Josh. He wore light-blue jeans, and a checked shirt, the sleeves rolled up to his elbows, the reins loose between his strong fingers. Beneath his own hat, his eyes shone brightly in his tanned face, his smile echoing Ash's. He gave the impression of being completely at home in the saddle, and no wonder, as he'd ridden horses all his life.

Mia's stomach gave a funny flip-flopping sensation which she put down to drinking the sparkling champagne in a moving vehicle. She exchanged a smile with Dotty before the other woman leant over her to show Calli the photo.

"*Well,*" Calli said and fanned herself with her free hand. "Would you *look* at them. I've never seen Ash so..." she trailed off, eyes wide.

"You're drooling, Calli," Claudia said with a laugh and tossed her a hot-pink napkin.

Calli laughed and pretended to dab her mouth. The other girls crowded around, and made appreciative noises. Mia shook her head in amusement and continued to sip her drink.

"That Josh is *fine,*" Audrey said. "Is he seeing anyone, Cal?"

Mia couldn't help but notice with some exasperation that Calli's eyes flicked to her before she answered. "Uh—no, he's a single pringle at the moment."

"Hmm," Audrey said, then finished her drink.

Mia realised it was a good thing she hadn't shared Josh's video with Calli—her matchmaking antenna would be twitching double-time. Even though she would be far, far, off the mark. It was just something a good friend would do.

"Don't get your hopes up though, Aud," Calli said in a breezy voice, "he's off to London for the summer."

Audrey pouted. "Bummer." Then she brightened. "Never mind. I'm sure we'll find some cute guys here too."

The conversation turned to what the girls had planned that weekend, and soon they were pulling up at Aunt Junie's beachside dance bar.

The girls filtered out of the limo, but Calli paused beside Mia. "You ready for this?"

Mia knew what she really meant; *are you ready to see Mae?* She gave her cousin a smile. "Sure. This weekend is going to be fun." And so jam-packed that she wouldn't have too much time for any intense one-on-one interactions with Mae if she didn't want it.

Calli searched her face for a moment, then smiled. "O-*K*. Then let the carnage begin!" She set off with a whoop of laughter towards her mum who waited for her in the doorway of the bar, and the other girls followed.

"Thank you," Mia said to the chauffeur, and he dipped his head.

"A pleasure, Miss."

Mia picked up her bag and followed more sedately over to the building's entrance, her heart suddenly pumping uncomfortably in her chest. She couldn't do it, she realised. She needed a moment first.

Stepping back before Aunt Junie spotted her, she veered off down a shady wooden-boarded path snaking around the building towards the beach. The waves crashed over the sand, its rhythm holding her focus much like Josh's video had done.

"Mia."

The familiar feminine voice from behind her had Mia closing her eyes on a shuddering sigh. She took another deep breath before turning around and getting her first good look at the woman who had chosen another life over her, for the first time in years.

"Hi, Mae," Mia said.

Mae's brown eyes flickered with what might have been pain,

before she smiled. Her hair—the same heavy pale-blonde as Mia's—had been cut short and danced in soft waves around her face. A face that was slightly more lined than the last time Mia had seen it, but still as familiar. The features were branded in Mia's mind, if not her heart. She wore a loose dress in bright colours, and her feet were bare. She was as Mia remembered her; carefree and bohemian.

"It's good to see you, sweetheart. You are looking so well. So beautiful," Mae said, and Mia had to battle back the resentment that threatened to burst out of her in a snarky comment.

Instead, she said, "And you, too. Putting down roots suits you."

Mae's smile faltered as if she was trying to detect some deeper meaning behind Mia's words. "Oh, well, I thought it was time...and Junie needed me, so..."

"Right, of course," Mia said. But *she* had needed Mae too. Where had she been then? Instead of voicing the questions, she gestured back to the building. "I better go and say hi to Aunt Junie."

"Certainly. We can catch up properly later." Mae gave her an encouraging smile, and Mia gave a small nod in return, fighting the urge to rub at her breastbone beneath her silky, yellow cropped vest top, and soothe her racing heart.

Mae led the way back to the building and Calli gave Mia a scrutinising look as they entered the large lounge area of the bar together. The girls had arranged themselves on the low, cushioned wicker seating and Aunt Junie was offering them brightly-coloured cocktails from the tray she held.

"Mia!" Aunt Junie said, and set down the empty tray once the girls had helped themselves.

Mia gave her aunt a genuine smile and moved in to hug her.

Her features were identical to Mae's—with them being twins—but she wore her hair in a longer style, and was dressed in shorts and a tee with sandals.

"So lovely to see you, Auntie, and thanks for helping me set everything up." Mia pulled back to speak with her.

"Of course. I'm so pleased Calli decided to come here to celebrate with you all. It's going to be a fun weekend."

"Speaking of which." Mia found a cocktail pressed into her hand by Calli. "Let's start as we mean to go on." Calli clinked her glass pointedly against Mia's.

Mia relaxed. "I can drink to that," she told her cousin and took a sip of the cool fruity drink.

The afternoon was made up of a pamper session for everyone, and Mia managed to be civil to Mae all while avoiding any solitary interactions with her. Calli had been treated like a queen, and her skin was glowing as she and Mia walked towards the small straw-roofed huts that served as guest accommodation for the site Aunt Junie's dance bar sat on.

"So, we're all set for the routine?" Calli asked. "It's going to be on Sunday night. As a finale for the fab weekend."

Mia paused. "I'm still a bit hesitant, to be honest."

"Mia! It's going to be fine. Enrique and Diego are going to go over it with us tomorrow, and I have the *best* song to do it to." Calli beamed at her, her enthusiasm lighting up her eyes.

"Oh, all right. When in Miami," Mia said with a laugh.

"Exactamente, mi prima," Calli said. "Oh, this is you." She stopped at Mia's door. "See you in an hour for dinner and drinks, OK?"

"Looking forward to it." Mia pressed a kiss to Calli's cheek and let herself into her room.

Inside, Mia debated over her choice of clothes. She'd forgotten how hot it was in Miami, even with the cooling sea breeze. She pulled out a short dress with a swing skirt, and spaghetti straps, in an electric blue, and matched it with a pair of blue-and-hot pink graphic opened-toed heeled sandals.

She took a quick cool shower, then got dressed, not bothering with full makeup just a layer of mascara, and lip gloss instead. She pulled her hair back into a half-up/half-down style, and used a beachy waves spray and scrunched the tresses in her hands.

Satisfied with her appearance, Mia took a selfie and sent it to Simi.

What do you think?

She'd debated sending it to Josh, but thought that might be a bit more than their friendship demanded, but Simi loved seeing what outfits she put together.

Ooh, Mami!

The reply came with an emoji of a pair of eyes, and Mia grinned at the screen, so looking forward to seeing her friend in person soon. Then another text came in:

Don't do anything I wouldn't do… no, scratch that, do all the things. Remember Thebes???

Mia snort-laughed, and typed back:

It's only dinner and drinks tonight.

Boo x

Mia sent him a kiss emoji before putting her phone into her small pink handbag and leaving.

Dotty, Claudia, and a few of the other girls were already walking along the path outside, so Mia joined them and they all headed to the bar together.

"Hi, girls," Aunt Junie said with a smile, from behind the bar. "Calli's already in the dining room, with the rest of the girls."

Mia smiled at her aunt, then led the way to the dining room. Calli sat at the head of a long table, and stood up with a squeal. "We're having lobster and steak tonight. Marlon is *the* best chef. Mom snaffled him from a restaurant in New Orleans."

Mia took a seat to the right of Calli. "Sounds yummy. Aunt Junie still goes to New Orleans then?"

Calli nodded. "She makes a point to visit Dad's parents once or twice a year. They're getting on a bit and Mom thinks they never recovered from Dad's passing, so she keeps an eye on them."

Mia laid a hand on Calli's arm. "It was tough on you all."

Calli's eyes sparkled with unshed tears. "Yeah."

Mia rubbed her arm, then said, "Shall I pour?" She gestured at the magnum of champagne set in the middle of the table.

Calli straightened and blinked away the tears. "We'll have a little toast to Dad too."

"Perfect," Mia said, then stood and picked up the bottle and poured out the shimmering liquid into the flutes of all the girls.

Aunt Junie and Mae joined them at the table; Junie on Calli's left and Mae at the other end and Mia ignored the tension in her stomach, and focused on enjoying the delicious food, with good company around her. She tapped her glass to Calli's and whispered, "To Reggie Lamone, beloved father of the most amazing bride-to-be ever."

"Oh, Mi," Calli said, and tapped her glass back, before taking a sip.

After the meal, Aunt Junie looked around at them all. "Now, who's for some Key Lime Pie?"

"Oh, one million percent," Calli said, back to her usual effervescent self. "I am indulging this weekend! Mia?"

"You don't have to ask me twice," Mia said, and the other girls made agreeable noises.

Mae and Aunt Junie rose. "Mia, would you like to help?" Mae asked.

Calli gave Mia a quick look, and Mia gave her a reassuring smile in return. This was Calli's weekend. She could do this.

Mia focused on Mae. "Certainly. Happy to."

CHAPTER FIFTEEN

"Mi, you have to hook your leg *over* Enrique's." Calli snapped her fingers in front of Mia. "Hello, Miami to Mia?"

"What? Oh, sorry. Hook my leg, got it." Mia had been lost in thought, her mind still going over the night before. She'd served the pie, made inane small-talk with Mae, and enjoyed a few cocktails and a dance with all the girls under the stars on the outside dancefloor. All in all, it had been a good night.

Calli re-set the music and they started again. They'd already gone over parts of it, but Calli wanted them to do the whole routine now. "That's it," Calli enthused. "Go for it, Mi."

Enrique gave her a white-toothed grin. "She's a bossy one, no?"

Mia leant in as he clasped her to him after a spin. "I feel sorry for her dance colleagues," she said in a mock whisper, and Calli narrowed her eyes at her.

"I heard that, Davenport."

Mia grinned at her cousin, as she hooked her leg perfectly over Enrique's upper thigh.

"All right, you're forgiven," Calli said with an eye-roll. "OK, I think we've got it. Oh, I'm so excited. They are going to love it."

"They?"

Calli's eyes slid away. "You know, the girls."

"Right. Of course." Mia said, hoping her cousin would stick to her promise and not record it. She smiled at Enrique. "Thanks, that was fun. It's good to see you again, and congrats on your wedding." She included Diego—stood next to Calli—in her smile.

"Gracias," Enrique said.

"We might see you in the bar later?" Diego said.

"Mia has planned games tonight, but we'll stop by for a few afterwards," Calli said and the two men smiled. With a wave, they left the dancefloor.

Mia checked her phone. "Speaking of which, the girls are probably waiting for us now."

"Let's go then," Calli said and together they stepped onto the path towards the bar lounge.

"Oh, damn, I've left some of the prizes in my room. I won't be a minute," Mia told Calli. "You go on ahead and get your mum to make a start."

"Sure thing," Calli said with a smile and carried on, while Mia veered off.

She collected the bag of small ornate bottles filled with perfume, and headed back towards the bar. Mia's phone rang and she stopped to answer it.

"Hi, there," Josh's warm voice came through the video call, and she thought it sounded even more drawling, and his eyes appeared even bluer in his tanned face. Perhaps his being back home triggered the change.

"Hi, yourself," Mia said. "How are you?" She wandered off

the path and onto the beach as she talked, stopping beneath a shady palm tree.

"I'm good, thanks. I'm phoning on behalf of the groom-to-be. He wants to make sure the bride-to-be is behaving herself."

Mia giggled. "She's being very well behaved...so far."

"That's good. I shall reassure my friend. And what about the maid of honour? Is she behaving herself too?" Josh's voice took on a teasing tone.

"Oh, no," Mia said, smiling, "she's a total nightmare."

"Now, I can't believe that," Josh returned. "But seriously, how's things going with your mom?"

Mia sat in the sand beneath the palm tree, and focused on the waves beneath the evening sky. "It's weird, we're like two polite strangers. I don't know what to say or how to act around her, and her smile seems fixed on, and her voice too cheery."

"That's tough. Maybe it's going to take a little time to ease back into it?"

"Time is one thing we don't have. I'll be back in New York in two days." Mia removed her slip-on sandals and pushed her feet through the sand. "Maybe I'm expecting too much too soon."

"Maybe," Josh murmured. "But she'll be in New York for the wedding, so now you've broken the ice so to speak, it might be easier then?"

"You could be right," Mia said. "Anyway, you all seem to be having fun—Dotty showed me the photo of you all on horseback."

"It's been a great couple of days. Do you ride?"

"Yes, I ride...Dad overcompensated, I think. I can ride, sing, dance, play piano and speak a fair bit of French. He put me in for all the activities in an attempt to keep me busy—distracted—so I wouldn't miss her too much..." Mia trailed off, leaning her head against the trunk of the palm tree. *And* they were back on the subject of her non-relationship with Mae. "God."

"What is it?"

Mia met Josh's blue gaze through the screen. "It didn't work," she said quietly. "I still bloody missed her. She was such a larger-than-life character, always creating something or singing or dancing around with floaty scarves...and then, she was gone."

"Of course you missed her, Mia. What little girl wouldn't miss her mom?"

"I tried not to. I tried to make it a big game—my mum was a great adventurer, and I was going to be exactly like her when I grew up." One tear snuck out to streak down her face. "Ironic isn't it? The best activity my father gave me wasn't one he paid for—no, it was treasure hunting with him using an old metal detector—best memories ever. Even then, I knew what I wanted to do with my life, but soon I realised Mae wasn't an adventurer...and I didn't want to be like her. I wanted to be like me."

"I wish I was there with you," Josh said after a moment.

Mia sniffled. "I could do with a hug right about now," she admitted.

Josh smiled, and somehow that was enough.

"So you ride, huh? You'd love it here," he told her.

"I haven't had a good horse ride in a while," Mia said.

"Then why don't we make a deal? After we both get back from England, I'll bring you here and you can take your pick of the horses—but not Hades, he's a bit of a diva—but any of the others, and you can just breathe and ride the plains."

Mia sighed, imagining the freedom. "That sounds perfect," she said.

"Perfect," Josh echoed. Someone said something to him in the background, and he twisted around. Mia heard a mumbled conversation take place before he turned to face her again. "I've got to go, Lance has somehow got entangled in his lasso."

Mia giggled, and Josh's gaze sharpened briefly. "OK," she said. "Thanks, Josh, I feel much better."

"Anytime," he said, with a smile. "I'll see you soon."

"See you soon," Mia murmured and disconnected the call.

She put her phone in her lap and stared out at the waves whispering in and out like the giant lungs of the sleeping earth.

Music, laughter, and muted voices filtered in from behind her and Mia knew she'd have to make an appearance soon. She *was* the maid of honour, and while she didn't have any unfortunates to un-entangle from errant lassos she did have a bride to entertain. *But just a moment more.*

The sea breeze wafted over her, teasing the tendrils of her hair. Mia breathed deep, filling up her lungs with enough air to make up for the imbalance of the panicky sensations that would be sure to plague her at some point that evening.

She pocketed her phone, picked up the bag of perfumes and stood, sliding her feet into her shoes, and headed for the bar. As she walked, Mia fixed a smile on her face and tried to relax her shoulders, but when Mae's face was the first she focused on as she stepped through the open doors, the air expelled from her lungs in a rush, scattering the last particles of the easy feeling. For a moment, Mia viewed her mother as she had been all those years ago; carefree and fun, and making Mia's early childhood magical.

"Mia! Come on, we're starting." Dotty grabbed her by the arm, and pulled her aside, staying Mae's half-risen position from her bar stool.

Mia and Dotty joined the other girls in the lounge area where Calli was standing in the centre, pink cards pinned to her clothes. She narrowed her eyes at Mia. "There you are! You're *supposed* to be running these games."

"Sorry, Cal. Had a phone call to take. But I'm all yours now." Mia tucked everything else deep into the recesses of her mind and focused on her cousin, and the games she and Aunt Junie had concocted.

"Goodie!"

"OK," Mia said, looking around. "Everyone takes a card off Calli—one at a time—and tries to answer the question on there. It's called 'How well do you know the bride?'. You get a point for each one you answer correctly."

"I hope you're not playing, Mia!" Audrey protested, tossing her long platinum blonde hair over the shoulder of her strapless minidress.

"I'll be hosting—so no unfair advantage," Mia said with a strained smile. She caught Calli's eye-roll but carried on. "Dotty, you go first."

Dotty sidled up to Calli and made a show of selecting the first card. "At what age did Calli have her first kiss?"

Mia and Calli exchanged a look. "Oh, god, I hope my mom's not still in here," Calli said craning her neck around to check, but Aunt Junie had gone back to the bar to get them a pitcher of cocktails.

"I'm going to go with fourteen?" Dotty said.

Calli let out a delighted laugh. "Ah, Dom Trenton, I remember it well...and yes, I was fourteen." And Mia remembered the long-distance phone call telling her all about it.

"Point for Dotty," Mia said, and made a note of it on the

board Aunt Junie had set up. "Next, Audrey..."

And so the night of games began. Mia forgot all about her problems with Mae for a little while, even when she and Aunt Junie joined them. Calli going beet red at the more colourful questions, and the girls sharing their own stories, were some of the highlights. And Mia was glad she was hosting and didn't have to delve deeply into her own past—that was a big plus.

"Next, pair up, and create a wedding dress out of toilet paper—Calli will be the judge."

As the other girls paired up, and Mae and Aunt Junie created a team, Mia sat next to Calli on one of the wicker sofas to view the chaotic fun.

"Hey, Miss Vega-Lamone—almost Mrs Sharma—who are you sneakily texting?" Mia teased when Calli peeked at her phone. "Not Ash, I hope?"

"But I miss him," Calli protested.

Mia softened. "He misses you too," she leant in to whisper. "He had Josh phone me on the pretence of asking if you were 'behaving yourself', but I know he's secretly pining too."

"Aww, he did?" Calli let out a contented sigh. "So you were on the phone to Josh, huh?"

"That's why I was late."

"A long phone call was it?" Calli raised one eyebrow.

Mia flicked a glance over to Mae and Aunt Junie, but Mae had only half-covered her sister, and was distracted as she laughingly twisted the paper roll, so Mia said, "He was just asking how things were going with—" She gestured her head in Mae's direction.

Calli fell silent, and Mia wondered what she was thinking until Calli patted her arm, and said, "He's such a good guy, isn't he? Always concerned about how you are doing."

"He's a good friend, and he gives good advice too," Mia said neutrally, before changing the subject. "They sound like they're having a great time on the ranch. Are they flying back Monday too?"

Calli's eyes flickered. "Oh, um, ah—I *think* most of the guys have to go back tomorrow. Don't forget they left a day before us."

"Oh, that's right." Mia gestured with her head towards the others. "Looks like the girls are finished. Time for a fashion show!"

The girls in their 'wedding dresses' assisted by their designers, walked up and down the lounge, strutting their stuff, until Calli crowned Audrey and Nicolette the winners. She handed Audrey a bouquet made from napkin roses and Audrey gave a faux-tearful speech thanking Nicolette. The others fell about giggling and toasting them with their cocktails.

"All right, last game," Mia said finally when the laughter had died down. "This one is 'Never Have I Ever'." She pulled out the sealed pack of pink cards Aunt Junie had picked up from the local mall. "You have to take a sip of your drink if you have done the thing I read out."

"Ooh, this is a surefire way to get tipsy." Dotty giggled, and Mia thought the petite redhead was already halfway there.

"Little sips should do," Mia said, and the other girls protested loudly. "OK, OK, on your heads be it," she amended with a grin.

"You *have* to play this one, Mi," Calli said.

"Yes, go on, I'll read them out," Mae said. "You should join in."

Mia hesitated then handed them over. "Thanks," she said, not meeting Mae's eyes.

"Right, first one...never have I ever...gone skinny-dipping," Mae said, and everyone—including Mia—took a sip.

Mae appeared surprised, but Mia merely gave a tight smile. Mae didn't *know* her, and that should—admittedly—be one of those things a mother didn't necessarily know about their daughter. But maybe, it was more than that, maybe she thought Mia didn't have the type of free spirit needed to do an act like that. Though, what if, Mae had unknowingly branded her daughter with more than just abandonment issues, maybe she had left a trace of her impulsiveness behind too. What a parting gift, Mia thought.

Mae continued. "Never have I ever...cheated on a partner."

And suddenly the game took a dark turn for Mia, and the cocktail sat heavily in her stomach. She couldn't bear to look around at the others and see who took a sip. She sat frozen, breaths shallow.

"Mi," Calli whispered, sitting closer, but Mia shook her head, heavily aware of Mae's curious gaze on her.

"I'm going to get some more cocktails for everyone," Mia said over-brightly, forcing herself to move. "No, no, you sit." She made a stay gesture to Aunt Junie who made to get up. "Maid of honour duties, you know."

Not meeting anyone's eyes, Mia hurried out of the lounge and into the corridor that led to the bar. *Shit*. Who the actual hell did she think she was fooling? Why couldn't she keep it together for one damn night?

She stayed pressed against the wall for as long as it took to get her breathing under control, then she carried on into the bar and collected another pitcher. By the time she returned to the lounge, Mia had plastered a fake smile on her face, desperately hoping the questions wouldn't get any worse.

She forced herself to join in for Calli, giving her cousin a reassuring squeeze of her hand when she resumed her seat next to her. Only seeing the happiness on Calli's face as the games progressed was enough to get Mia through the rest of the night.

CHAPTER SIXTEEN

"Were you OK after last night?" Calli asked Mia as the pair of them rifled Calli's closet in her old bedroom.

"Fine, Cal. You don't need to worry about me—concentrate on enjoying yourself." Mia gave her a wide smile and pulled out a top.

"Mi, seriously. I'm here for you." Calli took the top and set it on the pile they were accumulating.

"I know you are, but I'm fine, truly. I'm more nervous about the dance if I'm being honest," Mia said in a jokey tone, hoping to distract Calli.

It worked. "Pshaw, you'll have them all eating out of the palm of your hand. *Especially* in this..." Calli trailed off, triumphantly brandishing an iridescent silvery-pink sequined tiered miniskirt and matching cropped halter top at Mia.

Mia stared at it. "No, just no. There is no way I am getting into that again," she said, recognising the garments she had worn the last time they had performed the dance.

"The skirt might be a little shorter, and you'll definitely fill the top out better" — Calli raised an eyebrow emphatically, and Mia rolled her eyes — "but it'll fit. The top is a tie front and the skirt has a stretchy fabric. Go on."

"Honestly, Cal, the things I do for you," she said, with a narrow look, and took the clothes.

Calli threw her arms around Mia and squeezed her. "You know I'd do the same for you."

Mia blew out a breath of laughter. "Sure. If I have any hare-brained ideas, you'll be the first to know."

"I'll look forward to it," Calli said with a wink, then pulled out a similar outfit for herself, this time in a deep bronze-gold colour that would make her skin glow. "Let's get dressed! We don't want to miss our cue."

"Fine," Mia said and pulled off the short floaty summer dress she had worn for their last full day in Miami. They'd mostly spent it on the beach, relaxing, before they planned to dance the night away.

"Nuh-uh, no bra," Calli said, "It'll ruin the lines of the top."

"Jeez, Cal. Anything else?"

Calli tilted her head as if giving it considerable thought. "No you're fine, the skirt has little built-in shorts so you'll be covered on that front."

"Well that's a relief," Mia said sarcastically. But she took off her bra and slipped on the top, tying it in a firm double-knot at the front. She jumped up and down a few times, but everything stayed where it should albeit more pronounced than she would have normally liked.

"*Nice*," Calli said. "How do I look?"

"Hot," Mia said, and Calli beamed.

"Perfect!" She walked over to her dresser and hefted the bottle of tequila she had snaffled from the bar. "A bit of liquid courage?"

"Just one," Mia warned, "I want it to be *me* spinning, not the room."

Calli laughed appreciatively and poured out two shots. "Here's to the Paso Salsa 2.0. Cheers!"

"Cheers," Mia echoed, and then downed the shot with a slight wince.

Calli gave a wiggling shimmy, sending the sparkling tiers of her skirt fluttering. "Let's do this!"

Mia smiled; Calli's enthusiasm was infectious. "Lead the way, dancing queen," she said, and Calli grabbed one of her hands and led her from the room, dancing all the way.

Whoops and whistles surrounded Mia as she stepped up to Enrique and took her position; hip cocked, one hand on his shoulder, his at her waist. Calli mirrored Mia with Diego, and shot Mia a cheeky grin before her face took on a focused expression when the music began; a slower, yet hypnotic version of 'Hungry Eyes'.

Mia and Calli moved around the men in time to the slow rhythmic beats, while they in turn gripped the girls' hips and spun them away, and back to tilt them backwards at the waist in one fluid wave, one hand splayed wide across their upper chest pulsing like a breath.

The song moved through Mia like a heartbeat, and she began to enjoy herself. With the lights focused on them, the crowd were shadowy faces, yet she could still make out bright eyes and flashes of smiles as she spun around.

Enrique gripped the back of her knee as she lifted it exactly as Calli instructed her; in a perfect arc. She kicked it out, then dropped it sideways to the floor and traced up Enrique's body, until he spun her around and she pressed her back to his chest as they rolled their bodies as one.

Mia, eyes on the crowd, let out an intake of breath as Josh and Ash stood directly in her eyeline, just within the circle of lights. Ash was mesmerised by Calli to Mia's left, but Josh, Josh had his gaze firmly fixed on Mia; his bright blue eyes intense and watchful. Mia nearly missed a step, but recovered quickly as Enrique spun her back around to hold her against him. She caught Calli's eye over his shoulder and her cousin had a look on her face that told Mia all she needed to know. Calli had known they were coming. And conveniently neglected to mention it.

Mia managed to get through the rest of the sultry dance, finishing pressed up against Enrique. He patted her back and whispered, "Fantástica, Mia."

"Thanks, Riq," Mia said, and stepped back, taking her curtsey alongside Calli, who over-egged it, until, squealing, she ran forward and threw herself at Ash.

Mia walked more leisurely off the dancefloor, which was now filling with other couples and dancers as the music continued but in a more upbeat selection of songs.

"That was beautiful, Mia! A little different to how I remember it at Calli's Sweet Sixteen though," Aunt Junie said, intercepting her retreat.

Mia gave a sheepish laugh. "Just a bit," she agreed, "but thank you. Calli is a great choreographer as well as a dancer."

Aunt Junie beamed at her. "She takes after me," she said with a wink, and then sashayed over to Enrique and Diego. Mia watched her go; a smile on her face.

Mia turned then to go and say hi to Josh, but she could no

longer see him. Calli and Ash were hugging and talking to each other, so perhaps he had gone to the bar. Mia walked along the path to the bar on her strappy heels, wincing slightly, looking forward to removing them.

She rounded the corner. Josh leant against one of the wooden pillars supporting the entryway to the bar.

"Hi," she said, and he looked up, his eyes distant. They refocused on her, and a smile lit his face.

"Hi."

"How are you here? Calli didn't even mention you were coming," Mia said, a smile on her face.

"The guys had to go back today, but Calli was apparently *desperately* missing Ash, so he talked me in to diverting here for the night." He straightened and stepped forward into the lantern light. Dressed for the Miami weather, he wore a patterned short-sleeved shirt, linen shorts, and beige canvas shoes.

Mia now understood Calli's covert texts from the night before. She moved closer, intent on giving Josh a hug, but stopped when she viewed his shirt up close. "Oh my goodness, are those *crabs* wearing top hats and monocles on your shirt?" she asked with a delighted giggle.

Josh briefly inspected his shirt, a grin on his face. "They are. You like them?" He quirked one dark eyebrow.

"I *love* them," Mia said. "You and Simi would get on famously. Those type of shirts are all he wears."

"It seems I really need to meet this guy," Josh said.

"He's agreed to be on the dig team, so there's a chance you might," Mia hesitated, then added hastily, "I mean if I see you when we're both in England."

"I'll make sure of it," Josh said, his eyes intent on Mia's.

Mia dipped her head. “Great,” she said, then lifted her gaze and gestured to the bar. “Buy you a drink?”

“Sure,” Josh said.

They started walking and everything settled inside Mia as his scent wafted over to her on the gentle breeze. It all seemed better and brighter when Josh was around, she thought, and was grateful for his friendship, especially now that she’d have a buffer between her and Mae if things got too emotional.

They snagged two tall wicker stools at the bar and Mia ordered them spiced rum and cokes, before removing her shoes and tucking them beneath the stool. She wiggled her toes in relief.

Josh scanned the bar, and Mia followed his gaze. Mae talked with a group of people, a glass in her hand.

“I never realised Mae and Junie were twins,” Josh observed.

Mia nodded, this was a piece of her mother’s history that didn’t hurt her to share. “Yes. It’s quite a funny story. Mae was born first—just before midnight on May 31st, and Aunt Junie, just after, on June 1st.”

“Ah, I see, so that’s where their names come from?”

“Yes—but it’s not as cheesy as my name,” Mia said with a grimace, picking up her glass and taking a sip.

“What’s wrong with Mia? It’s a beautiful name.”

“Well, my full name is Mia-Mae. Mae wanted me to be named after where she grew up—Miami—but my dad was adamantly against it. But if you say Mia-Mae fast...”

Josh eye’s widened fractionally as he got it. “Oh—Mi-ah-may. *Almost* sounds like it.”

“Yeah, so Mae got her way after all.” God, she sounded bitter. And just like that, all her intentions of trying to not let the hurt win, vanished. Mia set her glass down. Perhaps she’d had too much of that this weekend.

"You OK?" Josh asked gently.

Mia focused on him. "Oh—yes—sure, ignore me." She gave a smile. "I'm a bit tired. It's been pretty full-on this weekend."

"Tell me about it," Josh said, then dropped his eyes to his glass. "As much as I enjoy being home, my dad gets a bit intense wanting to know about the contracts I've handled, whether I'm investing for my future, and so on."

Mia made a sympathetic noise.

Josh took a sip of his drink. "It was supposed to be *relaxing* but Dad was just in full on rancher-mode and had the guys helping him out at times."

"Hence the lasso incident?" Mia said, hoping to lighten his mood.

Josh set his drink down, and a grin pulled at his mouth. "Yeah, that was pretty funny," he admitted. "We had to spin Lance around to free him...speaking of which, that dance was pretty dynamic."

Surprised by the sudden segue, Mia flushed. "Hmm, ah, yeah, I can't believe I let Calli talk me into it, to be honest. It didn't look as—ah—*risqué* when we did it to an upbeat song. There's something about this version that hit a bit differently, though." Why the heck was she stumbling over her words, and her cheeks flaming? "Good job Enrique and Diego are married or I would have been embarrassed to dance like that with him otherwise."

Josh impaled her with his bright blue gaze. "It was compelling," he said softly.

"Oh...um, thank you," Mia said, and picked up her drink again, entirely forgetting her earlier decision that she'd had enough.

"Well, don't you two make a *lovely* couple." The moment was interrupted when Mae stumbled between them, half-finished cocktail raised high. "You'd sure make some beautiful grand-babies for me."

Mae eyed Mia and Josh—her gaze glassy—and embarrassment and anger flashed through Mia in twin prongs; embarrassment at Mae putting Josh in such an awkward position, and bitter anger at the thought that grand-babies would only be more children for her to abandon.

Uncomfortable at the acidic route her thoughts had taken, Mia sent Josh an apologetic grimace before saying to Mae, "Why don't you have some water, Mae," and went to take the glass off the older woman, which Mae deftly avoided. Perhaps, it was more luck on Mae's part, as she swung it around in her limp-wristed hand.

She raised an eyebrow, and ignored her daughter's suggestion by taking a long slurp of her cocktail. "It's time you got over that stuffy Englishman dumping you." She angled herself towards Mia. "You know what they say, Mia-Mae, to get over one man, you need to get under ano—"

"*Mae*!" Mia said, appalled. Is that how Mae thought it went down, that Henry had just dumped her?

"Oh, don't look so shocked, sweetheart—we are both women of the world." Mae winked at Josh as if they were compatriots, and said to him in a mock whisper, "I don't remember her being so snippy when she was a teenager."

Mia suddenly had had enough. Mortified at her mother for bringing Josh into their drama, she lashed out. "You can't *remember*, because you were never around!" She stood and glared at her mother, who froze, drink half-way to her lips, the laughter slowly dying in her brown eyes.

Mia pushed past Aunt Junie who had been on her way to join them. She had obviously overheard the last words as her gaze held pity and understanding. "Mia—" she started, but Mia shook her head. "I can't, Aunt Junie, I can't deal with her right now. I need a minute." *A damn minute.*

"OK, hun, go and clear your head," Aunt Junie said after her as Mia kept going out of the bar, leaving the rhythmic music, and Mae, far behind her.

"Mia, wait!" Josh caught up with her on the lantern-lit boardwalk. She kept walking, barefoot, along the wooden slats towards the whispering ocean and he kept pace.

"You think I was too hard on her?" she asked after a minute, giving Josh a sideways glance.

He shook his head. "No, your reactions are just that; *yours*. It's not for me—or anyone else—to tell you how to deal with what's happened with your mom. But what I *do* think was, she'd had too much to drink—perhaps, a bit of Dutch courage—and her misguided attempt at motherly advice went awry. The timing was poor—"

"That's Mae for you—poor timing, or none at all. " Mia stopped walking. "Look, Josh, I'm sorry Mae involved you in that. It was crass and..." she trailed off, her face flaming.

"Hey, it's OK, I wasn't offended." Josh offered a smile. "But you know what? She was right about one thing."

Mia stared at him, her mouth parted. "About which bit?" she asked in apprehension. *You know what they say; the best way to get over a man*...He wasn't suggesting?

"Our combined DNA *would* make cute kids," he said with a wink, and Mia relaxed. Of course he wasn't suggesting such a thing, merely teasing her to get her to smile again.

She let out a shaky laugh. "Thanks, Josh. You always know

how to cheer me up."

He stared at her for a moment, then his face relaxed into a grin. "Of course."

Mia started walking again along the boardwalk, stopping at the wicker beach bed set at the end on a circular platform. Four wooden posts rose around it with trailing gossamer curtains and twinkling fairy lights, but above, it was open to the elements. She sat down on the plump cushions and studied the full moon, glowing and round, nestled amongst the glittering star-strewn sky.

"Look." She pointed, and Josh wandered over to join her, sitting on the other side of the wide bed. "Orion's Belt."

"I don't see it," Josh said, so Mia lay back against the cushions and beckoned to him, and Josh followed suit. Heads nearly touching, she took his hand and used it to indicate the right direction. "Oh, now I do," he murmured.

"Did you know, the pyramids at Giza are exactly aligned with Orion's Belt above it," Mia told him in a quiet, musing voice. "I think there's something comforting in that. So much has changed in thousands of years, but the constancy of that vast fact—it makes you feel as though all your problems are small in comparison. Our lives are just a turning of the page in the history books" — she broke off as a small yawn escaped her, before continuing — "and those pyramids will stand beneath the watchful gaze of those three stars long after we are gone."

"That's beautiful and sad in equal measure," Josh said, his voice deepening, "but it's a great message that we should take advantage of every moment of happiness we can while we're here." Mia smiled softly, happy he understood what she had been trying to convey.

The stars above danced in front of her fluttering eyelids, as she murmured, “I agree, but some types of happiness are not for everyone.”

Josh moved closer; his elbow brushing hers. “I don’t believe that. Everyone deserves all the kinds...it just might take them longer to find it. But if you look, look really hard amongst those millions of stars, there’ll be that *one*, the one that’s for you alone.”

Mia turned her face, and caught a tantalising hint of his scent—now as familiar to her as her own scent—and breathed deep. “Now *that’s* beautiful, Joshie,” she murmured, her voice thickening with sleepiness. She had never felt so comfortable, so safe, in her whole life. She would close her eyes for a few moments.

As Mia did so, before slumber completely claimed her, she thought she heard Josh whispering about something else being beautiful. But it was lost to her as the soothing sound of the waves, and the remnants of the alcohol still coursing in her veins, took her deep under.

CHAPTER SEVENTEEN

Sunlight kissed Mia's eyelids, gently awakening her. She opened her eyes, and for a long moment, she couldn't remember where she was. Her right arm was trapped beneath something firm and warm. Upon closer scrutiny, she discovered she was cradled within Josh's arms, her arm stuck under him. *We're on the beach bed*, she understood with a start, recalling their hushed conversation the night before and how comfortable and sleepy she had been.

With a stifled gasp, Mia became acutely aware that her left leg was slung over his legs; the lightly bronzed skin beneath her tiered mini-skirt touching the tanned skin of his, visible beneath his shorts. *Oh god*, she thought. Carefully, and in tiny incremental movements, she lifted her leg off him. What would he have thought if he'd woken up and seen her sprawled all over him like that? She swallowed uncomfortably, then made shuffling movements backwards to increase the gap between their lower bodies, but her arm was a lost cause because her torso was still wrapped in the circle of his arms.

Mia risked a look up at Josh's sleeping face, and froze. His thick black eyelashes created a curving crescent shadow on his upper cheeks, while his breath came out in smooth waves beneath his slightly parted full lips. She was staring, she realised and blinked, knowing how creepy and inappropriate that was. She let out a squeak when his eyes shot open, impaling her with his bright blue gaze, as bright and sparkling as the stars they had discussed the night before.

Mia appreciated how close their faces were when he said, "Good morning," and his soft breath caressed her cheek.

"Ah, good morning," she replied in a slightly strangled voice, mortified at having been caught semi-staring. "Sorry, I was trying to extricate my arm...we kind of got a little tangled up."

Josh chuckled, a husky sound that did strange things to her insides. He unhooked his arms from around her, and lifted his body slightly, allowing her to pull out her tingling arm. She rubbed at it, encouraging the blood to start flowing freely again, and hastily sat up, turning away to shield her flaming face from him.

To calm her racing heart and rapid breathing, Mia focused on the glowing orange-red sun cresting the horizon above the ocean. Its scattered rays painted the surrounding sky in a peach-pink haze, while crystals danced across the shallow waves of the sea. She inhaled the sea breeze and the tsunami of emotion quietened inside.

She sensed Josh sitting up beside her, and turned to look at him over her shoulder; her long beachy curls partially hiding her face. "Sorry about falling asleep out here, and you being obliged to stay with me."

Josh's eyes crinkled at the corners as he smiled. "Don't be," he said with a stretch, his comical crab-patterned shirt riding up along his abs. "That was the best night's sleep I think I've ever had."

Mia paused. "Come to think of it. I don't think *I've* ever slept so soundly," she admitted. But, nope, she was not going to explore why. She would put it down to the sound of the soothing waves and the fresh air. Yes, that was definitely it.

"And what a view to wake up to," Josh said, a catch to his voice, and though he was still looking at her, she believed him to be referring to the glorious dawn canvas.

"I love watching the sunrise," she said agreeably.

Josh cleared his throat. "Me too."

Mia stood and pushed aside the gauzy curtains. At least they'd been hidden from view. "I guess we'd better return to our rooms before they send out a search party."

Josh gave another stretch. "I guess so," he said and stood. He moved around the bed and joined her.

Silently, they walked along the boardwalk, breaking off when they came to the fork in the path leading off to the separate beach hut accommodations.

"See you at breakfast," Josh said, catching Mia's eye.

"See you at breakfast," Mia repeated, then, "thanks for being there last night."

Their gaze held. "Anytime," Josh said, and then with a small smile, he turned away and headed for his hut.

After a moment, Mia did the same, a strange nagging pit in the centre of her stomach.

"And *where* have you been?"

The voice nearly had Mia jumping out of her skin. Calli stood in front of her on the path leading up to her hut.

"Oh, ah" – Mia avoided her cousin's gaze – "I went for a walk, to see the sunrise," she said lamely.

"In the exact same clothes as last night, hmm?"

"Thought it was easier to just throw them on," Mia said, taking a quick glimpse at her cousin.

Calli narrowed her eyes. "Tut, tut, tut, lying to your best cousin."

Mia grinned. "You're my only cousin."

"Semantics," Calli said, with a wave of her hand. "But seriously, I know a walk of shame when I see one."

"Why do they call it that? There's nothing to be shameful about. If it was a man, no one would bat an eyelid," Mia said, with a puff of outrage. "But, *nevertheless*, I have not been doing what you are implying I've been doing."

"Now that," Calli said, "is too bad."

"Cal," Mia said, a warning in her voice.

"I know, I know, but I can live in hope." Calli stepped forward and linked her arm through Mia's. "Anyway, I came to check up on you. Mom said you and Mae got into it last night."

Grateful for the change of subject, Mia sighed. "Stupid really, but sometimes, I get these little bursts of anger—I think it's grief masked, though—that I never had her when I should have. She *chose* to leave me, Cal."

"Oh, Mi," Calli said softly, stopping at the door to Mia's hut. She rubbed a comforting hand over her back, and Mia hadn't even realised she was crying. "You need to tell her this—and I'm sure Dr Carroll would agree with me—you *need* to, Mi. I know you bottle stuff up in typical Brit fashion, but it's not doing you—or her—any good. You'll go around in circles, with it eating you up inside like teeny, tiny piranhas."

Mia gave a watery smile. "You're very good at advice when you put your mind to it. And creative too."

"I have hidden depths," Calli said with a small smile.

“I know you do, and I value you more than anything.” Mia pulled her in for a hug. “Even if you sneaked Ash and Josh into our bachelorette party.”

They broke apart with Calli giving a little laugh. “Sorry, not sorry. I missed Ash, and their arrival at *just* the right time couldn’t have been planned any better. Ash thoroughly appreciated the routine...if you know what I mean?” She lifted an eyebrow, and Mia shook her head in amused exasperation, quickly realising the reason for her cousin’s radiant appearance.

“T.M.I, Cal, honestly.”

Calli gave a wicked laugh before her expression turned serious. “We’re all going snorkelling this morning—and I know you hate it, so I’ve booked you and Aunt Mae in for a massage.” Mia opened her mouth to protest, but Calli shook her head. “Tell her how you feel, Mi. She needs to know. How can she start making amends if she doesn’t know where to start?”

Mia nibbled her lip, considering whether she even wanted Mae to make amends. Was it too late? Had the hurt cut too deep, to ever be fixed? She stared into space, then said, “OK, I’ll give her a chance.”

“This is for *you*, Mia, not her. She made her choice. You never had one, but by giving her this chance, it’ll help you. And if you can’t repair it then at least you would have tried and you’ll never always be wondering.”

“Calli, you are wasted in the waitress-dancer sector.”

“But I’m a good waitress, and a damn good dancer,” Calli said.

“Preach,” Mia said. “I’ll see you at breakfast?”

Calli said, “Only for a quick one—our boat leaves with the tide.”

They shared another brief hug, before Mia pulled out her key from the pocket of her skirt and let herself into her accommodation, ready to take a quick shower and get changed.

Audrey slid into the seat next to Josh at breakfast, trapping him in the booth he sat at with Ash and Calli. Mia gave them all a friendly smile before moving on to sit with Dotty and Claudia, who beckoned her over to the booth they shared with Nicolette. Pouring herself a mimosa, Mia grasped that the fluttering in her stomach was nerves. Perhaps it was a good thing she had a reprieve from sitting so close to Josh and behaving normally after finding herself in his arms that morning.

"So you're not coming with us, Mia?" Nicolette asked, spearing a fluffy pancake, and placing it on her plate beside the heaping mound of berries.

Mia shuddered. "No, I'm not a fan of snorkelling, makes me feel claustrophobic," she explained.

"You could come on the boat though, apparently it's an hour's sail to the reef. Top up your tan?" Nicolette suggested.

"Thanks, but Calli's booked me and my–ah–Mae in for a massage." Mia still couldn't say mum, not that Mae cared. She'd always encouraged Mia to call her Mae once she'd left. Perhaps it assuaged her guilt, somehow.

"Ooh that sounds divine," Dotty said, bringing Mia's attention back to the breakfast table. "Heaven knows I don't want to top up my non-existent tan. Factor 50 for me, all the way."

Claudia laughed at her sister-in-law. "You'll be fine. The boat has a canopy, and you can lather up before you hit the water."

The three others talked about what swimsuits they planned to wear and Mia was finishing eating up her own pancakes when a familiar sea salt and coconut scent drifted her way. Josh stood beside their table.

Mia's stomach flip-flopped. Annoyed at her reaction she said brightly, "Hi."

"Hi, do you have a minute?" he asked.

"Sure. I've finished." Mia rose from her seat. "Have fun," she told the other women.

"See you later, Mia," Dotty said and the others said their goodbyes.

Mia waved to Calli and Ash as she passed them, and Audrey gave her and Josh a covert look from her position by the coffee machine as they headed outside.

"Calli tells me you're not coming with us this morning—that you're going to spend it with Mae," Josh said, stopping beneath a pergola.

Mia looked past him, and centred herself on the gentle rolling waves in the distance. "Yes. We leave this evening, so I guess this is the last chance for..." She turned her head to meet his gaze. "For what, I don't know."

Suddenly she found herself in Josh's arms again, his chin resting on her head. "You're being the bigger person here, Mia. You don't owe her anything, but perhaps you owe it to yourself."

Mia smiled sadly against his chest. "Calli said something along the same lines. That's why I'm going to try—for me, this time."

Josh eased back and let her go. He gave her an encouraging smile. "That's all you can do. I'll see you later, OK?"

"Sure. Have fun," she told him.

"Thanks." He looked behind Mia. "They're gesturing at me, I better go."

Mia nodded. "Oh, and Josh?" He turned, a question in his

eyes. "I like your shirt," she said, indicating the sea-blue shirt, printed with dolphins in cowboy hats, and lassos caught between their flippers.

"I thought you might," he said. Then with another smile, he moved away to join the others.

Mia and Mae sat in the small room off the massage parlour, and enjoyed tall glasses of cool lemon-and-lime-infused water after their massage, where they had made small talk, but now they were alone.

Mae took a sip of her water, then leant forward, her expression earnest. "Calli explained this morning what actually happened with your ex. Why didn't you tell me he cheated on you? And with little Nadia too—heavens, I was good friends with her mother!"

"Because" — Mia ignored the sharp pain that lanced behind her breastbone and bit back the sigh that wanted to escape — "seeking you out to confide in you is not my default, Mae."

Mae sat back, emotion rippling across her face. "And that's on me," she said slowly, obvious pain in her brown eyes.

Mia rubbed a hand across her face. She didn't know how to do this. *Why* was she even doing this? "Perhaps we should talk about something else."

"Sure, whatever you want, sweetheart. Tell me about your work." Mae gave her a faltering smile.

So Mia did. She told Mae briefly about the discovery of the ring and the planned expedition because of it, and how she was looking forward to doing fieldwork again.

"Boudicca? I know a little of her story—didn't she rise up because of what happened to her daughters?"

And in that moment, Mia knew why she was so drawn to the Iceni queen...because she had been the kind of mother Mia lacked. The one who would cause the ground beneath the feet of her daughters' betrayers to tremble, whose rallying cries would singe the ears of those who wronged them. *Shit.* Dr Carroll would call that a breakthrough. "Yes...that's the one," she said weakly, and then dissolved into tears. "You let me down, Mae," she sobbed. "I needed you. I needed a mother too."

"Oh! Oh, Mia," Mae said and then Mia found herself enveloped in her mother's arms, a soft cloud of patchouli-scented perfume surrounding her. "Sweetheart. I'm sorry. I'm so, so sorry," she uttered over and over. How long they sat together, clutching at each other as though making up for all the lost hugs, Mia had no idea. She only knew that when they pulled apart, she felt absolutely drained—but somehow a tiny bit better.

"Here." Mae handed her a tissue and Mia wiped her eyes. "Heavens, I think we needed that." She squeezed Mia's hand. "I know you go back to New York in a few hours, but maybe...maybe we can talk more at the wedding?"

Mia hesitated, knowing that sixteen years of hurt couldn't be erased in a few hours' worth of talking.

"I don't want to push you, Mia—and heaven knows I've got no right to any kind of proper relationship with you. I was a coward. I thought I couldn't be the kind of mother you needed, and so I left, but I *am* sorry that it caused you so much hurt, and I know nothing can make up for what we've lost, but I'd like to try and build something new, if you would have me."

Mia searched Mae's face. The words sounded sincere, but words from Mae were easy, she needed to see if Mae was willing to take action this time. "We'll talk at the wedding," Mia said neutrally, "and see where we go from there."

Mae's face softened. "Thank you," she said, and as Mia stood to leave, Mae reached out a hand to clasp to Mia's arm. "You are so much stronger and braver than I am, Mia. You're more like Boudicca than I ever could be. Remember that. Remember your inner strength."

Mia's lips parted in surprise. That was the most motherly thing Mae had ever said to her. "I will," she said finally. "Thank you."

Mae, eyes bright, let go of her arm. "And I'm sorry about last night, sweetheart. I shouldn't have tried to interfere in your life or offer unwanted advice."

Mia gave her a small smile. "I appreciate the apology. I'll see you later to say goodbye."

"OK," Mae said, her eyes crinkling as she smiled. "I'll see you later."

Mia left the room, pushing her way through the gauzy curtains and up the steps that led into a garden area. She walked through it, passed the fountain and its musical cadence, until she came out the other side.

She pressed her back against the stone wall encircling the garden, and doubled over, the heels of her hands pressing into her eyes as she tried to recover from the emotional onslaught.

"Mia?"

Mia straightened swiftly, and knuckled away the last of the tears. "Oh, Josh, hi," she said. "You're back from snorkelling."

"Everything OK?" The concern in his voice and etched on his tanned face almost undid her, but she forced back the last lapping waves of emotion and nodded briskly.

"Truthfully? Better than it was. While things are not reconciled completely between Mae and me—there's a long way to go until that happens—I'm more open to the possibility." As she spoke she realised it was true. She had been carrying around the rubble of her childhood abandonment for far too long, and twinned with everything else—well, something had to give.

"That's great." Josh smiled at her. "As long as it's what you want?"

"I'm open to it, and that's a start," Mia said. "But enough about me, how was snorkelling?"

"Wet," Josh said with a grin. "But no, seriously, it was great fun, until one of the girls thought she saw a shark and demanded I help her back up onto the boat."

"Let me guess," Mia said dryly. "Audrey?"

"How did you figure that out?" he said.

Mia laughed. "Call it intuition." She gestured to the path back to the accommodation huts. "You walking back?"

"I was looking for you, but we can head this way."

"Oh?"

"Yeah. Ash and I have to leave now. We couldn't get on your flight, and found two seats on another airline, so we'll see you at home later," Josh said, and Mia experienced a swoop of disappointment. He leant in and said, "Don't forget you have the video if you need it."

Mia stared up at him, and their eyes held for a brief moment. "I appreciate you doing that, Josh. It helped more than you know."

"I'm glad to hear it." Josh stopped on the path that forked to the bar on the right and the accommodation on the left. "Ash is waiting with our luggage, and the Uber's on its way. So, I guess this is hug time?"

"Hug time," Mia agreed and stepped easily into the safety of his arms. She squeezed him for that one extra moment, then released him, knowing it was too easy to cling to him. "Have a safe flight."

"You too." He stepped back and regarded her; his eyes held a heaviness to them, despite his curving lips.

"Thanks." She returned his smile, then turned left and carried on to her hut to finish her own packing. The weird niggling pain was back behind her breastbone, and this time she did rub it with the heel of her hand until it subsided.

Mia was wrung out yet filled with so much feeling that she needed something to distract herself with, so decided to check her emails until it was time to get ready to leave with the girls.

CHAPTER EIGHTEEN

Mia stared out of the window at the rain lashing down, and sighed happily, before taking a sip of her tea. She loved the rain, especially if she was warm and safe inside, and the sound of it beating on the glass of the apartment windows had a soothing tempo to it.

Something fluttered in front of the window, tossed about like a piece of litter in the wind, and Mia took a closer look as the thing battled back against the torrent. *It's a little bird*, she realised and hastened to set her cup down. She hurried around the back of the sofa and pushed open the window to the small balcony area.

"Oh, you poor thing," Mia said, catching ahold of the drenched bird carefully and cradling it in the palms of her hands. "Got a bit windswept there, didn't you?"

She set the bird down inside the apartment on the wide window ledge and went to locate a box. She found an old shoe box in the bottom of her closet and layered it with a cloth, before gently lifting the bird and settling it inside. "There you go. Get warm and dry, then you can be on your way."

The bird shivered in the corner of the box, and Mia carefully pulled a piece of the cloth over its shivering form. Gradually, the shivering subsided and the bird closed its eyes. A notification sounded on Mia's phone and she moved away from her vigil to take a look.

Ready for Saturday?

Mia debated an answer to Josh's text and whether to just send a single emoji detailing the state of her mind where the wedding was concerned; the one that implied she was going slightly bonkers. Calli had switched gears as soon as their return flight had touched down. While Mia was still sending thanks to those on high for their uneventful flight, Calli had begun issuing maid of honour orders and had only ceased when Mia called her a 'bridezilla'. She did send the emoji, but added:

Seriously though, yes, everything on Calli's huge list has been ticked off. All I need to do is get her to the venue Friday night, settled into the bridal suite and encourage her to have a good night's sleep in preparation, while you keep Ash company.

Sounds straightforward enough.

Josh replied with a grimace emoji, then added...

What are you up to?

Calli and Ash are out for dinner with Ash's family, and I've just rescued a little bird.

Mia waited for his reply, and she could almost hear a smile in the words when they did come.

Of course you did. Shall I come over and birdsit with you?

Sure, some company would be nice.

Be over in 5.

While she waited for Josh to come around, Mia pulled out a bottle of wine from the fridge and grabbed two glasses from the shelf. She didn't think Josh would want to share her pot of tea. He was still not convinced by the taste, but she and Calli kept trying different brews on him.

Mia opened the door when the knock came a few minutes later and let Josh inside. He was dressed casually in navy joggers and a white tee that enhanced his tan and the blue of his eyes. He carried a small plastic tub.

"Another of Simi's gifts?" He gestured at her own tee with a smile. She wore a pale mint-green coloured one this time, with her black leggings, emblazoned with the phrase, 'Never Throw In the Trowel.'

Mia dimpled out a smile at him, and swept her loose long hair over her shoulder. "However did you guess?" she asked mock surprised.

"Call it intuition," he said, and she laughed.

"What's that?" Mia gestured to the tub he carried.

"Oh, bird seeds. Sylvie was on a mission to feed all the birds over winter and gave us all a tub at one of the card nights. These are left over from the ones she gave me," Josh explained.

Mia's heart melted. "You used them?"

Josh's face turned sheepish for a second. "Sure. Sylvie's terrifying," he said, but Mia knew better, and could imagine him sprinkling out little handfuls of seeds for the hungry birds on his own balcony.

"Sure," she repeated, and took the tub when he passed it over to her. "Come on, I'll introduce you to my little friend."

Josh followed her over and Mia stopped at the ledge and carefully pulled the corner of the cloth back to reveal the brown-feathered bird. "I don't think he's injured, but I can't really tell. I'm hoping with a bit of rest, he should be able to fly away soon."

Josh leant closer. "More than likely just battered by the wind. Give him a few seeds, see if he eats."

Mia did as Josh suggested and scattered a few seeds near the bird. A few moments later he was pecking at them. "That's a good sign," Mia said, turning her face to Josh's.

Josh cleared his throat. "Certainly is."

Mia eased back. "Wine? I was having tea, but thought you'd probably prefer something else?"

"You thought right," Josh said. "Wine would be great."

Mia walked over to the counter, leaving the bird to his supper, and poured out two glasses. She handed one to Josh and picked up the other and they settled themselves on the sofa.

"So, everything ready for your dig?" Josh asked after he'd taken a sip of the pinot grigio.

“Yes, thanks. Simi’s put together a team, we’ve found somewhere to stay and everything else is in order.”

“That’s good. Excited?”

“Very.” Mia smiled. “I can’t wait to get my hands dirty and see what we uncover there...and there’s something about stepping foot on land that’s steeped in history. It’s like magic.” As she spoke, Mia gazed off into space, her voice softening.

“Magic,” Josh repeated softly, and Mia came back to the present with a laugh.

“Sorry, there I go again.”

“Don’t be sorry, it’s great to have a passion for something,” Josh told her and leant over to tap her glass with his.

“Now that, is something to toast,” Mia said, and took a sip of her wine.

The door opened and Calli and Ash came in, slightly damp, but faces wreathed in happy smiles, and Calli with a slight flush to her cheeks.

“Hi,” Calli said and came over to sit beside Mia. “This looks cosy.”

Mia shot Calli a look, but said, “Josh brought over some birdseed for my new friend.” She gestured to the box. “He got blown about by the wind.”

“Didn’t we all,” Ash said, removing his jacket, then poured out wine for him and Calli, while Calli hopped up to take a peek at the bird.

“Aww, poor thing,” she said. “We used up all our seeds, we’ll have to get some more for winter or Sylvie’ll be haranguing us again.”

Ash took a seat in one of the armchairs. “She’s got a good heart,” he said.

Calli’s face softened. “She has. She and Carlos are going to look after our apartments when we are all away." Her eyes twinkled merrily. "I sense a little stirring of something there," she said.

"Cal—you and your matchmaking," Ash said indulgently, while Mia smirked into her glass, happy not to be on the receiving end of said matchmaking for once.

"But I'm so good at it, and," Calli said, resuming her seat and looking around at them all, "I am *never* wrong."

Calli's gaze lingered on Mia's cheek, erasing the happy sensation. Mia determinedly refused to meet her cousin's gaze, instead changing the subject to that of wedding preparations—which she instantly regretted when Calli said, "Oh, Mi, I forgot. I need you to do one more thing for me..."

Mia couldn't help but laugh in exasperation. "Of course, what is it?"

"*Well*...kidding. Everything is ready!" Calli said, the humour on her face suddenly fading. She met Ash's eyes and a look passed between them, one that had Mia almost breathless with the intensity in it, and knew it was made up of all the different ways the happy-couple-to-be fiercely loved each other.

Mia was intruding on something special, so she dragged her gaze away and inadvertently locked eyes with Josh. In his own gaze was a knowing, an understanding, and Mia suddenly felt exposed—vulnerable—as though her innermost wistful wishes had been revealed. Ones she didn't even know she still held dear.

To cover her discomfort, she stood and headed over to the counter. "Top up, anyone?" she asked.

Everyone else declined so Mia sensibly put the rest of the bottle in the fridge. She didn't want any further emotions pushing their way to the fore. Emotions were far easier to deal with buried.

Josh stood. “I’d better make a move. We’ve got that early meeting tomorrow, Ash. Seeing as it’s our last official day in the office we’d better not miss it.”

“That is a good point,” Ash said. “Early night, Cal?”

Calli raised one eyebrow suggestively, and Mia shook her head in amusement. “Sure,” Calli said.

“You all go on, I’ll clear up,” Mia told them.

Calli came over and pressed a kiss to Mia’s cheek. “Thanks. Night,” she said, then turned to look at Josh. “Bye Josh.”

“Night both,” he said, and Ash murmured in response then went into the bathroom, and Calli into their bedroom.

“I’ll see you out,” Mia told Josh and walked him to the door. “Thanks for the birdseed,” she added and opened the apartment door.

“No problem. Hope your little friend will be up and flying about soon,” Josh told her with a smile.

“Fingers crossed,” Mia said, leaning on the doorframe as Josh stepped out into the hallway.

“Sleep well,” Josh said.

“Night,” Mia returned. She closed the door when he turned to go to his own apartment, and rested against it for a moment.

She gave herself a shake then set to cleaning up the wine glasses and her earlier tea things, before going to check on the bird.

Its feathers had dried out, and it breathed evenly in its sleep. She would give it the night in the box and then set it out on the balcony in the morning. “Don’t worry, little one,” she told it in a whisper, “you’re safe here.”

Mia continued to monitor it for a few minutes more before she took herself off to bed, somehow soothed within herself too.

“Yes, Cal, everything is at the bridal suite already—Lisette sent the gowns over, hair and makeup are booked, and you and I are having a quiet girls’ pamper night,” Mia repeated, stroking a placating hand down Calli’s arm.

“Are you absolutely sure we haven’t forgotten anything?” Calli asked again.

Mia looked at Ash for support.

He turned Calli into the circle of his arms, while Mia waited at the open door to the apartment with her and Calli’s overnight bags.

“It’s all going to be fine, Cal, and tomorrow you and I are getting married...and the rest of our shared life will begin,” Ash said soothingly, and Mia stepped into the hallway with the bags to give them some privacy, when Calli murmured back to him.

“Problem?” Josh asked, coming out of his apartment, a bag in hand.

“Oh, hi, not really a problem exactly. Cal’s freaking out a *teeny* bit. Ash is doing damage control.” Mia smiled at him, and gestured at his bag. “You all set for your boys’ sleepover.”

“It’s been a long time since I had one of those, but yeah, we’ll probably put on a movie, play a few card games...and maybe have a whiskey or two.”

“No more than two, please,” Mia implored. “We need at least one of the happy couple on time and clear-headed.” She and Josh shared a grin.

“I heard that, traitor,” Calli said, coming out of the apartment.

Mia noted her cousin exuded happiness again, and gave Ash a relieved smile when he followed Calli out. “Sorry,” Mia said with a laugh. "You ready?"

Calli picked up her bag, and Mia did the same. "Yes," Calli said emphatically, "I am ready." She focused on Josh. "Look after my man, OK?"

Josh clapped a hand to Ash's shoulder. "Absolutely."

Mia hit the call button on the lift and, as the doors opened, she met Josh's eyes. "Have fun," she said. "See you at the wedding."

"See you at the wedding," he repeated, and Mia and Calli stepped into the lift, Calli blowing a barrage of kisses at Ash until the lift doors closed.

Calli shuffled over to Mia and leant her head on Mia's shoulder. "Thanks for being here, Mi."

"Oh, Cal. There's nowhere else I'd rather be. I'm so excited for this next chapter in your life," Mia told her as the lift stopped on the ground floor.

Calli lifted her head and the pair stepped out.

"Your Uber is here, Miss Vega-Lamone," Carlos said with a twinkle-eyed smile. "That's the last time I'll ever call you that."

Calli let out a shuddering laugh, and pulled Carlos in for a hug. "Oh wow," she said, and Mia stroked a prancing Lou, and observed the scene with tears in her eyes.

Carlos released her, tears shining in his own eyes. "Go on, now, you don't want to keep it waiting."

"Thanks, Carlos, and don't forget to stop by the evening reception if you can make it," Calli reminded him.

"I shall do my best," Carlos said, then with a smile to include Mia, he opened the door for them, and the two women stepped through with waves of goodbye.

The ride to the venue was short and before Mia even took a metaphorical full breath, they were ensconced in the bridal suite, dressed in matching silky pink pyjamas, facemasks on, and soft music playing in the background, while an array of nibbles sat on a tray on the low table in the lounge area where they had settled themselves.

"Remind me again," Calli instructed, selecting a carrot stick and dipping it into the dish of humous.

Mia humoured her. "The girls are arriving at nine, hair and make-up soon after. Your mum texted to say her and Mae's flight gets in at ten and will join us soon after. They've got a room here and will stay overnight and have brunch with us all on Sunday before you catch your flight."

"OK," Calli said and let out a breath. "OK."

"Calli, everything will go like clockwork. The wedding planner is efficient and thorough. All you need to do is put on that beautiful dress and get married."

Calli contemplated her words, then said, "I can do that."

"Good. Now, let's wash this goop off, and have *one* glass of wine."

Calli grinned, cracking the mask. "Spoilsport."

Mia giggled, cracking her own mask, and soon they were clutching their sides as hysterical laughter took over.

CHAPTER NINETEEN

"Calli, we are going to be late!" Aunt Junie pushed into the room and cast Mia a frustrated look.

"Auntie, why don't you go and tell them we'll be another five minutes and I'll hurry her along," Mia suggested seeing Calli's strained face and thought perhaps her aunt wasn't helping matters.

Aunt Junie eyed Mia gratefully. "Fine, thank you," she said. "Right, everyone but Mia clear the room."

The other bridesmaids and Aunt Junie left and Mia sat down next to Calli. She nudged her gently. "You OK?"

Calli blew out a breath and lifted one hand. "Look," she said, "why am I trembling?" She turned to Mia with eyes shining with tears.

"It's a big step, Cal." Mia took Calli's hand in her own and squeezed it. "But remember, downstairs is a man who loves you with his whole heart, and your shared future is waiting. All it takes is you to stand up and take that step."

Calli stared at her. "He does love me doesn't he?"

“More than anything,” Mia reassured her.

“And I love him.” Calli sniffed. “Oh god, my makeup.”

“You look beautiful, not a smudge in sight,” Mia said with a smile. “Come on let’s put poor Ash out of his misery.”

Calli laughed. “He should know by now that I would be late.”

Mia stood and smoothed down the silky gold dress, and adjusted the heart-shaped scoop neck and lacy straps until it sat straight, then held out a hand to Calli.

Calli rose, accepting Mia’s hand, and Mia had to sniff back tears herself as she took in the full effect of the wedding gown. “Oh, Cal, you’re going to knock his socks off.”

Calli gave her usual cheeky grin. “I intend to do more than that later,” she said.

Mia laughed. “Ready?”

“Ready,” Calli said.

Mia passed her the gold and ivory waterfall-style bouquet, before picking up her own smaller clutch of similar-toned flowers. She led Calli out and they met up with Dotty, Claudia, and Nicolette, who gave relieved smiles at Calli’s approach.

“Oh, thank god,” Aunt Junie said as the women made their way down the wide staircase with Calli in tow. “I’ll see you in there.” She blew Calli a kiss, and mouthed ‘thank you’ to Mia before ducking back into the room.

Calli had elected to not have anyone give her away. Her father had passed four years ago when she was twenty, and she deemed no one else was worthy enough, although Mia thought it had more to do with Calli’s strong views on women not being something to ‘give away’. She couldn’t argue with that...but still, she imagined Calli would rather have her father walk beside her if she could.

Moments later, stringed music filtered out from the open

doors and one by one Dotty, Claudia, then Nicolette began walking in a slow glide through the doorway. Mia winked at Calli before she began her own walk along the aisle.

Mia smiled as she stepped into the room. Light, smiling faces, and flowers filled the magnificent, domed space. She traversed the golden-carpeted path up to the front, nodding at the guests. Her eyes rested on a wan-faced Ash, and she gave him an encouraging smile, but her steps almost faltered when her gaze then flitted behind him to where Josh stood. He wore a tux *extremely* well, with the gold of the cravat and brocade waistcoat enhancing his golden, chiselled features.

His eyes caught hers and they held as she came to a stop at her designated position opposite the groomsmen. Mia pulled her gaze away—with some difficulty—in time to catch Calli's glowing progression up the aisle. Gold had been the perfect choice to accentuate the ivory-white of Calli's lace and silk gown. The tiny iridescent beads scattered across the bodice caught the light and turned molten, glittering as she moved.

Mia was close enough to Ash to hear his stunned gasp, and see Josh clap a bolstering hand to his friend's shoulder briefly. Mia couldn't hide her smile as Calli stepped up to meet her soon-to-be husband. When she turned to focus on the couple, Josh moved into her eyeline and once again their eyes locked. Mia's stomach gave a funny flip-flop before the registrar commanded her attention.

The ceremony passed in a blur of meaningful words, laughter, and applause, topped off by a very flamboyant kiss at the end to much cheering from those assembled. Calli let out a whoop as Ash bent her back and Mia wished she'd had the foresight to put a tissue in the pocket of her gown. Although, with its slinky silhouette it probably would have ruined the lines of the dress.

Calli and Ash—the new Mr and Mrs Sharma—walked back down the aisle together and Josh and Mia stepped out at the same time and Josh offered Mia his arm.

"Thank you," she said as they followed Calli and Ash.

"My pleasure," Josh said.

Mia smiled at her dad as she passed him in the crowd, and he beamed at her proudly.

"I was introduced to your dad earlier, he's a terrific guy," Josh said as they made their way out of the double doors.

"He is. I was lucky to have him," Mia said softly, and then accepted a glass of champagne from a server who turned from offering the first glasses to Calli and Ash.

The wedding planner intercepted the happy couple and offered congratulations as she stationed them to receive the exiting guests. Mia raised her glass in Calli's direction as her cousin glanced over at her, her face alight with happiness.

Josh accepted a drink and as he took a sip, Mia turned back to him. His eyes met hers over the rim of his glass. He lowered the glass slowly and cleared his throat. "You look very beautiful," he said. "I like your hair like that."

Mia smiled shyly, a flush staining her cheeks, and resisted the urge to put a hand up to her curls anchored on top of her head, held in place by sparkling gold-and-crystal hairpins. "Thank you. It's a lot of work to get it this way. I have a *lot* of hair." Why was she rambling? "Anyway, you're the one who looks very dashing, sir," she added.

"Dashing, you say? I'll take that," Josh said and soon they were laughing and the strange tension had dissipated.

"Mia, Calli wants you." Claudia came up beside them and gestured over to where Calli waved at Mia urgently.

"Duty calls," Mia said and set her champagne glass down on the table behind her, before weaving her way through the thronging mass of congratulating guests. "What's wrong?" she asked when she reached her cousin's side.

Out of the corner of her mouth, Calli said, "I gotta pee."

Mia hid her smile, and gauged the receiving line. "You're almost done, Mrs Sharma," she said and Calli's eyes widened.

"*Mrs Sharma*," she said in wonder, then turned back to the remaining guests with renewed energy, her full bladder forgotten.

When the last of the stragglers had gone through to the drinks reception room, Mia finally had a moment with the newly married couple. She took one of Calli's hands in one of her own and one of Ash's in the other. "Congratulations to you both," she said through teary eyes. "You both deserve all the happiness in the world."

Calli's own eyes filled with tears, and she sniffled out, "Thank you, Mi."

"Thank you, Mia, and thank you for getting my wife to me *almost* on time," Ash said, with a fond grin.

Mia smiled at them both and then sensed Josh coming up behind her. She let go of Calli and Ash's hands and stepped aside to let him have his minute with them.

"Oh, and Mia...you deserve all the happiness in the world too," Calli said, and Mia's heart skipped a beat as Josh turned to look at her with a suddenly intense gaze.

Mia stepped back, her heart beating faster. "I," she said, then shook her head, breaking the look, "I need to speak to your mum," she added lamely and turned towards the drinks' reception room.

Calli called after her, "Don't be long, I still need to pee, remember?"

Mia's heart settled as her cousin managed to turn the suddenly fraught moment into one of comedy. "I'll be right back," she said over her shoulder. *After I've taken a moment to gather myself.*

What was wrong with her? This was *Josh*, her best friend. Just because he scrubbed up real nice in a tux didn't mean she had to lose her head, and Calli's pointed comments meant nothing new. She'd been making them since the beginning. Get yourself together, Mia told herself, and made sure to put a friendly smile on her face as she weaved through the guests.

"Everything, OK, Mia?" Aunt Junie appeared, Mae in tow.

Mae leant in and pressed a kiss to Mia's cheek, as Mia said, "Yes, I came to see if you need me to do anything?"

Aunt Junie rolled her eyes. "Keep an eye on my daughter, and make sure she's on time for the dinner. The wedding organiser has a strict timetable."

Mia laughed. "Sure thing, Auntie," she said, then turned to Mae. "Hi. I never asked earlier; are you staying long?"

Mae shook her head. "Junie and I fly back tomorrow after the brunch. Unfortunately, we couldn't get staff to cover us for longer."

If she was disappointed that Mae didn't plan on seeing her words through to actively spend more time with her only daughter while they were in the same city, Mia didn't let it show. Even though Mae had requested they carve out some time together at the wedding—and while they had of a sort while helping Calli get ready—it hadn't been the time or the place for an emotional conversation.

Mia thought they'd made steps towards a tentative relationship in Miami, but was Mae reneging? Maybe Mia should be the mature one and reach out now. “OK, that’s unavoidable I guess,” she said, with an understanding smile. “Maybe when I’m back from England we could meet up properly? Just us.”

A surprised expression crossed Mae’s face for a moment, while Aunt Junie beamed approvingly. “I’d like that, Mia-Mae,” Mae said. “We’ll go somewhere and have some one-on-one time.”

Now it was Mia’s turn to be surprised at how readily Mae had agreed. She leant forward and pulled Mae into a hug, instigating contact for the first time in a long time. “Sounds like a plan, Mum,” she said softly, and Mae stiffened slightly at the use of the term, then squeezed her back. Hard.

They broke apart as Aunt Junie dabbed at her eyes.

“I’ll see you both later. I’ve got to go and supervise Calli in the toilet,” Mia told them, and Aunt Junie nodded.

Mia walked away somewhat lighter. She’d never have the relationship with Mae that Aunt Junie and Calli shared, too much time had passed, but they could make some sort of future relationship. She smiled slightly to herself as she made her way out into the foyer where Calli was dancing about. As soon as Mia drew near her cousin, Calli grabbed her hand and pulled her towards the bathrooms.

“Oh my god, Mia, what took you so long?” she said and thrust her bouquet, and Mia’s posy, at a passing Dotty. They made their way into the bathroom and headed for the wide cubicle at the end.

As they negotiated the intricacies of holding up a voluminous dress while backing up to the seat, Mia said, “Sorry, Mae was with your mum...we kind of had a moment, I guess.”

Calli sat down and made a face of relief, then said, “You did?

Perhaps it's something about weddings. They tend to bring people together."

"Ha," Mia said with a smile as she held the skirts up gently so as not to wrinkle them.

"Huh. That's actually a good joke, but I'm serious, Mi. I know she hasn't been the best mother, not by any stretch of the imagination, but I think she's trying." Calli made some movements beneath the skirts, then stood.

She hit the flush before Mia walked her out, let the skirts go carefully and smoothed them out.

"I think she is too," Mia agreed. "But what matters is that *I'm* going to try. I'm fed up with the past holding me back. I've even spoken about it a bit with Dr Carroll. She thinks I've got a bit of overlapping trauma."

Calli washed her hands, observing Mia in the reflection of the mirror. "God, I could have strong words with that pair," she said with a frown. "But you're right: you can't let the past hold you back from healing–I know I've been pushing you to move on, but it's only because I want you to be happy." She snagged a paper towel and dried her hands.

Mia ran a hand down her cousin's arm. "I *am* happy, Cal, seriously. I've got the best cousin, great friends, and a wonderful life here with you all." Calli smiled at her. "But, this is yours and Ash's day. Come on, let's stop chatting in the bathroom and go and celebrate!"

"I hear that," Calli said and together they walked towards the door. Calli stopped just as she was about to exit. "Last thing, I promise," she said, looking back at Mia. "Sometimes love finds you when you don't think you're ready for it, but broken or not, your heart–in the right hands–will beat regardless."

Mia stared at her cousin as Calli gave her a small smile and walked serenely out of the bathroom. When had Calli gotten so wonderfully poetic?

Mia followed but Calli had already joined Ash.

"They look so happy, don't they?" a deep voice said from behind Mia and she turned to see Josh leaning against the wall, two full champagne glasses in his hands. He offered her one.

"Thanks." She accepted the drink, as Calli set a tender hand against Ash's cheek. "So happy," Mia agreed.

"Shall we go in? They called the dinner when you and Calli were in the bathroom." Josh pushed off the wall.

"We better had or Aunt Junie will have my skin," Mia said with a smile. They walked to where Ash and Calli waited to be announced.

"See you inside," Mia said to them and they went in to find their seats in the dining room.

The domed dining room was a mirror to the ceremony room, and the circular dining tables were dressed in the same ivory-white and gold, with creamy linen tablecloths and a gold gauzy overlay, topped with candles in golden urns that reflected the light in glittering spears, while surrounded by greenery and crystals.

"We're over there, table two," Josh told Mia after checking the table plan on the board. He guided her through the tables with his hand on the small of her back. For some reason, Mia was acutely aware of the placement of every one of his fingers. They touched her skin just above where the low backless part of her dress sat.

At the table where the other bridesmaids and groomsmen sat, Josh pulled out Mia's chair and she sat with a murmured, "Thanks."

Josh sat next to her with a smile.

The next moment, the emcee was making an announcement. “Please be upstanding for your bride and groom, Mr and Mrs Sharma!”

CHAPTER TWENTY

Mia stood with everyone else, clapping and cheering as Calli and Ash waltzed through the double doorways, smiles adorning their faces. They headed for the top table where Ash's parents, Aunt Junie and Mae sat. In the absence of Calli's father, Calli had thought Mae would like to sit with her sister.

Calli met Mia's eyes as she and Ash sat between their families and Mia blew her a kiss.

The dinner was delicious, and by dessert—a chocolate and raspberry torte—Mia thought she might burst out of her dress.

"You not eating that?" Josh leant over and eyed the last bit of her torte.

Mia laughed. "Go ahead. I'm about to explode."

Josh speared the bite on his fork and lifted it to his lips. "Mmm," he said, drawing the appreciative noise out, and closed his eyes.

Why the heck was she following the motion of his throat as he swallowed? Mia set down her champagne glass. Once again, she had obviously had *far* too much of that, she decided.

"You OK?" Josh asked opening his eyes as soft chatter filled the room around them.

"Oh, yes, fine," Mia said airily. "Just wondered where you fit all that, I mean" – *Oh god* – "you know, you're very—ah—trim." *Shit, shit, shit.*

Josh gave her a long look, then amusement filled his eyes. "Ah, thanks?"

She gave him a wide smile. "No problem," she said, covering the acute embarrassment that wanted to make her toes curl in her gold satin strappy high heels. She pointed behind him to where the emcee gestured with the microphone. "You're up."

"I'm what?" he said, eyes widening.

"Your speech," Mia replied, and his eyes cleared.

"Oh, right, thanks." He dabbed his mouth with his napkin, then stood and went over to the top table to stand between Ash and Calli.

The room quietened down once the emcee announced the speeches, and servers moved ghost-like around the room, topping up champagne glasses ready for the toasts. Mia winced at the thought of yet more alcohol, but a few more tiny sips wouldn't hurt, surely?

"Good evening, everyone," Josh said, and Mia enjoyed the tone of his voice as the microphone amplified his smooth, Southern drawl nicely. "For those who don't know, I'm Josh, Ash's best man, although I'm sure Calli would disagree, and say that the best man title falls wholly to her new husband." He smiled down at the pair. "And I would have to agree. I might not have known Ash long, but it's as though I have known him my whole life. We immediately clicked and I have had the pleasure of getting to know him by working with him, and by being their neighbour. At Thursday night card nights I was introduced into their amazing circle of friends" – he flicked a look at the bridesmaids and groomsmen and a few little whoops rippled around the table. Mia gave him an encouraging smile and he continued – "and when I met Calli, I knew she was the perfect woman for Ash. Their love is vast and true and I wish them nothing but the happiest of futures together. I can think of none who deserve it more."

Mia swallowed back her tears as Calli dabbed at her own eyes, and Ash stood to shake Josh's hand, and then pull him in for a hug.

"To the bride and groom," Josh said, once Ash had re-taken his seat, and a server had handed Josh a champagne glass. He raised it high.

"To the bride and groom," echoed around the room.

Josh took his seat next to Mia again as the speeches continued. "That was lovely," Mia leant in to whisper. "I know who to ask if I ever need a best man," she added jokingly.

"I'll always be your best man, Mia," Josh said after a moment, then turned away to listen to Ash's father talk.

Mia sat back, unable to make out any of Dr Sharma's speech as a roaring noise filled her ears. *Best* friend, *he meant, of course he did*, she decided before the sounds rushed back in and she belatedly realised glasses were once again being raised.

She took a hasty sip and almost choked on it. *Smooth, Mia, real smooth.*

Somehow, she managed to get through Aunt Junie's funny speech without incident. As soon as the speeches were over, the tables were being cleared, and guests were invited to mingle in the garden area while the tables were rearranged to make room for the dance floor, Mia wasted no time in getting up and exiting the room. She sensed Josh's eyes following her but she needed a few minutes alone. She had no idea why exactly.

“Mi, wait up!”

She turned to see Calli hurrying after her, skirts of her gown gripped in her hands to help her haste.

“Hey there, Mrs Sharma,” Mia said with a smile, waiting for her on the staircase leading up to the accommodation rooms. Her minute alone could wait.

“Now don’t get mad at me,” Calli said as soon as she caught up with her cousin. “Remember it’s my wedding day.”

Mia closed her eyes briefly. “What have you done?” she asked.

Calli hesitated, then, “Well, you know you mentioned before that Stav kept pestering you to go out on a date with him?”

“*Ye-es*,” Mia dragged out the word, bracing herself.

“Well, I kinda told him you were already seeing someone. I thought it would never be an issue and it would get him off your back.”

“OK,” Mia said, thinking a little white lie couldn’t hurt. Then she realised. “That’s not all, is it?”

“Ah, um, I totally forgot but he overheard me talking about the wedding and well, sort of invited himself to the evening reception.”

“And you’re telling me this now?” Mia held her impatience in check. It was Calli’s wedding day after all, and she couldn’t get mad at who she chose to have attend her celebrations. Even if it was their overbearing—and over-interested—boss.

“I forgot! Claudia informed me a minute ago that he’s definitely coming.” Calli explained.

“What’s the rest?” Mia sighed.

“*Welllll*, the person I told him you were seeing is here too, and if they meet, well Stav might make a comment and it might be a teensy bit awkward."

"You didn't *make up* someone?" Mia pressed a hand to her temple, her stomach suddenly sinking.

"It just came out. You know I'm no good thinking on my feet. *I thought I was helping you out.*" The last part came out as a near-wail.

Mia patted her cousin on the hand. "Don't upset yourself, Cal. Tell me who it is and I'll have a word, see if they'll vaguely go along with it, in the unlikely event they might speak with Stav."

Calli swallowed. "Don't get mad," she repeated.

"*Calli.*"

"All right, all right—It's Josh."

Mia stared at her cousin. *Of course it was Josh.*

"What's Josh?" a deep voice asked from below. *Shit.*

Mia and Calli peered over the glossy bannister rail. Josh stood in the foyer below looking up at them.

"Ah, I'll leave you two to have a little chat then, bye-ee," Calli said and hurried back down the stairs and into the dining room.

Mia followed slowly down the stairs in resignation, prolonging the inevitable.

"Now where is your cousin going in such a hurry?" Josh asked once she had joined him.

"Not my cousin, I renounce her," Mia said darkly.

"That doesn't sound good," Josh remarked, slipping his hands into his trouser pockets.

Mia stared at him, and bit back a groan. He'd loosened his cravat and the top button of his shirt. Why did he have to look so devastatingly handsome now she had something to ask of him that went far beyond the realms of their friendship? *Um, excuse me, devastatingly handsome? Where had that come from?* She gave herself a mental shake. *Focus!* "It's *not* good, and sorry, she's kind of involved you in a bit of a pickle."

"A bit of a pickle?" Josh said with an amused smile. "That doesn't sound too bad. I like pickles."

"Just you wait," Mia warned and took a deep breath, then she noticed someone coming along the long driveway behind Josh through the open front doors. "Shit," she said out loud, and Josh's eyebrows rose.

It was now or never. Stav had arrived.

"*Miss* Davenport," Josh said with a laugh at the expletive, but he stopped laughing when Mia stepped up close to him and said urgently, "My boss asked me out" – she waved a hand in a 'doesn't matter' gesture when his brows knit together, and carried on – "and Calli thought she was helping me by telling him I was already seeing someone."

A serious expression clouded Josh's eyes. "Oh?"

Mia let out a noise of dismay as Stav gave his name at the door. She nodded. "Yes, and he's here."

"Who's here? The guy?"

"My boss." Mia gestured at Stav, who waited while his name was being checked on the evening guest list.

"O-*K*," Josh said slowly. Then his eyes widened as the realisation dropped. "Calli said it was me, didn't she?"

Mia nodded again. "I'm so sorry to involve you in all this, but if you could play along for a few minutes because he is *right there*."

Josh blinked slowly, then before Mia was fully aware of what was happening, he pulled her into his arms, his face nestled into the curve of her neck.

"What are you doing?" she squeaked out.

"Making it look believable," Josh whispered against her

skin, and a rush of sensation shot through her. For one still, silent moment, Mia was at peace. Safe in the arms of a man she knew would *never* hurt or betray her. She closed her eyes, breathing in his scent, and lost herself in the sensation.

A throat cleared behind them, and they eased apart. Mia could barely look at Josh as he kept his arm around her when they turned to face Stav.

"Stav, hi," she said, her voice breathy and high-pitched.

"Evening, Mia," Stav said. He was dressed in a dark grey suit and his brown hair had been neatly styled. "Who's your friend?"

Oh, ah. "This is my—ah—my...Josh. This is Josh." *Oh my god, Mia,* she thought. If she could've slapped a hand to her forehead she would've. "Josh, this is Stav—mine and Calli's boss at the restaurant."

"So you're Stav," Josh said with enough inflection to insinuate that it wasn't a good thing.

Stav, wisely, chose a quick retreat and said, "Nice to meet you, but I'd better go and congratulate the happy couple."

Josh gave him a stony glare and Mia had to bite back a laugh. He was overdoing the protective boyfriend act a bit too much. "Bye, Stav," she said as the other man scuttled off.

"My Josh, huh?" Josh said when they were alone again.

"Oh god, I'm never going to live that down, am I?"

Josh grinned. "Nope, Mia-mine."

Mia burst out laughing. "Now *we* have nicknames? I'll have to keep track. My dad calls me 'Mouse', and Simi has one for me, but yours has a cute ring to it," she said. The laughter stopped as their eyes met, and a flush worked its way up Mia's cheeks. "Seriously though, thanks for that. I wondered why Stav had backed off lately—I guess I'll have to reclaim Calli as my cousin and thank her too."

Josh toyed with one of her curls. "Entirely my pleasure," he said, his eyes bright. "Come on, let's go and get ready for our dance."

"Oh—yes." Mia had forgotten that Calli and Ash wanted the bridesmaids and groomsmen to pair up and dance, after they'd had their first dance.

Josh offered her his arm, and she took it with a small smile. He led her into the dining room which had now been transformed into a low-lit ballroom. The candlelight still speared out in glittering shafts and leant an ethereal, mystical aura to the area.

"So beautiful," Mia said.

"My thoughts exactly," Josh said, but his eyes were on her. He waited a beat then said, "Stav's watching."

Mia swallowed. "Oh, of course."

They found seats along the edge of the room and waited until Calli and Ash were to begin their dance.

Mia's foot bounced in agitation, and she had to press a hand to her leg to help it cease. Josh leant in close, and said, "Would you like a drink while we wait?"

"No—no, I think I've had more than enough," Mia said, then added a smile when she realised how harsh the words had come out. "Oh, look, here they come." She pointed to the doorway from the garden where Ash was leading Calli in to the room, followed by the remainder of the guests.

Josh's eyes traced her gesture, and she breathed a sigh of relief. What was wrong with her? She needed to get it together.

Mia forced herself to get to her feet and join the circle of guests surrounding the edge of the dancefloor as 'Crazy for You' by Madonna started playing and Ash and Calli began their slow, romantic swaying dance. Tears sprang up in Mia's eyes as she recalled Calli telling her that she and Ash had met at one of Kocktails' 80's nights when she had been murdering that song. But Ash hadn't cared as their eyes locked, and the rest was history.

The emcee invited the bridesmaids and groomsmen to join them, and suddenly Josh was at Mia's side holding out his hand. She knew she needed to keep the pretence going so as not to put Calli in an awkward position with their boss, so she accepted Josh's hand with a smile, and moved into the circle of his arms.

Mia looped her arms loosely around his neck, and his hooked her waist, and again she was acutely aware of every placement of his fingertips against her skin. She couldn't meet his eyes, so lay her head against his chest, and as they moved to the beat, her eyes captured Calli's who danced with Ash to the side of them.

Calli gave her a nervous grin and a thumbs up, and Mia rolled her eyes at her, but she wasn't truly that mad. She had to see it through now, and ignore the uncomfortable sensations happening within her. Sensations she had thought were dead and buried.

She closed her eyes and listened to the words of the music against the steady beat of Josh's heart, and thought what a truly good guy he was. Josh was always there for her, in ways Henry had never been. Perhaps that was the problem; she and Henry had never been friends, just straight into lovers.

Mia pulled back with a jolt at the direction her thoughts had taken her.

"All right?" Josh asked.

"F-fine," she said. The music ended and cheers and claps filled the room. Mia realised she was staring at Josh, and blinked. She was about to step back, as an upbeat song started playing, when her father appeared at Josh's shoulder.

"Might I cut in?" he asked.

Josh released Mia with an easy smile. "Of course. See you later, Mia. Thanks for the dance."

And he was gone, absorbed by the dancing couples.

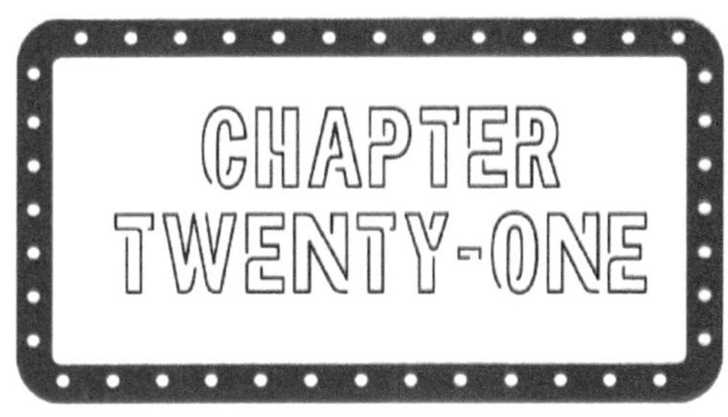

CHAPTER TWENTY-ONE

"Hi, Dad," Mia said as Stephen took her hand and twirled her around. "Sorry, I haven't had the chance to speak to you much."

He smiled. "Don't you worry about that. Alice and I have been well looked after, and you've been busy with maid of honour duties."

"We'll have more time tomorrow," Mia told him.

"I'm looking forward to it," her dad said. "How's your mother? Are you two getting along?"

Mia pursed her lips. "You know Mae," she said, "but, yes, we're both trying. I'm going to spend some time with her when I get back from England."

"That's good." Stephen's face rippled with pain for a moment. "I always thought I should have done more to get her to stay."

Mia stopped dancing and said, "No, Dad, she wasn't happy, and I see now that would have been worse for all of us if she'd stayed." She pulled him in for a tight hug. With eyes of an adult, she *could* see that, but the child in her wished that Mae hadn't just left and barely looked back at what she had left behind—that she'd made more of an effort to stay in touch. "You gave me the best childhood you could under the circumstances. I cherish every memory with you."

Stephen rubbed circles on her back. "I would have given you the moon, Mouse," he whispered, his voice gruff.

Mia pulled back. "All I needed was you to be there, Dad," she said.

"You'll always have me, but when you're ready, find yourself someone who'll give you the moon too."

Mia sniffed back tears. "Perhaps I'll get it myself," she said.

Her dad chuckled. "I have no doubt you could do anything you set your mind to...but it'll be lonely up there on the moon alone." He pressed a kiss to her cheek, and then seeing someone over her shoulder, he gave a little wave.

Mia turned. Alice stood on the edge of the dancefloor. "Go and dance with your wife," she urged.

"And you go and find your handsome friend and dance the night away yourself." Stephen gave her a narrow look. "Now, he's a good guy."

"Dad," she said warningly.

He gave her the cheeky smile she remembered from her childhood. "I'm going," he said and danced over to Alice, who laughingly accepted his hand.

Mia shook her head fondly, and then turned away, thinking she would find that few minutes of solitude. She smiled at various acquaintances and friends, including Carlos dancing with a blushing Sylvie, and Audrey who was cosied up to Ash's cousin, Addy, before winding her way through the remaining dancing couples, and out onto the terraced garden area.

Tall planters filled with fragrant white flowers and trailing greenery lined the edge of the outdoor space while hanging lanterns and fairy lights dangled from the white wooden beams of a gazebo. Mia avoided the gazebo as it was filled with a few chattering guests. Instead, she moved further along to a bench, mostly hidden by more flowers.

She sat down and tilted her face up the dusky sky, and breathed in the sweet-scented air. Why she suddenly felt like crying she had no idea. Damn, she should have brought a tissue—or a napkin at least.

"Mia?"

Mia sniffled and then focused on the figure before her. "Josh, hi."

He sat on the bench beside her, and silently withdrew a handkerchief from his pocket and offered it to her.

Of course Josh had a handkerchief. He always knew exactly what she needed. The thought only made her want to cry even harder.

She dabbed at her eyes, and took a deep breath.

"Anything you want to talk about?" Josh said after a few minutes. "Sorry if I came on a bit strong. I'm new to this undercover stuff."

A watery giggle escaped Mia. "Well, you do it very well, but it's not that." Well, not *only* that, she admitted to herself. "I had a bit of an emotional chat with my dad, and a semi-emotional one with Mae earlier, and I—I, oh, I don't know. It all seems a bit much. Everything's changing, but I'm stuck—if that makes sense?"

"Makes perfect sense. And perhaps, though your therapist would be better placed to talk about this, but perhaps, it's because you're returning to England soon, and it might make things resurface?"

Well, *damn*. Mia blinked at him. "Are you sure you're not an undercover therapist too?"

Josh let out his deep, throaty laugh. "Maybe." He tapped the side of his nose. "You can't expect me to reveal all of my secrets now."

Mia leant in teasingly. "Oh, so you have secrets, do you?"

Josh's throat worked before he answered. "One or two," he said and caught her gaze.

Mia felt as though she were falling into an ocean of the deepest, brightest blue. "Oh," she said finally, pulling away, "I guess we all do."

A silence fell between them, before Dotty came hurrying over. "Mia! I've been looking everywhere. Come on, Calli's about to throw her bouquet."

"Sorry, Dotty." Mia stood, then spoke to Josh, "Are you coming?"

"Go ahead, I'll be right there." His face was half hidden in the shadows, but Mia could sense a tension about him.

"OK," she said and offered him his handkerchief back.

"Keep it," he said, so Mia placed it inside her dress pocket, smoothing the bump down, hoping it wouldn't be too noticeable.

Mia followed Dotty back inside. In the foyer, they met up with Claudia and Nicolette who were organising those who wanted to take part in the bouquet catching. Mia smiled at Mae and Aunt Junie amongst the small crowd, but she had every intention of slipping to the side unnoticed once everyone was in place.

Calli emerged queen-like from the ballroom, displaying her throwing bouquet like a sceptre. The other guests followed and arranged themselves around the edge to spectate. Mia inched herself away before Calli clocked her. She wouldn't put it past her cousin to aim for her and do her best to nudge fate along.

Mia found a position on the edge of the cluster of women behind Calli's slightly taller college friend and deemed herself safe enough.

"Ready!" Calli shouted. "One…two…three!"

In slow-motion, the bouquet came sailing over the heads of the women in a graceful arc, and Mia realised how truly wily her cousin was. Calli had positioned herself in front of the long panels of mirrors gracing the wall in front of her. Her grin was obvious, as the bouquet began its descent straight at Mia's chest, and of course, she had no option but to clutch at it and plaster a smile of frozen faux-joy on her face.

She held it aloft as expected and only then did she see Josh leaning against the doorway of the ballroom. Their eyes met as Mia slowly lowered the bouquet, and then her view was cut off as she was surrounded by shrieking and giggling women. Mia sought out Calli amongst them, and thought seriously, once again, about renouncing her. She gave her a long look that spoke volumes, and Calli gave a little smiling shrug that wasn't apologetic in the slightest.

Mia endured the comments with good grace until the emcee announced that the evening canapés were ready, and she found herself alone clutching Calli's beautiful throwing bouquet; a miniature of the one she had carried down the aisle.

"Looks like I'll be attending your wedding next," Stav said, sauntering over from the direction of the bathrooms. "Your fella seems ready to put you on lockdown already."

Mia smiled weakly, while inwardly cringing inside. "It's far too early for that," she hedged.

"So, it's not serious then?" Stav said, his hazel eyes lighting up like a hound sighting its prey.

Shit.

"Oh, she's being far too modest, aren't you, darlin'." Josh's drawling voice rippled over Mia's skin and her lips parted, as he casually dropped an arm around her shoulders, joining them.

She looked up at him. "You know me," she said faintly.

Josh leant down and pressed a kiss to the top of her hair. "Yes, ma'am, I do," he murmured and Mia's mind went completely blank, wiped clean by the husky drawling statement. *Oh my.* Her knees turned to jelly and she vaguely heard Stav mutter something about a drink.

Once they were alone, Mia gathered the remnants of her scattered mind and said in a shaky voice, "You have got that act down well."

Josh removed his arm, and gave a dry laugh. "You know me," he repeated her words.

Mia was suddenly unsure of their dynamic. "Josh—"

They stood together, the bouquet between them. "Yes?"

"I..." What did she even want to say? *Thanks for always being there, thanks for being the buffer between me and my real-world problems. Thanks for being a listening ear, and giving great advice.* Instead, she dropped the hand holding the bouquet and leant in to give him a one-armed hug, and said, simply, "Thank you."

He relaxed against her. "Anytime, Mia-mine," he said.

And suddenly they were back on an even keel.

"Hungry?" Mia asked when she released him.

"Always," Josh said with a grin, and together they walked into the dance room and headed for the tables set out with the evening nibbles.

For the rest of the evening and well into the night, Mia found she could relax and enjoy herself. She danced with her friends and family, took fun pictures in the photo booth, and sang along with the other bridesmaids on the karaoke machine. She even dragged Josh up for a song, knowing it was probably the one and only time he would do so; at his friends' wedding. His deep timbre was a great foil for the 'Islands in the Stream' song picked for them.

She forgave Calli at some point during their rendition of 'Girls Just Wanna Have Fun' as they linked arms and belted it out along with Dotty, Claudia, Nicolette, Sylvie, some of the Valkyries, Aunt Junie, Mae, Ash's mum, and even Alice.

At the end of the night, giggling, Mia hopped up the stairs on bare feet after Dotty and Claudia. Calli and Ash had vanished at around midnight and most of the guests took their leave soon after, and Josh had retired to his room. But Mia had decided to embrace the contented state she found herself in and lingered over cocktails—which she'd probably regret in the morning—with Dotty and Claudia. Nicolette had decided to turn in with Lance.

"*Shh,*" Claudia whispered louder than Mia's giggling as they crept along the hallways of the accommodation part of the venue.

"Sozzy, I mean, *sorry,*" Mia said affecting a cultured voice, then stopped dead. "Dotty, what are you doing?"

Dotty stood before a door, peering at it. "Is this my room?"

Claudia and Mia walked back along the corridor and linked arms with her, one either side. "No...and neither were the other five doors you stopped at." The three women collapsed into peals of giggles again.

"I am queen of the key cards!" Mia said. "Follow me." She stopped at an intersection and started right. Then stopped. The other women were slow to follow suit and they wobbled on their heels. "Nope, this way." She dragged them left and carried on until they got to the end. She unclasped her small, beaded bag and pulled out the three cards she had put inside before their cocktail binge. Mia examined them and then handed them out like sweets. "One for you, and one for you..."

Dotty tried three times to insert her key card, but missed every time, until the door was yanked open and a rumpled, sleepy Benito stood in the doorway. "You three are making enough noise to wake the dead."

"My hero!" Dotty exclaimed and stumbled into his arms.

Claudia leant forward and patted him on the shoulder. "Sorry about that, bro, she's had one or two *teensy* cocktails."

Benito groaned. "Thanks, Claud."

"You, my dearest brother, are most welcome."

As Mia and Claudia continued on their rolling journey, Mia leant in and mock whispered, "I think he was being starcasic—ah—*sarcastic*."

Claudia peered at her as she stopped at her door. "Was he now? How rude." She made to turn back.

Mia grabbed her. "I would sleep on it," she suggested wisely.

"That, is great advice," Claudia said through a wide yawn. "I am a bit tired." Mia giggled as Claudia inserted her key. "A-ha, first try."

"See you on the morrow, dear lady," Mia said, trying to affect a curtsey, but forgetting what she was trying to accomplish halfway, so instead froze in a parody of a crouch, arms outstretched.

Claudia bobbed her head. "Night!" she said and closed her door.

"Ah, do you need a little help?"

Mia turned her head and managed to pull herself upright. She tried to focus on Josh, who observed her from further along the corridor, a bottle of water in hand. "Oh, Sir Josh," she said. "No, no, I am quite well."

"Are you sure about that?" Josh came forward and took her arm when she almost wobbled into the wall.

She frowned at him. "Indeed. I am not some silly damsel in distress."

"Of course you're not. What's with all the medieval jargon?"

Mia stopped and tilted her head at him. "I'm an archaelologist, don't you know?"

"An archae...*lologist*, you say?"

"Are you laughing at me, sir?"

"Nope, nope, not in the least. Where's your key card?" He held out his hand when they stopped outside the door to her room.

Mia inspected her empty hand then rifled in her bag again and ferreted it out. Somehow it had *teleported* back into her bag. She handed it over. "Bleurgh," she said, "I shouldn't have had *Sex on the Beach.*"

Josh dropped the key card, then bent to retrieve it. "I—what?"

"*You know*," she said, leaning in as if conspiratorially, "that evil drink—they even put in a mini sword! That should have told me everything."

"Cocktail, of course. A sword? Don't you mean umbrella?" Josh opened her door and gestured her inside.

"They *tried* to disguise it with a frilly paper thing, but *I* know a miniature sword when I see one. I'm an archra—archaelol—a thingy, after all." Mia set her bag on the dressing table and peered down at her feet. "Oh, I've lost my shoes." She giggled.

"I'm like Cinderella."

She wriggled her toes a few times, then blinked up at Josh. "I nearly did once...but it was a dig in...in Theee—Thebes, so not a beach, but the sand gets *everywhere* so I decided not to. Ten out of ten would *not* recommend...but" – she sighed – "Musafa, with the dreamy eyes." She stumbled over to Josh. "Oh, but your eyes, Joshie...a girl could drown in your eyes."

Josh swallowed a few times then said in a strangled voice, "Come on, let's get you into bed."

Mia stared at him with wide eyes. "Sir Josh!" she said.

He blew out a long breath, and added, "So you can *sleep*."

"Ah—sleep, sleep. To sleep is to dream," Mia misquoted in a sing-song voice, and allowed him to lead her over to the bed.

"In you get, Cinders," Josh said, and she slithered into the cool sheets still in her dress.

Mia laid down and as he leant over to pull the covers over her, she speared him with an intense look. "You know, Cinderella didn't want a prince as such, she just wanted to go to the ball..." her eyes fluttered, then re-opened "...but I always used to think it must be nice to have both."

Silence met her words, then as she was drifting off to sleep, a feather-light touch brushed the top of her head. "Sweet dreams, princess," Josh murmured, and then the door clicked shut.

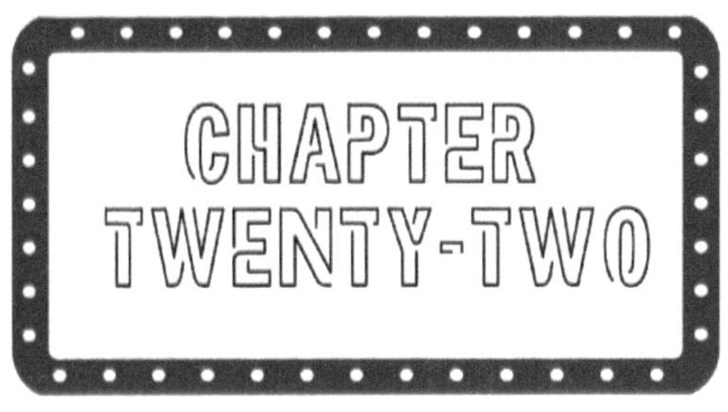

CHAPTER TWENTY-TWO

Mia awoke with ringing in her ears and a tongue like a carpet. She sat up and her head swam, but the ringing didn't abate. She peered blearily across the room, and realised the ringing was coming from her small bag on the dressing table. It was her phone making the noise, and thankfully not her head.

Mia pushed back the covers gingerly and swung her legs around. She noticed with surprise she was still in the slinky bridesmaid's dress, and with a horrible clarity, everything came rushing back.

Oh yes, it was all fun and games until she'd started rambling to Josh about—god, she couldn't even *remember* exactly what, but knew it was mortifying. And then he'd obviously tucked her into bed like a drunken teenager. Their next meeting was going to be fun...now, who was being 'starcasic', she mused with a laugh, then thought better of it as her stomach protested.

Experimentally, Mia stood, and her organs stayed where they belonged so she took small steps over to retrieve her phone—the ringing increasing to a piercing pitch. With a groan of relief, she turned off the alarm she had so optimistically set the day before for 8am. She had two hours to get herself together before the after-wedding brunch to see Calli and Ash off on their honeymoon.

Her phone beeped in her hand with a text message. *Josh.*

Good morning, Cinders, how are you feeling?

Cinders? Mia met her pale-faced gaze in the mirror. Oh, god, *now* she remembered...*A girl could drown in your eyes...*

I'm dead. Only a pint of orange juice and a one-hour shower will resurrect me.

She sent the text back with a skull and cross bones emoji. *That, and hiding away for the next decade*, she mentally added.

You sort the shower, I'll sort the OJ.

Thanks.

Mia smiled at her phone. Josh was such a great friend. And that was where she was going to leave her thoughts. Safely tucked up in the confines of her mind in a nice tidy friendship bow. Anything else that happened was a result of far too much champagne, cocktails, and a bit of interference from Calli.

Mia tackled the shower, carefully covering her still pinned-up curls with a shower cap before turning the temperature of the water up to near-boiling. She braced herself against the shower wall and allowed the spray to pelt her whole body back to life, before she lathered up with her peach-and-vanilla shower gel, and rinsed off.

Marginally better, she pulled on a soft towelling robe and went to shoot off quick texts to Dotty and Claudia, checking on their mortal status.

Benito answered for Dotty stating she was still snoring like a freight train, and Claudia's reply came back with an unintelligible stream of letters; an accurate representation of Mia's brain, so she could sympathise wholly.

Mia set her phone down when a knock came at the door. Hastily pulling off the shower cap, she made sure the belt of her robe was tied tightly before opening it. Seeing the giant jug of freshly squeezed orange juice on the tray, she almost hallucinated it had a healing aura around it like a golden halo.

"Lifesaver," she murmured, making a grab for the tray, then hesitated with a flush thinking the room service person would think she'd gone mad. Slowly raising her gaze, the flush did not abate when Josh stared back at her in amusement.

"I intercepted the room service guy," he said, offering her the tray.

Mia took it gratefully and backed into the room to set it down on her dressing table. She noticed a plate with two pieces of plain toast was set beside the juice jug and glass.

Josh leant against the doorframe. "Nibble it," he advised, "but definitely drink as much juice as you want."

"Thanks, Josh." She poured out a glass to the brim, took a life-giving gulp, and her carpet-y tongue absorbed the sweet, smooth—just as she preferred—orange juice like a sponge. She set the glass down. "About last night—ah—most of it is hazy, but thanks for looking after me. Claud, Dotty, and I *might* have had a few cocktails in the bar after everyone left."

"Not on the beach?" Josh said, one innocent eyebrow quirked.

Shit. Please don't mention the drowning in the eyes bit! "Ha, no. Remind me to lay off *that* particular cocktail in the future." Mia winced, and avoided his eyes.

"Noted. And the sword umbrellas—most lethal."

"Oh, god. No more, please!" she implored, but by now had begun laughing along with him.

He straightened up, raising both hands in a surrender pose. "Absolutely. I wouldn't want to upset the *archaelologist.*"

"Out!" Mia said, mock crossly, her lips twitching as he butchered the word the same way she had done the night before. She joined him at the door and shooed him out.

"I'm going, I'm going," he said. "But at least you have some colour in your cheeks now."

Mia closed the door on his grinning face and returned to nibble the toast and drink the rest of the juice. Catching a look at herself in the mirror, she saw he was absolutely right.

When she felt slightly more human, Mia dressed in a pink and white ensemble of flowy pastel pink wide-legged trousers, and pink-and-white gingham cropped halter-neck top, and open-toed wedge sandals. She put her phone in her pink, basket-style handbag, and inspected her face critically in the mirror. She'd added a little bit of bronzer on her cheekbones, some shimmery gold eyeshadow over her lids, a layer of mascara on her lashes, and finished off with a slick of matte pink lipstick.

She'd unpinned her curls and carefully finger-combed them into soft waves. A pink twisted headband in a shimmery fabric held the loose tresses back from her face and pearl drop earrings completed the casual-yet-put-together look. Just right for a lovely brunch.

After convincing herself she could power through it, all that needed to be done was see the happy couple off, check out of the venue, and go back to the apartment to rest before meeting up with her dad and Alice that evening.

Mia placed her key card in her bag, then left her room, pulling the door behind her with a click. Quickening her steps, not wanting to take over Calli's mantle and be late, she found her way to the small dining room, where the brunch was taking place. In the doorway, a member of staff pulled her aside.

"Oh, Miss, are these yours?" She held out the strappy gold shoes Mia had been wearing at the wedding.

Mia accepted them with a hasty, "Thanks," and made her way over to the table where the rest of Calli and Ash's party sat. Surprisingly, Calli was already there, smiling and glowing, between Ash and her mother.

Josh eyed the shoes and mouthed '*Cinders*' to Mia, from his seat next to Ash's parents.

Mia flushed and took the vacant chair opposite, between her father and Alice, and Mae who was seated next to Aunt Junie. She murmured greetings to everyone, and exchanged covert grimacing looks with her cocktail-buddies: Claudia and a green-looking Dotty, who along with Benito, Lance, Nicolette, and the third groomsman, Ash's cousin, Addy, made up the remainder of the party.

Mia managed to eat some of the fruit salad and a bit of croissant, while inhaling a large cup of extra-shot cappuccino.

"So, we'll come to your apartment later?" Stephen said as the meal was wrapping up.

Mia nodded, and pushed her plate away. "Are you sure you don't want me to come and get you from your hotel?"

Alice leant over Stephen. "We're getting to grips with the subway now, it's quite fun," she said. Her soft blue eyes sparkled beneath the fringe of her bobbed light-brown hair.

Mia smiled at her in genuine affection. "OK, as long as you're sure?"

Stephen and Alice both nodded. "We'll see you at six," Stephen said.

They all stood when Calli and Ash did. Calli, somewhat teary-eyed, rounded the table and pulled Mia to one side, while Ash spoke to the others.

"Sorry about last night, about the whole Stav-Josh thing," she said.

Mia pulled her in for a hug. "*That's* the least of my worries," she said. "I got myself in my own predicament after that."

"Oh?" Calli said, pulling back. "Do tell."

Mia shook her head, and indicated a waiting Ash. "You have a plane to catch, Mrs Sharma," she reminded her cousin.

Calli pouted. "When I see you next, I want all the details." She wagged one French-manicured-tipped finger at her. "I won't forget."

Mia laughed. "I know you won't. But seriously, have an amazing time in Europe and I'll see you in England in a few weeks." They planned to meet up briefly on the happy couple's return stopover.

Calli pressed a kiss to her cheek. "Looking forward to it. Have fun on your dig."

"Thanks. Now go! You'll be late for your plane."

Calli grinned, and then with another round of waves, and 'goodbyes', she allowed her new husband to drag her outside to their waiting Uber.

"We're going to head off too, Mia," Stephen said and gave her a quick kiss goodbye.

"See you later," she said and watched her beloved dad and his wife say a slightly awkward—but not as awkward as she thought it might have been—goodbye to Mae, and to the others.

"That's progress," Josh observed as he stepped up beside Mia.

She turned to him. "I was thinking something along those lines," she said.

The rest of the party dispersed around them, heading back up the stairs to ready themselves for checking out, with Mae calling over her shoulder, "I'll see you before Junie and I head to the airport," to Mia.

"OK," Mia called back.

She and Josh followed along slowly, Mia cradling the gold shoes awkwardly.

"Do you want a lift back to the apartment?" Josh asked. "I have my car outside."

"That would be great," Mia said. "I plan on doing nothing but resting this afternoon, and checking on my little bird friend." She'd put it out on the balcony, but when she'd left the day before the wedding it still hadn't made any moves to leave itself.

"It was fine when I checked yesterday before I came here. Hopping about on the ledge. I think it'll be good to go soon," Josh said.

Mia dimpled out a smile at him, and nudged him with her elbow. "Aww, you checked. See, you're as big a softie as I am."

Josh affected an airy expression. "I was at the apartment with Ash, and thought I might as well make sure it was all right."

Mia gave him a knowing smile. "Uh-huh," she said. "I bet you even put out a few seeds too."

Josh laughed. "Get your things. I'll meet you in the parking lot."

"OK, thanks," Mia said, and he left her at her door and carried on to his own further down the corridor.

After she had packed up her things, she went to find Mae, who was exiting her room along with Aunt Junie.

"There's my beautiful girl," Mae said when she spotted Mia. "I'm truly sorry it's been such a short visit, but I promise I'll be all yours when we meet up."

Aunt Junie said, "I'll make sure of it."

Mia smiled. She'd heard words to that effect from Mae many times over the years but this time she was inclined to believe it. "Have a safe flight home," she said. "I'll speak to you soon, and let you know when I'm free."

"Okie dokes, Mia-Mae. Have fun in England," Mae said.

Mia leant over and pressed a kiss to her cheek, before doing the same with Aunt Junie. "Bye," she said, and after the older women returned the farewell, she headed down the stairs with her small overnight bag.

In the car park, Josh leant against his white Prius with his arms folded, his face tilted up towards the sunny sky. Mia took the opportunity to study him, now that she wasn't being distracted by his intense blue eyes. He appeared relaxed and at ease; a stark contrast to the usual contained chaos inside herself—chaos she had controlled for so long. Contained and controlled it, because she had no desire to fully feel any of it. It was simply too painful.

Dr Carroll would say, 'Let it out, Mia,' and encourage her to find a secluded spot and scream out her lungs, but, as Josh opened his eyes, perhaps, sensing her standing there, she didn't feel so contained. As if, little by little—the more she interacted with Mae, the more she talked things through with Dr Carroll, and with Josh—it was leaking out in manageable dribbles of emotion and not in an unbearable rush.

"Hi," Josh said. "You ready to go home?"

"Yes, Sir Josh." Mia winked at him and laughter burst from him in a deep, rolling wave, and the knot loosened a little more inside of her.

He opened the passenger side door with a bow, before taking her bag. She slid into the seat and buckled up her seatbelt.

He got in and with a sideways grin at her, he started up the car and drove out of the car park. "Although I do like Sir Josh—it has a certain ring to it—I think I much prefer my other nickname." *My Josh.*

Mia double-downed on her earlier thought and firmly tied that friendship bow even tighter, and gave a lively laugh. "You cannot hold me to anything said under the influence of too many bubbles or cocktails," she protested.

He pulled into a gap in the heavy traffic, and sighed. "Now that, is truly a shame," he said, shaking his head teasingly.

He leant over and fiddled with the radio and when Mia noticed she was concentrating on his long, tanned fingers...*fingers that had grazed her skin last night*...she gave herself a mental shake, and was relieved when they pulled into their apartment block's underground parking garage.

CHAPTER TWENTY-THREE

Mia woke the next morning and stretched, and it took her a moment to place what was different. Ah, that was right, Calli wasn't fervently crashing about the place, after her two coffees, muttering, *I'm late, where's my shoes...or bag...or insert random misplaced item here.*

She'd had a lovely pre-show dinner with her dad and Alice, before they went to see *Camelot* on Broadway. It was the perfect musical, especially for Mia and Stephen who shared a love of history, and they all enjoyed this comedy-drama version. She'd invited Josh to tag along, but he elected to let her have some alone time with her dad and step-mum, and while she missed his company, it was very thoughtful of him. And it excused her from dealing with any residual awkwardness over the events of the wedding.

Mia rolled over and grabbed her phone and scrolled through the various text messages, and notifications, and liked every one of Calli's numerous posts on her Instagram page. The honeymooners had only arrived in Rome the day before, but still

Calli had managed to fit lots in. Poor Ash, Mia thought, knowing how Calli liked to photograph every tiny little moment. But then this time she had a great excuse; it was her honeymoon, and a once-in-a-lifetime trip.

She got up and showered, taking her time. She didn't have to go to the university as the professor had given her the time off to get ready for their departure to England on Wednesday.

After she'd dressed in a comfy blue-and-white patterned jumpsuit, Mia brewed a pot of tea before going to see how the little bird was doing. It had been hopping about as Josh had said, and she hoped that today would be the day it finally flew free.

Taking her tea and phone with her—hoping to catch the event—Mia perched on the window ledge and carefully pushed up the window that led to the small balcony.

The bird was indeed hopping along the edge of the balcony again, making little fluttering motions, and Mia urged it on, "Go on, little one, you can do it." She opened her camera app and started recording when a knock came on the door.

She bit her lip, but carefully set the phone down, propping it in position before she hurried over to answer it. Josh stood in the doorway looking as if he'd been for a run. "Come in, quick," she urged and he quirked an eyebrow. "It's time."

Without waiting, Mia rushed back over to the window, and resumed her position, picking up the phone and aiming it at the bird just as it found its confidence.

"Oh," she breathed out as Josh joined her in time to see the bird soar away. She stopped recording, emotion brimming inside her.

She turned her head and Josh was right there next to her, his eyes bright. "He found his courage. He did it," he said.

Mia gave a watery laugh. "He did."

"Then why do you look sad?" Josh asked quietly.

She leant back against the glass, and picked up her tea to take a fortifying sip. "Because it's bittersweet isn't it? Letting things you care about go." Josh sat on the back of the sofa and watched her intently. "Everything is changing...I can't stay here," she said.

"What, in New York?" Josh asked, a frown on his face.

"Oh, no. I haven't made any firm decision there. I meant here, in this apartment. I've been thinking that it's not fair for me to come back here after the dig and cramp Calli and Ash's style. They're married now, they should have some privacy. Maybe it's time I spread my wings—just like the little bird."

Josh's look turned thoughtful. "You could move in with me," he said slowly.

"You want me to live with you?" Why did her voice come out so breathy and high-pitched? "I thought you didn't want a roommate?"

Josh grinned. "I'd make an exception for you."

Mia took another sip of tea, her mind racing. Seeing Josh regularly was one thing, but living with him? Sleeping under the same roof as him. A vivid memory of her curled up in his arms on the beach bed in Miami flooded her mind, and she hastily pushed it away. That was *not* what he was insinuating. His apartment was exactly the same layout as Calli and Ash's, so he was obviously offering her the other room.

Astutely noticing her hesitation, Josh said, "You don't have to decide now. It's an open offer. Think about it when you're in England and we can talk about it again when we're home."

Home? Mia wasn't truly sure where that was now. Here, in the city of her heart? Or the land of her birth? But she found herself nodding. "Thanks, Josh, that's so generous of you. I'll give it serious consideration."

"Sure. No problem," he said easily.

Mia jumped down from the ledge with her empty tea cup and made her way into the kitchen area. "Would you like a coffee?"

Josh shook his head. "I better go and shower. I stopped by to ask if you wanted to come to Kocktails tonight—the guys are giving me a little send-off."

"Tonight?" Mia tilted her head in thought. "I would love to but I'm going out for a meal with my friends from the university. Axel's girlfriend is over from Sweden, so we're going to combine it with a welcome to New York for her—and a 'see you soon' for me."

"Sounds fun," Josh said, but Mia could see the disappointment in his eyes.

"I'll text them and see if they want to pop into Kocktails afterwards though," Mia said and Josh's face cleared.

"I'll be there." He smiled and pushed up off his position from the back of the sofa.

"Great. Well, hopefully, I'll see you later then."

Josh moved over to the door. "Hopefully see you later," he said before he let himself out, and closed the door behind him.

Mia made herself a breakfast of waffles and fruit before returning to her room and finishing up her packing, pushing Josh's quite-tempting-yet-somehow-terrifying offer of moving in with him to the back of her mind to think about at a later date.

"Those pants are divine, Mia, they really accentuate your long legs," Annika said, taking in Mia's tight black leather-look jeans.

She had paired them with a black lace corset top that bared

an inch of midriff below it and added a pair of block-heeled black suede ankle boots with cut-outs on the side. For her hair, Mia had taken a section of the middle and braided it from hairline to crown, then left the rest loose and rippling in wide waves. A smoky eye, dark-red lips, and dangling star-cluster silver earrings at her lobes finished off the look. Mia had gone all-out knowing she'd be spending the next few weeks in cargo shorts and muddy boots—not that she really minded that.

"Thanks, Annika," Mia said with a smile as they all walked along the pavement towards Kocktails after they'd enjoyed a fun meal together at a little Italian restaurant near the university.

Annika gave her a smooth-browed smile before moving on to catch up with Pieter who held the door to the karaoke bar open for her.

"After you," Mia said to Ingrid, Axel's girlfriend, and the petite blonde gave Mia a smile of thanks and moved ahead of her into the bar. "She's so lovely," Mia added to Axel as she passed him by. "I hope you convince her to stay."

"Me too," he said with feeling, and Mia laughed.

Mia stepped into the bar and cast a glance around. Despite there being no theme on a Monday, it was still busy with most of the tables and booths filled, but Annika managed to secure a booth when a group left. Mia and her friends settled themselves in, using the QR code on the table to order drinks. Mia hadn't immediately noticed Josh's group, but thought he might be on the other side of the circular bar out of sight.

She pulled out her phone and shot him a quick text, letting him know she was there.

"Still not your boyfriend, hmm?" Annika said, leaning in and looking over her shoulder.

Mia bit back the retort. She liked Pieter's girlfriend, but

sometimes her brusque and slightly imperious manner was a bit much. "Nope. Best friends," she told her. "I'm going to use the restroom," she added and slid out of the booth, thinking she'd look for Josh on the way.

A hand grazed the exposed skin on her waist, stopping her progress. Mia pivoted at the touch. Josh stood with a group of men at the bar near the entrance to the restrooms, dressed sharply in fitted black trousers and a silvery-grey shirt, with his black curls flopping loosely over his brow.

"Hi," she said with a smile.

"Hi yourself," he returned. "Let me introduce you. Guys, this is Mia, Ash's wife's cousin. Mia this is..." he rattled off a list of names as he pointed out his colleagues, and Mia smiled politely around at them all. "You just missed Lance—he had to go and pick up Nicolette."

"Nice to meet you all," she said.

"That accent is so sexy," one of the men—*Barty*, Mia thought—said. "Very Downton Abbey."

She couldn't be too cross. The man did have great taste in TV shows. She gave an easy smile and exchanged a covert eye-roll with Josh, who said, "That's your wife's favourite show isn't it?"

Barty flushed, and returned to his drink, while the other men sniggered.

Josh turned back to Mia. "Get you a drink?"

"I'm taking it easy tonight," she told him. "I've ordered a sparkling water to my booth."

Josh leant in. "What, no *Sex on the Beach*?"

He was in a teasing mood, Mia thought, perhaps it was his turn to succumb to too many drinks. She reached up and patted his cheek, "Not tonight, Joshie," she said with a wink, and his eyes glinted as she stepped around him. "I'm off to the ladies' room."

As Mia walked away, she heard Barty say, "Did she call you Joshie?" and Josh answered, "She's the only one who gets to call me that, so don't get any ideas." Mia's lips curved into a smile.

In the restroom, she dodged around a group of giggling women who appeared to be part of a bachelorette party, and Mia remembered fondly the fun she'd had with Calli. Feeling reminiscent, she shot off a quick text to her cousin once in the cubicle.

Hope you're having fun in Rome. I'm in Kocktails with the uni gang and thinking of you. M x

She smiled when Calli's reply came back despite the time difference.

You're in Kocktails? Josh is in Kocktails - he texted Ash.

What a co-inky-dink.

I have a severe case of FOMO. You better phone me tomorrow and tell me what I'm missing. C x

You're on your honeymoon, Cal. You're not missing out, you're experiencing new things! But I will phone you tomorrow. Love you xx

You're right, I'm on my honeymoon!!! Love you back, and speak to you tomorrow xx

After using the facilities, a small pang of loneliness shot through Mia as she exited the cubicle and washed and dried her hands. She hadn't realised how much she would miss Calli, but it wasn't for long, she reasoned.

When Mia left the restroom the group of bachelorettes were now mingling with Josh's group. She hesitated, then when Josh glanced her way she pointed to her table and mimed taking a drink.

After a brief moment, he gave her a thumbs-up, so she left him and his colleagues to chatting with the group of women, and went back to her own friends.

"Get lost did you?" Annika said when Mia seated herself again. The other woman had a smirk on her lips, but a knowing look in her eyes.

"No. I stopped to chat with Josh, but he's busy with his colleagues," Mia explained and leant forward to pick up her sparkling water and take a sip.

"I'd say he's busier with something else," Annika observed and gestured with her cocktail glass. The two mingled groups had moved around the bar and were heading towards the stairs to the elevated dancefloor. One woman leant in close to Josh and chatted animatedly up at him. He flashed her a smile, and something twisted in Mia's chest.

Mia took another sip, and turned away from Annika's scrutiny to speak with Axel and Ingrid about their sightseeing plans. Josh was perfectly entitled to enjoy himself with other people.

A few minutes later Mia's phone beeped, and she cast a quick glance down at it. It was one word.

Her lips twitched, thinking Josh was joking, but then another one came through:

Remember the wedding? I need you to return the favor.

Then another.

ASAP.

"I'm sorry, but I have to go and rescue my friend," Mia told the group. Ignoring Annika's self-satisfied smile, she left the booth and headed up to the dancefloor to locate Josh's group. They were all dancing with most of the bachelorettes, while some, including the bride-to-be, danced with each other. One girl was trying to drape herself over Josh, and with a deep breath, Mia made her way over.

This was going to be tough sober, she thought, swallowing her nerves.

"Hi, handsome," Mia said in her best sultry tone and moved up close to him, laying one hand over his shoulder.

"Darlin', there you are," he said, relief in his eyes.

The girl gave Mia a glare and moved away to her friends.

"I thought you said you weren't dating her," Barty said, dancing nearby, giving Josh and Mia a puzzled look.

“Just go with it, Barty,” Josh hissed out the corner of his mouth before turning to Mia and pulling her into his arms to dance with her. “*Thank* you,” he said.

Mia swayed her hips to the beat of Jennifer Lopez’s rhythmic, ‘Waiting For Tonight’, keeping up the pretence, but still enjoying herself. “You helped me, it’s only fair,” she said.

“Ah, you know I’d do anything for you,” Josh said, his voice deepening, and Mia had to remind herself he’d probably ingested enough alcohol to cause the intense words and slightly flirty manner.

“Ditto,” Mia said lightly. “But maybe you’ll meet someone in England and won’t need my help,” she said.

Josh stared at her intently for a moment. “And perhaps you’ll discover more than ancient relics,” he said.

Their eyes held, and Mia suddenly forgot what they were talking about, but when a slower song came on, she forced herself to ease back. Dancing separately but still close enough to him to maintain their cover, his scent washed over her. He was wearing the slightly spicy, bitter chocolate one this time. Perfect for dark nights on the dancefloor.

“Axel, buddy!” Josh said, looking behind her, and Mia turned to see Axel, Ingrid, Pieter, and Annika had joined them.

Soon they were all dancing and enjoying themselves together—one big multi-cultural group—and Mia relaxed, and went with the flow.

The bachelorette party moved on and bit by bit Josh’s colleagues dispersed, having work the next day, soon followed by Mia’s friends.

“See you when you get back, Mia!” Pieter said, and Axel nodded his large shaggy blonde head, echoing the sentiment.

“Nice to meet you, Mia,” Ingrid added, while Annika air-kissed Mia, dosing her in her signature Dior scent. She whispered in her ear, "Enjoy the rest of the night with your *best friend.*"

"I will," Mia said brightly, pointedly ignoring the insinuation. "Lovely to meet you too, Ingrid," she told the newest addition to their group, and then waved to them all when they moved away.

"Just you and me now," Josh remarked as they moved to the door of the bar. "Thanks again for rescuing me."

"Actually, it was kind of fun being the knight errant for a change instead of the damsel in distress," Mia said with a laugh once they were out on the street.

They began walking towards the apartment block, and Josh said, "I think you've come a long way."

"'We're not in Kansas anymore'," Mia quoted in a murmur, looking around at the busy street full of yellow cabs and meandering people.

"I meant figuratively, but yeah, you've crossed oceans to start anew."

Mia pushed open the apartment complex's door and said a 'hello' to the night concierge, before answering Josh. "And now I'm going back," she said.

They stepped into the lift and both leant back against the mirrored walls opposite each other. "You'll do fine, you're stronger than you think," Josh said.

Mia let out a small laugh. "Funny, Mae said something like that to me too."

"She did, huh?" Josh grinned at her, and gestured for her to go before him when the lift doors opened. "Then it must be true."

Mia stopped at Calli and Ash's apartment door, and rifled for her key. “Perhaps,” she said.

“Mia,” Josh said when she’d inserted the key. She looked up at him questioningly. He shook his head then smiled. “You look nice tonight...though I’m sure Calli would call it something else.”

“Oh. Thank you...so do you,” she said, startled by the compliment.

“Good night, Mia,” he said after a long moment.

Mia unlocked the door and stepped in. “Night, Josh.”

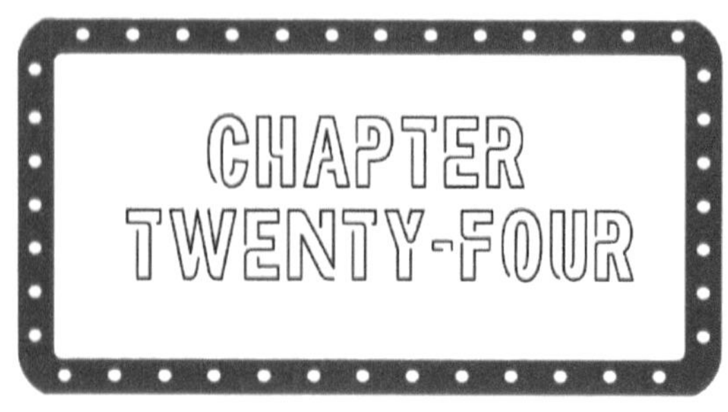

Mia stared down at her laptop. *This cannot be happening*. She re-read the email again and there it was in black and white. Professor Deacon had changed his flight. He was going to come a day later because he had meetings he needed to attend. However, he insisted on Mia still going as planned. And so she must go—*alone*.

Mia had bolstered herself up, knowing that she must look professional in front of the professor—and so, she'd reasoned, she would be able to force her fear of flying back. *Along with a whole bottle of herbal calming spray, and sneakily watching Josh's video*. But now she would have to watch the video on repeat, while praying to the gods of flying.

Apprehension roiled through her stomach, as she stared at her bags, ready for her flight the next day. *Shit*.

"Something wrong?" Josh asked her from his position on the sofa. He'd come over to make his goodbyes.

"Oh, no," she said brightly, "I have to face my imminent demise alone, that's all."

"Your what?"

Mia gave him a sheepish look. "I'll be flying to England without the professor. He's being held back a day."

"Ah, I see." Josh unfolded his long legs and came over to the kitchen area where she'd been checking last-minute details on her laptop.

He rubbed her back in a comforting gesture. "It'll be OK. Flying is safer than driving, you know."

"Is it? Is it though?" Mia stared up at him. "It doesn't feel like it," she moaned.

"You've got my video?" She nodded. "Then play it however many times you need, OK. Doing things when you're scared is brave. Remember what I said to you last night. You're strong. You can do this."

She grimaced. "I have little choice. I should have booked myself on a cargo ship," she muttered under her breath, and Josh laughed.

"I've got a few things to take care of myself, so I'm going to have to go now," he said.

Mia's heart began thudding in a strange cadence before swooping into her stomach. "So this is goodbye," she said softly, that disconcerting realisation replacing her apprehension about flying.

Josh stared down at her, then pulled her in for a hug. "Not for long," he said quietly.

Mia squeezed him back. "You look after yourself," she told him, and was annoyed at herself when tears prickled the back of her eyes.

"I will," he said, "and I want you to promise me that you'll keep being strong, OK?"

"I shall try my best," she said with a weak smile, pulling

back.

The air hung heavy between them. Josh lifted his hand and it hovered next to her face as if he wanted to touch her cheek. "That's all any of us can do," he said finally, before dropping his hand, eyes guarded.

"See you on the other side." Mia's joke cut through the strange tension and Josh let out a smile.

"Bye, Mia-mine," he said huskily and then he was gone and Mia was left alone, surrounded by her bags and the ghost of his sea salt and coconut scent.

The next day, Mia texted Simi with shaking hands:

OK, step one, I made it onto the plane.

Good girl. What's step two?

Mia didn't hesitate with her reply:

Don't die.

An eye-roll emoji came back, then:

No, but that's always a good idea anyway.

Mia stood in the aisle to let an older lady get into the middle seat, before she resumed her seat and texted Simi back.

Step two, practice my breathing and distract myself.

Nice… then?

Step three, arrive in London, and meet my partner-in-crime.

She smiled down at her phone, and firmly ignored her trembling fingers.

Atta girl. Me and the Juice Machine will be waiting.

Disconcertingly, Simi had added an orange emoji to his reply, and she knew better than to question it. All would be revealed when she crossed the ocean…in a metal tube, that had no right being airborne. *Don't think about it, don't think about it…*

"Everything all right, dear?" the lady next to Mia asked.

Mia tried to smile, but she feared it came out more of a grimace. The lady gazed at her in understanding.

"It's very unnatural isn't it?"

"What is?" Mia asked through teeth that threatened to chatter together. She rifled through her bag, searching for her lavender-scented pulse point roll-on.

The woman leant in. "Flying. My husband always said, 'If

people were meant to fly, they'd have wings'." She let out a laugh, eyes bright, and Mia stared at her in horror. She was getting off this ridiculous transportation right now.

Standing, she clutched her bag to her chest, and noticed a flight attendant coming down the aisle towards her. She'd beg her if need be to get her off the plane.

"Miss Davenport?" the attendant asked, and Mia nodded in a jerky motion. "Could you come with me please?"

Oh god, now what? Mia thought, and followed the attendant along the rows of seats. Were they kicking her off anyway? The hope died when she was led into first class, and was replaced by confusion.

"You've been upgraded," the attendant said with a smile and gestured to the twin pod, one seat already occupied. "Enjoy your flight, Miss."

Mia was so shocked at seeing Josh beaming up at her that she could barely answer.

"Josh...what?" she said and lowered into the seat.

"Surprise," he said.

"But how?" She couldn't formulate coherent thoughts.

"After our conversation yesterday, I knew I couldn't let you fly alone, so I switched things around a bit and managed to get on this flight and booked two seats."

"But *first class*, Josh." Mia had never flown first class in her life. Even on holidays with Henry.

Josh shrugged. "You're worth it."

Staring at him, she sat back and scanned around. "It doesn't even *look* like we're on a plane," she said in awe.

"That's the idea," Josh said with a smile.

Mia leant over the table separating them and grabbed him in an awkward hug. "I don't know what to say," she whispered.

"You don't have to say anything. Pick a movie and relax, OK," Josh said into her loosely braided hair.

"I get to pick the movie too? Any movie?" She pulled back to goggle at him.

"Any movie," he agreed.

Mia shook her head and stowed her bag. "Seriously, Josh, how you haven't been snapped up already, I have no idea," she said, settled enough to tease him.

"Maybe I'm waiting for the one," he said lightly, yet something made her look closely at him, but his open gaze revealed nothing.

Mia smiled, but the smile dropped when the engines started and the announcements came over the speakers.

She found her hand clutched tightly. "Eyes on me, remember," Josh said softly, and Mia locked eyes with him, breathing slowly through the ascent and levelling off. "That's it. The worst part's over. Now, what shall we watch?"

"Thanks," Mia said, giving a shuddering breath. She focused on searching through the catalogue of films. "Oh, you are in for a treat," she said, selecting one and pressing play.

"*Pride & Prejudice*, hmm?" Josh said. "I haven't seen this one."

"It's one of my comfort-watch films," Mia admitted with a sheepish smile.

"Then it's perfect," Josh said.

"Wait until we get to the 'hand-flex scene'," Mia said and Josh raised an eyebrow.

"The hand-flex scene. Now, I'm intrigued." Josh sat back in his seat as the movie started.

Mia, more at ease than any other flight ever, lost herself in the film. "Oh, here it comes," she said, a bit later on.

"What's the significance?" Josh murmured as the scene played out.

Mia hit pause, and turned to face Josh, an enthusiastic smile on her face. "I'll set the scene. Imagine we're in Regency times, and you're secretly in love with a young lady—"

"Secretly in love?" Josh repeated.

Mia nodded. "Yes, *secretly*, and skin-to-skin touches are not permitted. Most ladies would wear gloves to discourage it anyway, and ladies and gentlemen were closely chaperoned...but in that scene for a brief moment—but that's all it took—Darcy takes Lizzy's bare hand to help her up into the carriage, and he felt *it*."

"It?"

"Yes, that thing, that *magic*."

Josh considered Mia's hand as it lay beside him. "Ah. I get it," he said softly and Mia beamed.

"It's such an iconic scene—and I believe it wasn't even supposed to be in the film. But, goodness, it says so much with one tiny action." Mia turned back to play the rest of the film.

"It certainly does," Josh said as the film began once again.

Mia lost herself further, unconsciously clasping her hands together in delight as they came to the 'most ardently' scene.

"Now, there's tension," Josh observed as Darcy towered over Lizzy and she—breathing heavily—stood her ground, but with eyes that churned with so much emotion.

"It's my favourite scene—and look at the location," Mia murmured, staring at the rain-washed many-pillared structure.

"It's stunning," Josh agreed, "and perfect for a romantic encounter."

Mia flashed him a delighted smile, pleased he was seemingly enjoying the film as much as she. "Indeed."

The film came to its epic conclusion, and Mia sighed at the reunion of Darcy and Lizzy under the backdrop of a muted—yet somehow vibrant—misty landscape. She mouthed Darcy's iconic declaration along with him and broke off with a laugh when she noticed Josh watching her intently instead of the film.

"Sorry, I have a habit of doing that," she said. "But I wish Lizzy had said something more poignant."

Josh dropped his gaze, then back up to the screen where Mr Bennet was now laughingly inviting more gentlemen to come and ask for his other daughters' hands. "It was a bit anticlimactic after Darcy had valiantly declared his soul to her."

"Why, Mr Cavanaugh, I do believe you are a hopeless romantic," Mia said, a touch of teasing laughter in her voice.

"I prefer hopeful," Josh corrected, blue eyes bright.

"Hopeful," Mia repeated softly. "I like that."

"Champagne?" The attendant appeared beside them, and poured them out two flutes when they both agreed.

"So," Josh said after a moment when they were alone again, "what shall we watch next?"

Mia took a sip of her champagne, barely even noticing the motion of the plane. "I shall spare you another Austen film now—but I do recommend *Sense and Sensibility*. That is another exemplary piece of filmography. *And* it has the bad guy from *Die Hard* in it."

"Really? Well, that's a recommendation in itself," Josh said and toasted her with his champagne.

Mia toasted him back, then set her flute down. "I'm going to use the restroom, then we can choose the next film—ah—movie," she added with a smile.

"Go ahead," Josh said, looking perfectly at ease.

Mia took a deep breath, bracing herself for the walk to the

restroom but found the plane continued steadily on, and she was able to use the facilities without losing her mind. Josh's company, one of her favourite feel-good films, and bubbly champagne, all helped immensely.

She stepped out of the restroom, and the attendant who had brought her up from economy, stopped beside her. "Oh, Miss Davenport, I hope you are enjoying your flight? How lovely of your boyfriend to surprise you like that."

Mia hid the frustration with a polite smile. Why did everyone assume a man and a woman couldn't simply be friends? "He was very kind to do so," she said, "But he's just a friend—a very good friend," she amended. Hating the 'just' part. He had come to mean so much more to her than *just* anything.

"Oh, forgive me," the attendant said, then leant in. "I've seen real couples less attentive to each other. You must have a very good friendship."

"We do." Mia smiled.

"He reminds me of someone," the attendant mused, then said, "I've got it—a younger version of the guy in *A Knight's Tale.*"

"Oh, I know who you mean," Mia said. "The one who plays the count."

The attendant clicked her fingers. "That's the one." She sighed a little dreamily and Mia couldn't help but smile at the expression. The attendant's face cleared. "Anyway, duty calls. Lunch will be served soon."

"Thanks," Mia said and went back to take her seat, still smiling.

"Not that I'm complaining, but what's got you so amused?" Josh asked taking in her face.

"Oh, we were talking about you," Mia said airily.

"You were?"

"Yes, the attendant thinks you look a bit like one of the actors in *A Knight's Tale.*" Mia leant in and whispered, "It's mostly a good thing—he's very handsome, but unfortunately, the character is a bit of a rogue."

"*A Knight's Tale*?"

"Don't tell me you haven't seen that one either?" Mia said aghast and Josh laughed.

"Don't punish me," he said, holding up his hands. "So...do you happen to agree with her?"

Mia searched his face. "You do a little, although his eyes are compelling, I far prefer yours. That bright piercing blue is such a striking contrast to your black curls. And of course, you are very handsome too." She dimpled out a smile, but Josh only stared back at her slightly wide-eyed and Mia flushed.

She grabbed her champagne and unwisely took a large sip, and hiccupped.

"Well, I think it only right we should watch it now, don't you?" Josh said finally and Mia set her glass down to search for the film.

"You are certainly getting an education in cinematic mastery today," Mia said, finding the film. "Do you like the music of Queen?"

"Who doesn't?" Josh said.

"Well, you are going to love this," Mia said pressing play. But for some reason, she couldn't completely concentrate on the film, even if it was another of her favourites.

"That was good," Josh said once they'd finished it, pausing it halfway to eat their delicious lunch of beef wellington. "You're right—he is a bit of a what did you call him? A rogue?" Mia nodded. "But I sure didn't see the resemblance." His eyes twinkled.

"Ah, but there's only one of you, Josh," Mia said then wished she'd bitten her tongue. God, she was being very free with her compliments. Perhaps the altitude had gone to her head.

"My mom is very grateful for that fact," Josh said with a smile, showing he was joking.

"You've mentioned your Dad a few times, but what's your mum like?" Mia asked, grateful for a segue to change the subject.

A thoughtful expression crossed Josh's face. "She's great, they complement each other perfectly. Where my dad can be hard-headed at times, my mom is kind, and caring—but is strong with it. They met when they were teenagers—love at first sight, as my dad actually tells it—and are still very much in love now. They were attentive parents, but I was never spoiled. Working the ranch was a part of my childhood chores, and I adored it. Getting dirty, bull-wrangling and horse-riding—it was idyllic." He smiled at Mia. "They'd love you," he said. "Even my dad—he'd thoroughly approve of your work ethic." His smile faltered slightly.

"I'd like to meet them—if the offer still stands to visit?" Mia asked, recalling their phone conversation where he invited her to visit after their return from England...before she had ended up curled up in his arms on the beach bed.

"Of course," Josh said softly. "You'd always be welcome. Dad would put you out to work with the foals, I'm sure."

"Aww, sign me up." She beamed, hoping to ease some of the tension. "Well then, I have plenty to look forward to—horse riding with you, re-connecting with Mae. More than enough to keep me busy on my return," Mia said, firmly shoving away the memory of the beach and her confusing reactions.

"And what about the restaurant—will you go back there?" Josh asked.

Mia shook her head. "Even if the renovations are complete, I don't know if I will. Stav's been a bit intense," she admitted.

Josh's brows drew together. "You should put in a complaint for him harassing you."

"He'd stopped, and I have Calli to thank for that. But he only backed off because he thought I was seeing...you." Mia nibbled her lip. "As far as I could tell from Calli, he'd never asked anyone else out who worked for him, so maybe it was a one-off thing, but it's still not acceptable behaviour."

"No, it's not," Josh stated. "You shouldn't have to hide behind a faux-relationship. No should mean no, end of."

"You're a good guy, Josh," Mia said sincerely, "and I appreciate your support."

"You'll always have it," he promised.

Mia leant in with a smile. "And you, shall always have mine...oh, *aargh*, we're landing already?" she added with a gasp.

Josh smiled. "You didn't even notice," he said.

She met his eyes. "Oh my gosh, that was the best plane journey ever," she said with a breathy laugh. "Thank you for doing this."

"Glad to hear it," Josh said. "It was my pleasure."

They collected their things, and readied to disembark, Mia in a dull kind of shock that she'd actually—*actually*—enjoyed herself.

She exchanged a smile with the flight attendant on her way past her.

Outside Heathrow, a silence fell as Mia and Josh stood on the pavement; the easy camaraderie of the flight dissipating into something heavy and serious. Mia's heart beat hard in her chest. Why was she panicking now? She forced a deep inhale, an idea occurring to her.

Reaching down to unzip the large side pocket on the outside of her suitcase, she said, her voice coming out shaky and breathless, "I have a gift for you. I'd planned to give it to you when we met up here, but as you surprised me with the flight, you can have it now." She pulled out an art pad, and a selection of paints and paintbrushes in a mahogany case.

Josh mutely stared down at them.

"It's not my place to tell you to speak with your dad about how much you enjoy art—god knows, I have my own issues with my mum, but I thought..." Mia trailed off as he met her eyes again. Emotion swam in his blue irises. She continued softly, "I thought that while you were here, you might have the time to pick up a paintbrush again, and these could start you off." She pressed the gift into his hands. "Do something for yourself for a change."

He had helped her in so many ways and hoped he would accept this gesture as her way of potentially helping him.

"Mia, I don't know what to say," Josh said, his voice husky.

"Don't say anything, just paint," she told him with a soft smile, pressing a hand over his.

Their eyes clashed, and held, and the air around them hummed with intensity. "I—" he was interrupted as the beep of a vehicle drowned out his words.

"Coo-ee, Lady Croft! Your chariot awaits!"

Josh stared at the bright orange campervan pulling up beside them, driven by a young man with a huge smile beaming out of his tanned face, set beneath a cloud of black hair. "Who is that?" he asked.

"That, is *the* famed Simi, my friend from uni." Mia gave Josh a sideways look. "His nickname for me is Lara Croft—or Lady Croft. Hey, Indy!" she said louder to her friend, then took another look at the orange van. *Ah, Juice Machine, of course.* She shook her head in amusement.

Simi jumped out of the van, dressed in one of his usual brightly patterned short-sleeved shirts, cargo shorts, and boots, and grabbed Mia in an exuberant hug, before pulling back and giving Josh a long look. "Introduce me to your friend, Mi," he said.

"This is Josh Cavanaugh. Remember—my friend from New York? He's working at his London branch for a month, so we travelled over together. Josh, this is Simeon Jones, or Indiana Jones to his friends." Mia ended with an affectionate laugh.

Josh grinned in greeting, set the art pad and case on top of his suitcase, and offered his hand.

"No handshakes here, man, only hugs allowed," Simi said and gave Josh a quick hug, while mouthing, 'Oh my god," to Mia over his shoulder.

Mia rolled her eyes in affection as Josh pulled back, with a somewhat thunderstruck look, and said with a laugh, "Now I know why Mia's such a hugger too."

"Mia gives the *best* hugs," Simi agreed. "Right, I'll leave you to say your goodbyes," he added with a suggestive look at Mia. "Nice to meet you, Josh."

"Likewise," Josh said with a bemused smile. "Look after our girl."

"Oh, don't you worry, we're going to have the best time." Simi turned a smile on Mia. "Our cottages are right next to each other. It's all so quaint, Mia; you're going to love it!"

"I can't wait." Mia relinquished her suitcase as Simi took it to put inside the campervan. As Simi busied himself, Mia turned to Josh. "You sure you don't want a lift anywhere? Simi's going to take me to my dad's house so I can pick up my own car to use while I'm here," she babbled. Was she trying to prolong their inevitable goodbye?

Josh shook his head. "Thanks, but I'm collecting my rental here, so I'm good."

"OK then." It would be strange; not seeing Josh every day. "Right, well, we'd better get going." Mia met his gaze again, detecting a similar wistful sentiment in his eyes too.

He stepped forward and pulled her into a tight hug. "Look after yourself, Mia-mine," he said. "I'll call you later?"

She squeezed him back, inhaling his scent. "OK," and added, "my Josh," in a whisper.

Simi honking on the campervan's horn had them breaking apart, with Mia suddenly unable to look Josh directly in the eye.

"Bye," she said, and made to round the back of the van to get in the passenger seat.

"Oh, wait. I've left a gift for you in your bag," Josh said. "I snuck it in when you went to the bathroom."

Mia stopped, blowing out a breathy laugh at how in sync they were at times. "I'm intrigued."

"Open it later." He gave her one final look. "See you soon."

"All right...thanks. See you soon," Mia said, tears inexplicably threatening. Knowing she was being ridiculous, she hurried around the van and got in next to Simi.

"Ready?" Simi asked, giving her a scrutinising look.

"Yes." Mia buckled her seatbelt, then turned in her seat to wave at Josh when they pulled away. Josh waved back and watched them go.

"Ooh, lady, he is *hot*. Does he have a brother?"

Mia relaxed and let out a laugh. "No, sorry," she told her friend.

Simi gave an exaggerated sigh. "That, is a shame." He gave her a quick sideways glance as they pulled out of the airport. "Soooo, *why* are you 'just friends' again?"

Mia flushed. "Because, nosy, he sees me as just a friend, and I—I'm not looking for a relationship anyway."

"But if you were...?"

"He's the best man I know—aside from you and my dad, of course," she added when Simi gave her another side-eyed look, "and I'm honoured to have him as my friend. It's safer that way."

"Safer? Mia!" Simi's look was longer this time and outraged. "That bloody weasel did a number on you for sure. Seriously, let's stop off at his house on the way. I've got a few choice words for him. And as for that *snake*—you know Indy *hates* snakes."

Mia placed a placating hand on Simi's tanned arm, with a

grim smile at his joke. "I appreciate the thought, but I'm all right. I'm talking things through with a therapist and I'm getting there. Perhaps, I shouldn't have said *safer*. I just meant that those kind of feelings are dead and buried inside me; I only have friendship to offer, and I repeat, *he* only sees me as a friend."

"Mmm-hmm," was all Simi said in response. He leant forward and fiddled with the radio, and turned it up when 'Miracle' by Calvin Harris and Ellie Goulding came on.

As Simi sang along at the top of his lungs, Mia twisted around and pulled her carry-on bag onto her lap and unzipped it. Josh's familiar sea salt and coconut scent wafted out. Speechless, she pulled out the soft black hoodie and buried her face in it.

"What's that?" Simi asked as she set it on her lap and toyed with the hand-written tag attached to it. As she read to herself, *For hugs, when I'm not there, J x,* she told Simi in a murmur, her vision tunnelling, "It's Josh's."

"He left it for you?" Simi asked.

"He knows how fond I am of his hugs," Mia said, then glanced at Simi as he fell quiet. "What?"

"Nothing, nothing," Simi said, but a knowing smile played around his lips.

Mia ignored him and instead pulled out her phone and shot off a quick text to Josh.

Found your gift – thanks... but I'd rather have the real thing haha.

As soon as she'd sent the innocently worded truth, Mia regretted it. Would he think she was implying something? *God*, she thought in frustration, Simi was putting silly ideas into her head. She was overthinking it, that was all. She added another message, this time a light-hearted one:

Don't forget we drive on the left over here.

Mia bit her lip as she saw Josh was typing back, but then relaxed at the message:

You're welcome, and thank you for my gift - your encouragement means the world. And happy to meet up for real hugs any time

Oh, and thanks for the head's up.

He added the second message with a screaming emoji that had Mia giggling.

"You finished over there, Lady Croft?"

Mia, a smile still playing around her lips, put her phone away and re-focused on her friend. "Sorry, Indy, all yours."

"Good, because we have songs to siiinnnggg," Simi said, belting out the last word like an opera aria.

"You have to come to New York—you and Calli would make a great duo at our local karaoke bar," Mia said.

"Say when, and I'm there," Simi enthused.

He turned up the radio dial further and Mia joined in with him when Sheppard's 'Geronimo' blared out.

Mia's sadness at missing Josh evaporated as she reconnected with her old friend, and by the time they were pulling into her father's driveway, it was like they were back in uni and just come back from fieldwork.

She and Simi hopped out of the van and made their way inside to have an early dinner with Stephen and Alice before making the two-hour drive to the outskirts of the village of Mancetter where the dig site was situated.

Mia followed Simi's campervan up a narrow tree-lined track towards a row of eight neat little terraced cottages. She parked up behind him and got out, taking a good look at the charming ivy-covered accommodation. She'd hit gold when Professor Deacon asked her to find them somewhere to stay while on the excavation. The little cottages had been part of the plot of land the farmer had bought, and was only too happy to make some extra revenue by renting them out for the month before he decided what to do with them.

"Told you. Aren't they quaint?" Simi said, joining Mia.

Mia nodded. "They look so much better in person. I only saw them through the computer screen."

"Great find," Simi said, "and hey, thanks again for getting me and the others this gig. I mean I love my job at the department, but I've been itching for some fieldwork."

"You're welcome, and same. There's nothing like getting your hands dirty and being the first one to touch something that's lain hidden for perhaps centuries."

"Leave it to you to get excited about dirt," Simi said and gave her an affectionate hip-bump.

"It's what's *in* the dirt," Mia corrected him with an eye-roll.

"True that," Simi agreed. "Why don't you go unpack, and I'll come around in a bit. I've got a nice cold crisp chardonnay that won't drink itself."

Mia let out a sigh of pleasure. "Now that sounds like a plan."

"Great. I'll bring the others with me and you can all get acquainted. When's the prof arriving?"

"Early tomorrow. He had a few meetings first, but he'll be raring to go when he arrives so be prepared," Mia warned her friend.

"Hey, I was a cub scout, you know. I'm *always* prepared."

Mia gave an appreciative laugh, then pulled out her luggage from the campervan. "Thanks for the lift to my dad's," she said.

"You're welcome, lady." Simi grinned.

With the key he gave her, Mia let herself into the cottage at the end of the terrace next to his and made a noise of delight. The sparsely decorated open-plan layout still somehow evoked a homely and cosy scene; a wooden table and chairs were set in front of the floral-curtained window next to the front door, and opposite—in front of narrow, white-painted wood and glass patio doors—was a squashy sofa and a low wooden coffee table. Atop it sat a potted plant bursting with sunny yellow flowers and a few aged magazines. A small kitchen area with all the basic necessary amenities framed the back wall, while the remaining wall boasted two interior doors.

Mia set her bags down and inspected behind the two doors. First, she found a small bathroom that had, to her delight, both a shower and a bath. The other room was the bedroom. A quirky, uneven ceiling sloped above a metal-framed bed, already dressed with a dainty floral print quilt set, that echoed the faded wallpaper. Plump pillows and cushions gave the impression of it being an inviting and restful place to sleep, while an oak wood set of chest-of-drawers was positioned neatly beneath the window.

"This'll do nicely," Mia murmured to herself, and set about unpacking. Most of her clothes consisted of cargo trousers and shorts, plenty of t-shirts and linen shirts, and boots, with a few floaty dresses and skirts and sandals in case they went for a night out, or she visited her dad, or Josh in London.

A knock came at the door as Mia was setting her toiletries out in the bathroom. She hastened to open it and found a smiling Simi, cradling the aforementioned chardonnay, surrounded by five other men and women.

"Hi, come in," Mia invited, pulling the door wider.

Soon the small kitchen area was full of chatting voices and chardonnay being sipped from an array of mugs and glasses.

"So, Rigs," Mia said to the tall, burly, bearded young man daintily sipping his wine from a porcelain tea cup, "this your first dig?"

Rigs nodded. "Me and Connie" — he gestured to the auburn-haired woman beside him — "got picked by Simi for this."

"Then he must be impressed with you. Not everyone gets Simi's approval this early." Mia gave Simi a teasing look, which he returned with a mock scowl.

"I am very impressed with them," Simi said loftily, then indicated the other three people in the room. "And Colm, Erica, and Priti are all in their second year. I gave them a shot in the first year too. When you know, you know. I like to go with my gut."

Mia gave a shudder. "*Please* don't tell Professor Deacon that. *We deal with facts, not instinct, Miss Davenport*," she said with a laugh.

The others joined in. "I'll remember that," Simi said putting on his serious face. He leant over and tapped his glass to Mia's mug. "It's good to be working with you again, LC."

"Likewise, IJ," she murmured back.

"LC, IJ?" Connie scrunched up her nose and regarded them

curiously through green eyes.

"Just nicknames," Mia said.

"Oh cool, do we get nicknames too?" Priti asked, tossing her long silky black braid over her shoulder.

Mia cast Simi a sideways look. "Work with Simi long enough and you will."

Simi laughed. "Hey, you never complained before."

"I'm not complaining. You know I love being referred to as Lady C." Mia rose her mug, her pinkie finger stretched out.

Simi rolled his eyes. "Top up, my lady?"

"Perhaps not. We'd better have an early night," Mia said setting her mug down, and the others followed suit.

"If what you said about Professor Deacon is true then perhaps you're right," Colm said. He wore his blonde hair cropped close to his head, and with his solemn hazel eyes, he appeared to be the most serious of the group.

Simi set the wine bottle down regretfully. "Always the party-pooper," he said with a grin at Mia. "But yes, better get our beauty sleep."

The others filed out with variations on 'goodnight' and Simi paused on the threshold to pull Mia into a tight hug.

"Seriously, Mi, it's so good to see you. I've missed you."

Mia squeezed her friend back. "I've missed you too." She let him go and he gave a soft smile.

"Night. See you in the morning, bright-eyed and bushy-tailed." He wiggled his butt as he left.

"Night, Simi," Mia said, giggling, then waited until he headed to his own cottage before she closed the door and locked it.

CHAPTER TWENTY-SIX

Mia washed up the mugs and glasses, and then got ready for bed.

As she came out of the bathroom, a small shape darted across the living area floor. She had cracked open the patio door to let some air in, *not* a tiny visitor. Surrendering to the inevitable with a small sigh, Mia knelt on the floor, scanning for the unknown intruder. From her position on the floor, she pressed the accept button when her phone began to ring.

Josh's voice came through the speaker. "What are you doing?" he asked. "Some kind of strange archaeology ritual?"

Mia said out of the side of her mouth, "There's something in here."

"What! Are you OK?" Josh's voice turned from amusement to worried in an instant and a glance at the screen revealed his alarmed face.

"It's an animal," she said to reassure him, touched by his concern.

"Oh, OK."

"A-ha, *there* you are," Mia said to the bedraggled ginger cat. It crept out from beneath the sofa and meowed at her plaintively.

Josh's husky laugh filled the room. "Only you, Mia. Been there a matter of hours and already you're making friends with animals in need."

Mia straightened and gave him a helpless smile. "They find me," she protested. But still, she searched the fridge and was relieved to find the basics stocked inside. With her phone propped up against the toaster, so she could still speak to Josh, Mia simultaneously poured out a splash of milk onto a saucer. She offered it to the cat, who lapped it up hungrily. "It's probably come over from the farm. I'll ask around tomorrow."

"So, you all settled in?" Josh asked.

"Just about. I met the students who are helping on the dig earlier, they're a great bunch, and Simi picked them himself, so I know they'll be up to the task. How about you?"

"My apartment's nice, and only a few blocks—ah *streets*—from the office. Seems like a busy, vibrant area too," Josh said. "I'll shoot you the address in case you ever need it."

Mia smiled. "Thanks, and same, I'll send you the address to the cottage. Perhaps you could pop down one weekend. There's a nice little pub that serves food nearby." Somewhere that served homecooked-style food had been top of Professor Deacon's list. He'd been living in New York for a decade and was determined to indulge in as much English food as possible on his return home.

Josh's eyes crinkled as he smiled through the screen at her. "It's a date," he said, then added, "I meant, that sounds great. Let me know when works for you."

A knot of tension worked through Mia's stomach. Did he

think his innocently worded agreement would upset her? She forced a smile, hating that everyone thought they needed to walk on eggshells around her feelings. "Sure. I'll let you know. Well, I better let you go, you've probably got an early morning tomorrow too."

Josh frowned at her tone. "I do, actually. Sleep well, Mia."

"Thanks. You too," Mia said, then disconnected the call. She leant against the counter while the cat tried to lick the pattern off the saucer. "It's all gone," she told the cat gently, and with slow movements hunkered down beside it.

The cat sniffed at her before coming over and nuzzling against her with a rumbling purr. "You're welcome," Mia said, and not for the first time in her life, wondered why humans couldn't be as straightforward as animals.

Mia stood and rifled through the cupboards in the kitchen area. In a tall cupboard next to the fridge, she found what she was looking for; clean linen. She pulled out a towel and spread it on top of the sofa. "You can sleep here tonight...but only for tonight," she added, trying for a stern tone.

The cat blinked up at her, before walking straight past the sofa and towards the bedroom and meowing at the closed door. Mia huffed out a breath but knew it was in vain. "Oh for goodness sake, you probably have fleas," she said, snatching up the towel. The cat pinned her with what Mia could only determine was an outraged look, and then batted at the door with one delicate paw.

"Fine, fine," Mia said, knowing from the very beginning she was no match for a fluffy friend with oversized green eyes. She closed and locked the patio doors before opening the bedroom door. No sooner had she done so than the cat had jumped onto the bed and was kneading the duvet. Mia set the towel down, carefully picked up the cat and placed it on the towel. She and the cat had a staring contest for a few long minutes, before the cat, obviously knowing what a soft touch he or she had found, settled down on the towel with a soft meow, and a flick of its tail.

Mia turned on the bedside lamp, set her alarm for seven the next morning then put her phone on charge, before getting into bed. Sleep would probably elude her due to the time difference, but at least she could close her eyes and rest. But she hadn't banked on having her own soothing personal white-noise machine.

With the cat's rumbling purrs filling the small room, Mia drifted off to sleep.

Mia awoke suddenly, clawing at the sheets twisted around her. She sat up, her heart pounding. She'd dreamt of being stuck in an excavated hole, with Henry and Nadia standing above shovelling in sand on top of her. Mae stood beside them sipping a cocktail before she turned her back on the scene and walked away. Mia had screamed until the sand filled her lungs, and then a large, tanned hand was pulling her out and bright blue eyes were peering down at her...*I've got you, Mia!*

What would Dr Carroll have to say about that particular dream?

After unravelling herself from the sheets and duvet, she peered blearily around the room. The poor cat was standing by the bedroom door; its back arched.

"Sorry, puss," Mia said. "That one frightened me too."

With slow movements, she got up and aimed for the door, making soothing sounds. The cat relaxed enough so that when Mia opened the door it sauntered through as if it owned the place.

Mia followed the cat, refilled the saucer with water, recalling how milk should be given sparingly, and had another look in the cupboards. Finding a tin of tuna, she opened it and emptied it into a bowl before setting it beside the milk.

With a yawn, Mia padded over to the bathroom to take a shower.

The shower revived her enough that the last vestiges of the nightmare drifted away as the water sluiced off her. She squeezed out her hair and wrapped herself up in a towel before walking out into the kitchen area.

The cat meowed at her, and Mia shook her head. "That's all for now. I'll ask around later to see if anyone knows where you belong."

The cat blinked its green eyes as if to say, 'Here. I belong here.'

Mia chuckled and returned to her room when her phone alarm went off. She silenced it and returned to the kitchen area with the phone in hand. A text message came in as she flipped the kettle's on switch.

Good morning. Hope you slept well.

She smiled stupidly at her phone, before motivating herself into answering.

Morning, Joshie. Not as well as I have done, but it's a new place, so probably to be expected. How about you?

Mia didn't mention the nightmare; that was far too much to

unpack over text message.

Tossed and Turned a bit - probably jetlag, but I've done a Calli and had two coffees, so things are looking up.

Mia sent a laughing emoji and added:

I'm brewing tea and having breakfast with my new friend.

Oh?

She sent a cat emoji and a hug.

Right, of course. Well, have a great first day. I get out at 6. I'll call you then?

You too, Josh. I'll look forward to it. M x

Mia stared at her phone for a moment, before setting it down to finish making her tea and toasting a few pieces of thick bread. She took her last piece, heavily slathered in dripping salty butter, into her room and nibbled on it thoughtfully, debating what to wear. The sun was already shining so she decided on a pair of beige shorts, a white vest top tucked into them, comfy socks, and her trusty battered boots.

After braiding her hair into one long swinging tail, she added suncream to her exposed skin and face, before grabbing her sunglasses and hooking them into the neckline of her top.

"Come on, puss," Mia said as she opened the front door to the cottage, but the cat regarded her lazily from her position on the sofa. They stared at each other for one long minute, before Mia huffed out a breath. "OK, you win." Of course, the cat did. She set down a pile of newspaper near the patio doors. "Do your business on there, please."

Laughing at her own soft heart, she fastened her field kit tool belt around her waist, slotting her phone into the attached pouch. After leaving the cottage, she locked the door behind her and stowed the key in the zippered pocket of her shorts.

"Ooh-ee—Lara Croft has *arrived*!" Simi's voice had Mia turning to see him, and the others, congregated around Simi's orange campervan in front of the cottages.

"Oh, LC—Lara Croft—I get it," Connie said, taking in Mia's outfit and hairstyle.

"Go on, Mi, do it," Simi said and Mia flushed, and shook her head.

"No way. We are far too old and dignified," she said.

"*Do it, do it, do it*," Simi chanted. *OK, maybe not that dignified*, Mia amended.

"Fine," Mia huffed. "But only for you, and it's a one-time only deal."

Simi clapped his hands together as Mia spun around dropping low with one leg stretched out. From her tool belt, she whipped out her trowel in one hand, and a brush in the other and aimed them at Simi, who crowed with laughter along with the others.

Mia rose, her face burning, but soon she was laughing too.

"So glad to see you all in good spirits, team." Professor

Deacon's booming voice sobered them up quick.

Striding along from the direction of the furthest cottage away, he was dressed in a pair of brown corduroy trousers, a checked short-sleeved shirt, and a canvas hat over his brow with a leather bag slung over his shoulder. "Shall we?"

Mia made the introductions and soon they were all loading up boxes of equipment and piling into Simi's van and Rigs' 4 x 4, and driving the half-mile to the dig site on the farmer's land.

After taking her first look at the site, a shiver ghosted her spine at the enormity of the opportunity she—and the others—had been given. The geophysical surveys had already been completed and the ground marked, and the top layer of the grass had been removed before they had arrived. Everything was primed ready for them to begin.

Professor Deacon assessed the area with keen eyes. The others fell silent at the sudden reverent expression on the older man's face. Mia knew, despite his shrewd mind, inside of him beat a heart filled with the same respectful passion for the past as beat in hers—the only difference was she wore her love of the past on her sleeve.

He reached into the box he had carried from the campervan, and pulled out squat brown bottles of beer. He handed them out. "Low alcohol, of course," he said with a wink, "but I think we should have a little opening ceremony. Now, I am certainly not as eloquent as Miss Davenport, but I will say this: what we do is an honour. An honour to those who came before us. Standing here, on the precipice of—hopefully—many great discoveries, is its own reward." He focused on the students. "Be humble, be respectful, but be thorough. We owe it to them, and to future generations, to tell the story...and to tell it *well*."

Simi and Mia exchanged a look. "Wow," Simi mouthed, and

Mia blinked back the tears in her eyes. This happened to her on every dig. When the team assembled before they began and paid their own respects to those whose past they were about to uncover. Emotion stirred deep within her, and she could almost feel the curtains of the past parting briefly. Two different timelines colliding in a moment of shared purposes.

"Miss Davenport?" Professor Deacon was looking at her. "Any words?"

Mia cleared her throat. "Oh—I...I would like to say something about Boudicca if I may?" The professor nodded. She spoke to the soil revealed before her. "You left this world with your heart broken...you were betrayed horribly, your daughters violated, and your army decimated. But it was not in vain. Yours is the name we remember." She looked up and around at the others. "Boudicca is the name we remember, and the reason why we are all here today. Your cause echoes across time, and what we find here today—or in the days after—will help it *continue* to be remembered."

Mia shared a tremulous smile with Simi, as he added, looking meaningfully at Mia, "Yes, your heart was broken...but your spirit never was."

Trying valiantly to compose herself, Mia lifted her beer bottle and the others followed suit. "To Boudicca, queen with the warrior spirit!"

They all drank deep, and the sound returned. Mia hadn't noticed the silence until the birds started chirping again, and distant traffic noises filtered back in.

Professor Deacon gave her an indulgent smile, and Mia returned it sheepishly. He then began ordering the students about, and Simi turned to Mia.

"LC, that was...I don't even know how to describe

it...supernatural. It literally gave me goosebumps." Simi pointed to the dimpled skin of his forearm.

"The words felt right, somehow. I feel a bit of an affinity with her, I guess."

Simi searched her eyes. "I know why," he said. "You're a lot like her...fight on, Mi." His voice lowered to a whisper.

They smiled at each other. "Mr Jones," the professor called over, and Simi whispered sotto voce to Mia, "I prefer *Dr* Jones."

"Then make it so," she said pointedly. "Fight on, Indy."

Simi puffed out a breath, and quirked an eyebrow. "I'll make you a deal—you start on your doctorate, and I will too." He then sauntered over to Professor Deacon.

Mia stared after him. Now that wasn't the worst idea Simi had ever had. She joined him and the others as the professor doled out their duties.

Mia, keen to get her hands dirty, smiled in anticipation. This was going to be a good day.

CHAPTER TWENTY-SEVEN

The first week passed by in a rapid blur of long hot sweaty and dusty days. The first find was always a cause for celebration and by the Friday the small team congregated at the local pub, toasting their success.

"A spearhead. So appropriate," Simi said scrolling through the photos on his phone. Pinching the screen to enlarge the detail, he let out a contented sigh. "God, I love my job."

Mia smiled at his bowed head fondly, and took a sip of the cool white wine-lemonade spritzer she had ordered while they waited for their meal of chicken and chips. She pulled out her own phone and discovered Josh had texted her. They had both been so busy that phone calls had been scarce and messages brief. But she missed him.

> Are you free tomorrow? I could drive down for a few hours.

Before Mia could reply, Simi whipped the phone out of her hand. "Hey! What are you doing?" she demanded, trying to grab it back.

"Telling him that yes, you are free, and he should definitely come."

Mia narrowed her eyes. "I can do that myself," she said, and Simi reluctantly handed her the phone back. "Back to your drooling." She pointed at his phone.

"Oh, but yours is so much more entertaining," Simi returned.

A snort escaped. "You are incorrigible."

"*Encourageable?* Hmm, with the right guy, yes." Simi nodded seriously, then gave her a wink and returned to his scrolling.

Mia shook her head, lips twitching. She re-read Josh's message and her fingers hovered over the text buttons.

"You're *hes*itating," Simi sing-songed, eyes still on his phone.

"I'm not," Mia told him defensively—she was but had no idea why—then hastily typed:

Sure. Come down in the afternoon, I'll show you around the site x

Josh replied straightaway.

Great. I'll see you around 2pm.

"There, that wasn't so hard was it?" Simi said, and Mia shoved a fat chip in his mouth when the waiter set down their food. Simi mumbled something and Mia smiled sweetly at him.

"Don't talk with your mouth full." She waggled a finger at

him.

He swallowed and stared morosely at her. "That was a dirty trick, silencing me with sustenance."

"Just testing if it still worked." Mia grinned, then set about attacking her meal. She was suddenly ravenous.

The next morning, Mia answered the knock on her cottage door. Professor Deacon waited on the doorstep. "I am going up to London to show the spearhead to the British Museum. You are in charge until my return this evening, Miss Davenport. This morning, if you and the others could finish up the corner we were working in, then you can all have the afternoon off as previously agreed."

"Of course, Professor."

"I want to say what a fine job you are all doing—professional yet passionate about the subject. A great combination." The professor gave her a crinkled-eyed smile.

"Thank you," Mia said, pleased.

"Very good." He turned and made his way down the short path, whistling as he went.

Mia closed the door and the cat twined around her ankles. She'd asked at the farm, the pub, and the local village shop, but no one seemed to be missing a cat. So it appeared Mia had an unofficial housemate—at least for the duration of her stay. She wasn't sure what she was going to do when they left and had been hesitant to give the cat a name...but the urge was strong; she wouldn't be able to hold out for long. "Well, that was a nice surprise," Mia told the cat. She was so enjoying working with the small team, under Professor Deacon's instruction, and to have him compliment them all was a huge boost.

"Meow," the cat agreed.

Mia, already dressed in a pair of khaki shorts and a beige tee, sat and laced up her boots. She'd texted Josh the postcode of the dig site and he planned to meet her there so she could show him around.

Ready for the day, she left her cottage and met the others, filling them in on the professor's whereabouts before they all headed out to the site.

"Eager to see your hug-buddy?" Simi asked, leaning in on the pretext of changing the radio dial and speaking to her quietly.

"Hug-buddy?" Mia laughed. "Sure. I'm looking forward to catching up with him."

"Uh-huh," Simi said.

Mia rolled her eyes, but Simi turned up the music and they all sang along to 'Bones' by Imagine Dragons, bopping along until they reached the dig site.

She, Simi, Colm, and Erica hopped out of the campervan, while Rigs, Connie and Priti exited Rigs' 4 x 4. Mia looked around at them. "The plan is to finish up the corner we've been working on this morning, OK?"

The others nodded and organised themselves. Erica set off with her camera—the official photographer—to take some shots for the university's website, and the others got into the excavated hole.

Mia followed and soon lost herself in the delicate and time-consuming task of carefully trowelling away soil, listening to Simi humming to himself.

"Hydration break!" Priti called and Mia blinked herself back to the present, not realising they'd been at it for an hour already.

She clambered out of the hole and wiped the back of her neck with a bandana. “Ooh, it’s hot.”

Priti handed her a bottle of water, and she took it gratefully, before chugging half of it down.

“You can say that again,” Simi said joining her and accepting his own bottle. “How’s everyone doing?”

“Nothing to report,” Rigs said, joining them with Erica.

Colm, Connie, and Priti shook their heads. “Same,” Colm said.

“What do you think, Mi? Should we call it done and mark it off?” Simi asked Mia, but for some reason, Mia was reluctant to close that corner down yet.

“We’ll give it another hour,” she said.

“You’re the boss, boss,” he said, and after everyone had finished their water they all returned to their spots, and continued.

“You feeling something in your jellies?” Simi asked in an undertone when they had clambered back into the hole.

Mia hesitated before answering him. “Don’t tell the prof, but yeah—call it instinct, or something cosmic—but I feel there’s something here.”

“All right.” Simi shrugged. “Keep at it. Rigs can take the others back at lunchtime. I know they’ve planned a bit of sightseeing and shopping this afternoon.”

“What about you?” Mia asked.

“I’ll stay and be the Clyde to your Bonnie,” Simi said, “and besides someone has to be a chaperone.”

“Bonnie and Clyde?” Mia blinked, steadfastly ignoring the ‘chaperone’ part. “I think you’re mixing up your genre duos. How about the Jonathan to my Evelyn.”

Simi tilted his head thoughtfully. “That does make much more sense,” he agreed. He grinned, and gave her a shoulder bump. "It'll be like old times."

She waited.

"And then when 'Rick' shows up this afternoon, the trio will be complete." And there it was. "*And* he's American too—huh, that worked out well."

Mia hid her own grin. "We are *not* waking up a mummy," she said.

"Wrong continent, sweetie," Simi said.

"Thank god for that," she said, remembering the last time she and Simi were in North Africa. Not that they'd awakened a mummy, of course, but they'd had a bit of a good time with the locals.

Simi smiled and moved over to his own area, and Mia got back to work.

"See you later, Mia!"

Mia acknowledged the others as they packed away. "See you later, guys, enjoy your afternoon. Oh, and good work today."

They all headed up top and Mia heard the 4 x 4 start up as they left the site. She climbed out of the hole and found Simi rifling through his van. "What you looking for?" she asked.

"Food," he moaned. "I was sure I left some protein bars in here."

"Ugh, not those cardboard-tasting things?" Mia said.

"Hey, this is an emergency," Simi said, then something caught his eye. "A-ha." He reached into the pocket of the door and pulled out a bar. "Oh." His face fell. "Banana-peanut."

"Go and get something proper to eat, I'll be fine here," she told him. But he shook his head.

"Indy does not abandon his friends."

"I can't have you wasting away," Mia said, but was touched

that he would rather stay than leave her to go and find food.

"I won't," Simi said grimly, and ripped open the bar eyeing it with distaste.

As Mia watched him, lips twitching, a black car pulled in behind the campervan. It was Josh.

"Ooh, earning brownie points. He's early," Simi observed and lowered the bar away from his mouth.

Mia's heart gave a strange thump in her chest as Josh got out of the car, and their eyes met. He carried a paper bag. "Hi," he said, lifting the bag. "I brought food–wasn't sure if you guys would be hungry."

Mia's, "Hi," was drowned out by a strangled noise from Simi. "Simi, are you *crying*?" she asked, then in an aside, she explained to Josh, "He gets emotional when he's hungry."

"Do not judge me," Simi sniffled and Josh held out the bag with a straight face. Simi took the bag, then added to Mia in an undertone, "He brought food. Double brownie points." He gestured to the two of them. "You two get re-acquainted. I'll set up our little picnic. Thanks, Josh."

"No problem," Josh said, and he and Mia stared at each other as Simi moved away to a shady area beneath a tree, carrying an old blanket he pulled from the campervan.

"Hi," Mia said again. "I won't give you a hug." She gestured down at her soil-smeared clothes and then at his pristine black jeans and blue tee.

He let out a laugh and pulled her into him for a hug anyway. "I don't care about a bit of dirt, Mia," he said. "I was raised on a ranch, remember?"

Mia relaxed into him, and closed her eyes, breathing in his familiar scent, and the world righted itself. She wanted to cling to him, cling to the knowledge that if this had been Henry, he would have demanded she take a shower before even coming within touching distance of him. Realising she was comparing her friend to her *ex-boyfriend*, Mia stepped back, heat staining her cheeks.

"I've missed those," Josh said easily. "Shall we eat, then you can show me what you've been working on."

"That sounds like a plan," Mia responded, gathering her composure, and together they joined Simi.

"Look, Mia...real food." Tears sparkled in Simi's eyes as he gestured at the thick ham salad sandwiches, chicken legs, watermelon slices, and cans of still-cold lemonade.

"You've made a friend for life," Mia told Josh with a laugh as she pulled out her hand sanitiser from the tool belt and cleaned her hands. Simi held out his hands and she gave him a squirt too.

"I can live with that," Josh said and earned an adoring smile from Simi.

"Oof, you two go on. I'm going to rest for five," Simi said twenty minutes later when they'd finished the food.

Mia gave him an amused look as he laid back and closed his eyes, then turned to Josh. "Shall we?" He nodded, and the pair rose and headed over to the site. "How's work been?" Mia asked him.

"Terrific. It's great to see how contract law works over here. I'm enjoying it." Josh's eyes lit up as he spoke. "And I can see things are going well here too," he said as he took in the hole, sectioned out into areas.

"So well. The prof's gone up to London today to show the British Museum the spearhead we found yesterday. That was a good day," Mia told him with a smile.

"That's amazing," Josh said.

Mia studied the hole reminiscently, hearing the echo of Colm's shout as he'd uncovered the metal tip. She blinked and something caught her eye. "What the...?"

"What is it?" Josh asked.

But Mia was already climbing down into the hole and into the area she had been previously working in. Perhaps when she'd moved to climb out earlier, a portion of soil had shifted. She met Josh's eyes. "Now you are *my* good luck charm," she said. "Come down."

"You sure?" Josh asked, one eyebrow quirked.

"I'm the boss today," she said.

"OK," Josh said and joined her in the hole.

Mia offered him the brush. "Go on," she encouraged, and guided his hand with her own over to where she'd seen something in the dirt. Their shoulders skimmed against each other as they knelt in the soil, but Mia was too intent on the find. Josh brushed slowly and gently at the earth and Mia let go of his hand to let him continue.

Her breath hitched as the item was slowly revealed. Josh stopped. "This is your find," he said, and their eyes met. With a smile at his understanding, Mia took the brush and revealed the relic in its entirety. "Oh my," she breathed, seeing the twisted metal, "it's a cloak buckle." She threw herself at Josh, and grabbed him in a tight hug. "I knew there was something here," she said into his chest.

She released him and stood. "Simi Indiana Jones, get your butt down here!" she yelled.

Josh stared up at her. "Congrats," he said huskily.

Mia beamed back, excitement rippling from her in waves. Their eyes met and for one intense, disconcerting moment, she couldn't break the contact.

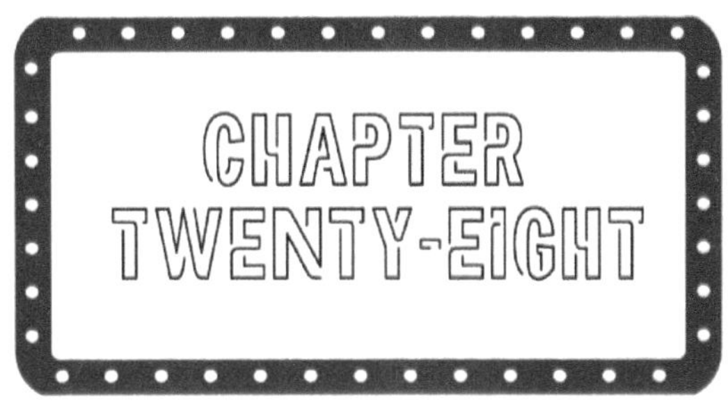

CHAPTER TWENTY-EIGHT

Simi clambered down and joined them. "What's all the hollering? I was catching zee's." He looked from one to the other. "Ooh, tension," he whispered to Mia, and the disconcerting moment passed.

She rolled her eyes and then pulled Simi down next to Josh. "Looky look," she said, pointing out the new find.

Simi fell silent, his mouth falling open. Then he clicked his fingers, and said, "See, the jellies are never wrong." He gave a whoop. "Group hug!" He slung an arm around Mia and then Josh. "This calls for a celebration. I'll be right back."

He released them abruptly, and climbed out of the hole. Mia and Josh followed him out. "I need to get the camera," Mia said. "Take a few photos while it's in situ."

"Go ahead," Josh said.

Mia passed Simi on the way as he returned with three bottles of the low-alcohol beer.

"I'm getting the camera," she told him. Erica had left it in Simi's van and, though she wasn't as great a photographer as

Erica was, Mia had had some practice on other digs, and knew the kind of shots Professor Deacon favoured.

Mia re-joined Josh and Simi and took a few photos before accepting the beer from Simi.

He tapped his bottle to hers. "Fortune and all that jazz, kid," he said in a deep voice, and Mia grinned in appreciation at the misquote.

"Fortune and all that jazz, Indy," she said.

"Congratulations on your find," Josh said and tapped each of their bottles.

"Thanks," Mia said. "Your arrival was very serendipitous."

"Ooh watch out, Josh, the big words are coming out." Simi grinned and Mia mock scowled at him.

"Watch it, or the big trowel will come out too."

Josh smiled at the exchange.

"Are you happy for me to remove it?" Simi asked, gesturing down into the hole.

"Go ahead," Mia invited.

Simi picked up a lidded box and a set of small tools and descended into the hole, while Josh and Mia sat on the grass surrounding the hole and sipped their beer.

A movement beside Mia attracted her attention. A slowworm slithered along sinuously, then, with a plop, fell into the hole—where Simi was working.

Uh-oh. She braced herself. *3... 2... 1...* "Aarghhhhhhh!"

"It's only a slowworm," Mia called down in a soothing voice, but handed her bottle to an amused-looking Josh in preparation.

"*Mi-aarghhhhh*!" Simi screamed again.

Mia got up and climbed down into the hole. Simi, eyes wide, brandished his trowel while backed up against the earth wall. "I got you," Mia murmured and Simi said, "*Thank you.*"

Mia stood, cradling the slowworm. "I was talking to this fine fella." She inspected the coppery-green colouring. "His skin looks like the patina on that Roman urn we found." She lifted the slowworm near her face, and a tiny tongue slipped out, scenting the air. "I think I'll name you Pat."

"Do *not* name it," Simi groaned out. "You know what happens when you name them. Please take it away."

Mia huffed out a mock sigh. "Very well. Pat, your beauty is underappreciated around here."

"My tolerance for serpents is underappreciated around here," Simi muttered.

Mia shot Simi a grin as she headed up to ground level one-handed, carefully cradling Pat in the other. "You should take that as a compliment, Pat, your worm status has been upgraded to 'serpent'."

"That wasn't a compliment!" Simi called after her.

With a laugh, Mia glanced at Josh. "Want to go for a walk?"

"Sure." Josh stood, and walked alongside her carrying their beer bottles, as they moved towards the wooded area. "So that's why Simi's nickname is Indy—because he doesn't like snakes?"

Mia stopped her murmuring to Pat and gave him a sideways look. "That...and he thinks Indiana Jones is cool."

Josh lifted his beer bottle. "I'll drink to that." He took a long gulp.

Mia stopped at a fallen log inside the treeline. "There we go, Pat, your new home." She set the little slowworm down, and it slithered underneath, taking refuge amongst the leafy, mossy floor. Taking a seat on the log, she accepted her beer bottle when Josh passed it to her.

She took a slow sip of the now lukewarm beer, then held out

a finger when a white butterfly flitted towards her. It landed—just the briefest of moments—on her fingertip before it floated off again.

"I'm beginning to think you *are* a secret princess," Josh said, eyes on her.

Mia laughed. "We all have our secrets," she said. "Archaeologist by day, princess by night." She shrugged. "Well, I'll never want for company—not with all my animal friends."

She stood and they headed back towards the dig site.

"You'll never want for company anyway, not with me around," Josh said quietly.

Mia gave him a shoulder bump. "Thanks. I might need some human contact to stop me spiralling into crazy cat lady—or crazy slowworm lady—territory." They shared a laugh, and carried on walking. "You know...speaking of princesses, I had a thought about Cinderella."

"Oh?"

"Yes. I think she should've stayed. Stayed past midnight."

"But...then the magic would have worn off and the prince would have seen her as she truly was," Josh said.

"Exactly! She should have shown him her true self from the very beginning; tattered gown, mouse friends and all—and if he'd accepted her as she was...then that's when the true magic would have happened." Mia smiled, stopping their walk.

Josh gave her a long, assessing look, as if he could see inside her soul, to the tiny broken parts of her heart, because in truth, her real self had never been completely accepted by Henry. And now she could see that.

"I would al—" Josh began but was interrupted by Simi on the radio on Mia's belt.

"Lady C, if you have finished frolicking through the forest

with Prince Charming, we have to close up for the day."

Mia rolled her eyes, a slight flush warming her cheeks.

"Could he hear us?" Josh asked in amazement, staring over at the excavation site, still ten or so metres away.

"I don't think so, he's a bit uncanny like that. Perhaps he picked up some sort of talisman somewhere," Mia said wryly, with a shake of her head. "Come on, if Simi's finished we can tidy everything away, then go and get cleaned up and have a proper drink at the pub."

"Sounds great," Josh said.

Mia grinned at that and, as she walked over to help Simi finish up, wondered what Josh had been about to say before they had been interrupted.

Later that evening, Mia slowly sipped her white wine from her seat in the cosy alcove they had commandeered in the corner of the Warrior Queen pub. Professor Deacon talked animatedly to Josh about US v UK finders' laws at the bar. The professor had arrived moments after the students had turned up and were ordering a meal. In an extremely jovial mood because of the new find, he had ordered a large whiskey and cornered Josh.

"Poor Lawyer-Man," Simi said, sitting down next to Mia. He doled out the drinks from the tray he had carried over.

"Thanks," Erica said from her seat opposite and sipped her Pimm's, while the other students accepted theirs.

"Lawyer-Man?" Mia asked, bemused.

"I'm trying out some new nicknames—but nothing's sticking yet. Any ideas?" Simi waggled his dark eyebrows at Mia.

Mia bit her tongue. She would not be disclosing what she called Josh. Simi would have a field day with that knowledge.

She shrugged. "I'm sure you'll come up with something," she said neutrally.

Simi clicked his fingers. "I have it, it's perfect—honourable, a bit like a superhero name, and steady. Just like our man…Sir Josh."

Mia choked on her drink, and Priti leant over to pat her on her back. "I'm fine," she gasped out, "thanks."

"No problem," Priti said, her dark eyes wide.

"So by that reaction—is it a yay or nay for Sir Josh? I think we should take votes." Simi looked around at everyone.

Seriously? Mia narrowed her eyes, very tempted to search her friend's pockets for the suspected telepathy-talisman. "It's a no, a very fervent, no," she said.

Simi pouted but took heed at the steely light in her eyes "OK, it's a nix on Sir Josh. I'll keep thinking."

"You do that," Mia said as Josh re-joined them, a slightly harassed look on his face. "Sorry about the prof," she said to him. "He is a bit overwhelming sometimes."

"Here, get this down you." Simi thrust a pint of cider at him. "It'll take the edge off."

Josh shook his head. "Thanks, but I better not. I've already had one and I have to get back to London."

"Why don't you stay—you could bunk at Mia's," Simi said, an innocent look on his face, and Mia had to restrain herself from locating his shin under the table and giving it a firm nudge.

Josh flicked a glance at Mia, then said, "Regretfully, I have meetings tomorrow, even though it's Sunday."

"Shame," Simi murmured.

"Oh, the pool table's free—anyone up for a game or two?" Colm said, and Rigs, Erica, Priti, and Connie all stood and picked up their drinks. "Simi?"

Simi waved a hand. "Go ahead, I might come over in a bit. I'm far too comfortable." He leant back in the squishy armchair.

Professor Deacon joined the students when he emerged from the bathroom, his booming voice informing them that he had been a champion pool player in his uni days.

"Do you want a game?" Mia asked Josh.

"Another time. I have to make a move soon," he said, but made no effort to move, and Mia was glad. She'd miss him again—more than she thought possible—once he'd gone.

Simi examined Mia and Josh through lazy eyes, then said, "So Josh, how's London? Made any friends?"

Josh toyed with a beermat. "One or two," he said.

"Oh, do tell—workmates—or you know, someone *hot*?"

What was Simi doing? Mia took another gulp of her wine, her eyes boring holes into Simi's face—completely unnoticed by him of course.

Josh laughed. "You're relentless," he said.

"Thank you," Simi said, and gestured with his hand. "But proceed."

"There's one woman at the office—Sabrina—we've kind of hit it off. I've known her awhile through online office meetings, and it's been nice getting to know her properly."

Don't react, Mia thought, then, *why would I even react anyway? Maybe because this is the first I'm hearing about it.*

This time Simi did look in Mia's direction, but she assumed an unconcerned air and continued to sip her drink. "That's...good," Simi said.

Josh sat up straighter, and his arm inadvertently brushed Mia's arm. "We're going out to dinner on Friday. She's from London so offered to be my guide around the city."

Mia's arm hummed from the touch, but her stomach twisted

itself into a knot at his innocent words. What was wrong with her? She set the wine down. "I'm going to use the bathroom," she said overbrightly, and when Josh stood up to let her move past him, Mia couldn't even meet his eyes.

She practically ran into the ladies' room. Thankfully it was empty, so she stepped up to the sink, ran her hands under the cold tap and dabbed her flushed cheeks. There was no reason—absolutely *no reason*—for the overreaction. Josh was a handsome man—a catch, her English nan would have said, so of course he would go on dates. He was free to live his life as he deemed fit. She wanted him to be happy. He deserved to be happy.

After that stern talking to, she used the facilities, before washing her hands and re-checking her appearance. The flush had died down, and her blue-green eyes weren't as shiny as they had been. Satisfied, Mia left the bathroom and serenely resumed her seat.

"Oh, good, Mia, you're back. Josh asked about my favourite dig—I think it was yours too." Simi grinned at her.

Mia's composed demeanour fled in an instant. *Shit*. "That's quite a change of conversation," she said weakly.

Josh gave her a searching look, but said, "There was a vague segue there somewhere."

Simi nodded. "Yeah, we were talking about you comfort-eating lemon sorbet, and how you'd discovered it on that expedition. It was three years ago in Thebes—Luxor, as it is now...oof, those Egyptian guys." He fanned himself.

Josh's eyes twinkled. "Thebes, huh?"

Mia turned desperate eyes on Simi, imploring him to not continue, vaguely wondering how they'd got onto her comfort-eating lemon sorbet, but he was lost in his swooning recollections.

"Thebes—where it smells of hot spiced sand and glitters with a thousand stars—"

"Sand," Josh murmured, laughter in his voice, and Mia almost crumbled into a mortified pile of it herself.

"—And who was that young professor who followed you around, Mi...you know the one with the—"

"*Simi*," Mimi said through clenched teeth.

"What did we call him? Oh, that's it" — Simi focused on Mia — "Dr Dreamy Eyes, that's it." He let out a triumphant laugh. *Shit, shit, shit.*

Had she teleported to Egypt? Her aflame face gave her the impression of being scorched to a frazzled crisp beneath the Egyptian sun right at that moment.

"No," she managed in a strangled voice. "It was Dr Harpocrates."

The smile fell off Simi's face. "Are you sure?"

"*Absolutely.*" Mia's teeth ground together.

Simi stared at her for a moment and she thought he was going to drag it out and get her back for the 'Pat' incident, but after a moment he grimaced. "Of course, *Harpocrates*, silly me."

He accepted the veiled command the name evoked. Harpocrates, being the Egyptian god of silence, was their code word to use when they wanted the conversation curtailed. Only to be used in dire circumstances, Mia deemed this discussion warranted it. She'd already drunkenly embarrassed herself once over 'Dr Dreamy Eyes' the night of Calli's wedding, and had no wish to re-live it again with Josh sitting next to her.

She and Simi needed to re-evaluate the terms of their friendship, she thought darkly.

"Right, I'll pop off and have a game with the others," Simi

said, astutely knowing his demise was imminent, and Mia gave him a strained smile.

Josh tilted his head, as if trying to puzzle something out. But Simi drained his drink and sauntered over to the others.

"That was *interesting*," Josh said finally. "Your friend's such a character."

Mia blew out a breath. "He's something all right," she said, but couldn't *really* blame Simi. While the story *was* somewhat embarrassing anyway, he didn't know that Mia had already divulged some of it to Josh in a mortifying episode.

"It's my fault we changed the subject—I thought the talk of me going out on a date was dredging stuff up for you. I know you have no interest in it right now," Josh said, his gaze earnest, yet slightly probing.

"Oh, god, don't think you have to spare my feelings, Josh, in order to live your life!" Mia said, horrified. "Just because I'm happy being an old spinster with my injured animals and cantankerous pets, doesn't mean you have to join my club."

"I'd be a fully paid-up member if it made you happy, Mia," Josh murmured, something flickering in his gaze.

Mia relaxed and placed a hand on his arm. "There's absolutely no way I want you to miss out on potential happiness because of keeping me company. You deserve to be happy, in fact, I order it. Josh Cavanaugh, you shall go forth and find your happiness."

"But what about you?" Josh asked, his voice husky.

"Me? I shall excavate the ruins of my heart until I find the building blocks needed to re-build it. Being here, doing what I love, with people I like and respect, having the *best* friends" — she squeezed his arm meaningfully — "and family, is a great foundation to start with," she said.

Pain swam in Josh's piercing blue gaze. He dropped his forehead to hers. "Oh, Mia-mine," he murmured.

Mia rubbed his arm. "I'll be fine, I promise. Now, you'd better set off. You don't want to get home too late." Her tone was brisk and business-like because she forced it to be. It helped cover the swirling emotions inside her. Conflicting, traitorous emotions that mocked her words. "I'll walk you out."

He pulled back, gave her another searching look, and then said, "OK." He stood, and she followed suit.

Josh walked over to the pool table to say his goodbyes. "See ya later, Law-Maker," Simi said, and when Josh raised one eyebrow, he carried on, "No? Right, I'll keep working on it."

"Don't forget what I said about the British Museum—they could use bright, young minds such as yourself," Professor Deacon said to Josh.

"I'll bear it in mind." Josh held out his hand and the professor shook it. "A pleasure to see you again."

"Likewise, Cavanaugh."

The students waved their goodbyes, and Mia followed Josh out into the lavender-coloured evening light. They stopped beside Josh's rental car.

"What was the professor talking about?" Mia asked.

"He thinks I should look into getting a job in the museum's acquisitions department—putting together the contracts, that sort of thing," Josh said.

"Oh. So you could potentially move to London then," Mia said, a strange ache behind her chest. Well, what did she expect? She'd urged him—no, *ordered* him—to go and find his happiness. And if that happiness included a woman from his office and a new job in London? Well, she had no right to comment on it.

Josh studied her. "Potentially," he agreed.

Mia had her heart set on staying in New York she now realised. She smiled sadly. Their roles would be wholly reversed, with Thursday night card night being completed over Zoom again, but this time, Josh in England, and her in New York. Oceans—chasms—apart.

She rubbed her bare arms, feeling a chill, despite the balmy weather. Josh noticed. "Go on in," he told her. "I'll give you a call tomorrow."

"OK, drive safe."

Josh pulled her in for a swift hug, but Mia noticed—and felt deeply—how brief it was. As if the divide had already started. "I will do. Thanks for a lovely day."

She stepped back to let him get into the car, and with a wave, and a quick one from him in return, she turned and made her way back into the pub, a weird hollow sensation in the pit of her stomach.

Mia battled with the tarpaulin as the wind tried to whip it out of her hand. The weather exactly matched her bad mood. The week had gone by once again quickly and with yet more excitement under the canopy of long sunny days. Arrowheads and a few coins had been found, along with broken pottery and another spearhead. But so far, no more jewellery. And now the weather had turned.

"I've got it," Rigs said, taking the tarpaulin from Mia and securing it with the tent pegs over the hole. "That's the last one."

"And just in time," Connie said as the clouds above opened and released a deluge of heavy rain.

"I'll start the Juice Machine," Simi shouted and the others hurried after him to where the campervan and the 4 x 4 were parked. The professor had already set off to London again with the latest finds.

"I'll be right there," Mia shouted after them, and Colm turned to give her a thumbs up. She headed over to where she had placed a box with pieces of pottery inside, battling to pull up her hood but it blew straight down, the rain plastering her braided hair to her head.

Her phone beeped with a notification, and she risked a peep at it, pulling it out of her inside pocket. As hoped it was Josh. Since he'd visited the Saturday before, their contact had been minimal again and Mia had tried not to read too much into it. They were both busy, that was all.

Can you talk?

Mia pulled up her hood and pressed video call, hunching over so the phone was protected by the hood, and this time the errant hood managed to stay over her head. She held the phone up close to her face while hefting the small box in the other hand.

"Are you OK?" Josh's voice was barely discernible over the rain.

Mia tried to focus on his face, and blow the raindrops out of her eyes at the same time. "Oh, sure, sure," Mia said, "just battling the good old British weather." She slipped on the mud and let out a little squeak of alarm.

"Perhaps you should go," Josh said.

Mia stamped her mud-caked boots, trying to loosen some of the clumps. "It is getting pretty treacherous out here," she agreed. "But what's up? You needed to speak with me?"

Josh shook his head. "It can wait," he said. "Go and get dry."

"Oh, your date!" Mia remembered. *But of course she hadn't forgotten.* Was he nervous? Did he need a morale boost? She diverted to the wooded area and stopped beneath the shelter of a wide oak, and raindrops dripped down the back of her neck when she pulled her hood down to focus on him properly. "Step back a bit, let me see what you're wearing."

Josh hesitated, then did as she asked. Mia inspected him through the screen. Her eyes roved over his styled curls—she preferred them flopping over his forehead—but approved of the sapphire blue shirt and black jacket. "Nice," she said, "the shirt brings out the beautiful blue of your eyes."

"You approve then?"

"Oh, definitely," she enthused, "any woman would." She bit back a wince. *Really, Mia,* you *are not going on a date with him.* "Channel your inner Darcy, and look at her intensely, you know like you do sometimes with m—" she broke off. *Shit.* "Hah, don't listen to me, what do I know about dating? Be your usual charming self and it'll be fine." *Oh, my god, could you dig a deeper hole*?

"OK. Look at her intensely, and be my usual charming self—got it. Thanks for the pep talk, Mia." His grin appeared forced and a line appeared between his brows.

"Anytime," she said, glad to help *him* for a change.

"Right, well I'd better be off. We have reservations at the Fern and Ivy."

"The Fern and Ivy?"

"What is it?" Josh must have noted the tone in her voice.

"Oh, nothing. I was thinking that's a good choice," she said lamely. It wasn't his fault that The Fern and Ivy brought back uncomfortable memories. Mostly Henry berating her about her career choice. She shook it off. "Go on, you'll be taking over from Calli and being late! Give me a call tomorrow and let me know how it went. Good luck."

Josh stared at her through the screen, perhaps practising his intense look, as his eyes shone even bluer. "Sure, and thanks."

"Bye, Josh," she said softly.

"Bye." He disconnected the call and Mia stared at the blank phone screen, the back of her neck frozen and mud seeping through her socks, from where it had overflowed into her boots.

With a sigh, Mia set off, squelching her way back towards the campervan, where the others waited for her.

"You are *not* getting in Juicy like that," Simi admonished taking in her bedraggled, muddy state.

"I'll sit on an empty artefact bag," she griped, suddenly not in the mood for Simi's banter.

"Mud in your socks?" Simi nodded wisely, knowing that was one of her bugbears.

Erica grabbed one of the larger clear bags and leant over to set it on the seat, and Mia pulled herself into the van, set the box at her feet, and threw Erica a grateful smile before sitting down with a muted squelch.

"I need a bath—no, a shower and a bath," Mia said.

"Lady, I got you, we'll be home in ten," Simi said, kinder now. He gave her a sideways look. "Oh *right*...it's Friday, isn't it."

"Last time I checked," Mia said, with a bemused smile.

"Mood check makes sense now," he murmured.

"What's that supposed to mean? You know I hate muddy socks."

"Uh-huh—sure, that's all it is." Simi rolled his eyes, then leant over to turn up the radio and 'Ivy' by Taylor Swift swelled out of the speakers. Mia resisted the urge to rest her weary head on the glass and have her brains rattle out as they traversed the rutted path.

Despite the title reminding her of the restaurant Josh had booked for his date, she lost herself in the beautiful lyrics of the song, while the others chatted softly in the back. She ignored the searching looks Simi shot her at intervals. *I'm not thinking of Josh, I'm not thinking of Josh...escorting a beautiful woman out to dinner and gazing at her intensely over candlelight.*

Mia practically wrenched open the door when Simi stopped in front of the cottages. Throwing, "Thanks," over her shoulder, she hurried through the rain to her accommodation.

Only once inside, dripping on the welcome mat, did she acknowledge that, yes, she was thinking of Josh and, with a sharp pain in her heart, knew, that without a doubt, he would not be thinking about her. And rightly so, he was on a *date*. A date she'd encouraged him to enjoy.

With a huff of impatience, Mia stripped down to her underwear where she stood, and then padded over to the bathroom, stopping her progress when she heard meowing from her feline houseguest. "Sorry, I'll replenish your food when I no longer resemble Bigfoot."

The cat swished its tail, and turned its face away, before stalking over to the sofa and lying down; back facing Mia.

Mia—her hand on the bathroom door handle—shook her head in wry amusement at the cantankerous nature of cats, before making her way to the shower. She stood beneath the hot-enough-to-peel-the-skin-off-your-bones water spray, and scrubbed at her skin until it pinked, then washed her hair thoroughly.

Wrapped in her towelling robe, with her hair bundled up in another towel, Mia went out into the living area and fed the cat before dealing with the detritus of her mud-splattered, rain-soaked clothes and boots. After she had hung the clothes over the tub and deposited the boots on some newspaper to clean afterwards, she pulled her phone out of the pocket of her dripping coat, and wiped the slightly damp screen.

Notifications popped up; one a photo message. She opened it and snorted out a laugh. Simi posed with a bottle of wine, a forlorn expression on his face. Question marks filled the text box below it.

Mia turned the camera on and posed with a smile and a thumbs up and sent it back, adding:

But I get to choose the film.

Dots moved along the screen, indicating Simi was typing either an excruciatingly long reply, or typing, deleting and then re-typing. Knowing Simi, it was probably the latter.

Mia grinned when the reply came back, first with an eye-roll emoji, then:

OK, Lady Bossy.

Yep, he'd definitely edited that message before sending it.

She brushed out her hair, and braided it into two braids; one on either side of her head, and put on a pair of soft black leggings and her 'I Dig You,' tee, knowing it would mollify Simi to see her wearing it. She pulled on a fluffy pink cardigan over the top, and slipped her feet into her slippers.

While she waited for Simi, Mia popped a frozen Hawaiian-style pizza in the oven and set the timer.

A tap came on the door as Mia pulled two glass tumblers out of the cupboard. She set them down on the counter and went to let Simi in and discovered the rain had softened to a soothing drizzle.

Simi strode in, holding the wine bottle aloft like a broadsword, and then set it down on the counter. He groaned at the empty pizza box, and sniffed the air. "Ugh, you get to choose the film, *and* I have to eat pineapple on pizza?" He mock scowled at her. "I'm really re-thinking the terms of our friendship, lady."

Mia laughed at his eerie nature; she had thought exactly the same thing the other night in the pub. She moved next to him and gave him a hip-bump. "It's fruit—it's good for you."

"Technically, so's wine—full of grapes, you know."

"Then we'll definitely be getting our quota today," Mia said, handing him the corkscrew.

Simi set to opening the bottle of shiraz, while Mia opened the laptop and selected the film. He joined her, looking over her shoulder. "*The Mummy*, thank god. I thought I'd have to sit through *Pride & Prejudice* again." He gave her a cheeky smirk.

"Hey, do not disparage P & P—you'll upset Mrs Bennet."

"Uh, sweetie, you know she's a fictional character right?" Simi gave her a strange look and patted her soothingly on the shoulder.

Mia, lips twitching, gestured to the cat sitting on the sofa behind them. "Mrs Bennet."

Simi gave her a narrow look. "You named it. What did I tell you about naming them?" He took a closer look at the cat. "But to be fair she does have a pinched my-daughters-*must*-marry-well look around her eyes."

"Simi!" Mia laughed. "Don't listen to him, Mrs Bennet, your eyes are perfectly un-pinched."

The cat fixed Simi with a gimlet stare, and Simi shuddered. "Cats, the Egyptian gods of the underworld. Perfect casting," he said.

Mia giggled and went over to the counter to collect their wine. She handed Simi a glass when the timer on the oven beeped.

"Oh, yummy," he said sarcastically when she pulled the steaming pizza out, cut it into six and put it on a large plate.

"Don't be fussy, Indy," Mia admonished and set the plate on the coffee table between them.

She settled down with her glass of wine and pressed play on the film. She hid her grin behind her glass when Simi devoured one piece of pizza and picked up a second before the opening credits had even finished.

Halfway through the film, Mrs Bennet snuck onto Mia's lap and distracted her suddenly wandering thoughts by plunging one hand into the cat's thick fur. *I bet Josh had something fancier than pizza...I wonder if they're watching a film...is he hooking an arm around his date's shoulder and pulling her in closer; so close she can smell his scent. Stop it, Mia!*

She refocused when Simi paused the film; Imhotep frozen in rage on the screen. "Come on, out with it."

"Out with what?"

Simi drained his glass and went to collect the bottle from the counter. He gave her a long look as he topped up their glasses. "You haven't *once* mouthed any of the lines...or pointed out any inaccuracies."

"I don't *always* do that," Mia protested.

Simi only continued to stare at her.

"Oh, all right, I admit it; I have a problem miming lines in movies."

"*Great*, that's step one, but that wasn't actually my point. Come on, kid, tell Uncle Indy what's the matter?"

"Nothing—I swear. It's just been a long, tiring week."

"That's true, but I know you, Mi," he paused, then, "look, I shall ask this one time, then I'll let it drop. It's Josh isn't it; the fact he's gone on a date?"

Mia straightened, almost dislodging Mrs Bennet, who gave a grumbling hiss. She laid a placating hand on the cat's back, and said. "Of course not! How many times do I have to tell you—we're just *friends*."

Simi took a slow sip, his eyes thoughtful. "So you are telling me, that there hasn't been any—not even a *frisson*—of anything intimate between you *at all*...ever?" Mia hesitated, only for a second, but that was enough for Simi to pounce. "Spill, lady."

She thought of Calli and Ash's wedding—but that was only acting so didn't truly count, but that night in Miami... "Well, we did sleep together one time—"

"*Lay-dee* Ceeeee," Simi said, drawing it out. "And I'm only hearing that prime deet now?"

Mia shook her head, frustrated at herself. *Damn, this lip-loosening wine*. "I meant *literally* slept. It was after I'd had an altercation with Mae, and Josh came after me on the beach...and then we were talking and stargazing on this woven beach bed and I fell asleep, and when I woke up he was still there."

Simi leant forward, chin cupped in his hand, rapt. "And?"

"And nothing. I extricated myself from his arms and we went to breakfast."

Disappointment wreathed Simi's expressive face, then he quirked an eyebrow. "In his arms, you say?"

Mia laughed. "Enough, Detective Jones. Stop making more to it than there was. I obviously rolled into him in the night and he naturally held on."

"Uh-huh, naturally. Well, he knows you like his hugs, eh?"

Mia swatted Simi with a cushion. "Everyone likes hugs," she

protested. "Nice friendly hugs."

"Sure," Simi said, then took a long slurp of his wine. "So...do you think this Sabrina is enjoying Lawyer Hottie's 'hugs' right now?"

Mia nearly choked on her own sip of wine. She pushed down the sudden disquieting image, and affected a careless air. "I have no idea. But if she is, it's certainly no business of ours. I told Josh to go and find his happiness."

Simi stared at her, eyes wide, and muttered, "Jeez," under his breath. He pouted at his glass. "Shame. We've been drinking."

"Why?" Mia asked, perplexed.

He set his near-empty glass down with a clink on the coffee table, making Mrs Bennet jump on Mia's lap. "*Because*, I would be getting in the Juice Machine and driving up to Kent and having words with a certain someone. Extremely stern words."

"Henry? Why?"

Simi leant forward again, and in the most serious voice Mia had ever heard from him, said, "Because he stole my best friend's happiness." He squeezed her free hand. "Indy does not let such dishonour go."

"Simi," Mia whispered, tears springing up in her eyes.

"Don't you dare. Don't you dare cry on me," Simi said, then, "Oh, now you've done it." He stood and walked across to the kitchen counter and grabbed two sheets of paper towel. On his return, he thrust one at Mia, and wiped furtively at his own dark eyes.

"Simi. I'm fine, seriously. I'm having the time of my life. I mean, I get to live in New York with Calli, Ash, and their friends, and now I'm doing fieldwork with my favourite archaeologist." She toasted him with her glass. "You know how Henry felt about me doing fieldwork—most unsuitable for the girlfriend of a man of his breeding—so I wouldn't be here with you right now." She sipped her wine, and added as an afterthought, "I don't *need* romantic happiness."

"What about Josh? You never mentioned Josh in all that," Simi pointed out quietly, resuming his seat.

Mia nibbled her lip. "He's my friend—Calli and Ash's friend. And that's all he sees me as too. So" — she narrowed her eyes at Simi — "put away that giant spoon, Dr Jones, and stop stirring the pot."

Simi blew out a long puff of breath. "Fine, fine. I shall cease and desist. *Such* a party-pooper," he said morosely.

"I have a better idea. Why don't we talk about *your* love life?" Mia teased.

With a violent shudder, Simi acted as if he'd been thrown into a pit of vipers. "Oh, hell no. We are going nowhere near that temple of doom," he said and Mia burst out snort-laughing.

"Oh, sure, it's all fun and games over my lack of a love life."

Mia stopped laughing with a hiccup, and patted her friend's arm. "What about Colm? You two seemed pretty cosy at the pub the other night."

Simi shook his head. "Nah, never raid where you excavate, LC. You, of all diggers, should know that—remember Dr Dreamy Eyes?"

Mia nearly snorted again at the—quite fitting—analogy, but the mention of the young Egyptian professor was enough to sober her. "Oh, yes. I remember all right. What was with throwing me under the bus the other night when Josh was here?"

"*Throwing you under the bus*?" Simi said slowly, looking innocent. "Why would it even matter about you and your past almost-hook-ups? You're *just friends*, remember?" And with a smug smile, he stood and gave a bow. "And that, is my cue to leave."

Mia's mouth dropped open. *Well-played, my friend.*

Simi leant over and pressed a kiss to her cheek. "You know I love you, Mi, I'm simply trying to stop you from becoming 'Lara Croft: crazy cat lady'." He stepped back when Mrs Bennet hissed out her disapproval.

Mia soothed the cat, and smiled up at her friend. "A bit too late for that, but likewise. Love you too."

Simi smiled back, but cast a disparaging look at her cardigan. "I see that. That cardi has 'crazy cat lady' written all over it, but I approve of the tee." He laughed and ducked the cushion she tossed at his head. "Nighty-night then."

"Night, Simi," Mia said, her lips twitching, knowing if she'd worn Josh's hoodie instead of the cardigan, it would have set her up for a different kind of ridicule. She lifted Mrs Bennet into her arms as she stood to see Simi out.

Locking the door behind him, she spoke to the cat, "What's wrong with being a crazy cat lady anyway?"

Mrs Bennet let out a plaintive meow.

"Exactly what I thought," Mia said and put the cat down to fill up her saucer with fresh water, and to enjoy the rest of the film. Fully intending to mimic her favourite lines to her heart's content.

CHAPTER THIRTY

Mia couldn't sleep.

She'd checked her phone numerous times, and finally had set it on the kitchen counter so she wouldn't be tempted to keep checking it. She was being ridiculous. Of course Josh wouldn't text her until the morning, or even later in the day. And why was she even so invested? Because Josh was her friend, she told herself stubbornly.

Mia kicked the blanket off, and Mrs Bennet gave her a narrow stare before closing her eyes and going back to sleep on the bottom of the bed. Getting up, Mia padded across the bedroom to gaze out of the window and caught the sun creeping over the horizon; the sky a perfect shade of dusky lavender tinged with pinky-peach.

Resigning herself to the futility of trying to sleep now, Mia got dressed in a pair of khaki shorts, a cream linen shirt, and her hiking boots. She pulled her hair into a low braid, before going out into the kitchen, brewing up a cup of tea and pouring into a lidded travel mug. She pocketed her phone and left the cottage, mug in hand. Locking the door behind her, Mia set off along the cottage path.

She aimed for a trail running alongside the field opposite that would take her to a wooded area and a small waterfall. As Mia walked, she sipped the honey-sweetened tea, and listened to the sound of the birds serenading the dawn.

The disquiet within her settled as she clambered over moss-covered logs, rounded trees that had seen more with their ancient eyes than she could ever fathom, and strolled through the lacy, dappled sunbeams filtering through the canopy overhead.

The musical sound of the waterfall reached Mia's ears long before she spotted it. But her first look had an awed smile blossoming. She pulled out her phone and took a few shots, then climbed down to a flat stone next to the sparkling water.

She sat cross-legged on the stone and sipped the rest of her tea, serene and at peace. A little brown sparrow fluttered down from the trees and landed nearby so Mia kept perfectly still, moving her phone in tiny movements until she could line up the picture. She took a well-timed shot when the bird looked directly at her and tilted its head. *Perfect.*

Her phone rang in her hand, and the little bird flew away. Mia answered Josh's video-call with her stomach suddenly twisting itself into a knot.

"Good morning," she said.

"Morning. Where are you?" Josh asked.

Mia smiled. "I couldn't sleep, so I decided to go for a walk. You're up early too," she pointed out.

The dark smudges beneath his eyes had her wondering if he had been up all night. The thought was somehow unsettling, but she couldn't put her finger on why it bothered her so much.

“I had trouble sleeping too,” he admitted. It seemed a lot of that was going around. “So where exactly are you? I can hear water.”

“Want to see?” Mia asked him.

“Sure.” He gave his usual grin and Mia stood, turning the phone’s camera around and aiming it at the waterfall.

“Oh, that’s lovely,” he said. “Looks peaceful. Take a photo of it and send it to me—I could do with a bit of peace.”

“It is, and sure,” Mia murmured, wondering what had happened to disrupt his peace. Perhaps he was homesick. “I made a little sparrow friend but he flew off,” she told him, hoping it would elicit a smile from him.

It worked; it was evident in his voice as he said softly, “Of course you did.”

Silence fell, punctuated only by the cadence of the tinkling water, and Mia knew she needed to ask him the question. She turned the camera back around.

“So, how did last night go?” She injected a light note into her voice.

“You want to know, huh?”

“Of course I do, Josh. I’m living vicariously through everyone else’s love lives, you know.” Her laughter sounded forced, but Josh didn’t seem to notice.

“It was...nice,” he said. “Sabrina’s really nice, and we had a nice time.”

OK. “You used the word ‘nice’ three times there, Josh,” Mia observed.

He grinned. “I am not as eloquent with words as you, Miss Davenport,” he said.

Oh, but you are, Mia thought. She recalled his words on the Miami beach, beneath a glittering sky...*But if you look, look really hard amongst those millions of stars, there'll be that one, the one that's for you alone*. Had he found his one?

Shit, she was morose this morning.

"Do not belittle yourself, Joshie, you have a romantic heart, remember?" Mia said mock sternly.

"Mmm-hmm," Josh said in a neutral tone. "Anyway, how are you? Have you recovered from the drenching yesterday?"

So they were changing the subject, alrighty-then. "Yes, I was fine. On digs you're at the mercy of Mother Nature, so you have to learn to roll with it. Simi and I shared a pizza and a nice Shiraz and watched *The Mummy*."

"Now that one I have seen," Josh said. His gaze appeared wistful. "Sounds like a fun night."

"Most nights are fun with Simi. He's a great guy, and so loyal. I'm so lucky that, despite the time, or distance, we take up as if we only saw each other the day before."

"You are lucky to have him in your corner," Josh said.

"He's in yours now too, you brought him food–he's easily won over." Mia's smile was genuine this time.

"Then I'm honoured." Josh smiled back.

A text notification popped up on the top of her screen. "Speak of the uncanny devil," Mia said, "he's texting me now. I'd better go, we need to see what state the site is in before we get back to it. What's your plans for today?"

"Oh, I intend to catch up on some paperwork at the apartment, and then I'll probably videochat with my mom and dad later."

"That sounds nice. Speaking of which, have you opened the art set yet?" She didn't want to push, but he seemed sad and in need of an outlet.

Their eyes met through the screen, and Mia felt wistful now

at the distance separating them.

"Ah...not really, but before you go, I wanted to show you something..." Josh vanished from the screen for a moment, then popped back into view. He held up a tiny Union Jack-printed bowtie. "It's a present for Lou."

Mia melted, belatedly realising he had deftly evaded talking about his art. "You got Lou a teeny bowtie? Oh my goodness, he is going to look *adorable*." She beamed at Josh, and a sheepish expression crossed his face.

"I thought he'd look dapper when you take him out on one of your breakfast walks."

"Aww, Joshie," Mia said softly.

"I'd better let you go," he said after a moment, and Mia nodded reluctantly.

"You're right or Simi'll be sending out a search party for me with Mrs Bennet leading the way," she said wryly.

"Uh, Mrs Bennet?"

"Oh, I never told you—I named the cat. She's Mrs Bennet now." It was Mia's turn for a sheepish look.

Josh let out a laugh. "That's perfect," he said, eyes sparkling.

"I'll speak to you soon, OK?" Mia said. "Don't forget we're meeting up with Calli and Ash next weekend."

"I won't forget," he promised. "Speak soon."

"Bye, Josh," Mia said and disconnected.

She took a minute more next to the waterfall, taking a few more pictures and sending the best image to Josh, then wended her way back through the forest and to the row of cottages.

"And what time do you call this?" Simi said, leaning against the campervan, tapping his smartwatch.

"Sorry, *Mum*. I was taking a walk." Mia smiled in amusement.

Simi rolled his eyes. "More frolicking through the forests, eh?"

She gave him an arch look. "I do not frolic," she said. "Give me five, I've got to grab my tools."

"Go ahead, I've got to wait for the others anyway," Simi said, then called after her, "Spoken to Contract Cutie this morning?"

This time Mia snort-laughed and turned around to look at her friend. "Contract Cutie? Oh, he'd love that one, I'm sure."

"*So*?"

"I have, and he's well, and his date was nice," Mia said, answering Simi's true question.

"Ugh, *nice*? Nice! How bland," Simi said. "I am very disappointed in him." He shook his head, then he brightened. "Hmm, no, actually that's good."

Mia narrowed her eyes. "Good. Why?"

Simi waved her question away. "What? Oh, here's the others now. Go and get your stuff, Lara. Chop chop."

Mia stared at him for a moment, then blew out an exasperated breath, and let herself into her cottage. She quickly fed Mrs Bennet, washed out her mug, grabbed a banana and a granola bar, along with her tool belt, before rejoining the others.

They divided into the Juice Machine and the 4 x 4 and set off to see what damage the rain had caused. Mia hoped the tarpaulin covers had done their job and protected the site.

"Ooh, this is a banger," Simi said and turned the radio up to 'Mysterious Times' and, with the sun lighting a path before them, they drove off, music blaring.

The following weekend, the professor, buoyed up by so much success, gave the whole team the weekend off, which worked out perfectly for Mia. She could drive up to Kent Saturday afternoon for the family meal with her dad, Alice, Calli and Ash—who were breaking their journey and staying with Stephen and Alice on the Friday night—and Josh who had promised to join them, and then rest the next day.

For some reason, Mia had been hesitant to contact Josh as frequently as normal. Knowing he was enjoying the company of another woman made her feel as though she would be imposing, which was ridiculous. They were *friends*, she reminded herself, so had texted him that morning with the postcode of the pub, and he had replied straightaway, telling her he was looking forward to it, which eased something within her somewhat.

Simi had driven back to Oxford to see his family, and most of the others had plans too but Connie had offered to look after Mrs Bennet. The other girl had a bit of a head cold and had decided to hole up in her cottage, so wanted the company. Mrs B had surprisingly gone without a fuss, and Mia was once again taken aback by the cat's contrary manner.

Simi gave Mia the once over before he left, approving of her long dress in silvery sage-green, with a lace band around the middle joining the top and skirt portions. Thin spaghetti straps held the dress up, and Mia paired it with silver block-heeled sandals. She left her hair loose except for one braid wrapped around the crown of her head. She kept her makeup minimal and natural except for lengthening mascara and a pinky-brown lipstick.

Mia's companion was named excitement as she made the drive up to Kent. It was one hundred times better than the ghost of betrayal that had shadowed her when she had previously left the county.

She pulled into the car park of The Rose and Thorn pub and

turned off her engine. Though slightly early, she didn't mind as it would give her time to calm herself before seeing Josh again.

Mia stepped out of the car, locked it, and made her way over to a bench set beneath a rose-covered arbour to wait. No sooner had she sat down than a black BMW pulled in and, with a sudden swoop in her stomach, she recognised it as Josh's rental car.

Mia stood, unclenching her hands from the skirts of her dress as Josh walked towards her. Dressed in fitted black trousers and a deep blue shirt, he directed a brilliant smile her way.

"Mia," he said, a soft drawl, and pulled her into his arms. She closed her eyes, feeling the bonds of their friendship knit back together.

"Hi, Josh," she said, smiling at him as he let her go. "You found the place with no problems, then?"

"Sure did," he said. "I'm getting used to driving around England—but the country lanes are a bit hairy." He laughed.

Mia let out a giggle and Josh's eyes momentarily lingered on her mouth.

"There's my girl."

Mia turned away from the intensity in Josh's gaze to see Stephen and Alice walking towards them. She wasted no time in slipping into his familiar hug. "Hi, Dad."

He let her go and shook Josh's hand. "Josh, a pleasure to see you again."

"Likewise, sir," Josh said, then smiled at Alice. "Lovely to see you too, Mrs Davenport."

"And you, Josh, and Mia—you are looking beautiful."

"Hi, Alice," Mia said and hugged her stepmother.

"Calli and Ash are behind us. Calli will probably blame the

Satnav but you know...” Stephen trailed off, an amused twitch to his lips, the insinuation clear. Calli’s tardiness was legendary. “But I better go inside and give our names so we don’t lose our reservation—we’re booked in the garden area, it’s lovely out there,” he carried on.

“OK, Dad—and don’t forget it’s my treat today,” Mia reminded him.

Stephen gave her a mock stern glare. “Oh, all right, Mouse, but just this time.”

Mia blew him a kiss as he headed inside with Alice.

“I never asked you before—why does your dad call you Mouse?” Josh asked.

Mia smiled. “It’s a cute story, but my dad probably wouldn’t agree. It involved me vanishing on him when we were treasure-hunting one day.”

Josh raised an eyebrow. “Yeah, I can imagine he wouldn’t find that cute—probably terrifying in reality. So what happened?”

“We were in a field and I took off at a run aiming for a cluster of trees, thinking they were a portal to fairyland” – she gave Josh a side-eyed sheepish look – “but when Dad got there, I’d vanished. It was only a few minutes, but apparently, that was enough to knock five years off Dad’s life. But, anyway, I popped up from a hole beneath the exposed roots of one of the trees. Probably an old badger’s sett, but I was convinced I had made a magical discovery—especially when a little fieldmouse ran up my arm.” Mia giggled at the memory. “And from that day on I became Mouse...and that was also the day I made my first true find—a Roman coin, and the rest is history.”

She finished her tale to find Josh staring at her, his eyes impossibly blue. “Now, I am convinced, more than ever, that you are *definitely* a fairytale princess."

"I'm not helping my cause am I?" she said, but then shrugged with an easy smile. "It's not a bad thing to be."

They smiled at each other.

Josh opened his mouth to say something but was interrupted by an excited squeal from across the car park.

"Mia!!!"

Mia turned as Calli emerged from a silver rental car, and then she was running to meet her halfway.

The two cousins clutched at each other, laughing and crying.

"There she is: Mrs Sharma. God, Cal, you look beautiful." Mia pulled back and searched her cousin's face. Her thick golden-brown curls had been secured on one side revealing a silver and crystal cuff earring twinned with a long dangling drop. Her cheeks were bronzed and her lips coated in a red lipstick that matched the red of her long cotton maxi dress.

"You're a fine one to talk! *Look* at you...you're like a glowing goddess in that getup, with your hair all loose and flowy, and that dress is stunning." Calli linked arms with Mia and spoke to Josh who was now chatting with Ash. "Isn't she glowing?"

Mia resisted the urge to elbow her cousin, knowing Calli couldn't help herself.

Josh smiled. "She sure is...but I'd expect nothing less from a storybook princess," he said, and Calli looked from one to the other; brow furrowed.

"Am I missing something?" she said.

Mia patted her on the arm. "Only a joke, Cal," she said and moved over to give Ash a hug after he'd finished greeting Josh. "Hi, Ash, hope you had a good honeymoon."

"It was great," he said.

"It was *perfect*," Calli corrected with a contented sigh.

"Come on, Mi, let me show you the photos." She dragged Mia towards the pub and Mia mouthed, "Help," over her shoulder to Josh and Ash.

They found Stephen and Alice in the outside eating area, and joined them at the oval table. Mia consented to ten minutes of scrolling through Calli's photo gallery while everyone else chatted and perused the menus.

"That's enough now, Cal," Ash said when the waitress came over to take their order, and Mia caught Josh's eye when she sat back slightly shell-shocked. An amused glint sparkled in his eye, but Mia would have the last laugh, knowing Calli would corner him at some point and make him look at all the images too.

"So, Josh, how's London been treating you?" Stephen asked once they were all cutting into their steaks.

"I'm enjoying my time here. The work's fulfilling, I've been sightseeing with a colleague and out to dinner a few times," he said, and Mia's small bite of sirloin turned to dust in her mouth. She took a sip of water and forced down the ashes of her sudden, and completely unexpected, reaction.

"Oh?" Calli said, a frown on her face, which she aimed at Ash, who shrugged in return. Was Josh keeping his deepening friendship incredibly close to his chest? Or did Calli and Ash already know and were surprised he was talking about it?

"Yes, remember—she's mine and Ash's London contact," Josh said to Calli. "I've become quite close with her, and with our boss too."

Calli flicked Mia a glance, perhaps gauging her reaction, and Mia gave her an unconcerned smile in return. "I think it's great you're having such a good time, and everyone's been so welcoming to you," Mia told Josh, and Calli's brows raised.

"You do?" Josh asked, his piece of steak halfway to his

mouth.

"Of course, having a good team around you is everything," she said, then resolutely returned to her own meal.

"Too true," Stephen said.

They carried on with small talk, enjoying the meal, with Mia ignoring Calli's pointed looks, knowing her cousin was dying to know all the details of all of the minutiae she may have missed out on.

"Well, I hate to love you and leave you all before dessert, but Alice and I must be getting back. Alice needs to visit her mum in the nursing home tonight," Stephen said, and stood, helping Alice up. Calli followed suit and gave him a huge hug.

"So good to see you, Uncle Steph, and thanks, both, for putting us up last night," she said, smiling at Alice.

"Always a pleasure, Calli." He turned to Ash and held out his hand. "Enjoy married life," he said with a smile.

"Thank you, sir."

Mia joined them, and after she had pressed a kiss to Alice's cheek, Stephen enfolded her into his arms. "Keep me posted on your plans, Mouse, but come and see us before you fly off again."

"I will. Love you, Dad."

"Love you more," he said. He let her go to shake Josh's hand.

"Josh, enjoy the rest of your stay in London. And you are always welcome to stay any time too." Mia hid her groan. *One matchmaker in the family was more than enough*, she thought wryly, but with some affection.

Josh smiled. "Thank you, sir, appreciate the offer of hospitality."

Stephen nodded, his blue-green eyes twinkling, then pressed a final kiss to Mia's cheek, and moved away with Alice, who waved a goodbye to them all.

Mia, Josh, Calli and Ash resumed their seats. "That was delicious," Ash said and leant back in the wooden chair, and placed his hands over his stomach.

Calli gave him a sideways look. "No room for dessert?" she teased.

He straightened. "Oh, I don't know about that. There's always room for dessert."

Mia raised her wine glass and toasted to that. She looked around in contentment at her cousin and friends, but the pleasant feeling disappeared when Calli's face suddenly fell and she went rigid in her seat.

"Mia—don't," she said but it was too late, Mia had already turned to see what her cousin was looking at.

She almost dropped her wine glass in shock as Henry weaved through the flower planters towards them. A sheen of cold sweat covered her body; her fight-or-flight response kicking in. Mia stood, fully ready to flee before it was too late.

Henry glanced up and their eyes met. *Shit*, Mia thought and froze—unable to separate the image of him before her from the horrific final one in her memories.

"Mia, darling!" Henry said in surprise. "Fancy seeing you here. But I'm so glad I bumped into you. I've been trying to get an invite to you and your dad has been strangely unforthcoming with your address." He reached inside the pocket of his pristine grey suit jacket and pulled out a stack of thick cream-coloured cards. He pressed one into Mia's hand.

The arrogant tone was enough to un-freeze Mia, but only so she could drop her gaze and suck in a shuddering breath, the sessions with Dr Carroll unravelling in an instant.

"Mia is not *your* darling, Henry," Calli said angrily.

"She was once," Henry carried on in silky tones, completely unconcerned, and Mia flinched away as he fleetingly settled a hand on her bare arm. "Calli, always a pleasure to see you again," he added, sounding anything but pleased to see her.

Mia sensed Josh standing and moving beside her and she lifted her gaze to look at him. "Don't," she said to him, "he isn't worth it."

"And who's this? Your new boyfriend? Didn't take you long to move on." Henry gave a tight, yet white-toothed, smile. "Why don't you bring him as your plus one to the wedding. Nadia would love to see you again. She misses you."

Mia's eyes widened at the audacity, as Josh uttered, "You sonofabitch."

Henry laughed. "You're welcome to her, Yank. Although, Mia, I have to say how lovely you are looking. Radiant, in fact." She knew he was only saying that to garner a reaction, he had never approved of her wearing her hair in the braided style, or wearing such whimsical clothing.

But Mia had frozen again, unable to say anything—*why*

couldn't she say anything?—but Calli had no such qualms. "Piss off, Henry," she said sweetly.

Henry curled his lip, before letting out a derisive laugh. "So well-mannered," he said and this time Ash stood too, looking as angry as Josh. "Oh, don't worry, I'm going. I have networking to do." He gave Mia a long look, and she flushed again in embarrassment before he strode away.

Mia slumped, her heart beating out of her chest, and let the invite flutter onto the wooden table.

"Mia—" Calli began, but Mia shook her head.

"I need air," she said, despite them being seated in the outdoor eating area. She turned on her heel and hurried away, through the planters, and into the secluded garden area beyond.

Josh followed her. "Mia," he said, turning her to face him, "you can't let that douchebag win! Don't give him the power."

"What do you want me to *do*, Josh? When I looked at him, I was back in that moment when I caught them. And it hurts. It bloody hurts!" She pressed a fisted hand to her chest, trying desperately to stay the galloping of her heart.

Josh scrubbed a hand over his face. "I *know* it does. But you can't let him continue to influence your life, Mia. As you said, he's not worth it. So don't let him be the cause of you missing out on so much happiness. I can see you retreating back into yourself." Emotion filled his voice. "Stop hiding away. Stop hiding your feelings."

Mia, hurt, shocked, and backed into a corner, lashed out. "Well, you're a fine one to talk, Josh. I don't see *you* out here expressing your feelings or making any commitments. You hide your true passions away, too scared to face them!"

They stared at each other, almost toe-to-toe, chests heaving. Josh searched her face, his features rearranging themselves into an attitude of pain. "Oh, Mia, you don't know anything. How can you be so blind?" he said almost bitterly. "As it happens I'm... I'm so in love with someone who has absolutely no idea. Don't talk to me about *commitment* or passion."

Mia took a physical step back in shock, the force of his words hitting her like a jolt to the heart. What? "You are? But...*who*?" she said, her suddenly exposed heart constricting painfully. Josh was in *love*, and he never told her about it. That fact hurt so much more than the encounter with Henry, she realised in devastation. What had happened with her ex was inconsequential now.

Relegated to the past.

Josh stared at her for one long searching moment. The fight seemed to drain out of him. "Figure it out, Mia," he said finally, wearily. "Figure it out and let me know when you do. Thanks for dinner." He turned away from her and started walking towards the car park.

"Josh," she called after him, but he kept going. "Josh!" Mia stared after her friend until he disappeared from sight. *What just happened*?

"Are you OK?" Calli joined her and put an arm around her waist.

Mia shook her head, but her mind wasn't on the scene with Henry but what had just occurred with Josh. That was all that mattered now. "Do *you* know who Josh is in love with?" she asked quietly, looking at her cousin, but Calli wouldn't meet her gaze. Did everyone know but her?

"It's not my place to say," Calli said in a defensive tone, exchanging a look with Ash who had come up beside them, a frozen expression on his face.

"Right. Fine," Mia said and blew out a breath.

Calli gave her a squeeze. "You'll figure it out," she told Mia, and Mia hid her wince. Why did everyone keep saying that, and why did she feel as though her heart had been excavated to its foundations? "Will you be all right? I hate leaving you like this but we have to get the rental back and catch our flight."

Mia forced a smile. "Of course I will." *Wasn't she always*? "I have to get back to the cottage and type up my dig notes anyway," she said as an excuse so Calli would feel all right about leaving her.

Calli gave her a scrutinising look. "You want me to find the weasel and shove that invite up his—"

"Cal," Ash interjected before she could finish the tempting offer.

"Thanks but no," Mia said, and took a deep breath. "I'll deal with it myself."

Admiration, twinned with respect, bloomed in Calli's eyes. "OK, then," she said. "I'll video call you later when we land."

Mia pulled Calli in for a hug. "All right, have a safe flight," she said before hugging Ash.

"Take care, Mia," Ash said, his eyes full of concern. "Don't let that confrontation dent your spirit OK?"

"I'll be fine," she assured them, and they headed towards the car park, Calli throwing a concerned look and a small wave over her shoulder.

When they had gone, Mia took a determined breath and returned to their table to collect the invite where it still sat; mocking her. She headed inside to take care of the bill—now sans dessert, thanks to Henry's rude interruption—searching for Henry as she went. He was at the bar, talking with two other similarly dressed men, and deduced they were his networking opportunities.

Mia paid the bill, then, with decided steps, strode over to Henry; a fire blazing within her. "Henry, a word," she said, and his face turned to one of angry impatience; she would never have dared to interrupt a business meeting of his like that before. "Or, we can do it here." She smiled sweetly, imitating Calli.

"Fine. Gentlemen, if you would excuse me a moment?"

The men regarded Mia with curious expressions but waved Henry on, so Mia led Henry out to the quiet garden area.

"Well?" Henry snapped, all pretence at his earlier genial nature completely evaporated, now he no longer had an audience.

Mia thought of what Josh had said, how she was still allowing Henry to have power over her. Well, no more. "I just wanted to say, I've put it all behind me. It's ancient history—and you know that's my favourite kind." She gave a whip-fast smile. "And I want to wish you and Nadia all the best. *Truly*" – she leant in close, her voice sweet, and mock friendly – "after all, I think you are going to need it. Because you are *both* marrying people who think cheating is perfectly acceptable." Henry's face dropped comically and, with a final smile of satisfaction, Mia ripped the invite in two, and placed it in her ex's hand, then patted him on the shoulder. "Goodbye, Henry," she said and sauntered away—with him spluttering after her—a wide smile on her face.

Mia unlocked her car, and sat in the driver's seat, suddenly shaking all over. Dropping her head in her hands, she let the emotions bubble to the surface this time. Let them come, experienced them all—each painful stab, and then allowed them to drift away. She was free of the ghost of Henry and Nadia's betrayal. It had power over her no longer.

Straightening up, she took a fortifying breath, and sat back against the seat for a moment. She'd wait until she was completely calm before driving back to the cottage. As Mia sat there waiting and steadying herself, her earlier conversation with Josh replayed in her mind like a movie scene. The fact that her best friend was *in love,* and she had no idea, unlocked something uncomfortable within her. How did she feel about that? She wanted Josh to be happy, *of course* she did, but something niggled at her. Something she couldn't quite put her finger on. She closed her eyes.

Figure it out, Mia...

Images burst through her mind in a kaleidoscope of memories. Josh's smiling face through the video screen on card night, winking at her when he won; him running with her, allowing her the freedom to give her banked emotions an outlet; listening and giving her great advice; his *amazing* hugs; his familiar, comforting scent; lying in his arms on the beach in Miami; of his face nuzzled into her neck as he held her tight at Calli and Ash's wedding...*making it look believable...*

The picture was so vivid that Mia could almost feel it. A frisson hummed along her neck as if the memory created a visceral caress upon her skin. Threads started to pull together, one by one until her eyes shot open. "Oh...my...god," she breathed out slowly. Did he mean...? She couldn't even finish the thought. It was too amazing, too wonderful, too *terrifying* to acknowledge, yet she couldn't deny it. Her hands shook as she fumbled with her phone. Mia hesitated over his name in her call list; her finger a trembling, hovering digit.

No.

Mia set the phone down and sucked in a breath, waiting until the trembling stopped, which took a few deep inhales. She inserted the key into the ignition. This revelation needed to be discussed in person, not via the phone. She needed to look into his eyes when she asked him if what she suspected was true. If what Mia, herself, had hidden for so long, and now suddenly *felt* in every fibre of her being, was true.

Mia picked up her phone again and scrolled through to Josh's rental apartment's address. After entering the postcode into her satnav app, she set off—her heart beating out of her chest in anticipation—to discover the truth.

The hour-long drive to Josh's apartment went by quickly as Mia focused on the journey and pushed away all and any other thoughts. She couldn't think about what would happen when she arrived at Josh's apartment, she needed to stay focused on the road and concentrate on getting there safely.

Finally, Mia pulled into the small car park outside Josh's apartment building and parked between Josh's black rental car, and a red convertible. Without taking the time to dissect whether this was the right course of action, she stepped out of her own car, locked it, and headed over to the outer door. As she approached, a man left the building and held the door open for her so she didn't have to press the intercom button. It was a relief, because if she heard Josh's voice, she might chicken out and turn tail and flee.

Mia made her way up the stairs to the next floor where she assumed Josh's apartment, 1A, to be.

She took a deep breath and pressed the doorbell. She stepped back in surprise when a woman's throaty voice said from behind the door, "I'll get it. I ordered us some dessert."

Oh god, Mia thought and checked the door number again. Definitely 1A. Before she could turn away, the door opened and a gorgeous brunette with deep-set chocolate brown eyes stood in the doorway. She leant against the doorframe, her left hand resting on it.

"Oh, you're not the delivery man," she said with a velvety laugh.

But Mia could only take in the enormous diamond ring on the finger of the woman's left hand. Mia was brought out of her staring gaze as Josh's voice filtered through from the interior of the apartment.

"Sab, come on. Stop chatting with the delivery guy, I've got the champagne open!"

Mia backed up in panic. She had gotten it terribly, horribly wrong. The woman's amused gaze turned to one of concern.

"I'm sorry," Mia gasped out, "wrong address." And she fled, clattering down the stairs in her heeled sandals, not stopping until she had let herself out, unlocked her car and thrown herself into her seat. She buckled her seatbelt and pulled out of the car park and into the quiet London street's traffic.

Oh god, oh god, oh god, she thought over and over until she found an empty spot further along the street and pulled in again. What had she been *thinking*? Mia smacked a hand against her head. She had jumped to a conclusion. She knew better than that. Professor Deacon was constantly telling her to gather the facts, not assumptions.

Sab?—*Sabrina?* Josh's dinner date had been a Sabrina from his office; the one he had spent months getting to know online, and now in person. That woman at his apartment, that 'Sab', must be her. *Oh god.* Perhaps...perhaps, things had progressed quicker and deeper and Josh hadn't wanted to say, and then...had she goaded him into making a commitment with this Sab? *I don't see you out here expressing your feelings or making any commitments!* But why wouldn't he have confided in her? Mia wanted him to be happy, surely he knew that. Just because she'd been broken-hearted didn't mean he had to walk on eggshells around her.

Mia put her own acute misery aside in her desire to try and salvage what was left of her and Josh's friendship. She *couldn't* lose him. It would break her. If it continued as only friendship, she would accept it. She would. He was far too important to her to lose him entirely.

She grabbed her phone, absentmindedly noticing it was now on low battery, and typed in a hasty message:

Josh, I'm sorry we argued. I figured it out. I wish you and Sabrina all the happiness in the world. You deserve it.

Mia added the emoji of two champagne glasses clinking together for good measure. She sent it, then, as an afterthought—because she needed him to believe she was all right—sent another:

You were right, it's time I start living my life again. I'll get Calli to put one of those dating apps on my phone when I get back to New York. Speak to you soon, M x

She sat immobile for a moment before a sudden sob burst out of her, surprising her. Why was she *crying*? Mia didn't want to admit to herself why, didn't want to admit that now she'd opened her eyes and her heart she'd hoped for a different outcome. But that was unfair of her. Josh had no idea she thought he had meant someone else entirely. Someone who had foolishly buried her heart, thinking it was safe that way. *Oh god*, what a fallacy.

Mia let the tears come until they numbed her.

Only then did she start the car again and head for the sanctuary of the cottage, fully intending to comfort-watch *Pride & Prejudice*, and eat a whole tub of lemon sorbet...while crying into Josh's hoodie and wrapping herself up in his scent.

Mia awoke to a rapid knocking on the front door, and the sound of rain coming through the open patio doors of her tiny cottage. She sat up in confusion. Her laptop had frozen on the rain-washed 'most ardently' scene of *Pride & Prejudice*. Mocking her.

The knocking came again. "Mia!"

Recognising Josh's voice, Mia got up. Pushing her hair—still slightly damp from the hot shower she had taken when she'd got home—over her shoulder, she padded across the room in her socks to unlock the door. She stared in surprise at Josh, at the way his black curls hung damply over his brow, enhancing the intense look in his piercing blue eyes.

"Josh?" She frowned; her heart beginning to thump painfully in her chest. "What are you doing here?"

"Can I come in?" he asked in return, gesturing to the rain.

Mia pulled the cottage door wider. "Oh—of course, sorry."

They stood in silence for a moment in the small entryway, until Mia mobilised herself enough to go and get Josh a towel from the laundry cupboard. She handed it over to him.

"Thanks," he said and rubbed his hair dry. When he had finished, he took in the garment around her shoulders, and his eyes shuttered.

Mia pulled the hoodie closer around herself, as though it was a piece of armour protecting her heart. She couldn't understand why he was *there* and not celebrating with Sabrina. So she asked again, "Why are you here?"

His lips twisted in a wry smile. "You can hardly send me those cryptic texts, and turn your phone off. You didn't even give me a chance to reply."

"But I didn't turn my phone off." Mia, puzzled, went to pick up her phone from the kitchen counter. She stared at the blank screen. "Oh, it died," she added apologetically. "But that still doesn't explain why you are here, and not back at your apartment with..." she trailed off, not wanting to say it out loud.

Josh searched her face for a long moment. "I think there's been a misunderstanding," he said gently.

Mia swallowed hard and gestured over to the sofa, and he walked across the room and took a seat. His eyes flicked to the laptop screen, and then to the half-eaten tub of lemon sorbet, and Mia hurried across to close the revealing depth-of-her-frazzled-emotions film down, leaving the laptop open on the home screen.

She sat on the other end of the sofa and they faced each other.

"Look, I'm so sorry about what I said to you earlier, Mia. I had no right, but I couldn't bear to see the defeated look on your face when you were confronted with that...*weasel*," Josh said, leaning towards her slightly. "Or as Calli would rightly say; that fucking idiot."

Mia sighed. "No, Josh, you were absolutely right. I *had* been letting him win. Until I faced him again I hadn't comprehended how much power I had been continuing to let him wield over me. He was still orchestrating my every move from afar." She gave a grim smile. "But don't worry—I had my say. He was still there when I went to leave."

"He was? What did you tell him?" Josh's blue eyes lit with intrigue.

"That I wished him and Nadia all the best—after all, they're both marrying people who believe cheating is OK. I walked away with my head held high; freer and lighter than I have ever experienced before. It was the final piece I needed to heal myself." Though what Mia had discovered at Josh's apartment had knocked her confidence, she had to believe, that, ultimately, she *would* be all right. She had been buried in a pit of quicksand for far too long, and had pulled herself out of it. Surely, she could do it again? She needed Josh in her life, even if it was only as her best friend, whatever happened.

"Nicely put, they'll always have suspicions about each other," Josh said with a dangerous smile, then paused before adding lightly, "So...you're ready to start dating again?"

Mia winced when she thought of the hasty second text she had sent to him. "Well, to be honest, I think I'll hold back on using a dating app just yet, but yes, it's time to move on with my life and see what happens naturally. I sat in my car and came to a few realisations." She took a deep breath and then forged on without thinking, rambling in her sudden nervousness around him. "I thought about what you said, and things started making sense, and I *thought* I had figured out who you meant, so I decided to go to your apartment and speak to you face-to-face about it."

"You came to my apartment?" Josh sat back against the

cushions, his face a picture of thought, and—curiously—*hope*?

Mia hesitated, realising she had revealed far more than she'd intended, then said, "Um—yes. Sabrina answered sporting a beautiful diamond ring and I heard you calling her back saying you'd opened the champagne."

"That was *you* at the door. Now it all makes sense," Josh said, almost to himself.

"I'm sorry for intruding into your private life. I realised I was interrupting something important, so told her I had the wrong address. I sent you the message because I want you to be happy, Josh. You so deserve it."

Josh stared at her, searching her face for one long breathless moment. "You want me to be happy with Sabrina? I think Berto will have something to say about that," he said finally, with a small smile.

"I truly do—wait, *what*? Who's Berto?"

Josh leant forward again, so close she could smell his rain-washed but still familiar scent. "Roberto Silva; Sab's fiancé. Our boss."

"Her what?" Mia blinked at him in confusion. "But...but you had a *date* with her, you were saying at the dinner how well you were getting on with her...she was at your *apartment*." Mia put her hands in her face, knowing she had jumped to conclusions *yet again*, and that—quite possibly—she might still have a bit of residual trauma left to deal with.

Josh gently pulled her hands away from her face, and rubbed one thumb over the back of her hand. "We did go on one date—one excruciatingly awkward date, because we were *both* in love with other people, and thought it would never happen with them. Sab and I quickly concluded that we should carry on as friends and colleagues. Nothing happened between us. If you'd stayed, you would have met Berto, he was at my apartment too; Sabrina finally plucked up the courage to tell him how she felt about him, which he had been waiting to hear, hence the ring. They came over after I arrived home to share their good news."

Mia stared at Josh, and that tiny kernel of hope began to blossom again. The one that had begun in her car as she had run through the entirety of their relationship in vivid detail. "So you are *not* engaged?" She heard that hope in the breathless tone of her voice.

Josh shook his head, his face suddenly serious. "My heart is, and always will be—"

"You watched *Sense and Sensibility*!" Mia broke in, her heart dancing in her chest.

Josh smiled. "Someone incredibly special recommended it."

Mia let out a laugh, of relief, of anticipation—she knew not which it was, probably a mixture of both, and their eyes met and held, something unfurling between them. Reaching out to close the gap.

"And if you had stayed you would have also seen this..." Josh pulled out his phone and showed her an image on the screen. It was a piece of artwork, hanging on the wall of what Mia supposed to be Josh's rental living room. She let out a gasp, recognising the waterfall; it exactly matched the one she had sat at when she'd gone for a walk and needed a time of reflection, the one she had sent a picture of to Josh. But it was the woman, sitting beside it, with her long blonde hair loose in waves around her face; her blue-green eyes wide and thoughtful, and the various array of animals around her feet, which grabbed her attention. With the long green warrior gown, and twisted circlet atop her head, the artist had captured her, and her essence, perfectly. As if he knew her very soul; her heart.

"You painted this?" Mia asked, tears thickening her voice.

Josh nodded. "You gave me the courage, Mia, and the inspiration to try and finish a painting. And this was the result." He met her eyes. "It's the best piece I have ever created."

Well, hell. "You have a real gift," she managed, overcome. Mia fell silent, staring at the picture, and everything seemed to fall into place with an audible click in her heart.

"So, *why* did you come to my apartment in the first place, Mia? What did you want to speak to me about?" Josh asked softly, slotting his phone back in his pocket, and breaking the silence.

Mia looked away, heat staining her cheeks. Now it was her turn for candour. "I thought I had figured out who you were talking about, and I realised you were right; I had been hiding my feelings. Hiding how I felt about..." she broke off, her heart beating faster.

"Felt about...?"

Mia sensed Josh moving closer, and suddenly she couldn't breathe. She leapt up and headed over to the kitchen counter to grab a glass and an unopened bottle of white wine, intent on filling the glass to the brim and inhaling it.

Josh followed quietly and his hand covered hers over the bottle. "No," he murmured, "we're doing this sober."

Mia let go of the bottle, and slowly turned to look up at him. "Doing what?" she asked, her voice a mere whisper.

Josh stared down at her, and moved his hands to gently frame her face. "This," he said.

And Mia knew. Her wonderful assumption about them was actually fact. The cobwebs of time blew away, revealing what was truly there, what had always been there, but she had been too blind—too afraid—to see. She was already rising up eagerly to her tiptoes as he bent down towards her. Their lips brushed tentatively at first, an electric skimming of sensation, before, as one, they deepened the kiss in a passionate dance of discovery and revelation, one that pulled them deep beneath the mantle of physical knowing. As though it had been ordained from the very first moment.

Mia pulled back, and breathlessly gazed up at Josh in a wide-eyed caress. The action had spoken volumes far beyond her imagining, but she needed—no—she longed for, the certainty of the words. "So...so this means?"

"This means, my darlin', Mia-mine," Josh said with a staggered look, "that you have bewitched me body and soul, and I love you. I have always loved you."

"Oh, Josh, *my Josh*," Mia murmured back, with a reminiscent smile, moved beyond measure. "I think—no, I *know*, I've always loved you too, but was too afraid to take the chance in case I lost you. I couldn't bear to lose you." She pressed a tremulous kiss to his lips. "So thank you for being my friend first."

Josh dropped his forehead to hers. "If that was all I could ever be, then it would have been an honour, but I had hope; sometimes I thought you felt it too. I mean how could you lie in my arms on that beach bed in Miami—and fit so perfectly—and not feel it too?" Mia nodded, a flush staining her cheeks at the memory of the magical night on the Miami beach. The night when she had indeed felt something powerful too; the first stirrings of a magnitude so terrifyingly wonderful, but had buried it before it had even taken breath. Josh continued softly, "For me, it was love at first sight, or first hug" – he smiled tenderly – "and I was always hopeful you'd catch up. Desperate for you to open your eyes and see what had always been in front of you."

"You hid it very well," Mia said. "But when you pulled me into your arms and said, '*making it look believable*', the night of Calli and Ash's wedding, in that moment, I imagined it *was* real. Craved for it, in truth."

"It was real for me," Josh stated. "It has *always* been real for me."

"When you nestled your face into my neck, it was real for me too," Mia admitted, to herself, to him, and Josh pulled back, showing her the awareness stealing into his eyes.

"It was?" He slowly lowered his face into her neck. "Like this?"

"Mmm-hmm," Mia said, then let out a noise of appreciation as his lips grazed her skin in a fiery trail of desire.

He lifted her up by her hips, his fingertips anchoring her, and set her onto the edge of the counter and they were silent for a few long minutes as they continued to discover each other with deep kisses and lingering caresses.

Mia clung to him as if her future depended on it. She thought she had lost him, and to find him, here, in her arms, was the greatest discovery of all, and more than she could ever have dreamed.

They eased slowly apart, eyes heavy on each other, when Mia's laptop began to ring. "That'll be Calli. I better answer it; she was worried about me."

Josh carefully set Mia back on her feet before threading his fingers through hers and leading her back over to the sofa. "Then we'd better answer it." He gave her a slow, loving smile as they both sat down side-by-side.

Mia smiled dazedly back, hardly able to believe what was happening. She leant forward to answer the video call, then sat back against Josh, and he pulled her close to him. Calli's face appeared on the screen. Her eyes flicked comically from Mia to Josh and then back again, before widening. "Ash, get in here!" she yelled, her gaze never leaving Mia's smiling face.

Ash sat down beside Calli and studied them through the screen. "It's about time," he said deadpan, not looking at all surprised, a smile starting on his face.

Calli began smiling too. "See, Mia. You figured it out," she said happily, then gave a slow-but-pointed wink, and Mia knew exactly what her cousin was getting at. Calli had been trying to get Mia and Josh together from the very beginning and, Mia acknowledged wryly, it appeared she hadn't been late in concluding that they did indeed belong together. As she had said once; she was *never* wrong.

Mia rolled her eyes in affection. "I see completely," she said softly.

Calli's eyes filled, and she pressed her hands up to her mouth in a gesture of composing herself. "I'll call you back later," she said after a few moments, meaning, 'I want to hear *all* the details'.

Josh leant forward. "*Much* later, Cal," he said, and Calli grinned in appreciation. Josh lowered the lid of the laptop and turned to Mia. "Now, where were we?"

Mia slowly pulled off the hoodie Josh had given to her, and said huskily, "Well, for a start, I won't be needing this anymore." She moved back into Josh's arms. "Now I've got the real thing."

Josh ran a hand through her hair as the rain continued to patter rhythmically outside the open patio doors. He smiled slowly. "Yes, ma'am," he murmured, and Mia's breath hitched, as heat pooled low in her stomach. "Real, true, eternal." He punctuated each word with a lingering kiss.

Mia blinked back happy tears. "Come on," she said finally, her voice a near-whisper, "the rain sounds even better from my room." She stood and held out her hand.

Josh's blue eyes lit with longing, and he rose to gently take her hand and link his fingers through hers. He pulled her hand up to his mouth and kissed it reverently. "Are you certain?"

Mia moved their combined hands until they pressed over her heart. "Feel that?" Josh nodded. "You were always in there, quietly helping it heal, and now it beats for you. For us." His eyes blazed aquamarine with emotion.

"Then show me the way, Mia-mine," he said thickly.

And Mia did just that. She pulled him through the door into the small bedroom, and the sound of the rain beating on the sloped roof above leant a magical, musical cadence to the atmosphere, almost like the distant drums of an otherworldly parade in honour of their spirited warrior queen.

Without awkwardness, or hesitation, Mia stepped into Josh's embrace—into her future—and finally laid the ghosts of her past to rest. She had secured the hand she could lay her whole heart in, and knew it was perfectly safe, as it moved in rhythm to its twin.

Mia opened her eyes and sat up with a stretch. She stared around the ornately decorated room, and clutched the silky sheet to her bare body. Josh had surprised her by booking a room at the fancy Meryton Manor in Wiltshire when they had returned to the UK for Sabrina and Roberto's wedding, and to also attend the opening of Professor Deacon's Boudicca exhibition at the British Museum.

She recalled the phone call she had shared with Calli the evening before and how her cousin had a wonderful excuse for being late this time. Mia was the first person Calli had told after Ash, and Mia couldn't wait to meet the reason in approximately nine months. Mia had moved in with Josh, after they had returned to New York, to give the newlyweds some privacy, and Mia loved her new life in the vibrant city, now working full-time as the professor's assistant while studying for her doctorate. To top it off, Simi had transferred over from Oxford and worked alongside Mia in the archaeology department. Karaoke nights had never sounded better, and he was a mean card-sharp too, totally dominating Thursday night card night. Even Mrs Bennet—who thoroughly approved of Josh—had gotten her happy-ever-after and was living her best life with Mia's dad and Alice.

But the real cherry on top of an already full cake was that Josh had talked with his dad when Mia had accompanied Josh to his parents' ranch. Following that heart-to-heart, when Josh's parents had subsequently visited Josh and Mia in New York his dad had—after seeing Josh's obvious talent for himself—commissioned him to paint scenes of the ranch; now proudly hung up in the ranch's living area, and study. Mia, having met Mr Cavanaugh now numerous times, knew that the display spoke more than words ever could, and had finally healed Josh's secret wounds.

All coherent thought left Mia when Josh came out of the bathroom, a thick white towel hooked around his hips. Drops of moisture clung to his chest, and to the curls of his floppy black hair. Mia's mouth dried up, and she longed to run her fingers through the damp tendrils, and scatter droplets like crystals.

"Good morning," he said, his lips moving into a smile when he caught her looking at him. "Sleep well?"

Mia crooked a finger at him and he walked slowly over to join her on the bed. "Extraordinarily well," she murmured and pressed a kiss to his lips as he leant over her. She lay back against the pillows bringing him with her.

Josh pulled back from the deepening kiss and looked at her regretfully. "Much as I would *really* love to continue this. There's somewhere we have to be."

Mia blinked up at him. "Oh?"

Josh grinned. "I think you're going to love it," he told her.

"I love you." She grinned back.

Nervousness entered Josh's eyes, and that intrigued her even more. "Shower, get dressed," he said, and helped her up. He groaned as he took in her naked form. "Rain-check on continuing this?" he said and Mia let out a delighted laugh.

"Absolutely," she agreed and walked towards the bathroom.

"I'll get room service sent up," he called after her. "I'm dying for a cup of 'proper' tea."

Mia turned around with a thrilled smirk. "See, I knew you'd become a convert."

He blew her a kiss as she vanished around the bathroom door.

After a quick shower, Mia dressed in a flowery, floaty maxi dress with halter neck in hues of pastel purple, blue and pink, and left half her waist-length hair down, while pulling the top half up into a high ponytail. She added purple leather sandals, and lavender tassel earrings to finish the look.

Josh let out a long whistle when she emerged. He walked slowly over to her and took her hand. "You look beautiful," he said.

"And you, sir, look most dashing," she said in return with a smile. He was dressed in beige chinos, and a loose pale blue shirt which enhanced the aquamarine of his eyes.

They ate a quick breakfast, before Mia, being terribly curious about what Josh had planned for them, asked, "Shall we go?"

Josh visibly swallowed and linked his fingers through hers, pulling her up from the table. "It would be my pleasure," he said.

They drove a short distance away in their rental car, and Mia sat up straighter when they passed through gates signposted, 'Stourhead'. She flicked an excited glance at Josh. "Oh my god. Is this what I think it is?"

"It might be." He smiled as he parked the car. They exited

the vehicle, with Mia growing more excited by the minute. She bounced on the cork heels of her sandals as Josh paid for the entry tickets.

"We'll join a tour later," he said, "but there's somewhere I think you'd like to see first?"

"You know me so well," Mia said happily and linked her arm through his. He pressed a kiss to the top of her head and murmured back, "I hope so."

They climbed up a hill and Mia held one hand to her chest in awe as 'Apollo's Temple' came into view. She stopped and eagerly took in the location of her favourite scene from *Pride & Prejudice* when rain-soaked Lizzy and Darcy had their most tension-filled encounter.

Mia sensed Josh's eyes on her and she turned to lean up and press a kiss to his lips. "Thank you," she said.

"Let's get closer," he replied, his voice husky, and together they approached the temple.

Josh released Mia to let her go on ahead and she walked slowly around the stone structure, running her hand along the wall. She revelled in the fact that it was entirely deserted and they could enjoy the place all to themselves. She leant against the wall, as Lizzy had done, and turned to speak to Josh.

Her eyes widened as she took him in, knelt on one knee before her, a ring in his outstretched hand.

Mia pushed off from the wall with a soft gasp, but not in frightened surprise as Lizzy had done, but in a burst of joy.

"Marry me, Mia-mine. Belong to me, as I have always belonged to you."

"Josh, oh, Josh." Mia's eyes filled with tears as she joined him. "Yes, a thousand times yes!" she exclaimed and he erupted to lift her up into his arms, pressing fervent kisses along her face and neck.

Minutes later, Josh set her back on her feet and took her left hand reverently in his. He placed the ring on her third finger and Mia gazed down at the platinum band with emeralds, topaz and diamonds swirled together in an intricate design. "Oh my…Is that…?"

"A replica of Boudicca's ring?" He gazed lovingly down at her. "Yes, I had it made specially. It's even inscribed with 'Body and Soul' along the inside."

Mia melted, her eyes once again filling with tears at how he had combined her favourite things together. "Oh, Joshie, could you be any more perfect?"

"I'm not perfect," he said softly, "just perfect for you."

Mia gave a watery laugh, and pulled his beloved face down to hers and pressed her forehead to his. "Well then," she said as the sun burst through the gaps in the temple pillars and painted their skin golden.

Josh let out a husky laugh, exactly as Mia had hoped, he too obviously recalling the memory, the memory of them on a plane—the first time she had never been afraid of flying, because he had been by her side. *He had always been by her side*—and they both remembered the discussion of Lizzy's uttered words from the ending of Mia's favourite movie.

But this wasn't the ending…this was only the beginning. Of a love story that continued long after the proposal was made, long after the words were uttered…the breath fading out to mingle on the wind eternal.

Josh took her hand and ran a thumb over the ring. "Let's take a *quick* tour then we can return to the hotel and celebrate."

"I love the sound of that." Mia smiled with a suggestive rise of one eyebrow, and allowed Josh to pull her away from the temple, after taking a selfie together to honour the memory. She could hear Calli's, and Simi's, squeals in her mind already. And Mia also couldn't wait to tell Mae—after a lot of time and effort, they'd finally reached a semblance of a mother-daughter relationship.

She glanced back at the temple, a wistful smile on her face.

"You know, you can get married here," Josh said, and Mia turned to him, her eyes wide.

"I love the sound of that too," she said, and, with the temple behind them, a backdrop to their love, Josh pulled Mia into his arms and kissed her until they were both breathless, just as it softly began to rain.

SONG LIST

Waiting for Tonight ~ Jennifer Lopez
What a Feeling ~ Irene Cara
I Want to Know What Love Is ~ Foreigner
Unstoppable ~ Sia
Wind Beneath My Wings ~ Bette Midler
Crazy For You ~ Madonna
Islands in the Stream ~ Dolly Parton & Kenny Rogers
Girls Just Wanna Have Fun - Cyndi Lauper
Miracle ~ Calvin Harris & Ellie Goulding
Geronimo ~ Sheppard
Bones ~ Imagine Dragons
Mysterious Times ~ Sash!
Ivy ~ Taylor Swift
Hungry Eyes ~Eric Carmen
We Will Rock You ~ Queen

WATCH LIST

Friends
Pride & Prejudice
Beaches
A Knight's Tale
Sense and Sensibility
The Mummy
Die Hard
Jurassic Park
The Wizard of Oz
Tomb Raider
Indiana Jones and the Temple of Doom

AUTHOR NOTE

Having been born and bred in the true land of myth and legend—Wales—history and magic is steeped in my veins. Fascinated by the past, I was fortunate enough to work at Cardiff Castle for six years, prior to having my children. The Castle has a Roman foundation, and there sparked my interest in the Roman Era and the Celtic tribes.

The fortress Mia mentions in discussion with the professor—Caerleon—is real, and I heartily recommend a visit if you are ever lucky enough to visit the Welsh borders and wish to learn more about the Romans in Wales.

The village of Mancetter is also real, but I have taken artistic licence in adding an impromptu dig and the discovery of the ring, and other items, there. Boudicca's tale is legendary, one that drew me (and Mia, of course) in, and I have loved weaving a bit of the 'what if' into this tale.

I hope you have enjoyed this love story to the past, to our animal friends whose short lives lengthen ours immeasurably, to those who fought for the ones they loved, and to those who despite being broken-hearted found the strength to forge onwards and earn the love they deserve. Love is the strongest magic of all...

Cardiff Castle

Caerleon Fortress & Baths

Mancetter Heritage Centre

As Mia astutely said, 'Having a good team around you is everything', and I couldn't agree more.

My team consists of a small but veritable army of champions. Huge thanks:

Firstly, to Jordan, who so kindly edited my book to such a high standard—her insightful suggestions, comments and amendments made this book that much stronger.

To Sophie, who crafted an enticing, perfect blurb for the back of this book.

To Julia Scott and her book that keeps on giving: 'The Book Formatting Formula'. It has been a huge help in helping me prettify this book in a way that I am proud to publish.

To my critique partner, Aerin, who reads whatever I throw her way and somehow—amazingly—enjoys it all. Your comments and read-throughs lift my spirits and inspire me every time.

To my X buddies: Emma, Sally, Marie, Alex, Daisy, and Loz who take the time to share my indie book tweets and help my little whisper become a shout. Though we be small, we be mighty.

To my Instagram Mystic Sis, Madonna, who encourages and lifts me up from afar. Keep shining that light, Sis! And to Shauna for ARC reading and being a fantastic writing inspiration.

To my family: My wonderful husband and four amazing children, who have allowed me to not only follow my dreams but achieve them too. I do this to show you that anything is possible if you believe high enough and work hard enough. Love you x

And lastly, to you, my fellow bookdragons, with one opening of a cover we can time-travel, realm-skip, or find true love.

Though our time here is just the turning of a page, we can live lifetimes. Thank you for choosing to live a life within my book. Your support and reviews mean the world!

Estelle x

Twitter/X: @E_G_Tudor
Instagram: @from_the_garret_of_e_g_tudor
TikTok: @egtudor_author

OTHER BOOKS

Middle Grade Fantasy

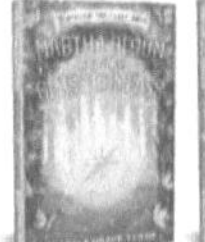

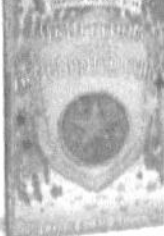

Upper YA Romantasy

Estelle Grace Tudor
Through the Fairy Door

E.G. Tudor
The Fated Partners Trilogy

www.ingramcontent.com/pod-product-compliance
Lightning Source LLC
Chambersburg PA
CBHW020523310726
48979CB00014B/2183/J
* 9 7 8 1 9 1 5 9 5 0 1 6 1 *